"This book is for those who've dreamed about dating a man with wings or squealed silently when a fae warrior removed his bracers to reveal his forearms—yes, I'm talking about *you*—the fangirls and fanguys who know that fantasy isn't just an escape, but a reminder that we can be the main characters in our real lives, too. Thank you, Emily Wibberley and Austin Siegemund-Broka, for this glorious love letter to readers of romantasy."

—#1 *New York Times* bestselling author Jodi Picoult

"Absolutely sparkling! With delicious friction and deft use of our most cherished tropes, *Book Boyfriend* is a love letter to the swooning, hopeful romance reader hearts out there, who are worthy not just of the lowest bar but of the highest, most magical love story imaginable."

—Christina Lauren, *New York Times* bestselling author of *The Paradise Problem*

"Whimsical, hilarious, and wholly original, *Book Boyfriend* is an ode not just to fandom and the bookish community but to the incomparable, rapturous feeling of falling in love with a story. You won't be able to put this one down." —Kate Golden, author of *A Dawn of Onyx*

"*Book Boyfriend* is a delightful story, an ode to any booklover who has fallen hard for fictional characters and worlds. Charmingly funny, sensually sexy, and full of absolute joy, this magical blend of *The Hating Game* meets *The Princess Bride* will enchant and immerse you, reminding you to be the hero of your own story."

—Sophie Sullivan, award-winning author of *Ten Rules for Faking It* and *How to Love Your Neighbor*

"With prose that sings, *The Breakup Tour* is an utterly romantic second-chance story that will have you running for your closest Taylor Swift playlist as soon as Riley and Max reach their swoon-worthy HEA. Emily Wibberley and Austin Siegemund-Broka write with deep, nuanced emotion, and the poignant original lyrics they weave throughout the story only amplify the characters' journey. This is an absolute hit!"

—Jessica Joyce, *USA Today* bestselling author of *The Ex Vows*

"*The Breakup Tour* is the single most romantic book I've ever read. Epic in its scope and wise in its emotional depth, it made me feel every breath and hear every perfect note. I devoured it."

—Annabel Monaghan, bestselling author of *Summer Romance*

"An ode to those brave enough to love deeply despite the risk of heartbreak, *The Breakup Tour* is as full of feeling as your favorite Taylor Swift song. My only regret after reading this swoony, sensitive novel is that I can't actually listen to the fictional album at its center."

—Laura Hankin, author of *The Daydreams*

"If Taylor Swift wrote a second-chance romance, it would be *The Breakup Tour*! This sparkling romance will make you swoon, laugh, and want to sing at the top of your lungs. It is definitely a must read!"

—Alexa Martin, author of *Next-Door Nemesis*

"Wibberley and Siegemund-Broka prove they are masters of the second-chance romance, getting the essentials just right—lingering chemistry, intense longing, and two people who have regrets about the past and one more chance to make it right." —*Booklist*

"Wibberley and Siegemund-Broka bring readers a sweet second-chance romance set in the music world.... The authors dedicate the novel 'to the Swifties, and Miss Swift,' making the inspiration for Riley clear. Equally apparent is how well suited Max and Riley are. Fans will have no trouble rooting for these two."

—*Publishers Weekly*

PRAISE FOR
Do I Know You?

"*Do I Know You?* shows the pure magic of that pivotal moment when two people make the choice to fight for each other. This book is more than a story of a marriage in trouble. It's the story of a spark rekindled, and the new flames deliver all the warmth you could want in a novel. Full of humor and heart, *Do I Know You?* had me in my feelings!"

—Denise Williams, author of *Technically Yours*

"*Do I Know You?* offers the fresh twist on a marriage in crisis that I didn't know I needed! Wibbroka does it again with a magnetically raw and intimate portrayal of where love begins, fades, and begins again. Flirty, sweeping, and hopeful; readers will clutch their chests and root for Eliza and Graham until the very last page."

—Amy Lea, international bestselling author of *The Catch*

PRAISE FOR
The Roughest Draft

"Real, raw, and heartfelt."   —*USA Today*

"*The Roughest Draft* is a book about books, and a breathtaking meditation on the ways in which fiction can be a space to expose and write large our most vulnerable truths. . . . Complex and achingly romantic, *The Roughest Draft* feels as if it's a palimpsest for Wibberley and Siegemund-Broka's most deeply held beliefs about writing and each other—a profound collective story inked out for all of us to find ourselves on its pages." —*Entertainment Weekly*

"*The Roughest Draft* has it all: romance, rumor, and intrigue, and you won't want to put it down." —Shondaland

"Wibberley and Siegemund-Broka deliver on what they've always done best: imperfect characters who you want to follow all the way to the end. There's fire-hot tension and yearning and resentfulness and fights and steamy romance, but there's also beauty in the way the story depicts the uncertainty of creative careers, working as a team, and individual growth." —BuzzFeed

"Emily Wibberley and Austin Siegemund-Broka are the dream team from heaven, starting as YA authors and shifting their powerhouse kingdom into adult. *The Roughest Draft* absolutely gives me *The Hating Game* vibes for a new generation, but sweeter. And maybe steamier?" —Oprah Daily

"I love, love, LOVED this book. It sucks you into a slow, sexy burn from page one and keeps you hooked with its layered, heart-wrenching honesty. This is contemporary romance at its best!" —Lyssa Kay Adams, author of *A Very Merry Bromance*

"Together, Emily Wibberley and Austin Siegemund-Broka produce a seamless voice that is compulsively readable. Their characters spark to life immediately on the page and are so real and relatable that I'm still thinking about them days later."

—Jen DeLuca, *USA Today* bestselling author of *Haunted Ever After*

"There isn't a single page of *The Roughest Draft*, not one, that doesn't contain a sentence I had to reread twice just to savor. I'm going to be thinking about this heartbreakingly lovely, vividly emotional book for a long time. These authors are masters of their craft, and their writing is such a treat to read."

—Sarah Hogle, author of *Old Flames and New Fortunes*

"*The Roughest Draft* turns the act of cowriting a novel into one of the most soulful expressions of love I've ever read. Smart, tender, and deeply romantic, this book is an unforgettable, page-turning knock-out."

—Bridget Morrissey, author of *That Summer Feeling*

Titles by Emily Wibberley & Austin Siegemund-Broka

The Roughest Draft
Do I Know You?
The Breakup Tour
Book Boyfriend
Seeing Other People

SEEING OTHER PEOPLE

EMILY WIBBERLEY &
AUSTIN SIEGEMUND-BROKA

BERKLEY ROMANCE

NEW YORK

BERKLEY ROMANCE
Published by Berkley
An imprint of Penguin Random House LLC
1745 Broadway, New York, NY 10019
penguinrandomhouse.com

Library of Congress Cataloging-in-Publication Data

Names: Wibberley, Emily, author. | Siegemund-Broka, Austin, author.
Title: Seeing other people / Emily Wibberley and Austin Siegemund-Broka.
Description: First edition. | New York: Berkley Romance, 2025.
Identifiers: LCCN 2025007646 (print) | LCCN 2025007647 (ebook) |
ISBN 9780593954263 (trade paperback) | ISBN 9780593954270 (ebook)
Subjects: LCGFT: Romance fiction. | Humorous fiction. | Novels.
Classification: LCC PS3623.I24 S44 2025 (print) | LCC PS3623.I24 (ebook) |
DDC 813/.6—dc23/eng/20250325
LC record available at https://lccn.loc.gov/2025007646
LC ebook record available at https://lccn.loc.gov/2025007647

First Edition: December 2025

Printed in the United States of America
1st Printing

The authorized representative in the EU for product safety and compliance is Penguin
Random House Ireland, Morrison Chambers, 32 Nassau Street, Dublin D02 YH68, Ireland,
https://eu-contact.penguin.ie.

SEEING OTHER PEOPLE

1

My life is a graveyard of failed dates.

I'm hoping this evening's outing won't end the way of my past few unfortunate romantic misadventures. *Hoping.* Not optimistic. Huge difference.

I stand in front of my small closet, stressed. The guy I'm meeting for our first date has undoubtedly illegally double-parked outside my West Hollywood apartment. I'm six-going-on-seven minutes late, which means I'm mere moments from receiving one of those impatient Everything okay? texts. Or worse, he'll just drive off, deciding my lateness or flakiness isn't worth skipping football or jerking off to French cinema or whatever single men in LA do.

I *want* to make a good first in-person impression. I really do. This isn't self-sabotage. Dan was nice when we messaged on Tinder. I would gladly go rock climbing with him, if only I could get my shoes out of my closet.

Which just happens to be haunted.

Inside, my hangers rattle ominously on their own. I chew my

lip. The haunting isn't confined to the small closet opposite my luxurious double bed, of course. My entire place is haunted. Everywhere I go is haunted.

I'm haunted.

It's the worst.

Often, the paranormal fuckery is focused on my closet, though. Something clatters in there, probably one of my hangers tumbling to the floor.

I could rent shoes from the semi-trendy Echo Park climbing gym where we're heading, I guess. But . . . rented shoes? Ew. I shouldn't be spending frivolously right now, either. No, I need to grab the gray pair shoved in the back.

I just know my ghost won't make it easy.

I jump when my phone vibrates loudly in the pocket of my leggings. Heart sinking, I check my screen.

Hey

any eta on when you'll be ready?

Right on cue, the closet rattles ferociously.

Groaning, I fire off a frankly overpromising reply.

One sec

Here goes nothing. I inhale deeply, summoning my courage.

"Please be cool, okay?" I say out loud into my empty room. "Let me have this. I haven't gotten laid in months."

I grab the knob—

The closet door swings open easily.

I exhale in relief. No scalding-hot knob. No slamming door. No clothes flying in my face.

"Thank you," I murmur.

Slowly, I reach for the gym bag containing the rock-climbing shoes I got when I lived in Colorado for my freshman and sophomore years of college. Rock climbing is one of my go-to first dates. I've gone on plenty over the past few years. Plenty of first dates, that is, not just ones involving multicolored handholds and climbing-gym harnesses.

They're kind of my specialty—or they were before my haunting—though the honor feels questionable. Like the romantic equivalent of rescuing my phone battery from sub-five-percent levels more often than most people I know.

Casual intimacy is where I'm most comfortable, though. Connection without commitment. Flings and fun, with a side of rough polyurethane handholds.

It's perfect, or so I promise myself. I get to experience *everything* the men of the cities where I live have to offer without putting pressure on myself to find love. Or worrying I'll screw something up, the likelier result. I can't ruin everything if there's no everything to ruin.

Do I ever wonder if someone out there will make commitment easy? Someone who'll replace flings with forever? Who will make me feel like I'm home, instead of just happily on the move?

I don't know. Maybe.

Believing in forever feels a little like believing in ghosts. But stranger things have happened.

For now, I'm holding on to those first dates like they're colorful handholds on indoor slabs of vertical limestone. They're fun. They're enough.

Hence, the five rock-climbing outings I've undertaken in Echo Park since I moved to West Hollywood. Eleven months into living here, it's the sort of shit I've found goes over well with men in LA, the low-key presumption of outdoorsiness.

I just . . . haven't gone on a rock-climbing date in a while.

I let myself look forward to this one. Which was stupid, I now recognize. Dan is undoubtedly checking the clock in his car—3:39 p.m., *Nice going, Morgan*—while I'm weighing whether I can retrieve my gym bag without risking living out *The Conjuring*.

The hangers shake, making my decision for me. I withdraw my hand hastily. *You win, okay?* Rented shoes it is.

The moment I close the closet door, my roommate screams.

I sigh. Savannah rushes into the room, eyes wide, hair disheveled, face ghostly pale.

"Dude," she starts, sounding the peculiar combination of pissed and remorseful I've become unfortunately familiar with recently. "I'm sorry, but I can't do this anymore."

Momentarily she eyes my rock-climbing outfit, then decides this is more important than my date. Which I understand. I wait wearily for her to continue.

"I went to sleep with my laptop open," she says, "and when I woke up, *Shark Week* reruns were playing *again*. I tried to close the tab and it just wouldn't."

I wince. "Maybe your laptop is buggy? You did spill water on it that one time," I venture hopefully.

Not optimistically.

Savannah's eyes round even wider. "You mean like a year ago?" she retorts.

I shrug.

"*Then*, when I closed my laptop, my door flew open and slammed back shut," she continues.

"Dang," I venture. "Drafts are the worst!"

"No." Savannah's eyes are stern.

I know what's coming. I knew what was coming when I brought Kyle—or Lyle, or something—to my bedroom, only for him to claim my sheets were trying to suffocate him. I knew what was coming when Lee insisted he saw a shadow in my rearview mirror sitting in my Honda's back seat.

"This place is haunted and I can't stand it anymore. I'm going to go stay with my parents. If you haven't exorcised your ghost by the end of the month," she declares, "I'm moving out."

Panic shoots through my tardiness worries. My roommate's constant, reasonable complaining is one thing. But moving out? "Savvy. Please."

I use our oldest nickname, hoping to win friend points. We were roommates when I transferred to UNC for my last year of college, way before my lovely little haunting. I never forgot how decidedly cool she was when I dropped out. When I shared my plans in our junior-year dorm room, I expected maudlin sympathy or judgment or, if I was lucky, complete carelessness.

Instead, Savvy hugged me and said, "You're awesome. You're going to be fine," and it was the last conversation we had on the subject. It was kind of perfect. Naturally, we kept loosely in touch, leading me to hit her up when I was figuring out my LA plans.

"I can't afford this lease on my own," I remind her. "Seriously. And how am I supposed to get a new roommate when"—I swallow— "when . . ."

Savvy looks smug.

"When you're haunted?" she finishes.

Not cool. My shoulders slump in defeat, and her wild-eyed expression softens.

"I'm really sorry, Morgan. But, like, this shit is scary," she explains. "I can't live like this."

My heart starts to pound in a way not even rattling hangers or poltergeisted rearview mirrors can provoke. You know what's spooky? Ghosts. You know what's *scary*? Rent in Los Fucking Angeles.

"I know," I say softly. "I get it."

I really do. The truth is, I can't live like this, either, but I can't escape it. I *wish* my romantic failures or my roommate's computer were the only haunted parts of my life. Instead, the paranormal follows me everywhere. When I go to work or the grocery store or the spicy noodle restaurant three blocks down from my building—where I'm no longer welcome on soy-sauce-eruption-related charges. Even the dentist. When the water tube squirted on poor Dr. Parsekian three times unprompted, I knew what was up.

Savannah—whose friendly nickname I revoke, the traitor—smiles sympathetically. "Thanks," she says. "I really hope you find a way to get rid of . . . it."

I nod in defeat. *Me too.*

While she grabs her laptop and keys and hastens out the door, I sink onto my bed. With miserable timing, my phone hums once more in my leggings. Whatever. Dan will have to wait one more minute while I wrestle with my misfortune.

I'm fucked, honestly. I cannot afford my rent without Savannah's half, and I can't get out of my lease for five more months. My parents can't help me. They haven't been able to retire due to still living paycheck to paycheck.

No, that's . . . not true. They do live paycheck to paycheck. But they would help me.

Which is exactly why I can't beg them to. I've imposed much, much too much on Ellen and Steven Lane of Jefferson City, Missouri. Or finally of Jefferson City. My dad worked in "location sur-veying and management" for most of my life, only retiring last year. Yearslong contracts would move our entire family from city to city, state to state, where he would coordinate land contracting, con-struction, and ongoing maintenance for new hotels or superstores.

The everywhere-and-nowhere upbringing earned me my itch for never sitting still. Which earned me my itch for . . . dropping out of college. I spent my freshman year studying social anthropol-ogy, then switched to video production for my sophomore year. Then, for my junior year, I switched from University of Colorado Boulder to University of North Carolina, where I met Savvy.

The whole while, I felt this . . . pressure mounting. To *become someone*. To know who I was. To make decisions that would lead me or force me to stop making decisions. My mental health suf-fered. Until one day, I worked up my courage or my selfishness and called my parents with my decision. To my enormous guilty sur-prise, they supported me. Three years of tuition, hard-scraped from my dad's moderate salary, just . . . gone.

I promised them I would get myself together. I would be inde-pendent. Established. Adult. The words people use for *not your problem.*

Then there was the whole shit with Michael. I didn't plan on breaking our engagement, obviously. I just got in over my head. I was desperate to prove I'd dropped out for the right reasons, to prove I was self-sufficient, to prove I was on my own path—which, funnily enough, were the wrong reasons for overcommitting my-self to Michael Hanover-Erickson, who was seven years my senior.

It took my panicky retreat from the life I planned with him for me to understand what I know now. When I commit, other people get hurt. Keeping my relationships casual isn't just fun or easy. It's mercy.

When I fucked everything up with Michael, my parents were there. Despite everything they put into my happiness, the promises I made them—the promises I made everyone—when I needed to run, they understood, or pretended they did. They were ready to waste more money and effort and compassion on me.

It's enough to make a girl feel like a living, breathing problem instead of a daughter. Enough to keep her from visiting home very often, which ironically—or helpfully—only makes her feel even less entitled to demand more help from people she's burdened plenty. If I could pay for therapy, I'd go. But I'd start with paying rent first.

I close my eyes, exhausted. The weight of my housing problem quietly overwhelms me. I literally don't know what I'm going to do.

Which is when I feel the familiar tingling sensation of someone's hand hovering over my shoulder. Except I know there's no one. My room—my entire apartment, unfortunately—is completely empty.

Sort of.

I shiver. "Can you please just *try* to be less creepy?"

Opening my eyes, I know what I'm going to find.

He's seated next to me on my bed, leaving my floral comforter undisturbed by his weightless presence. He's maybe six one, stocky, sort of boyishly handsome, with floppy chestnut hair he flips from side to side and unshaven stubble. Forever unshaven, now. I doubt he cares.

Next to me in my empty room sits the ghost of the last man I went rock climbing with.

"I prefer *spooky* to *creepy*," Zach says. "It's not like I watch you when you sleep."

He doesn't sound indignant despite my characterization. If there's one minuscule silver lining in my haunting situation, it's this. I have, somehow, wound up with the chillest ghost in the history of hauntings.

Obviously it's a small comfort when his incessant shenanigans have cost me my dating life, my favorite noodle restaurant, and now, my roommate and my financial stability. "Why were you tormenting Savannah?" I demand.

Whenever Zach feels an emotion, his entire face responds. Right now, indignant incredulity rounds his blue eyes and shoots his eyebrows up. "I wasn't!" he insists. "I swear. You know I can't control this stuff. I love Savannah," he says to me about the woman who's never spoken to him because she never knew him in life. "Even if it stung when she called me 'it,'" he complains. "I'm not an 'it.'"

"You're so an 'it,'" I shoot back in frustration.

"That hurts, Morgan. That cuts me deep."

"Nothing cuts you deep. It would go right through you."

Amused by my admittedly good comeback, Zach grins.

I groan. "Could you just go haunt someone else? I mean, we had a nice enough first date, but I wasn't even planning to go on a second date with you. No offense," I add.

Zach shrugs with equanimity.

Our first and only date was three months ago. We went rock climbing. I wore the shoes in my closet without fretting over supernatural phenomena. Imagine that! I made out with him in my car afterward, but I never felt the need to see him again.

I doubt he did, either, but I suppose we don't know for sure, because apparently, he died shortly thereafter. Shortly after *that*, he appeared in my bathroom mirror and scared the holy living fuck out of me.

"There have to be people who knew you better who you could spend your afterlife with," I press him.

Now Zach looks petulant in the fake way he does, like frustration never fully reaches his happy-go-lucky vibe. "Like I want to spend eternity with you!" he shoots back. "But for whatever reason, we're stuck together. Our shitty date is the only thing I can remember. If *you* had bothered to learn my last name, then maybe we could look me up and find my family."

I wilt. Okay, Zach has me there.

Frankly, I did not expect my noncommittal dating style would leave me with the surname-less specter who is presently, if unintentionally, ruining my life. "Hey, I'm sure I learned your last name," I reply weakly. "I just . . . forgot it."

Zach shakes his head in consternation. "Honestly, you deserve to be haunted," he declares. "I literally died. It's like you don't even care!"

The light bulb over my bed flickers. One of my houseplants wobbles on my desk, perilously close to the edge. I grab the pot mid-wobble and return the small philodendron to securer purchase.

Zach doesn't seem to notice. While he never haunts maliciously, sometimes his emotions don't show only on his face.

"It's very sad you died," I say. "To . . . other people. I'm sure."

Zach glares. I wince. I deserve that.

"No, look, I *am* sorry, Zach. I know it's unfair," I say. "It's just also unfair that I'm being haunted."

The legs of my bed shake, knocking sharply on my fake hardwood like we're going to levitate.

"*Less* unfair," I qualify hastily. The clattering stops. "But still unfair."

My correction satisfies him. He's nodding in half understanding when I hear footsteps from my living room. Heart leaping, I start for the door. Even if Savannah is only returning for her

clothes or computer charger or something, maybe I can convince
her a little involuntary Netflix isn't the end of the world—

"Morgan?"

The voice is not Savannah's. It's one I've never heard.

I stop short in my open doorway, recognizing Dan from his
Tinder picture. He's shaved his hipster mustache—god bless—
and I honestly have no idea why he wore that lovely brown leather
jacket for a rock-climbing date. Nevertheless, I haven't had sex in
thirteen weeks, and Dan's noticeably large hands have me hating
the supernatural.

He's standing uncomfortably next to our entryway table with
the empty glass dish where Savannah keeps—kept—her keys. He
looks like he doesn't know what to do with himself, which makes
two of us. Or two plus one ghost.

"The door was unlocked," he explains. "Sorry."

Overcoming my surprise, I soften. It's sort of sweet he didn't
just drive off, given I'm now fifteen minutes late.

My gratitude dies when Dan cranes his neck to look behind me.
I know what he *won't* find. Nobody can see Zach except for me.

"Um, were you talking to someone?" He sounds suspicious,
which is fair. I *was* talking to someone.

"Seriously, Morgan?" Right on cue, Zach pops up next to the
oblivious Dan. "This guy? He's wearing a company T-shirt." Zach
points to where—*Yes, fine*—under his leather jacket, Dan's gray
shirt shows the logo for Cynergy Systems. "You can do better," my
ghost insists.

"Nope!" I say cheerfully to Dan. "Just talking to myself! I'm
ready to go now!" I double back into my bedroom, where I grab my
phone.

"Who's Zach?"

I freeze in my doorway.

"This should be good," Zach interjects. "Who *is* Zach? Inquiring minds!"

Rounding slowly, I face Dan, praying the next few seconds deliver me something wholly sensible, completely innocent, and entirely non-supernatural to say.

Nothing comes. So here goes nothing. "Would you believe me if I told you my apartment is haunted and . . . he's my ghost?" I smile, going for quirky and bashful. It's Los Angeles. The men here love that, don't they?

Dan frowns. Not this one, apparently. "That's a new one. Look, if you have other guys you're seeing, that's fine," he says. "I'd just like to know."

Fine. The word sounds like a closing door. "No, really," I insist. "I went on one date with Zach and it didn't go anywhere."

In the dim entryway of my sparse living room, Dan shifts uncomfortably. Zach imitates him, unseen, then pantomimes pulling on his own leather jacket. I shoot my ghost a glare.

Come on, Dan, I consider joking, *I can't be the only LA girl you've ever met who swears the supernatural is ruining her dating life!*

"So, he's your ex?" Dan ventures.

"Yep!" Zach says proudly.

"No. He's dead," I correct.

Zach shrugs like, *Fair.*

Unfortunately, Dan's suspicion only deepens.

"Morgan, I think this guy is going from thinking you're a cheater to a murderer," Zach comments. He walks directly through Dan, coming to lean his weightlessness on the entryway end table.

"*I* didn't kill him!" I hasten to clarify. "I don't know how he died, actually." Hearing myself say what someone who did kill their ex would say, I cringe. I strategize fast. "If you give me one second, I could call my roommate back here," I offer—okay, I *plead*. "She'll corroborate that this place is, like, super haunted." It's the least Savvy could do, right?

"You know what . . ." Dan starts, and I have this shining moment of relief, like the Santa Monica sun parting from the surprisingly common California clouds—Dan's a nice guy, company shirt notwithstanding! He'll laugh it off and we'll enjoy rock climbing! And other pastimes!—and then his expression closes off. "I think I probably should go before I get a parking ticket."

Something quiet curls up in me.

"Yep. Sure. Sounds good," I say, knowing what he means.

"Um. Yeah," Dan says. "See you, Morgan."

He closes my front door when he goes—the second person to leave my apartment for ghost-related reasons in the past five minutes.

Retreating into my room, I'm surprised how upset I feel. I collapse heavily onto my floral comforter. I wasn't writing wedding vows in my head for Dan from Tinder, obviously. I just feel lonely enough *without* the fucking spectral interference.

It's why I throw myself into my dating life. Whenever the loneliness gets unmanageable, I put myself out there. Whenever the idea of commitment—of something real and loving and enduring out there for me—creeps in like a vine to wrap around my hopeful—not optimistic—heart, I plant those hopes in the possibility of a Dan or a Lee or a Michael.

Now my haunting has ruined even that.

When Zach flickers into visibility next to me, he has the grace to look somewhat guilty. "Honestly, I think I saved you on that one," he musters. "He was going to be a dud."

"You've driven off the last *five* duds," I shoot back.

Zach shrugs slowly. "You need higher standards."

I round on him. "You do know you're dissing yourself, right?"

When Zach grins, called out once more, I stomp into my room's bathroom, where I frustratedly fill the drinking glass I use to water my houseplant collection. When I'm stressed or pissed, tending to them is one thing I've found helps.

"Why do you even care?" I continue in exasperation. "Let me date my shitty men in peace."

"I'm bored!" Zach protests. "What else am I supposed to do? You know, maybe you should try a second date for once," he counsels.

I scoff while carefully moving my watering glass to the philodendron and her counterpart, the spider plant, each content in its ceramic home on my desk.

They're my closest *living* companions, which is fucking sad, frankly, but sort of comforting. They're pretty forgiving. If I forget to water them sometimes, I just make it up to them later. They come with no dropouts or graduations. No breakups or engagements. Easy, low-key commitment.

"I draw the line at advice from a dead guy," I say, chastening Zach.

He puts his hand over his nonexistent wounded heart. "Harsh!" he complains. "I'm going to rip your shower curtain off for that one."

Sure enough, from the small bathroom where I filled my glass, I hear the tearing of polyester fabric and fearsome clattering.

Not just clattering, though. Out of nowhere, I hear something else. The opening strains of "Call Me Maybe." It's not out loud. It's more like it's forcibly stuck in my head.

I groan in frustration. Now, I have no objections to "Call Me Maybe"—except when my ghost ex is using Carly Rae's certified bop to torment me. It's Zach's favorite song, he explained, and he's capable of running it through my head using his ghost powers, which he conveniently employs when I'm committing grievous misdeeds like concentrating on work emails for several hours instead of entertaining him.

"You're ruining this song for me," I inform him sternly.

"Be honest and take some accountability," he replies, unmoved.

I shake my head while I water the pair of *Zamioculcas zamiifolia* on my windowsill, their gorgeous waxy leaves shining in the uncharitable overhead lighting of my unaffordable room. No, I decide. No more ruined dates. No more fucking "Call Me Maybe." No more roommate crises or ripped shower curtains. I do need accountability—for my haunting.

"You don't know me," I declare. "Savannah was right."

No more comfort-watering. No more languishing on my bedspread like a fainting Victorian lady, either. No more contending with the eldritch horrors of my closet whenever I want my goddamn rock-climbing shoes. Zach watches me warily as I face him, flush with new resolve.

"I'm getting rid of you," I say. "I'm going to exorcise you from my life once and for all."

2

When we moved in, I worried the heat radiating off the hillside of Los Angeles's Silver Lake neighborhood would suffocate us or kill our electricity bill. Everything else was ideal—the view, the eclectic nearby restaurants, the layout ready for the renovation we'd planned. *Would we hate the heat?* I worried, wanting everything to be perfect.

Kennedy only scoffed lovingly. "It *is* perfect," my fiancée had promised. "We just don't know it yet."

Nowadays, even in summer, our home is always cold. In the past five years, I've never once used the air-conditioning.

Honestly, no one ever mentions the perks of living in a haunted house.

Wearing my favorite sweater—the one Kennedy got me on our first ski trip—I strike a match. Carefully, I hold the flickering flame to the tall candles I've set out on our dining table. The moment I reach the wick, the flame flutters out.

Patiently, and not entirely surprised, I strike another match. I don't mind if the evening I've planned requires a little persistence.

Love often does. Nevertheless, this is admittedly one of the *downsides* of haunted homeownership.

"You all right in there?" she calls from the living room.

I light my next match. The flame holds steady. I gently move the fire to the wicks, lighting one candle, then the next.

My success is short-lived. Without warning, the candles suddenly extinguish.

Undaunted, I pull out the next match. "All good! You know how drafty this house is," I reply.

"You know it's not a draft."

Hearing the undercurrent in Kennedy's voice, I hesitate, unlit match in hand. Yes, of course I know. I just don't want to have the conversation I know is coming.

She walks into the room, and I diligently renew my efforts. The flame steadies when I strike the match . . . the first candle . . . the second.

When I meet her eyes, I fight the familiar hollow clench in my chest. Kennedy's unhappiness distresses me but doesn't dim her beauty. Her long elegant cheekbones, her sensitive deep-brown eyes. Forget heaven-sent. Kennedy Raymond looks heaven-sculpted.

Unfortunately, she also looks disappointed.

"Of course it's drafty," I insist. "I need to patch that drywall and replace the back door. It's so close to being done, though," I say to her, fighting to remind her of the enthusiasm she once felt for the renovation. It feels a little like striking matches that won't light.

When Kennedy's eyes slip from mine, it's as if those phantom gusts have dashed my efforts. She gazes out the front window.

I know what she sees. Not the work we've done or the dream we shared when we bought this place. Though perfectly located, the two-bedroom was a total fixer-upper. Which was the plan. With Kennedy's design experience, we would overhaul the house into our forever home. We've made so much progress, even if unfinished patches of drywall, exposed outlets here or there, the unpainted interior of the guesthouse, and other details exist as lingering reminders of how recent events have somewhat stalled us.

No, what Kennedy sees is the front yard. The vines climbing on the rotting fence have overstayed their welcome. The weeds carpet the ground in high grasses of overgrown California green. It's the most unfinished part of our home.

"We'll get to it," I reassure her.

Kennedy blinks. Her keen gaze returns to me. "Get to what?"

"The yard," I say, feeling guilty. I've put off the project, which honestly intimidates me.

Kennedy's expression doesn't change. Her eyes return to the window. "Okay," she says.

My stomach sinks. She looks . . . wistful. Restless. *Dissatisfied*, a frightened voice says in my head.

I wish I could blame the unwelcome whisper on the supernatural. It's no ghost, though. It's something much scarier—the truth.

I'm desperate to make Kennedy happy. To . . . keep her here. With me. Especially tonight. She's absent more often. Like she can't stand to be here. I don't ask her where she goes. I'm afraid of the answer.

"So . . ." I start, moving toward the candlelit table.

Kennedy looks back. When her eyes focus on mine, it's like she's just remembered I'm here. "I got something for you," she says. She gestures to the credenza in the living room.

I remember when we found the piece out on the curb in Mid-Wilshire's residential neighborhood. Kennedy prefers old music, but when we found the handsome mid-century modern piece, she was so excited she cranked the radio up and sang P!nk the whole way home.

Under the mirror we hung together when we moved in, I notice a folded piece of paper on the credenza.

I smile. We used to exchange cards every anniversary. We started when we were in art school, where we met, Kennedy for design and me for pottery. Kennedy would rarely use her considerable drawing skills except on those occasions. We haven't recently, and light leaps into my heart finding she's restarted the custom.

Except when I unfold what she's left on the credenza, no drawing awaits. Only unfamiliar words.

Support and Resource Group for the Haunted

My excitement extinguishes. Kennedy has printed out a social media post publicizing the group, which meets in nearby Atwater Village. I drop the paper onto the credenza.

"We can't keep ignoring this," Kennedy insists. Her voice strains.

"I'm not ignoring it," I reply.

The candles whoosh out on the table.

"I just don't think it's a problem," I continue.

"How can you say that?"

The sadness in her voice pulls my gaze from the flyer. Kennedy sounds desperate. Broken. It breaks *me* more every time we have this discussion. I don't want her to hurt. I only want her to be happy.

I just don't know what else to do.

"Can't we just enjoy today?" I implore her.

I reach urgently for the matchbox on the dining table.

"I don't care if I have to light these candles a hundred times. You're worth it," I say.

The candles endure. Kennedy's smile offers the same warmth their flames do—none. Her heart isn't in it. I know what my fiancée looks like when she smiles for real. I remember from the day I proposed to her. The day we got the keys to this house. The day she sledgehammered through the wall to expand the living room. She looked like nothing in the world could steal her joy.

"This isn't working, Sawyer," she says somberly. "I . . . I know you feel the same even if you can't admit it."

"I don't," I insist, stubborn. I don't need support groups or interventions. I just need her.

"Please," Kennedy implores. "Really look at your life."

"I have. All I want is for you to be happy." I move closer to her. "Please. That's . . . everything to me. Nothing else matters."

I reach for her hand. She steps back.

"I think going"—she nods to the folded flyer—"would help us both."

"They won't be able to help. You know that." The chill in the house drops several degrees, making me shiver in my sweater. I never knew wind chimes could ring ominously. I don't care—I'm getting angry now. I don't want to fight with Kennedy on our anniversary, but I do need her to understand me. "There's no changing this. I like our life, our home. I guess what you're telling me is you don't."

Kennedy is opening her mouth when the doorbell rings.

"Dinner," I preempt her. "Hold on."

I head quickly through the living room, calming my pounding heart—not easy when I pass the wall in our entryway where we planned to hang our wedding photos. Only the framed invitation hangs there now, promising *Kennedy Raymond and Sawyer Wilson* would be wed.

The whole house is this way. Every room *looks* right, renovated minus a few finishing touches, lovingly rendered in geometric white with wood furniture and indulgent flourishes—"Mid-century modern meets minimalist boho," Kennedy would enthuse, her eyes dancing like she loved the sound of the words themselves. But everywhere, longing haunts our halls.

On the porch, I find the delivery guy clad in the usual uniform of our longtime go-to neighborhood-institution pizza place fifteen minutes down the hillside on that wonderful winding stretch of Sunset Boulevard nestled with tattoo parlors and independent bakeries, where Kennedy and I had our first date.

The delivery guy is looking nervously over his shoulder. I understand. Nighttime leaves the overgrown garden downright spooky. Ironic when the front yard, I've noticed, is the least haunted part of our home.

He startles when I open the door, probably expecting a knife-wielding serial killer to live here. He hastens to hand over the flat white boxes holding our margherita and Sunset Special pies, the same combo Kennedy and I have ordered forever.

"It's a fixer-upper," I say grumpily. "My fiancée is a house flipper. We've just hit some unexpected roadblocks."

He nods while I sign the receipt. "Do house flippers also handle exorcisms? 'Cause this place looks mad haunted."

I return the pen, smiling humorlessly. First Kennedy's flyer, now judgmental pizza delivery? Everyone's a critic or comedian of my relationship with the paranormal.

I close the door, dinner in hand. Sighing, I release my frustration. I just want to lay this fight to rest.

When I reenter the dining room, however, Kennedy looks somehow more unhappy. I persevere. "Happy anniversary, baby. Nine years ago today, my life changed forever. I'm the luckiest man in the whole world."

Kennedy finally moves forward, closer to me. I'm convinced she's forgiven me, she understands—

Until she steps right through me.

The cold rush shakes me. Kennedy knew it would. Fighting for composure, I turn, finding her watching me from the living room.

"No. You're not lucky," she says. "Neither of us are. We don't have an anniversary, Sawyer. We haven't in five years."

Then Kennedy—Kennedy Claire Raymond, my fiancée, who died five years ago on November 5 from undiagnosed heart conditions—walks through the wall. She vanishes somewhere on the other side.

She'll be back, I console myself. *She'll be back*.

My Kennedy. My fiancée. My ghost.

She'll be back. It's one of the perks of living in a haunted house. The rest of the world said goodbye to Kennedy Raymond. I haven't.

Still . . . I can't ignore how miserable she looked. How empty. How haunted.

Despite myself, I leave pizza for one on the candlelit table. I return to the credenza, no longer hungry, where I pick up the paper my dead fiancée left for me.

3

MORGAN

So far, the worst part of accountability is finding parking. In my inexhaustible Honda, I circle the narrow streets of dusty Atwater Village for fifteen minutes.

The inscrutable signs of parking permissions and restrictions don't help. I've found their overcomplicated directions one of my least favorite parts of Los Angeles. THREE HOURS, MONDAY–WEDNESDAY, WITH PERMIT 3R. EXCEPT, PAST 8 P.M., SIX HOURS. NO PARKING FRIDAY, EXCEPT WHEN THE PALE MOON RISES AND THE MARK OF THE SERPENT SHINES IN THE SILVER CLOUDS.

Whatever. Parking, I remind myself, is part of life here.

I'm not in the most pleasant mood, parking problems notwithstanding. I drove over here from work, where I *would have* enjoyed picking up soil samples directly from our local supplier for the afternoon's client meeting—a rare reprieve from operating DiCrescenzo Landscaping's scheduling and ordering software. *Would have*, had Zach not exploded soil on me in retribution for our fight yesterday.

I want to work with plants professionally—I honestly do. Given the job market, I feel genuinely grateful to work for the DiCre-scenzo brothers. Still, I get restless spending ninety-five percent of my workdays in their office on Wilshire Boulevard in my very in-door cubicle under their unforgiving fluorescent overheads, where the majority of pruning I do these days is on cancellations from the company calendar.

Handling the greenery and evaluating the health and the qual-ity of the soil we receive from various suppliers would have been invigorating.

Until *someone* decided to lash out at my support-group plans. I've spent the forty-minute drive swiping mulch off my shirt and out of my bra while muttering threats like "exorcism" and "Ghost-busters."

Finally, once I've wedged myself close enough to someone's dented Prius in order to not hang over the gated driveway of some sort of construction yard, I hustle down the hot uneven sidewalk. I'm late for my very first haunting support group.

Do I love this option? No. No more than Zach does.

Is it the only real resource I found in hours of miserable googling last night? Yes. Otherwise, I learned absolutely nothing helpful. Most online resources instructed me to "tell the ghost to go away."

I wish I could, Zach had responded, then opened every cup-board in my kitchen out of spite.

Real mature, I'd admonished him.

I tried leaving borders of salt on my floor, only for him to step easily over them. I did wonder if ghosts only respond to the pink Himalayan kind from Trader Joe's, whereas Morton's iodized salt doesn't pack enough punch. I tried ignoring Zach—the worst idea, prompting him to invade my head with "Call Me Maybe" for hours. I was frustratedly murmur-singing of wishes and wells and hot night winds blowing until my head hit the pillow.

None of the cleansing rituals I found worked. The group was my only recourse. *Support and Resource Group for the Haunted*, proclaimed the social media post from the crystal shop where I'm headed.

If this doesn't work, I'm going to have to hire one young priest and one elderly priest for a proper exorcism. Considering I've never once set foot in a church, I'm hoping Zach can be resolved secularly.

The only silver lining is my locale. Los Angeles seems like the right city for my sort of problem. Tarot cards, haunted hotels, crystal shops . . . people embrace the supernatural here, more than any other city I've lived in in my life. In my eleven-month residency in West Hollywood, I've learned the perils of Mercury in retrograde, how to read auras, and what candles to light for manifestations.

I would've dismissed it as superstitious crap, but the literal ghost I live with—who played the license plate game on the drive out here, exultant when he found Ohio—won't let me.

It leaves me optimistic that *someone* in Gwyneth's Crystals will have something helpful to say. Sweating in the merciless summer heat, my sneakers starting to shred the blister on my heel from yard work, I finally reach the small shabby storefront. Glass windows display shelves of crystals and glittery candles. There's a fish tank supply store next door on one side, Vietnamese sandwiches on the other.

The doorbell chimes when I enter. Making my way to the rear of the store, I wonder whether the powerful mystical energies of the decorative crystals might interfere with Zach's presence— until he pops up nearby, examining the shelves. "Ooh, I love crystals," he enthuses. "We should get some blue quartz for the apartment."

My spirit sinking, I do not dignify his suggestion with a response.

He, for his part, offers no contrition for or other mention of the DiCrescenzo Landscaping soil carpeting the front seat of my car.

The meeting has not yet started despite my lateness. I guess no one else could find parking, either.

I evaluate my surroundings. Dim lighting from very old windows. Shelves of overstock lining one wall. Plastic folding table with, shall we say, minimalist drink offerings. It's giving church community center meets Dungeons & Dragons session.

However, East LA heat is East LA heat. I notice Spindrift on the folding table. Lemon—the everyman's flavor. Nothing exciting, like raspberry or mango, but decent. Next to the drink offerings stand two elder millennial men in dark clothing.

I've come here for resources. Guidance. Inspiration.

The room is filling up with more presumed hauntees. I remind myself that everyone is here for their own reasons, and any one of them could hold the key to my own haunting. If the millennial goths don't want to chat, I'll find someone who does.

I have to start somewhere, though, and these guys look like they're hoping to audition authentic ghost members for their dark-wave synthpop band. I approach the promising pair, planning on making conversation.

"Hi, I'm Morgan . . ." I start.

I'm reaching for the lemon Spindrift when the can ruptures, hissing lemony carbonation from gashes in the metal and spraying all over my shirt.

Zach. Probably because I ignored his crystal request.

"Sorry!" I say, grabbing for napkins to blot my shirt. "Sorry. My ghost is here," I explain. Not the strongest start to my first support-group reconnaissance conversation, I have to concede. Yet, unlike Street Noodle or Dan from Tinder, perhaps this group will prove receptive to ghost-related excuses.

The goths do not look pleased. Tough supernaturally inclined crowd.

They find seats in the folding chair circle far from me. In fairness, I wouldn't want lemon Spindrift on a vintage Sisters of Mercy shirt if I were them. Either they don't really know any ghosts, or their ghosts are way less annoying than Zach.

I take my seat, noticing coupons on every chair for Serving Spirits. Thirty percent off food for what looks like a ghost-themed restaurant and bar in the neighborhood. I pocket mine, then examine my haunted new friends.

Besides the goths is a middle-aged couple who exchange judgmental glances when they notice my wet T-shirt. There's also a beleaguered woman on her phone chaperoning three teenage girls, who giggle while they peruse the merchandise, and a young guy whose leather notebook and elegant wireframe glasses scream, *aspiring screenwriter here for research.* Finally, a genial older guy is passing out the coupons and wearing his very own Serving Spirits shirt.

I fight to keep my hopes up. They seem like hobbyists, lookie-loos, and self-promoters, but I have nowhere else to go.

I head straight for the open seat next to a guy here on his own. Praying I do not have unnoticed dirt on my hair or sleeves, I sit down next to him.

He eyes me warily, which, okay, if he saw my Spindrift mishap, is fair. Reassurance is due. "I promise not to open any carbonated beverages by you," I say, going for cheeky and cheerful.

But he only blinks, looking up from his empty contemplativeness like he's surprised I spoke to him. He has the most guarded vibe of anyone I've ever met. His stony solemnity seems purposefully defensive.

Unfortunately—for him—it only makes me more curious.

"I'm not worried about carbonated beverages," he replies. His voice matches his demeanor. Low, humming with quiet intensity, yet impenetrable. He sounds like he's carving every word into a headstone.

"Oh, thank god," I reply gamely. "Then *maybe* I'll risk one. I'm Morgan," I introduce myself, smiling my winningest smile.

Honestly, I pride myself on how well I can get to know new people. Moving states every few years my entire life, I've needed to win over landlords, human resource departments, neighbors, roommates, gas station clerks, convenience store owners, you name it. I've developed near-supernatural powers of easy friendliness.

So I'm surprised when they only barely prevail on my new acquaintance. He hesitates. He does not extend his hand. He does not smile. When he speaks, I only just catch the name his hardened voice offers.

"Sawyer," he says.

"Sawyer," I repeat. He's dressed simply, in jeans and a brown sweater that is way too warm for this hot day. He's pushed the sleeves up, revealing corded forearms and large hands. His hair is short, dark above his stone-cut jaw. There's something downcast, even guarded, in his shuttered expression, sadness in his blue eyes. They're like fog obscuring the ocean, so thick the sun can't get in.

He is, I notice, the only person in this room who *looks* haunted. Figuratively and literally.

What, I wonder, has summoned Sawyer here, looking haunted or ghostly himself in the midst of LA's finest paranormal hobbyists? I'm chasing meaningless hope now, but something makes me feel like I'm more similar to Sawyer than he wants to let on.

Searching for insight, I look at his hands in his lap. I recognize what he's holding—sort of—a flyer. A printout of the advertisement I found online for this group.

I doubt he notices how his restless fingers have softened the warped edges of the folded paper with fidgeting. He's . . . not unfriendly, I realize. Or not only unfriendly. He's nervous. Nobody wants to chat when they're nervous, but sometimes if you get through to them, it helps. I just need to be persistent.

"How long have you been haunted?" I ask.

Once more, my friendliness visibly surprises Sawyer. With each question, he eyes me like I'm speaking in a language he thought no one else could understand. It's sort of funny, although I obviously don't laugh. It's a support group. Did he expect the support to be . . . silent? Unspoken, meditative commiseration?

"Five years," he replies. Despite his effortful monotone, I hear conflicting emotion in his voice. Like five years is nothing and forever.

Now I'm the one to startle. Five *years*?

Sawyer's answer raises another question I'm desperate to ask. If he's endured his haunting for five years, why come to a supernatural support group *now*?

"You?" he asks in return.

A question! From somber Sawyer himself! A real, ordinarily human effort at conversation! I hide my delight. "A couple months," I reply. "Got any tips for newbies?"

Sawyer doesn't shut down like I'm expecting. Instead, he seems very seriously to consider my question. *Hmm, how must I distill five years of haunted wisdom into concise counsel for this strange woman who definitely does not have dirt in her hair?*

"Wool sweaters," he finally replies. "Lots of wool sweaters."

My eyebrows rise.

Not only is Sawyer's reply utterly cryptic—*like, is he joking?*—his tone is unbothered. Even. As if he wants to dispense his sincere recommendations for long-haul haunting, nothing more, nothing less, with no interest in the more obvious emotional or logistical problems our supernatural situation presents.

"Maybe I should take up knitting," I dare to joke.

Sawyer nods thoughtfully. "That would be smart," he replies.

He's so serious I have to stifle a laugh. *Okay, dude, wool sweaters it is.*

Unfortunately, I do not get to continue my inquiry. Interruption comes in the form of, presumably, Gwyneth, the proprietress, who emerges from the nearby storage room. Wearing crystal earrings, her skin decorated with beautiful colored tattoos, she looks us over with calm, welcoming confidence. Honestly, if she can't fix my haunting, I wonder if she could help me decorate the interior of the apartment I can no longer afford.

"I think we're ready to begin," she starts, her voice soothing.

She enters our folding chair circle. The screenwriter's gaze sharpens. The judgmental couple relaxes. Even the millennial goths' spirits seem to improve, so to speak.

"This is a chance for people to share their experiences with spirits on the other side in a safe place, without judgment," Gwyneth continues. "I saw my first ghost when I was a child. Everywhere I've gone, I've encountered evidence of supernatural energies. I've warded away evil ones and ignored harmless ones."

I find myself nodding. Zach is nowhere to be seen. Promising.

Or promising until Gwyneth produces chunky crystal necklaces with price stickers on them from the woven hip pouch she's wearing.

"If you'd like to protect yourself from dark energies, please browse my collection of amethyst, selenite, and black tourmaline," she encourages us. "Discount for purchases made today only!"

This meeting is starting to feel less paranormal and more promotional. *Well, salespeople can be haunted, too,* I reassure myself.

I'm not flush with cash, but if investing in some black tourmaline means my roommate won't leave, then so be it!

"Do you have crystals that do the opposite?" I look toward the source of the interruption. Serving Spirits guy has raised his hand eagerly.

Gwyneth eyes him. "You . . . wish to summon evil?"

"Doesn't have to be evil," he replies. "I just want to attract paranormal activity."

Sawyer *hmm*s.

Gwyneth looks delighted. "Yes, of course. See me afterward," she says.

My heart sinks further. If these people want to conjure hauntings, they have no idea what I'm going through.

"Who wants to share first?" Gwyneth invites the group.

I sit back, fighting discouragement. The teenagers stand and begin describing a recent sleepover, exaggerating lurid details that feel ripped from every horror movie of the past five years. I'm not even mad—I would've done the same shit in high school. *Wait until you nearly drop your phone in the toilet because your ghost surprises you when you're doing your scrollies while brushing your teeth*, I would say, except then I would sound like a crotchety old haunted grown-up.

The middle-aged couple nervously share stories of what sound like the quirks and malfunctions of a home needing repairs. The screenwriter, like the goths, stays silently observant. Sawyer sits glumly, facing forward, continuing his half-hearted fidgeting of the program in his hands.

I'm going to share, then leave, I decide. My last-ditch effort. If it doesn't work, then RIP my chances of paying rent.

I raise my hand. When Gwyneth nods welcomingly, I stand. "Hi. I'm Morgan Lane," I introduce myself. "Um. I didn't believe in ghosts until one showed up in my apartment. His name is Zach and he follows me everywhere. Of course, right now he's hiding because he's a bit of a prankster. In fact, he was responsible for the exploding Spindrift."

No one laughs. No one nods in commiseration. Not even Zach pops up to offer me well-intentioned words of encouragement.

The only change in the crowd comes from Sawyer. He doesn't look happy to be here, but his expression has opened up ever so slightly. He probably doesn't even register the change himself.

I do. Despite his demeanor, no less standoffish, he watches me with new interest.

I continue on, feeling self-conscious. "Yeah, um, so," I say eloquently, "Zach is . . . sort of ruining everything. I'm desperate to find a way to"—I whisper, just in case—"*get rid of him.*"

No exploding Spindrifts greet my declaration. Whew.

"Go on, Morgan," Gwyneth urges, delighted.

"My roommate is fed up with the haunting, and she's going to move out, leaving me with a lease I can't afford," I continue, appreciating the shopkeeper's support. "Unless anyone here has any leads on roommates who are cool and also looking to move in with one nice roommate and one ghost, I'm about to go into credit card debt to pay my rent."

Sawyer stares—nay, glares—straight forward, glumly examining the linoleum floor.

I feel incredibly ridiculous. As I'm standing here in my wet shirt, my cheeks flame.

The wannabe screenwriter raises his hand. "You could film your paranormal activity," he says zealously when I call on him, "and post it on social media to make your rent money."

I deflate. *Why do I feel like I've just heard young Spielberg's own elevator pitch?* Before he starts saying words like "cinema verité" or "new media," I nod. "Thanks for the suggestion."

"What if—"

Do my ears deceive me? I look sharply to Sawyer, who's spoken up. Given our earlier conversation—putting it generously—I did not expect voluntary input from the man watching me contemplatively, frowning in real concentration.

"What if instead of getting rid of him, you give him what he wants?" he continues. "He's probably trying to communicate with you."

"I can't just let him watch *Shark Week* on my roommate's computer whenever he's bored," I say, not certain Sawyer is fully comprehending the Zach situation. Zach is not yearning for release from some tortured grievance. My ghost is no yearner, I know that much.

But Sawyer is unmoved by my protest. He shrugs. "Then tell him," he replies. "If he's reasonable, you can work out a system that both of you like."

I'm opening my mouth to reject the well-intentioned recommendation when I realize it's . . . not the worst idea. I've tolerated Zach. I've tried to predict his outbursts and control them. I have not tried to deliberately schedule TV time or hangouts with my spectral sidekick. I mean, I've had *worse* roommates.

Gwyneth, for one, looks rapt, pausing in her crystal peddling with genuine interest in our exchange. Maybe, I concede, I've been a little hard on my ghost. To be fair, he hasn't made it easy to be easy on him, and I remain unconvinced anyone here knows what it's really like to have to share their life haunted. Even wool-sweater Sawyer.

Still, I nod. "I can try," I say reluctantly. "I'd rather evict him than work out roommate agreements, though."

Sawyer says nothing, but one of the millennial goths interjects. "A spirit is not something to evict. You have no more right to existence than your ghost," he pronounces, stern.

Gwyneth nods sagely.

"Of course," I say. I don't want to get into it with the guy whose shirt I hosed in citrusy sparkling water.

No one has more to offer. Discouraged, not to mention somewhat embarrassed, I return to my seat.

I'm contemplating walking out early when Gwyneth speaks up. "We want everyone to have the opportunity to join our community."

She rounds encouragingly on Sawyer, eyeing him in front of the group. I hold my breath, my curiosity rushing back.

"Would you like to share your experience with haunting?" she invites him.

Sawyer looks startled, like he never imagined participating. He seems to hesitate. "Fine. Sure," he says.

Way to go, Gwyneth. I disavow my earlier skepticism for our enthusiastic hostess. I'm going to buy some black tourmaline in thanks.

He stands slowly. "Hi, um. My name is Sawyer. I've been . . . haunted for a couple years now," he starts. "At first, I guess it could be a little unsettling. But . . . I don't know." Sawyer shrugs.

I frown. *He . . . doesn't know?* He's fine with slamming computers, rattling closet doors, and wholly unfortunate soy sauce explosions? I guess he's just got it very easy where his haunting is concerned. Or he's full of shit, like everyone else here.

"It's just life," Sawyer goes on. I resist the urge to point out we are, in fact, discussing the literal opposite of life. "It's fine. It's good, even," he says. "I don't mind unexplained drafts or cold temperatures. Or specific songs getting stuck in my head."

I'm strongly considering ducking out of here in discouragement when Sawyer's last words stop me dead.

Specific . . .

"Songs?" I repeat.

He looks over, surprised I've interrupted him. Finally, clarity parts the somber emptiness in his blue eyes.

Yeah, well, I'm surprised, too. I really, really expected today would prove nothing but Bullshit-R-Us with bad parking.

But I thought the song stuck in my head was Zach's thing. I didn't even know it was something ghosts could do until it happened to me.

"It's not like the normal way a song gets stuck in your head," Sawyer explains, under the reasonable impression I'm confused instead of understanding him perfectly. "It's not something I've listened to lately, or caught a strain of at the grocery store. It's a song I haven't thought about at all, but I know it's . . . It usually means . . . It's . . ."

I know what he's trying to say. "The ghost's favorite song," I finish.

I have Sawyer's full focus now. He holds my gaze, and I watch him realize what I have. We're both haunted—for real.

"Yeah," he confirms reluctantly. "For mine, it's 'A Sunday Kind of Love.' Etta James."

"I got 'Call Me Maybe,'" I say.

He blinks. I think I've thrown him off. I don't know why he came here, but clearly, like me, he didn't really expect to find someone who shares his experiences. He tugs his sweater sleeve like it's instinct to roll it down, then thinks better of it. His *wool* sweater, I realize, remembering his unexpected words of wisdom. I figured he was just trying to shut me up with useless advice.

He wasn't. It was real.

It *is* real.

"Whenever it plays in my head, I know, um, the ghost wants to communicate something or is nearby," Sawyer continues. "Honestly, I find it—"

"Really annoying." I laugh.

Sawyer doesn't. My laughter dies when his expression hardens defensively. "I was going to say *comforting*," he says.

"Comforting?" Incredulous, I can't help repeating his overgenerous characterization. He's obviously never had to draft scheduling emails while Carly Rae—or his ghost's oh-so-romantic Etta James pick—clamors in his head. "Well, I just want it to stop," I say.

"I don't," he retorts.

I don't want to discount anyone's personal experience in a support group, but I cannot fucking believe this. I need immediate, useful help, not Ghost Appreciation Week. Yet the *one* guy who might know something real is just . . . at peace with being haunted? How is that going to help pay my rent?

The unfriendly goths observe our exchange with their customary scorn, though I don't know whether their judgment is for me or Sawyer. The teenagers have disengaged with their phones to watch us with open interest. I get it—we're two perfect strangers fighting over ghosts getting songs stuck in our heads.

"Your ghost doesn't use their song to bother you when you're ignoring them?" I press him.

"Why would I ignore my ghost?" Sawyer sounds as disbelieving as me.

"Because you're in the middle of living your life," I reply, "and . . . they're dead?"

Now something hot sears through the haze in Sawyer's eyes. He drops his guard, and resentment hardens his expression. "Dead doesn't mean gone," he returns.

"No. That's the whole problem, isn't it?" I feel my own temper starting to rise. I've had no one—*no one*—who I could turn to while my little paranormal problem eroded every part of my life. "It means whenever you want to relax or go out to dinner or *date* or just . . . be by yourself, they're there. It's—"

"It's a gift," Sawyer interjects.

"I was going to say *nightmare*," I shoot back. "I wish they'd just rest in peace like they're supposed to."

The comment bewilders Sawyer. Recovering his composure, he scowls. He's opening his mouth to reply when Gwyneth intercedes.

"Fear not. I believe I have crystals to help both of you," she says in her damn soothing voice.

Fear not? Yeah, I was really fearing you would not have the crystals I need, I restrain myself from saying.

"I encourage everyone to take advantage of the discount. Today only!" she goes on.

With her words, I hear faint clatter over my shoulder. From the overstock shelves, some blue stones seem to tumble inexplicably to the floor and roll right to my feet.

I sigh. Sawyer may be ridiculously content with his haunting, but he might be right when it comes to warding off Zach. *Give him what he wants*, Sawyer counseled, his one semi-useful idea. "Do these happen to be blue quartz?" I inquire, holding one of the stones up wearily for the shopkeeper's inspection.

Her eyes light up. "They are! I think you would benefit from their calming energy. Maybe I can interest you in some black tourmaline for protection, too?"

I collect my bag. Between me and my ghost, one of us is going home happy. "Might as well," I say.

The group disassembles, retreating to the snacks or to peruse the shelves. I follow Gwyneth to the register, where she rings up my crystals.

While she does, I glance out the front window.

Sawyer, shoulders hunched in the sunlight, is walking out the front door.

Despite our less than harmonious introduction, I make a quick decision. I can either leave Gwyneth's Crystals with nothing except my dubious geological purchases . . . or I can pursue my only real lead. Everyone else here is obviously a fraud, but Sawyer's unprompted description of his own haunting had enough in common with mine to convince me.

When I finish paying, I sweep the crystals hastily into my bag and chase after him. Sawyer may like his ghost—and he may be a sanctimonious grump—but he's the only person who might know something that could help.

4

SAWYER

"I went. Happy?"

I ask the question under my breath seemingly to no one. I don't feel Kennedy right now, but she has to be nearby. Of course, I get no reply. Only a car honking at someone blocking the intersection.

It's too hot out here. I hurry to my car, eager to get home. This whole outing was a waste of time. I don't know what Kennedy expected me to get out of it, but all I'm leaving with is a coupon to a restaurant I'll never go to. Maybe I can give it to the next delivery person who I scare with my yard.

"Sawyer! Hey, Sawyer, hold up for a second!"

I'm reaching for my keys when I hear my name called behind me. Maybe I left my phone or my wallet inside or something.

Except when I turn, I find the woman from the meeting who also seems to be genuinely haunted—although our similarities definitely end there. She's dressed for the summer heat in overall shorts and scuffed sneakers. Her nails are dark blue, and her earrings are studs in the shape of Arizona. Since coming outside, she's pulled her brown hair back into a messy bun.

She rushes up to me, her expression a mix of frantic and eager. "Can we talk?" she asks. "You, um . . . Well, you're the only one in there who seems to be actually haunted."

I wish I had pretended I hadn't heard her over the car honking.

"What do you want to talk about?" I ask stiffly, hoping the gruffness of my tone will communicate how little I want to discuss anything with her.

Either Morgan doesn't pick up on social cues or she just ignores them. She steps closer to me like I've just agreed to hang out in front of the driver's side door of my car on the edge of the road. She's carrying a tote bag covered in artful drawings of plants with sexual-sounding Latin names. *Clitoria. Bifora testiculata.* Inside, I can see a shopping bag from Gwyneth's Crystals on top, presumably full of crystals.

"I just think that if we share more of our haunting experiences with each other, we might be able to figure out how to get rid of our ghosts. Like, exorcise them," she says. She must notice how entirely uninterested I am in the suggestion, because she starts in again. "Or maybe we can . . . help them?" she amends hopefully.

"You want to help your ghost," I repeat flatly.

"No." She looks to the side like she's seeing someone who isn't there. "I mean, I want to *help* Zach move on."

I know when I look at where she's looking, I won't see *Zach*, but I look anyway. Still, I'm not in any position to doubt this woman, as much as I desperately wish I could.

It doesn't matter if Zach is real, I remind myself. There's nothing Morgan and I can offer each other.

"I don't need help," I tell her, then open my car door.

She puts her hand on the door's top, making her intention of not leaving clear. I wish I were in my haunted house. People are less chatty in haunted houses. I've lost my touch for extricating myself from unwanted conversations.

Morgan smiles, unabashed. "You must have come to this meeting for something."

Her words halt me. I'm not about to explain to Morgan with her plant sex puns and invisible Zach that I came to this meeting because my ghost fiancée wants to try to get me to accept I'm unhappy in our relationship.

But what if the distance I'm feeling from Kennedy has nothing to do with our un-living conditions and is because *she's* distant? Not emotionally but metaphysically? Kennedy has been distracted and absent more. I thought it was because of me, but what if . . . ?

"Do you think ghosts can fade away?" I ask Morgan softly.

Her eyes widen. "Do they?" Her voice is gratingly hopeful. "I've only been haunted for a couple months, and Zach seems as present as ever, but you said you've been haunted for five years, right?"

I nod. I've completely abandoned getting into my car, invested in this conversation against my better judgment.

"Maybe with enough time . . ." she muses, her gaze turning thoughtfully to the road. "But five years? I'm sorry. I cannot waste my thirties waiting for Zach to fade away." She meets my eyes again, sympathy entering her expression. "You don't want your ghost to leave and they've started fading. That must be really hard."

The muscles of my jaw clench. I'm used to pity. Doesn't mean I like it, though. It's the invisible specter hanging over every conversation I've had with loved ones and strangers over the years, haunting me worse than any ghost.

This Morgan with her crystals and her desire to be free of the dead doesn't know anything about me.

"Look," I say, my tone pickax-sharp once more. "I don't think we can help each other. I wish you luck with your . . . Zach problem. But I have to go. I'm late for a meeting."

I climb into my front seat, no longer caring if Morgan wants to hold my door open. I'll drive away with it open if I have to.

Except the second I bring my key to the ignition, I hear a loud pop. The car rocks violently, then sags distinctly forward and to the left. Morgan shrieks and jumps back—right into the street.

On instinct, I leap out of the car and yank her forward, out of oncoming traffic. Her eyes widen in stunned gratitude.

I hold on to her forearm until I'm confident she's found her footing again, then I release her. The indent of my fingers on her pale arm shocks me. My eyes linger on the streaks of pink and white quickly fading to flesh as her blood pumps through her veins. I forgot skin does that.

Pulling myself from my trance, I peer around the corner of my car to find—yes, my driver's side tire is somehow completely, spontaneously, shredded.

No, not *somehow*.

I can feel Kennedy nearby, her presence a comforting chill on this summer's day. I pull my sleeves down. *Finally* she's returned, only to destroy my tire. I fight the annoyance that surges in me. Why is she doing this to me?

Of course, I know the answer. She wants me to keep talking to Morgan. There's no other reason. She wouldn't just torture me with unwanted conversation otherwise. Kennedy isn't spiteful or malicious. Her spirit is only kindness and love.

She must think there's something Morgan can do for us. For her.

"Tough luck," Morgan says when she's caught her breath. "Well, it looks like you're going to be waiting around for Triple A. Want to grab some food?"

She pulls out the coupon for Serving Spirits and grins.

5

SAWYER

Kennedy would hate Serving Spirits. When I called AAA, only to find myself on hold, then learn from the dispassionate representative the wait time would leave me standing in the sweltering heat for nearly two hours, I reluctantly followed Morgan down the street.

The place has me close to returning to my popped tire. Everything is coated in dust—"intentionally," I have no doubt. The old-Hollywood feel, with gilt-framed mirrors over the wooden bar and hardened burgundy leather furniture, does not change the fact that nothing here looks renovated or repaired *since* the 1940s. The B health rating hangs unabashed in the window.

If the poor upkeep wasn't enough, the paranormal paraphernalia sets me on edge. Ouija boards wait ready for inquisitive summoners on the tables. EMF detectors, the cheap devices they use on ghost-hunting reality shows, rest on the hardwood bar, inviting patrons to probe the space for specters. Old photographs and paintings decorate the walls with plaques attesting to the ghosts in every image.

Morgan loves it. Her eyes go wide with giddy incredulity when we walk in. *I thought you found ghosts irritating*, I half want to say, except I don't want to be petty.

Nor do I really want to talk to Morgan Lane when I don't have to.

The guy from the meeting who handed out coupons waves enthusiastically when he sees us, no doubt pleased his marketing strategy seems to have worked.

Morgan beams. I do not.

I resentfully follow Morgan to one of the leather booths beneath a photograph of a classic California bungalow. Morgan leans in to read the plaque, then points to a smudge on the window. Maybe it is the spirit of some 1920s Hollywood ghost, or maybe the camera's flash caught in warped glass. We'll never know, and I don't care to speculate.

When Morgan opens a laminated menu, however, my disloyal stomach groans.

Reluctantly, I inspect our options. The Great Beyond Burgers. The Blair Sandwich Project. Wings with "haunt sauce." On Sundays they have Paranormal Flapjacktivity.

Of course.

Morgan eagerly orders the Blair Sandwich. I only muster enthusiasm for the least whimsically named menu item, fries with ghost-pepper ranch dip. The fact ghost peppers happen to be named that doesn't mean I'm disrespecting the dead.

While we wait, Morgan picks up an EMF detector nearby. She waves the plastic unit in our vicinity.

"Zach," she says to the empty seat next to her, "is there another ghost here?"

Obviously, no one replies. I keep wishing I could disbelieve her—it would mean I had gained nothing from the meeting Kennedy sent me to.

But everything Morgan has said is impossible to ignore. So here I find myself, in a ghost bar with a woman who is talking to someone invisible.

"He says he can't see one," Morgan informs her living lunch companion—me.

"Those don't work," I cannot help remarking, nodding to the EMF detector.

Morgan smiles. "You're such a skeptic for someone who lives with a ghost," she comments playfully.

"You don't need a device to measure where they are," I reply. "You just feel them. Haunting is . . ."

I hesitate. Is what? What wouldn't Morgan scoff at? *Haunting is the visible echo of countless dreams that won't happen. Haunting is the future you imagined playing out in the shadow of your worst fear.*

"Nothing like this," I conclude, hoping Morgan hears the finality in my voice.

If she does, she ignores it.

She studies me without judgment. "What's it like for you, then?"

I meet her gaze. Though I find the question silly—like wondering, *What's memory like?* or *What's feeling like?*—Morgan's interest seems genuine. It's sort of impressive. Openheartedness radiates from her like sunshine.

Despite the EMF detector she's clutching, her interest relaxes me. "It's love. Grief so real it's palpable. Not . . . jump scares and green slime," I say, gesturing to the menu references.

Morgan doesn't sneer like in the support group. Instead, she looks to her left. To no one. "I hope you know that if you ever green-slime me, I will re-kill you." She pauses. "You don't even want to know how." Seeming satisfied, she looks to me. "I don't grieve Zach, though," she replies. "I definitely didn't love him."

Her bag, perched on the table, starts to wobble suddenly. When it tumbles from the edge, Morgan catches it clumsily, looking relieved. "He doesn't like it when I'm mean to him, but I don't like it when he cock-blocks every date I've been on since he appeared," Morgan explains matter-of-factly. "Does your ghost ruin your sex life?"

I shift uncomfortably. "No," I say.

"You're lucky," Morgan informs me.

Unbeknownst to Morgan, I hear the phantom echo of my own promise to Kennedy. *I'm the luckiest man in the whole world.*

"Maybe Zach loves *you*," I say.

Morgan laughs.

"If you could see Zach's face right now," she replies. "I promise you. He doesn't. Okay, okay, dude"—she glances to her other side—"no need to rub it in! I have feelings!"

Our food is delivered. Promptly Morgan produces from her bag shining pieces of black crystal. She sets them up, forming a secure perimeter surrounding her sandwich.

"Leave my food alone," she warns. I know I'm not the person she's speaking to.

I start in slowly on my fries. The ghost-pepper sauce is decent, even if eating ranch from a B-rated restaurant may have me joining Kennedy on the other side real soon.

Morgan continues in between bites. "I went on one date with Zach three months ago, and neither of us wanted a second date. I didn't even know he died until he popped up in my bathroom mirror while I was brushing my teeth. I have no idea why he's haunting me. Was it similar for you?"

"Not really," I say, hoping one- or two-word responses will communicate that I do not want to elaborate.

No such luck.

"How did you first discover you were being haunted?" Morgan presses me.

I sigh. I keep to myself mostly these days. I've forgotten how pushy the living can be in conversation.

"Kennedy showed up shortly after she died. I didn't realize it was her at first. Things in my house just kept being moved around. A folded blanket. A dish I left out moved to the sink. Mail brought in," I explain.

"Man, I wish Zach was helpful like that," she says. She reaches for one of my fries, then clenches her hand, withdrawing in reconsideration.

"Maybe if he were, you wouldn't be in such a hurry to get rid of him," I reply.

Morgan considers. She grows serious, the sunlight quality of her eyes clouding. "I still would," she finally says. "He's . . . not supposed to be here," she explains. "I don't think he wants to be here, either. I mean, it's not really a life, just hovering around me. I think it's better he move on, or whatever."

She clutches the edge of her plate, expecting retribution from Zach, but nothing happens. Her bag sits motionless on the table. He . . . agrees with her.

My stomach knots.

It's different with us, I insist to myself. Kennedy and I had a life. *Have* a life.

"Maybe," I concede.

Morgan studies me more closely. I feel suddenly self-conscious, like when I shared in the support group. I offer her one of my fries, hoping to distract her.

She looks pleased and hits the ghost-pepper sauce unflinchingly. Her focus on me doesn't let up, however. "Doesn't Kennedy keep you from living a normal life? Surely it must be hard to explain to coworkers why the office feels haunted around you," she ventures. "Your friends must be creeped out at your place."

"I work from home," I say.

Morgan raises her eyebrows, unsatisfied. "And your friends?"

"Kennedy is my friend."

Morgan's shoulders slump. "Dude," she pronounces. "You need to have at least one friend who isn't dead."

I shrug. Defiantly, I dip my fry. "Why?"

Skepticism crosses Morgan's expression when she opens and then closes her mouth. She lifts the EMF detector up and waves the unit closer in front of me.

"What are you doing?" I ask.

"Making sure *you're* not a ghost," she informs me. "Can't end up in a *Sixth Sense* situation here."

I nearly laugh, surprising myself. "Well, what does the very science-backed ghost-hunting tool tell you?"

"According to this, you're alive, but I'm not convinced," she informs me. "You're right. Probably doesn't work."

"Tough luck," I reply.

Those clouds in Morgan's warm brown irises part. Our gazes lock, and I have the strangest feeling of her sunlight spilling into me. For one moment, I nearly forget I'm in a paranormal-themed bar with a woman and her ghost for company.

"So"—Morgan interrupts the pause—"you're happy with your one ghost friend in your haunted house, but you came to the support group because you're worried Kennedy is fading away?"

Her words summon the memory of what waits when I return to my overgrown garden and unfinished home. "I came because Kennedy wanted me to," I correct, then promptly change the subject. "If you want to send Zach away, I think you need to figure out why he's haunting *you*," I suggest. "There must be a deeper connection between you than you think."

"So there's a deeper connection between you and Kennedy?" Morgan replies. She's good at disarming my deflections, at digging up everything I'm trying to keep buried in this conversation.

I don't flinch or falter. I would have in the months following Kennedy's death.

In those months, however, our Silver Lake home was not the only remodel I undertook. I walled off my feelings, my dreams, my shattered heart. I knew the world would not have patience forever for how broken I was, so I practiced looking fixed. I learned how to pretend I had returned to a world I no longer recognized.

Working not with clay but with stone, I sculpted the image of someone who had *gone through something*, who was *doing better now*.

When Kennedy came to me, I was ready. With the only companion I would ever need, my emotional fallout shelter was complete.

"Yes," I say simply.

"What—" Morgan starts.

I interrupt her. "I think part of you hasn't let Zach go. Part of you wants him to stay."

Morgan softens. She returns her sandwich to her plate. "Look, I know you believe hauntings are like a metaphysical representation of grief, but I'm sorry to say you're wrong," she says. "Honestly, it should reassure you. Kennedy isn't fading away because you've stopped grieving her or something. It's not your pain that's holding her here," Morgan says, "and it's not your healing that's cutting her loose."

Startled, I meet her eyes. Morgan isn't just haunted, I realize.

She *understands* haunting—on a much deeper level than I expected. She has, impossibly, described exactly what I've subconsciously feared for months. That I was failing Kennedy somehow. Wasn't grieving enough. Wasn't holding on hard enough.

I couldn't even put it into words the way Morgan just did. "You're sure?" I venture, aware I'm exposing exactly what I was trying to hide from her, letting her peek over my walled-off pain. "You feel nothing for Zach?"

"Nothing," Morgan says. "And he can't even remember his life except for the shitty date we went on, and that he wishes he could forget."

I finish my final fry and realize I'm a little mournful there aren't more. "What a bleak way to go out," I remark.

Morgan laughs. "A date so mediocre, it'll haunt you forever," she says. "Maybe I should add it to my dating bios."

I feel myself smile. "You could spin it," I offer. "No matter what, you'll remember this date until after your dying day."

"Or please ghost me. Literally," Morgan suggests.

I laugh.

Morgan seems startled, then eyes me in sly satisfaction. "Finally. Proof of life," she says. "Guess the EMF reader was right."

I look down, self-conscious, still smiling. Honestly, I don't know how I'm feeling. None of today has gone the way I expected, including this ridiculous bar. I feel guilty in a way I can't explain. "I should go," I say.

"Wait," Morgan exclaims. "I need your help. We have two unexplained phenomena—Kennedy fading away and Zach haunting *me*, someone who has no emotional attachment to him."

The light flickers overhead.

Other patrons murmur excitedly.

The proprietor from the support group looks giddy behind the bar. "Don't worry, folks! Just regular paranormal activity at this haunted bar!" he crows.

Wisely, Morgan drops her voice. "It seems to me," she continues, "like they might have the same answer if we could just figure it out. They need something from us. Something specific."

I hesitate. I want to wait for Kennedy's reappearances, dwelling in the desperation I've convinced myself is hope.

But despite myself, Morgan has halfway convinced me. I haven't failed Kennedy in not grieving well enough. But I could fail her in other ways. I could withdraw from whatever nameless dissatisfaction she's struggling with. When I promised I only wanted her happiness, I meant it.

"I don't know what it is," I reply.

"But Kennedy wanted you to come to this meeting," Morgan insists. "Why? If she'd wanted you to make friends, she would have told you to go to a book club or something. She sent you to a haunting support group. She needs help."

She needs help. The words cut deep into me. It's one thing to hear them in my head, doubtful whispers following every drawn look in Kennedy's eyes. It's something else to hear them out loud. I can't handle it.

"I'm probably just picking up on nothing," I declare. "I'm sure she's fine."

Morgan's bag flies off the table.

The contents spill out everywhere on the floor. One woman in the corner shrieks out in shock.

"Jeez, Zach!" Morgan exclaims in frustration. "Cut it out!"

Dutifully, I start helping Morgan return her possessions to their rightful places. While I'm collecting loose change, however, Morgan hisses. "Ow. Fuck." She drops what she was holding. "It's burning hot," she explains. "I don't know why he's so mad—"

I notice what Morgan has dropped. A small packet of garden seeds.

Comforting cold shivers up my arms.

"It's not Zach," I say, reaching for the packet. Its temperature is perfectly normal when I pick it up. "Why do you have these?"

"I'm a landscaper," Morgan replies. "It's what I do for work."

My thoughts race. My heart follows. I hold on to the seeds while we retake our seats—the seeds Kennedy wanted me to find. "Like . . . a gardener," I say.

Morgan nods.

While I'm reckoning with what's happening here, the Serving Spirits proprietor exuberantly comes over to where we're seated. He's holding two plates with identical desserts, chocolate miniature bundt cakes with marshmallow glaze descending unevenly down the sides. On the dark chocolate, the white goo leaves the cake looking cartoon-ghost-shaped.

Kennedy would cringe. My stomach grumbles.

"You two are welcome back here anytime. Our signature dessert is on the house. You have to try it because, after all—"

Delightedly, he points to the poster on the wall next to the front door, which depicts the dessert.

Unfinished Business, the confection is called.

"—you can't leave until you've finished your Unfinished Business," the proprietor proclaims.

Morgan reaches for her fork.

I don't.

I never imagined revelation would be found in a novelty chocolate cake. Today truly has defied every expectation.

"I know what the ghosts want," I say.

6

One gooey, chocolaty, metaphorically resonant ghost cake later, I'm watching Sawyer thank the repair guy for replacing his Kennedy-damaged tire. The proprietor's words hum in my mind. *Unfinished business.*

For once, I feel not just hopeful. I feel *optimistic.*

It's fucking great.

While we paid our bill, Sawyer promised me he had a proposition. One that could help us *and* our ghosts. Obviously, I told him I was game for anything. I just bought fifty dollars' worth of crystals, after all. Why wouldn't I go to his haunted house and hear him out?

And I can't deny that my fellow hauntee is handsome. While I wasn't flirting with Sawyer—*Come to this ghost-themed bar often?*—under other circumstances, I could easily imagine doing so, with his short dark curls, the lean muscle he seems carved of, the way laughter leapt unexpectedly from his stern, strong-jawed profile.

With Sawyer's car situation resolved, I drive from my unfortunate parking space to his SUV, then follow behind his car to where he lives. It's not far. For fifteen minutes, Atwater Village's low strip malls and suburban flatlands fade into Silver Lake's verdant, palm-treed hipster hillside, until Sawyer pulls into his driveway.

I veer toward the curb, mentally psyching myself up for more parallel parking. Just as I'm about to abandon my effort, Zach pops into visibility next to the front of the vintage Bronco I'm wedging myself up to.

"You're good," he calls out for only me to hear. "Plenty of space. Keep backing up."

I start to smile. Only in Los Angeles is parallel parking guidance one of the upsides of haunting.

"Keep straightening out," he counsels. "Perfect. Remember to curb your wheels!"

"Thanks for being helpful for once," I say when Zach rematerializes in my rearview mirror.

"More helpful than collecting mail, wouldn't you say? Admit it. I'm way better than that guy's ghost," Zach replies haughtily.

Laughing, I step out of the car.

Honestly, even without Sawyer's SUV in his driveway, I could've picked out my destination on the street of cool, elegantly remodeled old California homes. One house on the block definitely looks haunted.

The front yard is . . . scary. Overgrown and dead, with just terrible curb appeal. It looks abandoned, with dry vines winding over each other in high clumped masses obscuring the house I can only glimpse past them.

Sawyer waits for me next to his car on the cracked sidewalk.

"Seriously, Morgan, be careful," Zach warns. "Judging from his yard, this guy is a serial killer."

I close my car door. Admittedly, I'm not feeling awesome about following the man I just met to a second location right now. "If he gets out a chain saw, maybe you could short-circuit it or something," I say.

Zach vanishes. *So much for helpful.* I remind myself why I'm here—unfinished business, no way to pay rent, "Call Me Maybe"—and walk over to Sawyer, mustering my courage.

I guess he notices the ghostly pallor of my face. "I know it looks bad," he preempts, sounding sincerely remorseful.

"Oh, your yard? It's lovely," I joke. "Who's your landscaper? Beetlejuice?"

Sawyer winces. "It was in bad shape when I bought it. Most of the interior is fixed up, and the yard was next. But . . ."

I hear the end of Sawyer's unfinished sentence. *Kennedy.*

He's grieving. This home was his project until loss overwhelmed his life, overgrowing like choking vines.

I feel shitty for making fun. Contrite, I step into the garden mess, wanting a better look.

Except there is no *better* look. The yard only gets worse. Above the dead grass, dried bushes of shriveled, dusty leaves intertwine chaotically. I'm pretty sure this is downtown for the neighborhood spiders. Light hardly pervades the shaggy mess, which is dense enough to get lost in.

Or . . . to lose yourself in. If I wanted to hide in plain sunlight, walled off from the world, I would welcome this plant portcullis Sawyer lives behind.

It's not as if he likes his horrific murder garden, I remind myself. He said so himself. He knows it needs—

I whirl, suddenly realizing. "You want me to *landscape* this?"

Sawyer puts his hands in his jeans pockets, sheepish.

"It's just . . . it's a huge job," I say gently, despite knowing I could slap on several more words for *huge* and still come out understating the calamity of this man's yard. "It would take . . . a lot of time. I'm not always great at long-term commitments," I admit.

Pathologically commitment-phobic is more like it. I pretty much wrecked my twenties, nearly drove my parents into debt, charging carelessly into commitments I couldn't keep. College. My premature engagement. I know renovating Sawyer's garden isn't equivalent to promising myself for marriage, but . . . still. I'm done getting people's hopes up.

It's just easier, I've found. Easier to get up every day. Easier to not judge myself. Every time I move cities with no money, no boyfriend, and no idea what I want, I'm not failing. I'm just starting over.

"But really," I emphasize. "I'm just the office manager for a landscaping firm. I barely handle my own projects. My bosses could totally do this, though," I encourage Sawyer. "They'd love it."

Now Sawyer hunches his shoulders. If he hunched them any more, his head would disappear into the cozy wool sweater he's wearing in the middle of July.

"I can't afford them," he explains.

Despite my remorse for mocking his landscaping, my eyes go wide. "You want me to fix your yard *for free*?"

Sawyer doesn't get defensive. He looks patient with my incredulity, actually. It suits him, like waiting comes naturally to my new prospective pro bono employer.

"Just hear me out," he implores me. The sun manages to filter past the thicket surrounding us, dappling him in light. "What if the ghosts have unfinished business that they need *our* help with?"

"You think Kennedy's unfinished business is your lawn?" I clarify.

Sawyer looks down. He speaks to the dead ground. "She was my fiancée," he says.

The guilty pit I was ignoring opens wide in my stomach. I replay my own words, every mocking dismissal I made of holding on to his ghost, every flippant joke about the dead. I practically owe him a fucking topiary out of his haunted thickets for the way I carried on.

"We bought this house together," he continues. "She was a contractor, and we did most of the renovations together to turn this into our dream home. But she died before we could finish. I haven't had the heart to work on it without her."

He pauses ever so slightly on the important words. Like he has to force his voice to form them. Of course he does. How would they ever get easier? While I complain about Zach opening my cupboards or putting songs in my head, Sawyer has carried unimaginable grief with him for years.

No wonder he likes being haunted.

"But if we do this, aren't you afraid Kennedy will . . . move on?" I ask gently. It's why I latched on to Sawyer's idea in Serving Spirits, after all. I'm hoping if I find whatever unfulfilled wish Zach needs fulfilling, he'll vanish from my life, not to mention my cupboards and my roommate's Netflix queue.

The same possibility has obviously occurred to Sawyer.

His breathing goes shallow. He looks nervous, his lips seeming to quaver when he speaks. Suddenly, the solidity of him, the stone-worked quality of his features I noticed immediately, disappears. He looks on the verge of crumbling to pieces.

"I . . . I would do anything for her," he says. "She wants me to do this. For some reason, she sent me to that meeting. She wanted me to find those seeds and ask what you do. She's been . . . fading," he explains. "Like you said—what if because she hasn't accomplished her unfinished business, she just . . . fades to nothing? I can't let that happen."

He's close to crying now, wrestling his tears like he's desperate to keep them from showing. His determination wins out, and his expression sets.

"If this is what she wants, I'll do it for her," he whispers. "No matter what."

I know what I need to say, even if it makes me feel horrible. I summon my own determination. Letting all my compassion into my expression, I speak softly to him under the fractured garden light.

"I'm really sorry, Sawyer," I say. "This has to be . . . impossible to face. I want to help. I do. It's just . . ." I struggle to explain myself. "This is a really big job."

I don't give voice to the clamor of whispers in my head, the ghosts I contended with long before Zach. *I'll screw it up. I'll disappoint you. I won't come through. Don't depend on Morgan Lane. A decision so bad, it'll haunt you forever.*

"I have my own problems right now," I say instead. The selfishness of my words makes my skin itch, but it's better than offering promises I can't keep. "Including my own ghost whose unfinished business I have no clue about. And I'm about to go severely into debt . . ."

Sawyer looks up. His eyes focus, like he's grasping onto this tether I've given him out of his emotions. "Let me show you one more thing," he says.

I half expect Zach to comment, *That's exactly what a serial killer would say.*

Instead, only quiet greets Sawyer's offer. I nod.

Sawyer leads me off to a side garden path that winds past the home. The foliage is somewhat less egregious here, fortunately. Chipping paint on the white wooden fence hems us in while I follow Sawyer to the back of the lot.

Our destination is a detached room on the other side of a small patio swallowed by a gorgeous bougainvillea. The renovation Sawyer mentioned is halfway complete—the walls look freshly clean of dirt and moss, but the trim on the windows is shabby, and the heavy handle on the door rusted.

Sawyer inserts his key, then proceeds to jostle the uncooperative lock vigorously. My cowardly hopes rise for a second—maybe Kennedy is interfering, and I can easily chalk my landscaping reluctance up to the clear evidence his ghost fiancée does not want me snooping in her spare room. *What a shame!*

For once in my life, however, paranormal activity doesn't seem to be the culprit. Sawyer manages to jog the lock while pushing his shoulder into the door, springing open the entry.

What waits inside is . . . very dusty. Serving Spirits has nothing on my new acquaintance's spooky-ass house.

When I examine the outline of the room in the dim sunlight filtering through the dirty window, I realize what I'm seeing is half mother-in-law unit, complete with tiny kitchenette and fancy sleeper sofa, and half . . . pottery studio. Dust covers the pottery wheel in one corner, while sculpted projects in various stages of completion line the shelves.

"It was my studio. I haven't worked in a while," Sawyer explains.

His studio. I remember Sawyer's deflection when I pressed him on Kennedy's interference in his professional life. *I work from home.*

I assumed Zoom and Slack. This is . . . intriguing. Not what I expected from the withdrawn, contemplative man whose home I'm touring.

"You could . . . stay here," Sawyer proposes. "Once I, um, clean.

We set this room up for friends and family to visit. You'd have your privacy. The lock even has a separate key that you can have, and I won't be able to access it without your permission." He steps in, gesturing past the kitchenette. "There's a small bathroom behind the kitchen. Your roommate could stay in your apartment, and you could live here, with Zach, rent-free."

Rent-free. The sweetest words in the English language. Two words, two syllables, eight letters. Say it and I'm yours. *Rent-free.* If I joined Zach in the spectral realm and could only communicate via Ouija board, Serving Spirits patrons could still find the ghost of Morgan Lane pushing the pointer to R-E-N-T-F-R-E-E.

Nonetheless. "Not completely rent-free," I say. "I'm guessing in exchange for the yard?"

Once more, I receive Sawyer's hunched shoulders. He nods, and in the crumbling interior, I'm forced to recognize haunted houses suit him.

"Yes," he concedes gently. "But you can take as much time as you need. I know you have a job and a life. Any time you can spare on the garden is great, and you can stay here as long as it takes."

I soften. When was the last time *anyone* said I could take as much time as I need?

Stepping into the space, I evaluate my potential new living conditions, available for the low, low price of landscaping the world's most horrific front yard. Under the overwhelming dust, I start to see how the space could be charming. Rustically simple with plenty of sunlight for my houseplants once we clean the windows. Savannah could come back to our apartment, and I could keep paying my share of the lease while staying here until I've exorcised Zach. It would solve my financial problems, for sure.

"A little cozy for us, don't you think?" I find Zach seated on the kitchenette countertop, swinging his feet. His see-through heels, clad in the dadcore New Balances I guess he died in, pass in and out of the cabinet.

"You don't get a say," I remind him. "This is your fault."

Sawyer startles.

"Sorry, talking to Zach," I say sheepishly, realizing how my outburst would have sounded. Sawyer very much does get a say in inviting the random woman he brought home from Ghost Therapy to live in his guesthouse. "It's weird you can't see him, although I guess no one else can," I say. "Just me."

"It's something we can figure out together," Sawyer replies. "Why our ghosts can only be perceived by us. Where is Zach?"

I point to the counter.

Sawyer very sincerely faces the general direction of Zach.

My spectral companion's eyebrows rise.

"Zach, I promise to try to help with your unfinished business, too," Sawyer declares.

Something unexpected crosses Zach's face. Something pained, and I realize it hasn't just been nine weeks of Zach haunting me. It's been nine weeks since anyone *else* has spoken to him.

It must be lonely.

Slowly, my ghost's easygoing cheer returns. He shrugs, looking to me. "Dude seems all right," he says, grudging. "No serial killer vibes detected. Anything to get free of you, honestly."

When I smile, Sawyer notices. "What did he say?" he asks.

I hold out my hand for the key. "When can we move in?"

7

SAWYER

I wash my hands in cold water. It'll eventually heat up, but I've gotten used to the cool. It's not paranormally cold, even—just a quirk of the pipes of a home built in the 1930s.

Grime sheds from my skin, pooling and then disappearing down the drain. I spent the rest of yesterday cleaning the studio, making minimal progress on the formidable job. Turns out five years of dirt takes more than one night to clean.

It's not like I was busy, though. My hopes of watching TV with Kennedy or having dinner while she sat nearby remained only that—hopes.

Determined, I finished the job today. I washed sheets, stocked the bathroom with soap, and bought a plunger from Target. I even hung a shower curtain. With everything else prepared, I returned to the exhausting fight to exorcise the studio's dust. I wish I'd found it cathartic or meditative or some shit like that.

I didn't. It was hard. Not physically or logistically—after helping Kennedy with our remodel, I'm fairly handy. No, it was hard emotionally. I haven't done work on the house since Kennedy was really here, when she played her favorite music from her phone instead of just running it through my head. It's why I've avoided patching and painting the remaining unfinished pieces of the house. I know it'll hurt.

But I'm doing this for her, I remind myself. To save her from fading to nothing.

When I shut off the water, I see lights outside my front window. Morgan's car is pulling up to the curb. I dry my hands, noticing how pale the cold water makes them.

"This is what you want, right?" I ask quietly.

The faintest hum of "A Sunday Kind of Love" enters my head. I smile and then hurry outside to help.

Morgan is hauling a worn suitcase from her car. She spent one more night in her place last night while I prepared the studio. I'm guessing she left work tonight, picked up her packed things, then headed here to move in. She shuts the trunk and starts walking toward my gnarled yard.

Pausing outside my door, I observe my new guest for a moment. Morgan is short, dresses in laid-back, effortlessly cool staples, and has extraordinary long, wavy brown hair. What I notice most, though, isn't these superficialities. She has an energy to her—half restless, half eager. Nothing seems to slow her down or dim her vigor.

It's reflected in her laissez-faire attitude on haunting. Most people would have gone catatonic or jittery if they genuinely experienced the supernatural. Not Morgan. Instead, she seems to . . . crack jokes with her ghost and ask his opinion on her—their—living conditions. It's unusual. Impressive, even.

Watching her wrestle her luggage up the path, I take a deep breath. Even though I spent two days preparing the studio for her, it's only now hitting me that someone is going to be *living* here.

"I can help grab the rest from your car," I call.

Morgan instantly startles, dropping the handle of her suitcase. "Dude!" Her eyes land on me. "You cannot sneak up on people in this yard." She bends down to pick up her suitcase.

"Sorry." I wince. "I figured you didn't spook easily, given your . . . circumstances."

"My circumstances? You mean the ghost of a himbo I live with? That's nothing compared to a strange man with a murder yard," she replies flippantly. "And no, this is everything. I just have a few plants in the car but, no offense, only I handle them. All the plants under your care are super fucking dead."

I stop in the middle of my, yes, super fucking dead lawn. "Wait. That's . . . everything? You're moving in here for an indefinite amount of time with one suitcase?"

Morgan doesn't stop walking. Her voice carries over her shoulder. "I don't have a lot of stuff. Never really believed in acquiring things that I'll just throw out one day. Besides, it makes moves like right now easier."

I don't even know where to begin with that statement. I suppose it's no surprise that the woman who is eager to get rid of her ghost ex considers physical possessions to be only future garbage.

I can't relate. I've bought and made many pieces of pottery that have gone on to sit collecting dust in the closet.

"Do you move a lot, then?" I ask as I catch up to her on the back patio, my feet crunching over the fallen bougainvillea petals.

Morgan shrugs one shoulder. "Every couple years or so. We moved a lot when I was growing up, and it sort of stuck. I was in Arizona last, but I needed a break from the heat."

My eyes trail to her earrings—the ones I noticed earlier. The outline of the state of Arizona. Perhaps she's not as unsentimental as she pretends to be.

"A little ironic, don't you think?" I ask. "A gardener who doesn't put down roots?"

Morgan flashes me a grin. "My plants travel with me just fine." Reaching into the pocket of her overalls, she pulls out the key I gave her earlier. She unlocks the door and seems surprised by how little resistance it gives her. I don't bother telling her I spent an hour today sanding down the warped part of the door under the lock.

"Do you need anything from the house? I set you up with some basic supplies, but if you need plates or silverware, I could bring some over," I offer, eyeing her regular-sized suitcase doubtfully.

"I'm good," Morgan replies cheerfully. "I brought my plate." She walks farther into the room, shivering slightly.

"Your . . . plate? Singular?"

"I only need the one. Zach doesn't eat," she says, laughing at her own joke.

I can't help it. I gape at her. I haven't had someone living come over to my house in years, and still I could never only have *one* plate. Not only because a good plate is a piece of art in itself, but because it's just inconvenient. Does she never cook? Does she not get satisfaction from adding a clean plate to a stack in the cupboard?

Morgan watches me, clearly amused. "I suppose that's vaguely horrifying to someone who makes pottery. You probably have a lot of plates."

"Cups and bowls, too," I add, puffing my chest up like I'm bragging.

She grins. Her smile is bright, her teeth just a tiny bit crooked on the top. The room seems a little warmer suddenly. Like whatever the opposite of haunting is, Morgan is doing it.

"It's good to know if Zach smashes my beloved plate, you'll have me covered." She lays her suitcase flat on the original hardwood.

When she speaks, it's seemingly to the empty room. "Well, buddy? Want to help me unpack?"

We wait. A breeze outside sways the open door.

Morgan sighs. "Didn't think so." She unzips her suitcase and starts pulling things out.

I step back, not wanting to intrude. I only just met this woman yesterday. We're not exactly friends. I'm not exactly her landlord. We're . . . I don't know. But I don't know her well enough to hover, even if I am fascinated by what she might have deemed worthy to travel with her.

"Have a good night. Come by sometime tomorrow and we can discuss yard plans," I say, holding the knob, ready to close the door behind me.

Morgan holds her hand up, waving while she continues to rummage.

I leave her to it and return to my dark and much colder house. I turn on the lights, chasing the shadows away as much as I can. Suddenly, I feel just how large this house is. I was never meant to live here alone. When Kennedy leaves, how much worse will it feel? I can't contemplate the question.

It's nearly nine. I'm not in the mood to read. I've done so much physical labor today that I know I'll sleep as soon as I lie down. Might as well surrender now. I drag myself up my creaky stairs and head for our—my—bedroom. The en suite bathroom was the first big renovation Kennedy did. We tiled the floor together. I worked on the mosaic while Kennedy watched from the arched doorway.

I push the memory from my head and reach for my toothbrush.

As soon as I have toothpaste all over my teeth, music suddenly blares through the small window overlooking the back patio. The Killers, I think, though I can't fully hear the melody. How very appropriate for Morgan.

I cool my instant irritation. I haven't had to live with a roommate since college. I didn't like it then. Kennedy and I moved in
together shortly after we started dating, and I never looked back.

But honestly, I haven't lived with *anyone* in five years. Ghosts
are one thing, but living people are a lot more . . . present. I'd like
to knock on Morgan's door and ask her to turn it down. It's her first
night, though. I don't want her to back out of our deal.

I also don't need her to know I'm a loser who goes to sleep at
nine p.m. I'm already the grieving haunted dude with a creepy
yard. I need to hold on to the shreds of dignity I have left.

I've survived worse than a night of falling asleep fitfully to
2000s hits. It'll be fine, I tell myself. Sleeping in an old haunted
house has trained me for this.

I spit and rinse. Suddenly, the music gets *louder.* I close my eyes.
No, wait, it's not just louder. I can make out the lyrics now, too.
"Smile Like You Mean It." I look out the window and find the studio door is open and a dark figure is crossing the flagstone to my
back door. This is no shadowy apparition.

I speed down my steps to meet her. *Of course* she's realized she
needs something. A cup or a towel. No one can really live out of
one suitcase.

When I open my door, I'm ready to gloat. Until Morgan holds
up a small ceramic mug in the shape of a dragon's head.

I recognize it instantly. I made it. Years and years ago.

"Sorry," Morgan begins. "Zach stole this. He hid it in my luggage. I think he must have found it in the studio? I'm afraid he'll
break it, so it might be better if you take it inside your house. Sometimes, he gets obsessed with things, and I really don't need his
latest prank fixation to feature something I'm guessing you made."

I reach out for the dark green mug. The front is sharpened into
a dragon's nose. The back features wings that I carefully sculpted

and applied. I haven't seen it in—I don't know how long. I made it before I started focusing on the vases and pottery I sold to hotel decorators for a living. "I did, yeah," I tell her. "A lifetime ago. I didn't know I still had it. I don't even know where he found it."

Morgan surrenders the dragon carefully. "Zach is good at turning up crap. *Not* that this is crap," she says, rushing to clarify. "It's actually very cool. I just mean he finds old forgotten stuff a lot. My roommate had this envelope of Polaroids she took with an ex and—you know what? I'm not going to tell that story, but suffice to say, Zach found what she never wanted found again."

I thumb the indentations I made for eyes, remembering the smell of fresh glaze, the paint I applied with a fine brush. It had been a random experiment, a challenge for myself to make something outside my comfort zone. Holding this relic from my past brings back memories I forgot I had. How can Morgan live with so few possessions? How many pieces of her own life are out of her sight and therefore entirely forgotten? Gone forever, now.

Maybe that's the point, I realize sadly.

"Thanks," I tell Morgan. "If he finds it again, or something else, it's okay. I'm not afraid of mugs breaking. It happens."

Morgan's gaze moves from the dragon to me. I have the sense she's seeing far more than I intended. "You said you don't do pottery anymore. Get bored?" she asks, her voice gentle but inquisitive.

I know what she's really asking. I decide to spare her having to come right out with it. "I haven't been able to since Kennedy died. I need to make her an urn, but I . . . can't. It's blocked me, I guess."

Her eyes, brown, soften in the moonlight. "Well, if you ever want to make anything less painful than the final resting place for your deceased fiancée, this dragon mug is cool as hell. You could try a unicorn next."

I'm instantly grateful she didn't linger on my wounds, didn't give me meaningless sympathy or empty aphorisms about how it'll get better one day. She acknowledged it without making it the focus. It lets me push it to the side, too.

"Would you make room for a unicorn mug in your single suitcase if I did make one?" I ask, the tide of grief that always rises when I think of Kennedy's urn subsiding just a little.

"Maybe," she replies with a half smile. "There's some toothpaste on your chin. I'll turn the music down." She waves and walks back to the studio, where, sure enough, the Killers are silenced.

I reach for my chin, rubbing toothpaste away self-consciously. When I return inside carrying a relic from my former life, I suddenly wish it weren't so quiet.

8

MORGAN

I sleep fitfully. Whenever I move somewhere new, I keep hoping the first night will get easier. It never does.

Tonight is exceptionally hard, though. Sawyer's studio is comfortable, thanks to his impressive cleaning efforts. His neighborhood is quieter than West Hollywood. I just can't get over the fact my new living space is now double-haunted.

I can't see Kennedy, like Sawyer can't see Zach, and she doesn't make her presence known. No rattling doorknobs or floating furniture startle me during the night. Still, I spend every moment wondering whether I'm hearing spooky creaks or garden-variety creaks from the old guesthouse.

I would pull up my favorite dating reality show on Netflix, except I forgot to get the Wi-Fi password from Sawyer. I consider guessing passwords like *hauntedandhappy* or something, except I don't want to piss off the home's incorporeal occupant with my irreverent efforts.

When sunrise comes, my phone glowing 5:57 from the nightstand, I've had enough. I'm ready to chase the shadows away. Exhausted, jittery, and wishing I'd packed melatonin in the suitcase

Sawyer found ridiculously light, I haul myself out from under the covers.

Ghost-related insomnia has left me with hours until I need to go work. Wanting to shake off my discomfort, I pull on shorts. I need distraction, and I know exactly where to start.

Outside, the morning calm relaxes me. The fog descending over Silver Lake will vanish when the sun heats the hillside in the early morning, but for now, the mist cools my shoulders while I unwind—

The guesthouse door slams behind me.

The sharp sound startles me, only for me to remember I'd left the door open when I stepped outside. Gravity, not ghosts, had swung the door closed.

Embarrassed, I let out my breath. I'm glad Zach couldn't see that. He would have laughed. I would have said *Not cool, man.* He would have frozen the water bottle on my nightstand solid in response. *How's this for cool?*

Pretending the incident never happened, I continue through the fog to Sawyer's front yard, where I do damage control.

Like yesterday, the job overwhelms me. It's . . . so much. The size and scale are instantly intimidating. I'm experienced in the garden, which got me my present job. When I was growing up, gardening was something I could do with my dad on weekend mornings no matter where his work deposited us. We shaped begonias in Baton Rouge, tended roses in Richmond, watered hydrangeas in Hartford.

It's why I know just exactly how unmanageable Sawyer's murder yard—*must stop calling it this while I'm here*—is.

The middle of the mess is what worries me. When I've sunk weeks into it and have weeks left to go. When Sawyer starts to *depend* on me.

The idea makes me shudder like no ghost ever has. I can already imagine what kind of fucked-up self-fulfilling prophecy I'll have locked myself into. I'll fear running out on Sawyer and his garden, disappointing him, and then the fear will make me *want* to leave. To get it over with—the failure I know is coming. I'll yearn for escape, for a fresh start on something else, somewhere else. Somewhere I'm not in deep enough to ruin everything. Like I did with Michael Hanover-Erickson.

Like I will here, the voices in my head whisper.

No, damn it. I may have something to lose if I commit to Sawyer's garden—what remains of my wounded self-respect—but I have more to lose if I don't. I remind myself of Zach spraying soy sauce everywhere in Street Noodle. If he lingers for five years, or forever . . . I need this chance to be free of my ghostly visitor.

Besides, I feel bad for Sawyer and his pained reminiscences. His desperation to make Kennedy content on the other side. I do want to help him. He hasn't been able to move on from Kennedy. He hasn't even been able to make her urn. It's like he's petrified in loss.

If I left here, how many more years would it take for Sawyer himself to wither like the weeds in his yard?

Determined, I venture forward, where I start on the dead shrubs. So, so many dead shrubs. I grasp them where they meet the ground, rip them from the soil, and pile them near where I'm working. It's not like it matters if my mound looks ugly or disorganized.

Soon, I hit my stride. It's cathartic, pulling up dead things that shouldn't be there anymore. The physical labor helps me shake off the night spent overanalyzing. I find an abandoned and obviously unused shovel on the side of the house and get to work on some of the bigger desiccated bushes. I move from patch to patch, working evenly, welcoming the soreness in my muscles.

Before I know it, hours have passed. The neighborhood starts to wake up. I stand, sweating, my shoulders aching, dirt coating my fingers. I feel good, though. Comfortable, even.

I pull out some of the shaggier bushes. With my confidence and determination growing, I set to the hardest obstacle I can find, the gnarled dead tree in one corner of Sawyer's yard. It's formidably sized but unquestionably worse for wear. Years of proximity to Sawyer's street have coated the dry bark with grime.

It has to go. I drive my shovel under the roots in the fresh soil my morning efforts have upturned, jostling the metal spade to loosen the trunk where I can. If I keep going—

My heart seizes when I notice a figure watching me from the window. I'm thinking *Haunting of Hill House* until I realize it's only Sawyer.

He . . . doesn't look happy.

I wave, confused. *What the hell, man?* I've just spent hours working my ass off on the job I'm doing for him pretty much for free.

Sawyer doesn't return the greeting. He only grimaces. He disappears from the windowsill.

Then, startling me, he storms outside. "What are you doing?" he demands. The sadness in his eyes hasn't changed, but restless urgency has joined it. His gaze sweeps over his desolate yard, like he finds everything somehow damningly familiar and frighteningly unknown.

Still, hours of pro bono yard work have me not feeling super charitable for his chastisement. "Um, the job you wanted me to do?" I say. "I have to clear the dead plants out to landscape."

"Not that one." Sawyer's reply is instantaneous. He's fixated on the decrepit tree. "Can't you"—frustration grasps in his voice— "nurse it back to health, or whatever?"

"I think that would require a necromancer," I say. "Not a gardener."

Sawyer scowls. He squints in the morning sun, focused on the tree.

Leaning on my shovel, I wait. I hold in my annoyance, realizing what's probably happening here. This tree is somehow a Kennedy thing.

Of course, I didn't move into a stranger's haunted house without googling him. I spent last night reconstructing Sawyer's shattered life out of search engine results and social media. His website for his pottery showed off the impressionistic, intriguing workmanship of a versatile creator. Except in the details—the site's copyright date, five years ago, which is when the photo gallery of commissioned pieces stops. When Kennedy's life ended, so did Sawyer's creative one.

His name led readily to obituaries for Kennedy Claire Raymond. Social media pages for Sawyer's late fiancée, now maintained in memoriam and full of commented condolences, revealed the woman who once shared this garden. Who still does, in her way. Or so says Sawyer.

Kennedy was what I expected. Vibrant, joyous, creative. Every photo she posted was magazine quality. Her and Sawyer on Joshua Tree getaways, her proud renovation handiwork combining antique flourishes with modern design, even just the Silver Lake sunset framed in the foliage I'm now clearing out.

A perfect pairing for Sawyer, in other words. They made a lovely couple, until Kennedy passed away. From natural causes—needless to say, I checked this detail carefully.

The more time I spend in Sawyer's company, the easier it is to feel him searching the world in frustration for wholeness he can no longer find. Sympathy dulls my defensiveness. I set my shovel down. "We can return to this one later," I concede.

To my surprise, Sawyer only glares harder. "Don't pity me," he snaps.

I narrow my eyes. "Okay . . ." I say. "Then don't ask me to save the deadest tree in all of Los Angeles."

Sawyer grumbles. "Landscape around it," he insists. "Make it look intentional."

"No."

He frowns. Despite myself, I wince. Whatever this tree's connection to Kennedy, I know it has to come out.

"Sorry," I go on. "Just . . . you told me not to pity you."

"And I meant it," he says.

He's not convinced; I hear it in his voice. Every word—or every day or every living moment—is ripping him slowly in half. "Are you sure?" I venture. "Because you seem . . ."

"I'm fine." The same instant insistence. His determination is unflinching, like the sun coming up over the hill, shining in our eyes.

"It's just—"

"*Morgan*," he interrupts. "No pity."

I meet Sawyer's hardened gaze. The moment stretches in silence.

"Good," I finally say, satisfied with Sawyer's resolve. Maybe he wasn't pulling himself in half—maybe he was fighting a necessary fight, and the stronger part of him won. "Well, then this tree is going to have to go," I announce. "It doesn't have to be now. You can say your goodbyes. But it's dead and not great for the other plants. And it doesn't align with the artistic vision of anyone living."

Sawyer is starting to reply when an unseasonably chilly wind rolls over the morning hillside. The punctuating gust shakes loose twigs from the dead tree.

When my eyes catch the form they've fallen into in the fresh dirt, I shiver. It's no jumble or cryptic pattern. The dislodged sticks spell words.

EXHUME ME

It's very creepy, obviously. However, it's also serving my creative choices.

"See?" I point out the words to Sawyer. "It clearly doesn't align with the dead's artistic vision, either. Cheeky word choice."

Sawyer does look amused. His gaze darts over the garden, his fragile demeanor returning. "Is Zach nearby?" he asks.

"Don't think so," I say honestly. "Plus, I mean, 'exhume'? I'm pretty sure Zach's spelling isn't that good." When Sawyer only grunts one of his usual *hmm*s, I know I'm making real progress. "I think Kennedy is on my side," I dare to say. "She wants the dead tree gone."

I'm hoping the mention of Kennedy cleanses Sawyer of his grumpy resistance. If he doesn't want to listen to the random woman he invited into his guesthouse, fine. Maybe he'll listen to supernatural signals from his dead fiancée.

Instead, the suggestion only worsens Sawyer's mood. That frustrated fog descends over his eyes. "Let me do it at least," he demands. "Later. I don't have it in me right now."

Without waiting for my reply, he stalks off, leaving me with the haunted sticks. Kennedy's message.

"Thanks, girl," I whisper to the wind.

Checking my phone, I realize I should start getting ready for work. Despite Sawyer's unhelpful interruption, I've made progress on the ghostly gardening.

When I return to the studio, I run the shower in the unit's small bathroom while my breathing evens out from the exertion. I strip off my clothes and step under the water. I have enough problems without my haunting, honestly. Shitty sleep in my temporary living space. Overwhelming gardening goals. Now my judgmental new landlord-slash-neighbor-slash-fellow-hauntee, who seems determined to slow down the job *he* wants—

Mid-shampoo, I scream when my water suddenly goes ice-cold.

9

SAWYER

I retreat inside, feeling guilty. I shouldn't have gotten mad at Morgan. I could have used my grown-up words instead of stomping and frowning. How hard would it have been to say, *Would you please postpone your efforts on this particular tree, which reminds me of Kennedy's and my first visit to this house in ways I can't stand to part with just yet?*

Never mind. It would have been extremely hard.

But Morgan deserved the effort. She's doing exactly what we said, working on my garden. What's more, she's doing what Kennedy wants, obviously.

It's just not what *I* want.

Watching Morgan from my window while she handled the mess in front, I couldn't stop wondering why everything needs to change. Why Kennedy's doing this. Things have been fine these past few years; I know they have. I know Kennedy hasn't hated our movie nights or when I'd put Etta James or Mazzy Star on the record player and we'd just dance, not caring if my hand slipped into the insubstantiality of hers while we spun. Once I got past the shock waves of grief followed by the realization my fiancée was haunting our house, everything has been perfectly fine.

We've been fine.

Morgan clearing the yard reminded me how, once her work is done, the view from my window will be unrecognizable. It won't be the view I saw with Kennedy when we toured the place or the one we woke up to on our first morning here. The one Kennedy glimpsed on the last day of her life.

I don't know if I'm ready for unrecognizable. Everyone else, from my parents and almost-in-laws to pizza delivery people, thinks my yard is an eyesore, but I never have. Those tangled thickets hold memories.

Memories Morgan is uprooting.

It's not her fault, I remind myself while I move to my mirror to comb my hair. I can't take my frustration out on my houseguest. What Kennedy needs is the most important thing to me. Morgan's only here to help.

I vow to act extra-friendly the next time I see her. Honestly, I probably should get to know the woman living in my spare room for the next few weeks or months. I've got nothing other than that she packs light, she's into plants, she likes the Killers, and—oh, right—she's haunted. I'll remark on her bag, maybe. Ask what *Bifora testiculata* is.

On second thought, maybe I won't.

I'll figure it out. While I'm rusty in conversations with the living, I'm not completely hopeless.

I'm pulling my shirt on, comforting myself about my social skills in a perfectly normal way for an adult man, when my door rattles like someone's pounding from outside. I ignore it— Kennedy is probably nearby, manifesting in her usual homey rustlings. My heart skips, and I wonder hopefully whether the room feels chillier.

Instead, the door flies open and a decidedly un-ghostly woman storms in.

Un-ghostly and . . . unclothed. Morgan is wrapped in a towel, dripping water everywhere on my restored hardwood floors.

"Morgan!" I exclaim. "What the hell?"

Damn. I really was planning on friendliness. Extenuating circumstances.

"I *knocked*," Morgan replies harshly.

"And I didn't tell you to come in!" I reply. "I especially didn't tell you to come in so . . . undressed and—"

I manage to stop myself short of saying *wet*.

Imperious, Morgan holds my gaze. Breathing hard, her hair hanging in soapy clumps over her shoulders, her skin splotchy, she looks . . . vibrant.

Not to mention pissed. "*Obviously*, it's an emergency," she hisses. "The water heater cut out while I was showering."

"Oh." *Ghosts,* I wonder, *or just shitty plumbing?* The house is old. While I've remodeled, I have not, surprisingly enough, replaced the entire water heater.

"Not *oh*," Morgan snaps. Water trails down her legs. She's barefoot. I swallow. "You need to fix the water heater. Now," she demands. "I have to leave for work in forty minutes."

"Right. Yes. Okay. Water heater," I repeat. I'm having difficulty forming words under the circumstances I find myself in. Beneath Morgan's expectant gaze, I step into my shoes and head downstairs.

I'm surprised to hear Morgan following me, matching my pace with the soft, watery footsteps her bare feet make on the hardwood.

She continues dauntlessly into the kitchen with me like we're infiltrating past enemy lines.

I pause near the pantry in front of the door leading downstairs into the garage. "You can't come down here," I say. "You could step on something sharp."

Morgan doesn't even hesitate. Defiance flashes in her chestnut eyes.

She walks to the back door, where my own work boots sit. They're several sizes too large for Morgan, which means they're easy for her to step into.

Impatient, she gestures to the door for me to lead the way.

The sight of Morgan glistening wet, wearing only her towel and my boots, is more than I can process right now. My chest tight, I force my gaze to the garage stairs.

When I open the door, icy cold greets me. The garage scares even me, frankly. As Morgan and I descend, the steps creak, the echoes seeming to lengthen and grow louder in the concrete space. Shadows move on the walls. The deeper we get, the more haunted it seems.

I wish I'd replaced or fixed the garage door so I could let some light in. Sort of like I wish I'd fixed the water heater. Unfortunately, the garage door remains immovable—manual and rusted— leaving Morgan and me to venture into the darkness.

Reluctantly, I reach the end of the stairs. I move a paint can to clear the way for Morgan and reach out to help her down the final steps.

She places her hand in mine. It's warm—shockingly warm. Flush with life.

"Okay," Morgan whispers unevenly. "I'm obviously pretty immune to haunting, but this is next level."

"I think maybe having two ghosts in the house is making it worse," I say. I'm only guessing. Putting clumsy patterns to impossible, unnatural events like I have for five years. Rationalizing in hopes of feeling some sense of control over my situation.

Grief does that to you, I've heard. Only Morgan makes me feel conscious of the effort.

I step sideways, only to nearly trip over the paint can. Because it's returned to where I moved it from.

Morgan notices. Our eyes meet.

"Let's do this quickly," she says.

For once, I couldn't agree with her more.

I walk deeper into the garage, determined to ignore the pounding of my heart. I hear Morgan following me, the heavy soles of my shoes thumping with her footsteps. Her breathing in the noiseless dark is conspicuous, her chest moving under her towel with every soft inhale—

"Zach, seriously. You're being scary right now. Can you knock it off?" she pleads.

In response, the stairwell door slams shut. Morgan jumps.

I nearly do the same. I don't feel Kennedy nearby. Etta James doesn't linger in my head.

Morgan told me her ghost was annoying, but she never said he was malicious. She also said she didn't know him very well, though. Who exactly *have* I invited to my home? What if Zach died some horribly gruesome death and is now taking out his pain on the living?

I reach the water heater, exhaling with relief that the garage hasn't swallowed me up somehow. Using my phone flashlight, I illuminate the heater's base where the instructions are printed.

Which . . . have warped and discolored into illegibility.

"Just do what you've done before," Morgan suggests desperately. Her eyes roam nervously over the space while she clutches her towel.

"I've never done this before," I reply, exasperated. "But be my guest."

"Dude, I've never owned property before!" Morgan shoots back. "You think I know how to fix your water heater? I'm an expert at calling the landlord, but when it comes to actual repairs, I've got nothing."

"Let me find a YouTube video." I fumble with my phone while the shadows thicken around us. There's something palpable in their ominous reach—something *intentional*.

Sure enough, the next moment my bars disappear. NO SERVICE, reads my screen.

"Shit," I mutter.

I don't know if I have the strength to return upstairs, resolve this with some hardcore internet research, and then venture back down here, like some vengeful water-heater-conquering hero—

Suddenly, Morgan gasps so sharply that I do jump. She nearly drops her towel, catching it only at the last second as I dart my gaze from her.

"What the hell?" I whisper.

Morgan stares into the shadows.

"Zach is in the corner," she replies, her voice breathy and soft.

Goose bumps prickle down my arms. While I worried for my sanity in the early days of Kennedy's manifestation, I've long felt haunting gets a really unfair reputation, because my ghost has never once scared me.

Morgan looks like she no longer shares my peaceful view on the paranormal—or she's playing a very effective practical joke on me.

She watches the empty darkness where she must see Zach, looking extra ghostly. "He's . . ." she exhales.

My heart hammers. *He's what?*

"He looks wrong," Morgan manages. "He's just . . . standing there. I don't think he's seeing us. Is this where the ghosts go when they disappear? To the creepiest fucking place nearby?"

She's half joking. Even so, I wonder if she's right. I search the garage—Kennedy is nowhere to be found.

"Has he ever done this before?" I murmur.

Morgan shakes her head. "No. Never. I wonder if all the paranormal activity in this house is . . . making him worse. Summoning the spookier side of Zach."

"Try to snap him out of it," I urge her.

Morgan whirls, hand clamped on her towel. "Why? That's a horrible idea," she admonishes me.

"*Why?*" I repeat. "Because he's cutting my cell service right now, and I can't fix this until he cools it."

"He looks like—like a real ghost. Like he'll, I don't know, rush me or do some horror movie shit." Morgan sighs. She knows I'm right. "Fine, but if I die of fear, I'm going to haunt the shit out of this garage, you know," she warns me. "You'll never be able to get repairmen in here, and you'll have cold showers forever."

I nod solemnly.

Her expression goes serious. She looks determined. Her gait uneven in my too-large boots, she ventures into the center of the garage.

"Hey, Zach," she greets the ghost with forced friendliness. "What's up?"

I wait, nervous. Nothing happens.

"Want to watch *Shark Week* reruns?" Morgan suggests.

Even scared shitless, I have to smile. No luck for Morgan, though. She shivers. I know it's not just from the cold garage climate meeting her wet hair.

"Or we could go through my Tinder matches and I'll let you choose who to swipe on," she says. Moments later, her posture relaxes slightly. "Honestly, thank god that one didn't work," she says to me. "I don't know if I could go out with anyone Zach approved of—"

"Morgan!" I interrupt her.

"Sorry. Right. I'm just . . ." She glances into the corner where Zach supposedly skulks. From the fear in her eyes, I know he hasn't vanished. "I'm out of ideas," she confesses.

I rub my face. The fact is, YouTube probably won't fix the results of ghostly interference. I don't want to shower in frigid water, either. We need to fix this—which means Morgan needs to fix this. I wish I could help, but I literally can't see the problem.

I'm wondering whether Google has hits for paranormal plumbers when Morgan's expression changes. She winces heavily, then faces Zach in the corner, resigned.

"Okay, last-ditch effort. I'm sorry in advance," she says.

I wait with bated breath.

Morgan faces Zach. She loosens her grip on her towel.

"I guess I have no choice," she says. "If you stop being spooky, I'll flash you."

I'm groaning—it's funny, I'm getting to know Zach without ever meeting him—when suddenly Morgan cheers.

"Zach!" she exclaims proudly. "I should have known boobs were the only thing that could bring you back!"

With Morgan's victorious laughter echoing from the walls, I can't help noticing that my haunted garage has started feeling a lot less scary. The dread in my chest lessens. My heart is slowing, though still pounding from the fresh fear. "What's he saying?" I ask Morgan when I notice her smiling into the corner.

"He's mad I'm not going through with the flashing. No way, dude," she chides. "You should have been a better first date if you wanted to see these."

The change in Morgan, gripping her towel reassuringly firmly, is pronounced. She's no longer shivering. The vivacious pink has returned to her cheeks.

She listens, like Zach is still speaking, then shoots me a furtive glance I don't miss. Her cheeks grow pinker.

"No, he wouldn't," she mutters to Zach.

I inspect the water heater with no doubt who the pronoun refers to.

Morgan clears her throat, then speaks normally. "Zach doesn't know why he's down here," she informs me. "He doesn't remember being scary." She looks back to him. "The water heater is out," she explains to her ghost. "We're trying to fix it, but we couldn't with you haunting the place to hell."

In the pause of Zach's reply, she straightens suddenly.

Her eyes fly to mine, fresh excitement in their caramel glow. "He says he knows how to fix the water heater. He . . ."

She listens.

"Oh my god, Zach. This is huge!" she enthuses. She sounds giddy when she continues. "He says he knows a lot about water heaters, actually. He's never remembered anything about his life except for our date, but—"

"Being in front of the water heater is bringing back a memory," I finish, reasoning out the revelation. "It's not that Zach has no memories. It's that they need to be brought back. Which is why Kennedy doesn't have memory gaps like he does. She's in her home, surrounded by everything from her life."

It makes sense. More importantly, it's useful. I meant what I said when I promised the *Shark Week*–loving, Carly Rae Jepsen–listening man haunting Morgan that we would work together to resolve his unfinished business. Well, we've just gotten one step closer.

Morgan nods, eager. "This is good, Zach. Keep remembering."

"What?" My heart is racing now for a different reason. A *good* reason. I've practically forgotten the feeling.

Morgan looks up.

"He's saying . . . He thinks his parents own a hardware store," she says. Her eyes dazzle in the darkness. "We have a clue about his actual life. If we find out who he is, we can complete Zach's unfinished business."

10

I'm ninety-nine percent certain I'm not the only one waiting in my living room while Morgan showers.

While I can't confirm Zach is nearby because he's invisible to me, I feel an unusual energy on my couch. It's not spooky, nothing like his accidental stunt in the garage. It's more . . . anxious.

I understand why. Soon, Zach's entire life—or rather his afterlife—could change.

With Zach's guidance, Morgan quickly relit the pilot light and then rushed to take a shower. We don't have long before she has to go to work, but she promised she would shower fast enough for a quick Zach recon session. Her exact words were *This will be the highest-stakes stalking of one of my exes, ever.*

The back door opens and clatters shut. Morgan sweeps inside, her hair still wet and piled on her head in a large clip. She's holding her laptop. "I need the Wi-Fi password," she says breathlessly.

Instantly, I feel bad. I should have remembered to give it to her last night. I just haven't had to share it with anyone in a long time. "Kintsugi," I say.

Morgan pauses before typing.

"It's spelled K-I—"

"I know how to spell it," she replies, darting a mildly offended look over her shoulder as she opens her laptop on the coffee table and starts typing. "It's a Death Cab album. Also a Lana Del Rey song. But I'm guessing you chose it to reference the pottery thing. Japanese art of repairing broken pottery with gold, right?"

I blink. For someone with one plate, she knows more about pottery than I expected. I suppose landscaping is art, though. In a way, both of us work with materials right from the earth—her plants and me clay.

Or I used to, at least.

"I do love the Death Cab album," I say. "Can't listen to it much anymore, though."

Morgan looks like she wants to say more. She opens her mouth only to close it and glare to my left. "All right, Zach, jeez. I'm doing it now."

The coasters on my coffee table rattle in reply.

Eager myself, I stand and move behind Morgan so I can get a clear view of her screen. The empty space next to me feels frigid. We, I'm assuming, watch as Morgan types in, *Los Angeles son of family-owned hardware store owners dead.* Seemingly as an afterthought, or maybe at insistence from our spectral spectator, she adds, *tragically.*

"Do you really think that will be enough detail?" I ask. If we can just find out Zach's full name, we can find his family. We can talk to them, learn about Zach's life. They're our best chance of discovering whatever Zach died having left unfinished.

Morgan glances at me. "You have clearly never tried to find the social media of the cute guy who you met at a bar whose only information you got was his first name and that he did tattoos."

"Admittedly, I have not," I reply.

Morgan presses enter. We wait as hits start to populate her screen.

"Told you," Morgan crows.

Near the top is a local paper's memorial announcement nearly three months ago. She opens it quickly.

> Join family and friends at a celebration of Zach Harrison's life at Harrison's Hardware from 1 to 4 on Saturday. There will be music, spicy foods, surfing stories, and all of Zach's favorite things. All are welcome. Speeches will be given by immediate family.

Everyone is silent for a moment. Or, I assume, Zach is silent. Morgan doesn't seem to be listening to him.

"Zach Harrison," Morgan repeats, reverent in her success. Then she glances over her shoulder. "Zach, look, you're a surfer and you like spicy food. You probably love the ocean, hence the *Shark Week* obsession. We already knew of your love of pop music, of course," Morgan says. She's smiling, genuinely pleased for her ghost. He's not just an invisible phantom. He was—is—a person.

I take out my phone, open a maps app, and plug in the hardware store. "It's only twenty minutes away. Open from nine to five."

Morgan's eyes light up. "His parents are probably there right now. We can talk to them—" She stops when she sees the time in the upper corner of her computer. "Crap. I'm going to be late for work. I won't get home in time, either. But I'll take tomorrow off and we can go first thing." She stands.

"I can't wait to hear what you find out," I say, stepping back to clear her path.

Morgan whirls, aghast. "You promised to help. You're coming with us!"

"I didn't know Zach," I protest. I shove my hands in my pockets, suddenly uncomfortable. "I don't need to intrude on this family in their grief."

I've been around enough grieving parents for one lifetime. Sitting with Kennedy's parents at her funeral was the hardest thing I ever had to do. They're nice people, and we remain friends. They've since moved away to be nearer to Kennedy's brother.

I was so glad when they told me they were leaving. Seeing them and how their loss affected them only made me feel mine more keenly.

It made it difficult to savor what I *did* have of Kennedy—her ghost. When it's just me and Kennedy together, it feels like she never left. Like she's still alive. But when we're in the room with her parents, it's . . . different. They couldn't see her. It was hard for me and harder for Kennedy.

"You think *I* want to intrude on their grief?" Morgan fires back. "I'm just a girl who hooked up with Zach in her car once. They aren't going to know who I am. I didn't even want to meet Zach's parents when he was alive. It's, like, a million times worse now that he's dead." She's speaking quickly, her voice rising in pitch.

I don't know where her fear is coming from. Morgan just faced down a scene from *The Blair Witch Project* in my garage, and it's Zach's parents that have her begging for my help? I thought she would be thrilled at getting closer to sending Zach on.

"You'll be fine," I reassure her. "You can say you and Zach were friends. I mean, you basically are now."

Her eyes are wide. The whites large in her small face. "They'll ask how we met and I'll say Tinder, and then they'll want to know why it didn't work out with us. I'll be the asshole who didn't love their dead son. What am I supposed to say? That he got me off in my car, but we weren't a personality fit?"

"I would maybe leave those details out—"

"No. Sawyer, please. *Please.*" She steps closer to me like she wants to grab my hands. "I can't do this on my own." She stops herself. "I'm not the girl who meets people's parents. I've never, like"—she stammers—"done that."

I feel my brow furrow. "You've never . . . met someone's parents?"

Morgan presses her restless palms to her work skirt. "Not someone I was, you know, involved with. I'm not like that."

"Like what?"

"Serious!" Morgan blurts. I've never seen her so frantic. There's no pink in her cheeks. She's as pale as—well, a ghost. "Committed. I don't *do* that. Never have," she snaps. "Never will."

Committed. Memories of record-player dancing and pizza-delivery nights in, of engagement photos and secondhand credenzas rush through my head. "It's not so bad," I say defensively before I can stop myself.

Morgan's eyes dart to mine. I see her grasp onto confrontation, her handhold to pull herself out of everything else she's feeling. "Please. I do *not* need more judgment from you."

"I wasn't—"

"I'm not some careless free spirit." Morgan charges on. "I'm a fucking liability, okay?"

This quiets me. I almost reach for her just to help her calm down. My surprise quickly gives way to sympathy when I see her visceral reaction. The instant open-faced pain of this statement is unhidden on Morgan's vivacious features. "I'm . . . sure that's not true," I muster, hearing how useless it sounds.

"Well." Morgan's voice is low. "It is. The closest I ever came to *meeting the parents* was when I got engaged. I was twenty-two. Look how that turned out."

I can't help myself. The sharp revelation, so out of place with the Morgan I know, intrigues me immediately. She obviously wouldn't welcome prying, though, which leaves me not knowing what to say.

When Morgan checks her phone, the fight seems to leave her. Her frame slumps. "Please, Sawyer," she repeats, sounding exhausted. "Don't make me do this on my own."

Suddenly, I know I have no choice. Of course I'm going to help her.

Her fear is bigger than her fleeting connection with Zach Harrison. Morgan—with her nomadic life, her dread of commitment—has never stuck around long enough for these sorts of conversations. This discomfort is what waits on the other side of her exuberant restlessness or is the reason for it. Maybe it's why she leaves so often, why she doesn't want memories of her former homes.

I can't say I don't see the appeal. Sometimes when people break, you can't glue them back together with gold and make them more beautiful than they were. Sometimes, people are just too shattered. When you've committed to them, though, you have to sit among the pieces. It's a consequence of commitment Morgan has no experience with.

I do, though.

"Okay. Okay," I say reassuringly. "I'll go with you."

Morgan exhales. Color returns to her cheeks. Her eyes. The brown of her irises is so warm. Like earth or clay.

She looks to my left, then back to me. "Zach says thanks. He doesn't trust me to do this on my own, and I'm not even offended. It means a lot to him. To . . . both of us."

I give her a small smile, self-conscious. Their gratitude warms me more than I expected. I haven't *helped* someone other than Kennedy in longer than I'd like to admit. I don't think it's selfish to focus on yourself when you're drowning, but I guess I didn't realize how helping someone else might calm the waters.

"I need some things for the house anyway," I say, not wanting them to feel indebted to me. "I should finish patching and painting while you're working on the yard."

"Of course," Morgan says, but some knowing quality in her voice tells me she's seeing through me.

When she starts to close her computer, I have this unexpected straining feeling. Like I can't let her leave. Not yet.

"You're not a liability," I say.

I feel Morgan's startled pause. She withdraws, then straightens to look me in the eye. Skepticism, worn and weary, joins with hesitant hope in her eyes. I watch her evaluate me, like she's gauging whether I give a shit.

I do, Morgan. I do.

I hold her gaze with everything I have. Zach, I figure, is probably nearby. I can't see him like Morgan can, but I'm guessing he's listening. I wonder what he thinks.

Finally, she sighs. "I am. I promise," she says. "I dropped out of college when I was twenty-one. Three years in. I was . . . really struggling. I was desperate to be my own person, to make my own choices. I wanted to prove to my parents I was independent, that I'd dropped out because I was ready to live in the real world."

"Dropping out of college does not make you a liability," I reply, going for the right combination of gentle and firm. "You're clearly great at what you do."

Morgan pinches her lips together. "That's only part of it," she says. "I was living in North Carolina on my own, and I met Michael. Michael Hanover-Erickson. He was seven years older. I thought it was perfect. We dated, fell in love, yada yada yada. When he proposed, I . . . said yes. We moved to Seattle for Michael's job, started planning the wedding, the whole nine yards. I didn't know if I was ready. I just knew I really wanted to be."

She shrugs.

I hate how hollowed out she looks. I hardly know Morgan, but innately, something in me wants to keep her from punishing herself like this. Kennedy, I guess. Love like ours didn't just make me happy. It made me want other people to be happy. It makes me want to fight whatever has Morgan convinced she's not worth hope or commitment.

"Of course my parents were supportive," she goes on. "They've only ever been supportive. They started helping us pay for wedding stuff. Everything was moving fast, but Michael didn't care. He wanted the rest of our lives to start. Then the date started getting nearer, Michael started mentioning trying for a baby . . . Suddenly I realized how not ready I was," she confesses. "I bailed. On everything. Michael was heartbroken. My parents were blindsided, but they helped me relocate."

She looks down. She's utterly crestfallen.

"I know better now," she says. "It's better when I don't commit."

I wrestle for something to say. It's comedic, garishly. World's loneliest man, who only converses with his personal ghost, called upon to comfort someone he hardly knows over the labyrinthine wounds of her love life. I wonder if Zach's heard this story. I wonder if he's extending her reassurances right now in a voice for only her to hear. I hope he is.

I have to offer her my own, though. Or try.

"I'm sure Michael wouldn't have wanted you to go through with a marriage you were uncertain of," I venture.

Morgan scoffs. I scold myself for the misstep. I just want to make her hurt less. "Sure," she replies drolly, "but I'm sure he'd have preferred he never wasted his time with me in the first place."

Now I know exactly what to say. "It wasn't wasted time," I reply. "Even when engagements don't lead to marriage, they're not wasted."

Morgan has no quick rejoinder. How can she when doing so would be telling me my engagement to Kennedy was wasted time?

I'm relieved when she seems to really hear me. The empty shame haunting her eyes seems to part, clarity emerging from its reaches.

She looks down, where she notices the time on her phone in her hand. "Shit," she says hastily. "Now I'm definitely late."

She reaches for her computer, then pauses.

"Zach," she addresses the cold corner of the room, confirming my guess—the ghost never left our midst. "If you want, I can search your name now and probably find out how you died," she offers.

I wait. Honestly, I don't want to know. I don't want to think of Zach as dead. I don't want some horrible thing to have happened to him, like I speculated in the garage. I can't even see him, but I like him.

But I won't be a coward. If Zach wants to find out what happened to him, I won't leave Morgan to read the details by herself.

The laptop slams shut on its own.

Morgan nods, her expression a mix of sadness and relief. I don't need her to convey whatever it is Zach's said.

Zach wants to learn about his life. Not his death.

11

MORGAN

On the morning we're set to drive out to Harrison's Hardware, Zach causes chaos. The sink shoots water on my shirt when I reach for the faucet. My shower curtain rattles nonstop. While I get dressed, my shoes fly from one side of the room to the other. My coffee nearly spills onto my laptop when I'm not looking. *How would we watch* Shark Week *then, Zach?*

I'm not even mad. Unlike in Sawyer's spooky garage, I feel Zach's eagerness in every paranormal episode. He's excited, but he's also nervous, and I understand. It's how family is—even when you're not dead. I've avoided home for longer and longer stretches, feeling guiltier every year for not having my shit together despite everything I've cost my parents. It's just easier when I'm on my own.

Zach, for his part, doesn't even know what he's walking into.

Waiting in my car for Sawyer, I watch the ghost in the rearview mirror. Miraculously, I'm wearing both my shoes and I'm not coffee-stained. With no seat belt to constrain him, Zach repositions restlessly. He's ninety-five percent opaque most days, and right now, the morning sunlight passes faintly through him.

"What if they hate me?" he worries. "What if we're estranged, and the reason I'm haunting you is because I was a weird loner who no one liked?"

I twist in the driver's seat so I can look sincerely into his ghostly eyes. "That's not true," I say to him.

"You don't know!" Zach protests. "You didn't even like me!"

"I liked you well enough to make out with you in this car," I remind him.

Our rock-climbing date was . . . memorable. The highlight was how flat-out horrible Zach was at scaling the colorful handholds on the fabricated rock walls. I mean, really horrible. Like he'd never even heard of rock climbing. He would reach hopelessly for handholds he had no chance of grasping only to—sure enough—fumble, leaving himself dangling in the Velcro harness.

I remember wondering what the hell was wrong with this guy, saying yes to a rock-climbing date with a woman he presumably wanted to impress, despite having this shitty of an intuition for rock climbing.

And . . . then it started to work on me. I stopped seeing Zach's utter ineptitude and started seeing his unashamed adventurousness. His reckless disregard for looking cool.

It was enough to inspire me to invite him into the back seat where he's hovering right now. I knew our personalities didn't mesh, our interests didn't match. Rock climbing spared us from disjointed conversation. Even so, Zach didn't hold back on the rock wall. What else would he do with complete conviction?

Zach gazes around my Honda, remembering. "It wasn't a bad hookup," he ventures.

I smile. "No," I concede. "Not bad at all."

My understated compliment wounds Zach. He slouches, his outline blurring into the seat. "Morgan, I'm having an existential crisis!" he exclaims, then pauses. "Wait, is it existential when you're dead? Do I *exist*? I don't know. I'm having a post-existential crisis. I need more than *not bad at all*."

I soften. Yeah, I wouldn't love knowing my posthumous hookup reputation consisted only of "not bad," either.

"Okay, honestly, Zach?" I start. "You were—"

Sawyer opens the passenger door and climbs inside.

"—a good kisser," I continue. My cheeks flush while Sawyer settles himself. Zach didn't let chagrin scare him on the rock wall. I won't, either. He deserves to hear this. "Very good," I elaborate. "We had a nice time. We just didn't have feelings for each other beyond the physical."

"Am I interrupting something?" Sawyer inquires.

"No," I reply while Sawyer pulls up the GPS on his phone. "*Someone* is just a little nervous about finding out who he was."

My chair reclines suddenly, startling me. I glare over my shoulder, righting my seat.

"I know you weren't some creepy loner," I reassure Zach. "I don't hook up with creepy loners. Okay?"

"Hey, not all creepy loners are a bad lay," Sawyer interjects.

I laugh, surprising myself. Sawyer smiles. He's dressed simply, his green sweater and jeans familiar to me now. He has several sets of this unseasonably cozy uniform, I think.

Since our conversation yesterday, Sawyer hasn't mentioned my frantic oversharing. It's for the best, really. No need for someone on whom I'm presently depending—not to mention who I'm sort of starting to like—to know exactly how undependable I am. If I know Sawyer, he's not being standoffish or judgmental of my outburst. He's being discreet. Giving me space.

When I pull away from the curb, Zach starts whistling. It's not "Call Me Maybe"—it's his own melody, meandering and disorganized. It seems like Sawyer's comment has distracted him from his momentary post-existential panic.

We follow Waze's dubious guidance from freeway to freeway through the dusty hills that surround Los Angeles, out to Zach's family's store. Thirty minutes later, we exit the off-ramp into the neighborhood where Zach grew up.

I've never heard the wistfulness in his voice when he speaks up. "I learned how to skateboard here," he says when I round a strip mall on the corner.

Glancing into the rearview mirror, I find him rapturous. He's watching the streets fly past our windows like he's seeing the Sistine Chapel.

"I used to skate down to the 7-Eleven with TJ and Oliver. My best friends growing up," he explains distractedly. He looks up, tears in his eyes when they meet mine in our reflections. "I had best friends!" he exclaims.

Sawyer hears nothing of our conversation but looks to me, noticing my smile.

"He's remembering," I explain.

Sawyer nods. "I'm glad," he says sincerely.

We pull into the parking lot. Waze informs us we've reached our destination.

Reaching for his seat belt, Sawyer hesitates. "Does Zach . . . need a moment?"

I look at the rearview mirror for guidance.

"Nah," Zach announces. "Let's go meet my family who probably thought I was a weirdo loner."

Shaking my head, I open my door. "Zach's good," I say to Sawyer.

Harrison's Hardware is old but well maintained. The sign looks hand-painted. The storefront windows have been polished to shine. On Wednesday morning, business is brisk. Men in painter's boots haul tarps out to their vans in the parking lot. Contractor types in Timberlands load freshly cut wood into their pickups.

I like the place immediately. Los Angeles is a city of dreams and dreamers, of vibes and manifestations, a city where Laurel Hardware is the name of a hip restaurant. It's nice to spend time somewhere unpretentious and real.

Like Zach is.

He materializes next to me on the curb. "I worked here all through high school on the weekends," he says. "My mom would bring home-cooked meals. Good shit like lasagna or meat loaf. I would eat them on my break."

"See?" I say. "I told you you were loved, Zach."

He only smiles in reply.

We walk inside. Unlike the vast high ceilings of Home Depot or Lowe's, the compact Harrison's Hardware fits shelves of screws, knobs, hinges, fixtures, fasteners, spigots, joists, hooks, nails, dowels, and you-name-it in the claustrophobic cement space. Under the minimal lighting—sunlight through the front windows and from the large lumberyard in back does most of the work—we navigate the labyrinth, figuring we'll know who we need when, or if, we find them.

And we do.

The man restocking the screwdriver shelf, wearing no uniform or name tag, looks just like Zach. Thirty years older, of course, but the same face.

Even if the resemblance was less pronounced, though, the withdrawn weariness in Mr. Harrison's expression—the way he looks when he thinks no one notices—would have clued me in. I've seen the same look on Sawyer.

He glances up when we come near. He looks right through

Zach, his gaze focusing on me instead. The sadness in his eyes is deep, and suddenly my throat closes up.

"Can I help you folks?" he asks.

I hope so, I nearly say. "No. I mean, um, yes. Maybe," I stammer. *Great start, Morgan.* "Sorry." I restart, composing myself. "I know this is awkward, but I'm here to see you. I, um, know—knew your son. Zach. I was hoping—"

In Zach's father's eyes, something seems to close up. I've seen Sawyer do that, too. "You a girlfriend or something?" he interrupts me.

"Not exactly," I say honestly.

"Good," Zach's father replies.

I draw back, stung. The rejection from my onetime hookup's dad shocks me.

When he notices my reaction, guilt draws heavily over Mr. Harrison's face. Its sharp resonance seemed to surprise Mr. Harrison himself. "Sorry. I didn't mean it like that. You look really nice. I'd want Zachy to date someone like you if he were . . ." He can't get the words out. "But he's not. It's good you're not missing him like that. That's all I meant," he promises me.

I soften, understanding his response now. He must see the world through broken glasses these days.

"It's okay," I say honestly, then swallow. "I was hoping we could . . . talk about him some? If you're not too busy."

Zach's father pauses. Slowly, he sets down the screwdrivers.

Zach watches everything the older man does, yet the shelves surrounding my ghostly one-night stand stay entirely silent. Memory is consuming him, I think. Quieting the vortex he felt this morning.

Mr. Harrison closes the distance between us. "He's gone," Zach's father says. "Talking about him just brings him back, and then I gotta lose him again." He pats me gently on the shoulder and walks past us.

Zach seems pulled from his trance—he goes just a little more translucent. His haunted hijinks stay quiet, though. He's worse than upset. He's sad.

In desperation, I spin. "Mr. Harrison," I start recklessly, feeling like Zach on that damn rock wall. Reaching for handholds I can't grasp. What should I say to his grieving father? Should I . . . say Zach's ghost is here? Would he just think I'm pranking him, trying to hurt him? Or I'm some wannabe witchy girl?

Fuck. I don't know how to talk to parents. Not even my own. I'm no good at this. Zach looks miserable next to me. I want to help—I just don't know how.

"I don't think you understand," Mr. Harrison replies. *Yeah, no shit.* Desperate impatience lingers on the edges of his weariness. "I can't. It's . . . it's like . . ." He stares off, facing the store counter like he's searching for words somewhere in the middle distance.

"Like he's just in the next room," Sawyer finishes his sentence.

I look behind me. So does Mr. Harrison.

I'd forgotten Sawyer was here. He pulls his eyes from the wall of hammers, meeting Zach's father's gaze.

"Right?" Sawyer prompts. His straight, serious mouth belies the compassion in his eyes. Grief and condolence in one. "When you're alone, it feels like he isn't gone," he continues. "Whoever you've lost, you feel like you'll just see them later. They're just not here right now. You'll pick them up from work or meet them for dinner. Or you'll just walk into the next room, and there they'll be."

He looks down. His breathing shudders.

"But there is no next room," Sawyer says, talking to the ground or what's buried beneath. "The place they've gone feels like it should be right there. Like it's so close. But it never is. Wherever you look, they're never there. Instead, it's like they're just in the next room, forever."

When he lifts his eyes, they're shining. So, I find, are Mr. Harrison's.

"Do I know you?" he asks. "Are you one of Zach's friends?"

"Not exactly," Sawyer says.

Zach's father hesitates. He looks like he doesn't want to stay, doesn't want to continue speaking with us, but he no longer wants to leave.

"I couldn't talk about my Kennedy for a while, either," Sawyer continues. "I lost my fiancée five years ago. I tried not to talk about her. I still can't, really."

With every word from Sawyer, the doors that closed in Zach's dad's eyes start to slowly open.

"I'm sorry for your loss. Really, I am. You're too young for it," he replies. The defensiveness in his voice is gone.

Of course. Sawyer knows how to talk to the grieving. He's one of them. If this is hard for him, it's a challenge he faces every day.

He steps up beside me, where Zach was.

"I don't think any age makes it better," Sawyer says. "I have one regret, though. I wish I talked about her more with the people who knew her. I'm . . . so afraid of losing her for good," he admits.

I say nothing. Only I know exactly what he means. Well, and Zach and Kennedy, if she's here. Sawyer is terrified of Kennedy moving on for good, of how powerful his grief will become when her mysterious tether to our world is gone.

"I'm afraid I've forgotten so much about her life already. I'll wake up in the middle of the night wondering if I'll always remember the way her hair smelled or what the backs of her knees looked like or the sound of her sneezes." His voice wavers just a little. He continues, courage and compassion in one. "I scour my phone for every photo, every video, hoping for forever proof of these pieces of her I took for granted. If I'd shared more with the people who knew her in the days after she'd passed, I might have helped preserve their memories," he says. "They might have helped preserve mine."

My heart cracks open for Sawyer. Finally, I understand just how vast the ocean of his grief is. Of course he wants to hold on to Kennedy's ghost.

And finally, I recognize how noble and self-sacrificial it is, how much a sign it is of Sawyer's love that he's willing to help her move on in order to save her from nothingness.

I don't know if I could do the same. No, I know I *couldn't*. I don't imagine many people could.

Sawyer . . . might be unlike anyone I've ever known.

Tears have begun streaming now down Mr. Harrison's cheeks. Boyish, like his son's. "His thumbs," he says suddenly. "It sounds so silly, but I can't picture them. I taught him how to hold a hammer, and I can't remember what his thumbs looked like."

Zach has rematerialized near the shelf of hammers. He gazes down, examining his hands, quiet pain riven through his expression. He wants to talk to his dad, to show him the shape of his thumbs. But he can't.

I'm not the one on Zach's rock wall. He is. No matter how he reaches out, he can never make contact. Except to me.

Or . . . *through* me.

I can do this, I remind myself firmly. *I have to do this.* Sawyer didn't need to come therapize grief with Zach's father, either. But he showed up.

"His thumbnails were large and square. Short," I say, staring at the translucent hands only I can see. "And he had that small scar on the left one. Like a perfect crescent."

Zach's father looks to me. His eyes go distant. The glimmer of memory enters them, the picture of Zach's hands returning, and he starts to smile.

Sawyer and I wait while something settles over Mr. Harrison. I catch Sawyer's eye, and in that moment, I'm grateful. I came here nervous and afraid to confront Zach's father's grief. Now I'm glad I have. Even if I didn't have a ghost to exorcise, I'm glad I got the chance to help this stranger remember his loved one.

Mr. Harrison's gaze clears, returning to us once more.

"Why don't I pour you both a cup of coffee in back," he says, "and tell you about my son."

12

MORGAN

Learning about my dead ex's life from his grieving father is surprisingly fun.

No one cries. In fact, we spend most of the time laughing as we sip the surprisingly good black coffee Bill—as he insists we call him when we're seated—pours for us. The break room is crammed with storage, and Sawyer and I are wedged on metal chairs close enough for our elbows to brush. On the other side of the small table, Bill sits on a flipped-over painter's bucket. If Zach were alive, he wouldn't fit, but as a ghost, he's able to perch on some boxes with half of his legs disappearing into the table.

It feels cozy. Homey. Like we're part of Zach's family. Somehow it makes me miss him even though he's sitting right next to me.

Bill fills the crowded room with stories about Zach. He speaks without a break for so long his coffee goes cold and he has to dump it and refill it, only to let that one go cold, too. It's like he's kept these reminiscences locked away since Zach died. Now they spill out of him.

Zach, of course, soaks them all in.

He laughs and cheers and adds anecdotes only I can hear as his memories return with his father's stories. I have to stop myself from smiling at the dusty corner too frequently, distracted by just how complete Zach suddenly is.

Bill tells us that Zach was always protective of his older sister, Ari. How, even though she was five years older than him, he insisted he was her big brother until he was crushed when he was old enough to realize he was actually her little brother. He details Zach's championship baseball team in sixth grade. His senior prom and how he caught Zach sneaking into the house later that night somehow having lost his pants. He tells us about the day Zach moved out. Then the day he moved back in two years later when he got laid off. How he switched jobs from sales to something he loved a lot more—being a lifeguard.

"He never hesitated to go after what he wanted," Bill says softly, after describing Zach's training for the lifeguard exam.

I catch Sawyer's eye. Bill's statement is lovely, but there has to be *something* Zach didn't get around to doing. Otherwise he wouldn't still be here. While part of me would surprisingly love to just keep hearing more of Bill's stories, we came here for a purpose.

"Was there anything he didn't get to finish when he was alive?" I ask. "Anything Zach was working on or dreaming of?"

Bill looks puzzled by the questions. His face scrunches in a way I can't help recognizing. His posture tightens defensively.

I feel my pulse pick up with nerves. I don't want to offend Bill. I certainly don't want to cause him more pain. But I'm not just the ex of a dead guy right now. I'm also the person responsible for making sure Zach isn't stuck in limbo for the rest of eternity. The problem is, I don't know how to ask about what Zach left unfinished without coming across as insensitive.

Sawyer rushes to rescue me. "We wanted to do a tribute to

him," he says quickly. "If there's something he had on his bucket list, we thought it might be nice if we do it for him. For closure."

Bill's face softens; his smile returns. He's touched.

I nudge Sawyer's knee with mine under the table, a silent thank-you for his quick thinking. He nudges back, and I smile into my coffee.

"That's real kind of you both." Bill beams at us. "I'm so glad Zachy had friends like you—friends I didn't even know about. Just imagine how many other people he must have touched, too. He lived a full life despite it being too short." His voice starts to waver with emotion.

Tentatively, I reach out to lay a comforting hand on his wrist. The gesture feels awkward and clumsy to me, but I owe it to Zach. I'm sure he wishes he could be the one to comfort his dad. He can't, and for whatever reason, I'm the one he can communicate through. He shoots me a grateful look.

Bill pats my hand, pulled from his sadness. It's such a dad gesture that I can't help thinking of my own father. Suddenly, I miss him in a way I don't normally dwell on.

"But no," Bill continues. "That's what was so inspiring about Zach. He lived in the moment, and he never let one pass him by."

My stomach twists. *Wonderful. Zach Harrison was the epitome of regretless joie de vivre. Love that for him. Exactly what we needed.*

I set my coffee down. "Were there . . . any grudges Zach had? Anything or anyone we shouldn't involve in our, um, tribute?" I ask.

Bill laughs amicably. "No, no. Nothing like that. You can't live in the moment if you're holding grudges, can you?" His eyes drift to the corner where Zach sits, like somehow he's pulled to his son even though he can't see him. "He gave people the benefit of the doubt, and it just made him freer. I"—he blinks a tear away—"I should be more like him, I think."

Zach doesn't say anything. He watches his father, and I swear I feel the temperature in the room rise just a little, like he's giving his dad the only hug he can.

"Zach loved you a lot," I tell Bill. "He said you were the best dad he could have had."

Zach has never said those words to me. But I know they're true.

"Thanks, Morgan," he whispers.

Bill squeezes my hand tighter as more tears overwhelm him. I know they're both happy and sad. It makes my heart hurt. I want to comfort him, but I also know that Sawyer and I, two strangers, are not who he needs right now. He needs to close the shop early. Go home. See his wife. Hug his daughter. He doesn't seem to know what Zach's unfinished business could be, and even if he did, it wouldn't be right to pry it out of him now. Even if we return home from Harrison's Hardware with nothing promising, we should leave Mr. Harrison to his family and his memories.

Clearly reaching the same conclusion, Sawyer stands from the table. "Thank you for sharing your stories with us," he says, his voice sympathetic. "Anyone who didn't know Zach would know just from hearing you talk how wonderful a person he was and how much he'll be missed."

Now I have to hold in my tears. I glance at Sawyer, moved. He means what he's said, too. It's not just that he knows the right things to say to the bereaved. He respects life and loss. He's not afraid to care for someone whose absence hurts.

Bill nods, grateful. He wipes his eyes on a rag in his shirt pocket. "You both come by anytime," he says. "I'd love to see the tribute you put together, too."

"We will," I promise, having no idea what that tribute will be, but confident we'll find a way to honor Zach and his family.

When we walk out of the hardware store, Zach trails behind us. I know he's reluctant to leave. I don't blame him. Why would he want to go with us to a house that was never his home?

For the thousandth time, I find myself wishing Zach were haunting someone else—his family—but for the first time, it's not because I want to get rid of him. It's because it's horribly unfair that he can't be with his loved ones. He shouldn't be tied to *me*. He should get to use this borrowed time to tell his dad himself how much he loved him.

Zach disappears when we reach the sidewalk.

"You okay?" Sawyer asks as we walk to the car.

I'm grateful Zach is gone for the moment. "It just sucks he's dead," I say, holding back tears. Immediately, I'm embarrassed by the simplicity of my words for the enormity of Zach's loss—*It "sucks"?*—and how unearned my grief feels.

But Sawyer doesn't see it that way. "Yeah," he agrees softly. Like he understands me perfectly.

We drive home in silence. I roll the windows down, needing to hear the sounds of birds and traffic, of the rest of the world moving forward. It helps. Zach's family will never forget him, but I guess it's for the best he isn't haunting them. Bill will go home, and maybe he and his wife will have Zach's favorite meal tonight, and they'll hold each other when they cry. Tomorrow the sun will rise on them. Their lives will continue.

By the time we get home, I feel slightly better. I'm glad I got to know Zach more, even in the most unconventional of ways, with his spirit peering down semi-visibly from his cardboard perch. Maybe the next time I have a boyfriend, I'll let him take me home to his parents. It's probably nicer when the boyfriend isn't dead.

Only, for there to *be* another boyfriend, I need to figure out how to help Zach.

Sawyer turns off the engine. "What now?" he asks.

"I have no idea," I reply. "Congrats to Zach for living a very fulfilling, beautiful life, but we are nowhere closer to learning what his unfinished business is."

Sawyer focuses earnestly. "Maybe more memories will unlock in him now that we know more about his life? We could just give him some time."

The hairs on my neck stand up like someone is behind me. Sure enough, I find Zach manifested in the back seat.

"At least now we know I was awesome and everyone loves me. That's comforting," Zach says sincerely.

I ignore him, distracted by Sawyer, who unexpectedly straightens up and stares in the rearview mirror. I twist to try to see what he's seeing. Maybe someone is walking up to our car or something. Except I don't see anything on the street behind us.

I look at Sawyer, confused.

He pulls his gaze from the mirror. He blinks.

"I think that hearing about Zach's life let me get to know him better," he says slowly. "I feel like I really met him."

"That's . . . nice?" I say, unclear where he's going with this.

Sawyer suddenly grins. The expression on his usually somber, contemplative, hard-sculpted face is revelatory.

"Well," he replies, "it's either that, or there's another ghost who bears a striking resemblance to Zach's father sitting in the back seat right now."

My eyes widen as I realize what he's saying.

Sawyer can *see* Zach.

13

Morgan's haunted hookup matches the impression I've developed of him from her one-sided conversations with the ghost. Zach is chatty, boyishly exuberant, with a streak of sincerity in everything he says. He's my height, with natural muscle—his former life-guarding vocation makes sense—and a now eternal easygoing LA dad sense of style.

"You know," he says to me when we get out of the car, "you're really lucky you can see me now. You have no idea how helpful I can be. Like, if you ever need someone to covertly investigate a murder, I would gladly provide my surveillance services."

"I'll keep you in mind for my next murder investigation," I promise.

"I mean it!" Zach insists. "What about problems with your neighbors? Missing lawn gnomes? Broken fences?"

"Unsurprisingly, my neighbors steer clear of my house."

Zach is undaunted. "Industrial espionage? Reading people's PIN numbers over their shoulders?"

I laugh. "I'm good, man," I say.

Zach seems disappointed. "I'm just . . . grateful you're helping me and Morgan. You don't have to."

Reaching my front steps, I soften, understanding now Zach's desire to commit various ghostly crimes for me. "How about I consult you when I need to know what hammer or screwdriver to use on the house?"

Morgan smiles.

"Deal," Zach says.

While I head inside, Morgan sets to yard work. I guess the hardware store inspired me, because I find myself invigorated to handle more of the house repairs. I start on the living room shelves, which have gathered years of dust on the floor in the corner instead of lining the wall where we intended them.

Deep down, I keep hoping my handiwork will summon Kennedy, who's been conspicuously evasive since her spelling stunt with the sticks under her tree. The cupboards have remained restful, the house's temperature tepid. She hasn't materialized to watch, or even half watch, TV with me or to supernaturally rearrange the furniture for the hundredth time.

Right now, I'm wondering if she might want to counsel me on proper hammering or leveling. Unfortunately, I guess my technique is perfect.

Sunset comes, lighting my workspace in vermilion. Out the front windows, I notice Morgan. She's made progress on clearing the yard. My heart clenches when I see it, and I selfishly start reassuring myself of just how many dead vines remain.

I want this, I remind myself furiously. *I should want this. I do want this.* If we're right, this garden separates Kennedy from passing peacefully into the hereafter instead of—I don't know—getting lost in a limbo of nothing.

I want this. I should want this.

I don't fucking want this.

The thought pierces me, making me suddenly angry. Now I can see Zach Harrison and not my own fucking fiancée? It's not fair. How often have I had that thought in the past five years? It's not fair. Yet somehow, Kennedy or the spirit world or something has found new ways to fuck with my head and my heart.

The last sign of Kennedy I saw was out in the front yard where Morgan's working. *EXHUME ME.*

Well, message received.

I stomp outside, down the porch steps, to where I noticed Morgan leaves the shovel against the railing. I seize the implement, heart heavy, and head straight for the tree, passing Morgan, who's clearing weeds on the other side of the yard. She straightens up in confusion. I ignore her.

Kennedy made her wishes perfectly clear. Mine certainly don't matter. I'm alive, right? It's the only happiness I'm entitled to.

If Kennedy wants me to dig up this fucking tree, I will. Reaching the withered old jacaranda, I slam the shovel's slanted mouth under the rotted trunk like I'm chopping off my own limb. I keep hammering the shovel in, searching for purchase, punishing myself. Punishing Kennedy.

I sense Morgan approaching cautiously. "I can do it," she ventures with heartbreaking kindness.

"No," I reply. "You can't."

While she watches, helpless, I exact my vengeance on the tree. I drive the shovel in harder, ramming the metal horizontally into the trunk. Over and over and over. Wood chips fly out like shrapnel from where I strike, dirt flinging up with my furious effort, coating me in years-old dust.

With my punishing repetition, the tree finally shifts. Roots lurch under me, disrupting my swing, unsteadying my footing. I stumble.

Morgan's there to catch me. I feel her grasping, clumsy embrace struggling to hold me.

I can't stay upright. In Morgan's unfairly caring hands, my strength leaves me. The shovel falls from my grip.

In the light of the setting sun, I let myself sink into the soil.

14

MORGAN

I join Sawyer in the dirt. I have no idea what's come over him. I just know he needs me now.

While we kneel, I remove the shovel from his reach. I say nothing. Sawyer stays silent. Eyes downcast, head hung. He doesn't look haunted now. He looks destroyed, like he must have when he lost Kennedy. I don't know what pushed him to his outburst, but I know it has to do with her.

The sun descends under the horizon. Like with every sunset, the final glimmers of light seem suddenly to shine brighter than the rest—their last flash of defiant life. Then twilight settles over us.

Sawyer looks similarly like some sustaining light in him has gone out.

Eventually, he speaks. "This tree was blooming when we first saw the house," he says.

I envision it—jacarandas blossom in pale purple popcorn covering their high outreaching limbs. On this hillside in this once verdant yard, the sight must have been gorgeous.

"The whole yard was a mess," he says. "The whole house was. I didn't want to buy it. I couldn't see what Kennedy saw. But Kennedy pointed to this jacaranda's purple flowers. She told me to look past the mess to the potential."

I just listen. Honestly, I cannot imagine what Sawyer's feeling. I focus on his words instead—on the Kennedy that no social media stalking or engagement photos on the minimalist mantel can capture. Only Sawyer's memories bring this Kennedy to life, hopeful and keen-eyed and wise.

"*One day our kids will play under these blooms*, she said," Sawyer recounts hollowly. His head droops to his chest once more. "But they won't," he says. "They won't, because . . . because she's dead."

I feel like I did in Harrison's Hardware, realizing what he plans on giving up for Kennedy's peace. Sawyer and I only share the same supernatural problem in the superficial sense, I know. Deeper down, our situations couldn't be more different. I'm dealing with the inconvenience of my mischievous specter. Sawyer is . . . wrestling with losing the woman he loves for the second time.

He reaches out, splaying his fingers into the dirt, like he imagines the soil can connect him with those memories. His own roots, desperate to return to the home he once hoped to cultivate.

"All the rot in this yard must have spread and choked it," he speculates.

Staring up, Sawyer studies the withered limbs of the ruined jacaranda. Their dead fingers look like roots in reverse. Reaching heavenward, finding nothing.

"Do you think that's happened to me, too?" he whispers. "What if I'm past saving? I mean, look at me. Furious with my dead fiancée for wanting peace." He shakes his head ruefully. "Surely there's something rotten in me already."

Something rotten in me. His self-loathing strikes the hateful sound of a familiar chord. How often have I punished myself for how I dealt with difficulties? *Something rotten in me. I'm a fucking liability.*

Sawyer's position is more understandable than mine. I dealt with the consequences of my own honest mistakes, while Sawyer is facing fate's harshest cruelties. Still, how much have I hated myself for letting people down, just like Sawyer hates himself for depending on Kennedy's ghost? He retreated from living while I just retreated from people.

I haven't retreated from him, though. I haven't wanted to, just like I don't want him to suffer in self-imposed isolation. He deserves to know what happened to him isn't his fault. He deserves salvation from self-loathing for how he coped.

I nudge him gently.

"You don't know a lot about plants," I say.

Slowly, he faces me, surprise settling over him, like he'd forgotten I was here. The twilight hues shade his stricken features in unruly, surrealistic swaths of pale color.

"Dead plants," I go on, "make great compost to fertilize living plants. It doesn't choke them. It only makes them stronger."

Now Sawyer's eyes lock with mine. He holds my gaze, and I know he's not merely seeing me in front of him. He's seeing the life I'm promising him. Where he doesn't have to resent himself for how grief's hold weakens his resolve. Where, in Kennedy's ghostly eyes, he has strength and selflessness.

I want him to. I want him to believe me, so bad. I want him to believe he'll come out of this.

When he laughs, sarcastic but not scornful, I feel glimmers of hope. "I'm hardly stronger," he replies. "I can't even dig up this tree." His voice's hollow fury has subsided. He's starting to sound like the Sawyer I've gotten to know.

I smile. "Let's do it together," I say.

I don't wait for Sawyer's reply, for whatever futile protest he'll make, insisting he's not up to this. He is. Even having only entered each other's lives recently, I know he's the strongest person I've ever met.

I stand, not bothering to swipe soil from my knees. I bend down to pick up the discarded shovel. With my other hand, I reach out to Sawyer.

He hesitates. He's not wavering, though. He's marshaling his spirit, summoning his strength. I don't know how I know it's what he's doing—I just do.

Finally, he puts his hand in mine.

When I help him up, he nods. I've seen Sawyer shattered, the fragile, fraught way he gets—it's not how he looks now. He's determined. His quiet strength has returned. Without speaking, I drive the shovel into the earth, under the jacaranda's loosest roots, pounding the head into the soil with my foot on the upper edge.

The root resists. I look over my shoulder at Sawyer.

Understanding, he steps closer to me. He places his hands on the shovel's grip, close to mine. Our forearms, mine wiry with gardening exertion, Sawyer's thick with cords of sculpting and home-improvement muscle, line up next to each other. I'm shoulder to shoulder with him. Together, we press our combined strength on the shovel.

It takes enormous effort. We're both straining, putting everything we have into it. The exertion unsteadies us. Sawyer has to put his hand briefly on my hip to rebalance us. I don't mind.

We push and push, and finally, the jacaranda starts to move.

Up the wavering shaft of the shovel, I literally feel the popping, ripping relief of the infinite root cords coming loose from the soil. It's kind of grotesque, the root-pulling, but kind of wonderful. The wrenching, consummating feeling of freedom.

Sawyer and I keep pushing, keep dredging for that freedom. My muscles sear. I hear Sawyer grunt from low in his stomach with the continued pressure. I let myself do the same, our voices joining while the tree dislodges, comes uprooted, and finally slides out of the soil.

Freed, it collapses into the dead weeds surrounding us.

Chests heaving, Sawyer and I retreat. I drop the shovel into the dirt, calluses—past, present, and future—stinging in fierce pink splotches on my palms.

Sawyer looks to me. He surprises me by raising his hand for a high five. With his palms looking similarly fucked up, the gesture makes me laugh. Gamely, I high-five him.

The moment we touch, Sawyer closes his fingers gently over mine, holding my hand.

"Thank you," he says quietly.

His gaze is downcast, not meeting my eyes. I don't think he's heartbroken, though. Or not exactly. He's solemn, peaceful in reconciliation with what we've done. In recognition that to keep living, sometimes you need to pull old dreams out by their roots.

I'm touched by the depth of the sincerity in his voice. When I nod, knowing there's nothing more I need to say, he releases my hand.

In the corner of my eye, I notice movement, and the flicker draws my gaze to Sawyer's front door. I see a shadow in the archway— there for a moment, then gone. *Kennedy?* I can't help but wonder, even though I feel like I know.

15

SAWYER

Dinnertime finds me fighting loneliness, hoping even for glimmers of Kennedy—tuneless wind chimes outside or doors drifting closed on their own—while my frozen lasagna spins slowly within my microwave.

I expected Morgan and me exhuming the withered jacaranda yesterday would summon signs of life after death, at least. Despite my outburst, I don't regret the decision. Morgan and Kennedy were right. It needed to go.

Of course, I understand the contradiction here. It's one of those ruthless equations of grief, I think. Letting go of some parts of them just makes you cling harder to others.

Suddenly, the power cuts out. It happens enough in a haunted house that I'm not startled, merely prepared to eat a half-frozen meal. I remove my lasagna, inspecting the microwave's lack of progress mournfully. When I set it on the counter, though, I hear knocking on my back door.

I abandon my lukewarm dinner and open the door, where I find Morgan and Zach.

Morgan *and* Zach. The latter startles me. I'm still getting used to having two houseguests instead of one.

Zach's mood has worsened since offering me his detective services yesterday. He stares glumly forward. I think he seems somewhat more translucent today than when we got home from yesterday's drive out to the hardware store.

The very not-translucent Morgan has showered since her gardening today. Her hair hangs slick over one shoulder. She is fully clothed this time, however.

"I need to use your stove," she announces. "Zach is moping and he keeps accidentally cutting the power. My hot plate cannot compete with his mood swings."

In keeping with her habit of wandering freely into my house, Morgan steps inside past me. She's holding packaged mac and cheese. On the counter, she spies my lasagna.

"Bringing Zach here has only killed my power, too," I explain.

Morgan looks undaunted. "But how is your stove?" she asks.

I gesture to the oven. "Be my guest." I guess Zach hears *Be my ghost*, because he rematerializes in my kitchen next to Morgan. He remains distracted, unmoved by his interference with our dinners.

Morgan clicks the knob. When the stove *whoosh*es softly with gas, she lets out a surprised little cheer. "Zach, stay away," she warns him as she pulls out a match and lights the burner.

Zach slouches. "I'm not *trying* to cut the power," he protests. "I'm sorry that me mourning the great life I had that is now over because I'm *dead* is getting in the way of your mac and cheese."

Morgan's shoulders slump. "Ugh, Zach, I'm sorry," she concedes. "I'm trying to help, but I'm *not* dead, so I do need to eat in order to, you know, stay that way."

She reaches down into my cabinets, rummaging through cookware until she finds my largest metal pot. I watch her, intrigued despite myself, while she makes herself at home in my kitchen. She dumps her orange cheese sauce mix into the pot, and soon the room fills with the heavy scent of cheesy goo.

My stomach grumbles. "Do you . . . have enough for two?" I venture. Honestly, mac and cheese—and company—sound pretty great.

Morgan grins. "I got you," she says, stirring the sauce.

"No one cares about me," Zach declares. "I'm nothing compared to mac and cheese."

"Buddy, what happened?" I ask him. "You were thrilled yesterday. Remember how relieved you were to learn that you had family who loved you?"

"I didn't realize it would make this . . . worse," Zach confesses. "It would be easier if I was just some dead miserable loser. But I had a great family. I had things I loved."

I nod, not expecting how well I understand Zach's sentiment. Sitting down with Bill Harrison was nice, yes. It was confusing, though, too, in ways I haven't shared with Morgan—not that I need to. Long before I met Kennedy, I wanted to distance myself from my parents. Growing up, I struggled with my father's impatience and unpredictability, my mom's glorified indignation and weaponized fragility. I couldn't wait to leave home.

I managed to graduate, found my way to Los Angeles, to art school. Found Kennedy. I shared her with my parents on infrequent, controlled conditions, short visits, enough to keep up the semblance of an ordinary relationship with my family.

Then Kennedy died. Foolishly, I visited home, groping for something like stability. Reassurance, even.

What I got was razor-wire smiles and claims of packed schedules. I persisted, spending time near them if not with them, until one night I found myself having dinner with my mom while my dad worked late, still his custom despite being in his sixties. I ventured to explain how I was feeling, how I was struggling to reshape my life.

Cheer up, my mother exhorted me. *Did you drive up here just to mope?*

I knew my mom wasn't cruel. She wasn't oblivious. She was just . . . emotionally limited. She couldn't manage my pain except to flippantly, dismissively distance herself from it. *To mope.* The word she used for my grief.

I left the next day politely but with certainty. I didn't need them.

I remember feeling relief hiding in my misery. Kennedy's death and their response was the final, irrefutable push I needed to reject the shitty parental hand I was dealt. Out of sight, out of mind, out of my life.

Zach has no such luck. He lost people worth holding on to. His frustration hides sadness, the cheated hurt of one robbed of his entire life.

"Now I just have watching you make mac and cheese while I accidentally kill the power," he says.

On cue, the kitchen lights dim. The room grows darker.

Having dealt with the electrical manifestations of unhappy ghosts, I reach into the drawer where I keep my candles. "It's unfair," I say. "I understand. I would be unhappy, too."

Zach nods. He seems grateful. Some of the lights flicker on.

Morgan notices. She gasps indignantly, twisting to face us at the stove. "I totally gave you sympathy," she chastens Zach, "and I didn't get any electricity!"

While she unceremoniously dumps the macaroni into the cheesy pot, I shrug. "Guess he likes me better."

Zach nearly smiles. The lights hum louder. "It *is* nice to be able to talk to someone else," Zach says.

"Dude, I'm *right here*," Morgan complains.

I feel the sudden responsibility to keep the peace before Zach escalates drastically by exploding our cheese sauce. "Morgan doesn't seem like that bad of company," I say.

She pauses in her stirring to meet my eyes. Something unfamiliar lights them. Like sunlight past garden vines.

"She snores loud enough to wake the dead," Zach comments. "Literally."

Morgan spins, aghast, with enough momentum to fling cheese on the wall. "That is *not* true!"

I can't help myself. I laugh. So does Zach. The light bulb overhead surges and then shines steadily.

"She does listen to music way too loud," I concede. "I mean, it's not college." Morgan won't mind if I partake in some supernatural reassurance via making fun of her. Probably.

"Yeah, and it's, like, *only* 2000s millennial iPod rock," Zach corroborates. "Have you not listened to new music since middle school?"

The lights stay on, the power holding strong. Morgan shakes her head.

"Oh, I see," she says. "Teasing me is the only way to liven you up. I expected it from Zach, but for you to partake of it so gleefully—"

She points to me with her cheesy spoon.

"I'm surprised," she chastens.

"Hey, when you're dealing with the paranormal, you have to play by their rules," I reply.

Morgan shakes her head, offering no concession to my defense.

"One thing that's been bothering me, though," Zach says. "If just getting to know me better let you see me, then why couldn't my dad see me?"

The light bulb dims momentarily, fading with Zach's sadness.

Morgan pauses her stirring.

I say nothing. It's a good question.

While our dinner bubbles, Morgan leans back on the counter, considering. "You're obviously haunting me for some mysterious reason, and it's not like I really knew you," she says. "Maybe it's not just that Sawyer got to know you. Maybe it's—" She stops herself. Pink invades her cheeks.

Zach, caught up in his malaise, doesn't notice.

I do. "It's what?" I prompt.

Morgan returns to stirring. "Maybe it . . . has to do with me *and Sawyer*. I got to know him better because he opened up to get your dad to trust us. *And* he also got to know you," she says.

I study her, surprise settling over me. She's right. I did open up. I spoke of the pain and fear and longing I haven't shared with anyone in years.

Morgan heard me. Not just in service of Zach. She listened to what *I* had to say, and now this stranger I met in ghost support group understands me like few people in my post-Kennedy existence do. We only entered each other's lives last week—now, like I've started to know Zach, Morgan has started to know me.

Honestly, I . . . don't know how it makes me feel.

I've gotten used to the walls of stone I use to conceal my emotions, my haunting, my functional-dysfunctional life. Don't all lonely people want someone like Morgan—vivacious, funny, optimistic—to penetrate those walls? It's how these stories go.

But those happy endings presume I *want* to change, even deep down, even subconsciously. I don't know if I do. It's comfortable in my haunted fortress of solitude. In fact, it's the only comfort I've found since life ripped my greatest love, my greatest hope, out of my grasp.

Morgan has dislodged the quiet complacency I've found, just

as she uprooted my yard's somber monument to Kennedy. In Morgan's persistent company, I not only feel seen. I feel . . . vulnerable.

I muster the best smile I can manage, wan and noncommittal. If Morgan notices my hesitation, she doesn't react or comment.

"So, you're saying . . . the three of us have a special connection," Zach summarizes proudly.

His enthusiasm pulls me from my rumination. Honestly, Morgan could have done worse for supernatural company. Zach's a genuinely cool ghost.

"Looks like," I reply, grateful for the change of topic.

The rest of the lights brighten to life.

Morgan grins. She shuts off the burner where our dinner simmers.

"I guess I have a pretty nice afterlife as well as a nice life," Zach says.

With our electricity and good moods restored, Morgan serves us dinner—"us" meaning the corporeal members of our promising trio.

It's delicious, especially so for stovetop mac and cheese. In the years since Kennedy died, I've withdrawn from dinner parties, unable to force pleasantries or play grieving widower when I'm not—when my Kennedy is just invisible to everyone else. Now, though, I suspect I may have missed eating with company.

Zach watches us without jealousy. Kennedy explained to me once that they couldn't taste or smell. "Do you think you could make a connection with my dad, too?" Zach asks, hopeful.

Morgan pauses over her steaming macaroni. Her mouth twists. "I don't know if that's a good idea," she replies gently. "If he were to see you, then . . ."

"He'd be like me," I finish, hearing what she's really saying. "Haunted by a loved one. Unable to move on. Forced to eventually say goodbye a second time." I can't help the edge in my voice. Is her reply out of compassion for Zach? Or pity for poor, wounded me? Pity can come perilously close to judgment.

Morgan hears the undercurrent in my voice. She looks over, finding me frowning at my mac and cheese. "You're doing the right thing," she says, trying to comfort me.

Then, why does the right thing hurt so fucking much?

The thought shoots sharply into my head. The pain in my chest is suddenly unbearable. I can't put on the calm, enduring face. Not now. Not with Morgan telling me how to say goodbye to the woman I love. In a flash, my pain turns to anger.

"How could you possibly know that?" I ask. "You think because we have enough of a connection that I can see Zach, it means you know everything about me?"

The lights hum and churn with Zach's surprise. Morgan holds my gaze. If my outburst startled her, her poker face is impressive. "I know you've tried to hide your grief in this haunted house for years," she shoots back. "You're just mad I've brought it into the light."

"Of course I am!" I shout. Everything is rushing out of me now, emotions and confessions I wanted to hide. It's the problem with stone walls—they can let horrible pressure mount before they crack. "I didn't ask for any of this. I was happy before," I fume, pain-choked, heart pounding.

"You weren't happy, Sawyer. I know you well enough to know that." Morgan's indignation has vanished. She only sounds sad. "This house is a mausoleum. You can't *live* here. You're surviving on savings that will run out eventually, and then what? Forget making pottery for money. What about making it for art? You used to be an artist. Now, you're . . ." She shakes her head.

Suffocating silence fills my haunted house.

"I don't know," Morgan finally says. "But you're not happy."

I feel suddenly like Kennedy or Zach. I'm not made of stone. I'm transparent. Morgan has stared right through me to my shattered heart.

I hate it. I hate how much I've let myself unravel over the past five years. My work history is nonexistent, my life funded by the savings from several major contracts I landed when Kennedy was still here. My friends were *our* friends—when they reached out to help me grieve, I let them. When they invited me to return to life, I ignored them, until eventually the invitations stopped coming. I speak to my parents in the platitudes they want to hear. *Everything's fine. House is coming together. No dating yet. Everything's fine, I promise.*

Morgan somehow sees everything.

It embarrasses me and enrages me. It's not my fault my life was destroyed.

It's not Morgan's, either, obviously, but sitting here, helplessly lonely, I want to fight whatever stole Kennedy from me. Since I can't, I'll settle for fighting with Morgan.

"Oh, so you're the expert on a perfect life? Come on," I shoot back. "You're so afraid of commitment you can't even buy a full set of plates. You move from city to city before anyone cares about you enough to want you to stay. That's not living, either. Hell—"

When I gesture to my other houseguest, the kitchen lights surge dangerously.

"—between the three of us, *Zach* is the most alive," I say.

Immediately I know I've wounded Morgan. Her face closes up like the withered leaves of the dead plants outside. Exuberant, daring Morgan, who marched into my kitchen with her macaroni and cheese like she owned the place.

She feels seen, too. She feels vulnerable, too.

She doesn't like it, either.

I'm guilty and I'm glad. Glad someone else is suffering with me. Guilty that I'm the cause. I wanted Morgan to understand the pain, yes, but I never, ever wanted to hurt her. Regret's cold shock consumes me instantly.

It only makes me want to retreat deeper into myself. Morgan wishes me free of my mausoleum, free to return to the world when Kennedy is gone. But why should I? What good would *I* do? This conversation proves I'm too damaged to rejoin the living. Like one of my own creations, once shattered, my sharp pieces are only capable of injury. What if there's not enough gold in the world to make me whole?

I've ruined my fragile friendship with Morgan, now. I'll inevitably drive her away. Maybe then things will go back to the way they were.

Except, when Morgan stands sharply, defiant, I realize I don't want her to leave.

The back door slams shut behind her, and I flinch.

Zach remains. So does the power in my house. "She'll forgive you, you know," he says softly.

I shrug. "I don't care," I lie.

Zach shakes his head. "Special connection, remember, dude? You care," he insists. "And I know more about Morgan than that she snores. She acts selfish, but when people need her, she's there for them. She shows up."

While I meet his ghostly gaze, Zach starts fading from visibility.

"You need her," he says.

Then he disappears, leaving me alone, wishing he wasn't right.

16

MORGAN

If I could leave this house now, I honestly would. I would leave Sawyer and his spooky studio and his nightmare garden and his dysfunctional water heater and his ghost fiancée and his uncomfortably perceptive observations right damn now. I would grab my one suitcase, which I still haven't unpacked, and abandon Sawyer to the miserable life to which he's so eager to return.

Unfortunately, I can't. I promised him I would clear his front yard. The stubborn need to defy his sharp words—*afraid of commitment, huh?*—won't let me abandon my horticultural undertaking.

This stubbornness pulls me out of bed early in the morning. I need to put in hours on Sawyer's dead yard if I'm going to leave here *as soon as possible*. Which I very much intend to.

With morning light invading my guesthouse windows—which Sawyer would have never cleaned without me, so really he should be thanking me instead of calling me commitment-phobic or whatever—I pull on my leggings and gardening boots. I put my hair up. Time to garden like I've never goddamn gardened before.

Determined, I march under the bougainvillea, down the dirt path, and reach for the shovel I left there yesterday.

The tool drops out of my hands when I glimpse the yard.

The dead plants have been cleared. Instead of shrouding Sawyer's home in messy hedges, they sit clipped and organized in impeccable piles in front of the house.

I gape. There's . . . no way Sawyer did this. Not to mention in one night. The job was weeks of painstaking work. *Nobody* could do this in one night.

Or . . . nobody living.

Zach materializes next to me, sunlight passing through him while he rubs his stubbled chin.

"Did . . . you do this?" I murmur, even though from his expression, I know he didn't.

"I think it was Kennedy," he replies.

He wanders into the front yard, examining the plant piles with visible fascination. I watch him. Zach is, of course, my expert on what ghosts can and cannot do.

"Didn't Sawyer mention he hasn't seen Kennedy in days?" he asks. "I wondered if she was . . . fading or something. But if she's able to manifest strongly enough to do *this* . . . I mean, I couldn't do this," he elaborates.

"Hey," I say. "Don't sell yourself short."

Zach smiles graciously. "No, seriously. If Kennedy is making short work of her own yard, then why hasn't she appeared to Sawyer in days? And," he says, "why didn't she do the yard herself sooner?"

I have no answers for my ghost's questions.

The front door opens. I see Sawyer coming downstairs in gray sweatpants, his hair mussed.

"You two didn't do this, did you?" he inquires.

I notice dark circles under his eyes. He slept even worse than I did. *Good*, I remind myself, except my own vindictiveness doesn't quite convince me.

Zach shakes his head, silent.

"No," Sawyer agrees, overlooking the yard like he's realizing what we have. "I feel her. She was here."

Then his sleep-deprived gaze moves to me.

"I was . . . worried you'd be leaving this morning," he muscles out.

I raise my eyebrows. "I'm not," I say. "Are you kicking me out?"

"I'm not," Sawyer says.

I nod, hiding my unexpected relief. We're not apologizing for the regrettable things we said about each other. Or I assume *Sawyer* regrets them. I'm not happy with him, and I know he's not happy with me.

Still, it's something. The start of something, instead of another ending. Like soil, cleared of dead weeds, where something, maybe, one day, could grow.

"Well, since the dead plants are gone," I say. "It's time to plant new ones. I have a couple hours before work. I could go to the nursery to pick some out for you, or you could tell me what you want. You'll just have to reimburse me for the purchases."

Sawyer pauses. "Can I . . ." He clears his throat like he's clearing out old resentments. "Can I come with you?"

I don't smile. I kind of want to, though. "I think I can *commit* to a car ride with you," I say pointedly. "Think you can drag yourself out of your depressing house for a couple hours?"

Sawyer cracks half a grin. "Only one way to find out," he replies.

17

SAWYER

The sun shines overhead when we park outside Morgan's chosen destination. It's hot—Hollywood Hills hot. Over the door, the nursery's logo depicts a child's crib entwined with flowering plants.

I follow Morgan inside, starting to sweat immediately. The place reminds me of Zach's family's store. The enormous gravel parking lot leads into the high-ceilinged metal warehouse, where flora crowd the verdant space. There's a fresh hopefulness in the uncomplicated hues of the young leaves on each plant.

It's ironic, I suppose. To commemorate and possibly help the dead, we've found ourselves in a place of new life.

We pass quick conversations and customers hauling heavy pots or packages of soil, heading directly through the space and out the back doors, where the sprawling garden extends in every direction. Endless varieties of swaying stalks, low shrubs, and pinprick flowers combining in a kaleidoscope of green.

I notice how everyone seems to know exactly what they're doing here. Morgan is no exception. While she points out plants on the shelves surrounding us, I struggle to keep up with her observations. Some plants will flourish on the north side of my yard, she explains, where there's more sunlight. Others should be tucked closer to the porch, where overexposure to sunlight won't ravage them.

I feel some kinship with those plants. I don't make this observation to Morgan.

Instead, I follow her unrelenting stride. I have six inches on her, but still I find myself struggling to match her eager pace. The exertion combined with the hot day has sweat prickling incessantly over my heating skin.

Morgan is unstoppable. It's like being here has brought her to life even more. She seems somehow to capture the sun, radiant with light. I'm soon out of breath, and I'm not convinced the summer weather is solely responsible.

Suddenly, she whirls. "So?" she demands. "Which will it be?"

I stumble and halt. "What?"

Morgan presses her lips together, looking impatient. Her hair has started to come free from the clip on the back of her head. Her sunglasses reveal a shadowed glimpse of her eyes. "Which *plants*?" she says. "Were you even listening?"

My shoulders slacken. Is she serious? I've heard auctioneers less loquacious. "Morgan," I start. "You—"

You belong among foliage. You love it here so much it's infectious. You have a wild strand of chestnut-gold hair falling into your face.

I startle. Where did *those* thoughts come from?

"You talk really fast," I say, recovering.

Morgan pauses to return the rogue strand to her clip. Seeming unsatisfied with her efforts, she releases the clip, letting her hair fall free.

I divert my gaze to the greenery.

"Sorry," Morgan replies. She sounds, well, not sorry. "It's just always inspiring being here. I wish I could plant everything. One day," she muses.

"Do you have a garden of your own?" I ask. My uneducated stare settles on the largest nearby plant—a cactus, limbs pointed resolutely up from the enormous round pot where the plant stands. I imagine Morgan ensuring the spiny megalith receives just enough water, not too much, or pruning unwieldy growth to ensure the stalk stands straight.

Morgan laughs. "I have a concrete walkway in front of my apartment," she replies. "I tried to put some plants out, and the landlord told me I couldn't have them. Fire hazard," she adds, sounding understandably dubious.

When she shrugs, I catch disappointment flicker in her expression. In the mere days I've known Morgan, one thing I've started to notice is how instinctually she fends off discouragement. Or hides it.

"It's fine," she insists. "I just like to look at them. That's what's so wonderful about gardens. They aren't just for you, are they? You don't have to own them to enjoy them," she goes on.

She surveys the plants, her stare lingering on one with clusters of purple flowers under an awning. I don't need to have known Morgan long to recognize her rapture, either.

"All your neighbors will get this gift. So if I design enough beautiful gardens and yards in the world, it'll be like they're mine," she says.

Hearing her explanation, I can't help huffing a "Huh."

Of course, Morgan looks up, expectant. "Now what?" she demands, deadpan.

I shake my head. "Nothing."

What I *would* say, if I wanted to share, was how I feel like I'm starting to put the pieces of Morgan Lane together. I'm realizing she doesn't just have commitment issues—no, Morgan doesn't need much stuff when the stuff that brings her joy doesn't have to be owned to be enjoyed. Gardens. Loud music. Mac and cheese.

New friends.

No, I'm flattering myself now.

Unsurprisingly, my nonanswer does not satisfy Morgan. She lifts her glasses to peer at me, questioning. "Nothing?" she repeats.

I hesitate. I don't want to share what I've observed. I don't want to resurrect our conversation—our resentful, wounded accusations, which have receded into the shadows on this sunlit day—and even more than that, I know my commentary would come off as too intimate. Morgan is someone who lives in my guesthouse. If she becomes someone I *know*, someone I want to keep getting to know, she'll be the first person in years who I've let in. I don't know what that means.

So I divert. "Use my yard then," I offer spontaneously.

Morgan cocks her head, not following.

"Pick whatever you want to plant most and design around that," I elaborate. "Anything you'd enjoy seeing."

Now her eyes widen. Her expression turns giddy. She may be evasive with disappointment, but she's wonderfully open with her excitement. "Really?" she asks.

I nod firmly. "Really. You're right. For too long my yard hasn't brightened anyone's days. I'd like to change that," I say. "Starting with you. I want it to make you happy."

Morgan takes in my words. Then she hugs me.

The warm impact of her surprises me. She smells like flowers. The corner of her sunglasses presses into my chest. She's so—solid. So real.

For a heartbeat, I put my arms around her.

We both withdraw quickly. The moment has made me bashful,

but I'm not expecting the same shyness on Morgan's face. Smiling past pink cheeks, she shoves her hands in the back pockets of her overalls.

"I think it won't just make *me* happy," she says of my future garden.

"Of course. I'll enjoy the view, too," I assure her. Shit, if Morgan manages to capture half of her own relentless vibrancy in the palette of petals she uses on my home, I'll have the loveliest yard in the neighborhood.

Morgan laughs. "I'd hope so. But that's not what I meant," she replies. Her voice softens when she continues. "I think it'll make Kennedy happy. She built a dream home with you. It deserves better than a nightmare yard."

I feel myself stiffen. The sunlight feels suddenly cold on my skin.

I guess my face falls, because Morgan instantly looks guilty. "Sorry. Sorry," she repeats. "I just mean . . . it's nice what you're doing. That's all. I'm not trying to reopen everything we said last night."

I shake my head. "No, I know," I say. "That's not—I'd just . . . forgotten for a moment that that's why we're here."

Feeling my throat thicken, I pull my gaze from Morgan, who doesn't deserve to know how her kindness has wounded me. Instead, my eyes find the immense cactus, lonesome in the corner.

"I'd forgotten this should make me sad," I confess.

The reminder is punishing. Everything, every fleeting hope and fond observation I've had this morning, is crushed under its enormous weight. I shouldn't be *excited* to see what Morgan does with the yard. I should be mourning. Funereal veils instead of flourishing color. Planting the yard is moving forward.

I don't want to move forward. I don't.

"It's okay to forget your grief for an hour," Morgan replies gently. "It doesn't mean you aren't always carrying it. That it isn't inside here."

She reaches forward to touch my chest, then stops herself.

"She'll always be with you," she says instead.

I nod. It's not *not* what I needed to hear. It's just hard to content myself with consolation, even if consolation is all I have now.

Morgan offers me a comforting smile, then wanders off toward the plant with the purple flowers.

Suspecting she's just giving me privacy, I don't follow. I just stare into the bright sky behind her until my eyes water.

18

MORGAN

The next Friday, I come home from work in high spirits.

Or so to speak. In one sense, I return home in *no* spirits, since Zach hasn't interrupted my workdays this week in his usual ways. I finished my purchase orders quickly, worked out some scheduling issues with minimal client fussiness, and even contributed notes Jason DiCrescenzo called "good garden intuition." Zach, for his part, has graciously understood I was having a good week and hasn't interfered.

It's Sawyer's doing. With my lifestyle, I'm used to considering my jobs more like stopgap solutions for the unfortunate requirement of earning a living wage. Instead, Sawyer's offer to let me design his yard to my green thumb's content reminded me I *like* what I do.

When I took that inspiration to work, it . . . helped. I spent the week starting to imagine myself doing well here. Even having my own company, maybe, one day.

Morgan Lane, Los Angeles landscaper. Ha. It still sounds kind of ridiculous to me.

Kind of real, though. Like a dream coming to life. Like something I never imagined possible becoming something I can see.

I'm not putting down roots in Los Angeles, metaphorically, despite doing so literally in Sawyer's front yard. Not yet. I'm just . . . less wary of settling into my life here, I guess.

Spring in my step, I climb Sawyer's porch. I have decided on the perfect way to celebrate career contentment and existential inspiration—pizza. I noticed a cool-looking old place on Sunset on my drive home, and I'm feeling ninety-nine percent certain I can convince Sawyer to go in on delivery with me. I knock eagerly on the front door.

The woman who opens it is not Sawyer.

She's older, with gray streaks in her dark hair. Her loose-fitting sundress combines patchwork swatches of patterned fabric. Her smile forms to the light wrinkles lining her cheeks.

"Hi!" she greets me cheerfully.

"Um," I say.

When she just smiles, I peer past her.

"Hi. Is, uh, Sawyer here?" I manage.

"He ran to the store to get stuff for dinner. I can pass a message to him when he gets back for you," she offers.

I guess she's some relative of his. Clearly it was a surprise drop-in, hence him not mentioning it to me and needing to run to the store for dinner. His mom, maybe? It's a quick reminder of how little we really know each other outside of our respective hauntings, despite his kindness in offering me his garden.

"Oh, it's fine," I say. "You have a nice night. I'll just catch him later. I'm his, um, tenant," I explain, not wanting this woman to be concerned when I hole up in the shed outside instead of leaving the property.

Surprisingly, however, this makes the visitor's eyes light up.

"You're Morgan!" she exclaims. "You have to come in and join us for dinner!"

Yes, I'm Morgan—Morgan, who is stunned Sawyer mentioned me to his family. My stomach does this inexplicable happy flip. In my years on the move, I've all but forgotten how it feels to be remembered.

"Um. Okay," I say. "Yeah." I'm relieved for the dinner invitation, honestly, since pizza with Sawyer is evidently a no-go.

I step into Sawyer's sitting room, where I find the woman isn't alone. On the sofa sits a sturdy-looking man—her husband, presumably. Sawyer's father?

"Joe," the woman says, "this is Morgan."

Only when Joe stands do I notice what he has in his hands. It's one of Sawyer's framed photographs—one of his engagement photos with Kennedy, who is laughing, luminous, her hand in Sawyer's.

Joe does not look as warmly welcoming as his wife, which is when I start to have a horrible suspicion.

Cold dread flushes through me right as the front door opens and Sawyer emerges carrying groceries.

He falters in the doorway. "Morgan," he says.

"Sawyer!" the good-natured woman greets him. "I invited Morgan to join us, if that's okay with you."

His eyes find mine. Then hers. His mouth flattens. His narrowed gaze pretty much confirms the situation I've stumbled into. "Of course," he says.

"It's fine," I hasten to interject. "I don't need to intrude." Honestly, a hot-plate dinner with Zach is sounding pretty good right now.

"You're not intruding!" the persistent woman replies. "We're the intruders." She laughs. "We dropped in on Sawyer to pick up some photos of Kennedy. He's terrible at returning calls, you know."

There it is—my fear confirmed. Forget hot-plate dinner. I would prefer dining in Sawyer's dark garage with spooky, no-memory, horror-movie Zach over having dinner with *Kennedy's parents*.

"Goodness, I didn't introduce myself," Kennedy's mother says, looking to me with wide-eyed contrition to match her enthusiastic welcome. "I'm Irene Raymond. Our son, Kennedy's brother Jordan, is having a baby, and we wanted to put up some photos of Kennedy through the years at the shower. Sawyer had one of her old albums. Hence the drop-in."

I nod, still not sure what to make of myself in this position.

Sawyer moves into the kitchen, depositing the groceries on the counter. "If you'd just told me you wanted the photos, I would have sent them over," he reminds them gently.

Joe and Irene pause, exchanging a complicated look.

"We wanted to see you, son," Joe finally says.

Sawyer stops unloading groceries.

I may not know his parents, may not know his former future in-laws, but I know Sawyer well enough to feel how Joe's words wreck him. He stares down, looking winded, like the weight of loss has felled him where he stands.

"We're so glad you're just too busy for us," Irene joins in, softer. "Instead of . . ."

She doesn't need to finish the sentence. Not with us. *Instead of being too grief-stricken to return our calls. Instead of rejecting the reminder of people you wanted to spend the rest of your life with.*

I recognize her hesitation. It's not just reluctance. No, Irene Raymond is merely speaking around the unspeakable. The loss of a soulmate or a child—like describing the feeling of Zach's hand slipping into my shoulder or the quality of sunlight filtering through him or the way he summons pop songs into my head—death extends into a realm past language itself.

Irene composes herself, chasing the worry from her expression. "Never mind that," she reassures Sawyer. She looks to me. "He told us you were helping him fix up the house finally. And that you're a real artist with plants."

I flush, flattered. When I glance at Sawyer, he's very determinedly preparing pasta in a pot on the stove. I have the sneaking suspicion grief is no longer the reason for his focus.

Well, while Sawyer can hide from my eyes, he can't change the way he's made me feel. I'm touched. Him thinking I'm gifted, thinking I'm skillful . . . it's not just kind. It's the way I want to be seen. "I don't know about *artist*," I demur. "Sawyer's the artist here."

Irene radiates pride for her nearly son-in-law. "Isn't his work just incredible?" she says. "Kennedy told us she fell in love with him for his hands," she adds half conspiratorially.

I laugh. I feel like Kennedy knew *exactly* what her praise implied. "I can understand that," I say.

Sawyer, I notice, is blushing furiously.

Joe shifts where he's seated. His manner is stiff, but not unkind. "How long have you two been together?"

Now Sawyer looks up.

I lock eyes with my roommate-slash-landlord-slash-fellow-hauntee. Holding my gaze, Sawyer dries his—yes, admirable—hands on a dishcloth and comes to lean in the archway. "We're not together," he says. His voice is patient yet firm in speaking to the parents of the woman death ripped from his life, and instantly I remember why I would have preferred dinner with Zach. "Morgan is my tenant. I told you," he says. "She's helping with the landscaping."

Kennedy's parents don't look convinced.

"You know you don't have to hide your love life from us, right?"

Irene says gently. "Just, if that was a story you constructed so you didn't have to tell your late fiancée's parents you have a girlfriend, you could just be honest."

"No, really," I interject, for I definitely owe Sawyer my help on this one. "We're just friends."

Irene's expression flickers like I've said the wrong thing. I look at Sawyer, unsure. Unsure about any of this—what to say, what he wants me to be in his life. Whatever it is, I really, genuinely do not want to intrude on Kennedy's lovely family.

"Friends is good," Joe finally comments. "Sawyer could use more friends."

Sawyer snorts, and I feel the tension in the room instantly release. "Way to make me sound like a loser, Joe," Sawyer says.

"I just call it like I see it," Kennedy's father replies, cracking a smile.

"Well, when we fix this yard up, Sawyer won't have his creepy house as his excuse not to have a social life," I chime in, glancing at Sawyer, wondering if I'm crossing invisible guardrails or if he'll welcome my joining in. I'm deeply relieved when he looks grateful.

"I'll have to fall back on my miserable personality, then," he replies.

I grin. "At least you have good hands, though."

Sawyer's warm eyes catch on mine. It's over the line we've carefully maintained—past friendship, into flirtation. Sawyer doesn't look regretful.

I feel the same way.

In the kitchen's soft yellow evening hue, with the scent of garlic and tomatoes filling the room, color lights his cheeks. For one fragile, wonderful moment, in the midst of loss and memory, everything is suspended, somehow, in the promise of new connection.

Kennedy's parents' smiles soften.

Irene passes me, squeezing my shoulder. "Let me help with that dinner," she offers to Sawyer.

Sawyer nods, his gaze remaining on me.

We imagine our friends and loved ones in the "afterlife" when they die. What I'm learning in Sawyer's company is that the rest of us experience our own afterlife. We're the ones who have passed on into somewhere else, this place without the ones we remember.

In the right company, maybe it doesn't have to hurt forever.

19

SAWYER

Memories of Kennedy surface late into the night, like they do whenever I spend time with her parents. Which isn't often—I love them dearly, but it's hard, withstanding the limbo of our relationship whenever we're together. The family we're not.

Morgan gracefully retires to the guesthouse when the rest of us lapse into reminiscing. *House looks good. Just like Kennedy designed. She'd have it no other way. Remember Thanksgiving?*

No discomfort spending time with my late fiancée's parents takes the fun out of that story. Kennedy and I spent exactly one Thanksgiving here during her life with her parents, her brother, and his girlfriend. Except the girlfriend was a surprise Kennedy's brother forgot to mention until the day of.

Kennedy and I had lived in the house mere months. Furnishing was very much unfinished. We literally did not have enough chairs for the new guest.

Not only was Kennedy undaunted, her design eye would not permit mismatched seating. With urgent calls to her favorite wholesaler, who *very* indulgently unlocked his warehouse at two p.m. on Thanksgiving, I was dispatched to pick up one more perfectly matching chair for our dining room. It's the one Morgan sat in earlier this evening.

With the night drawing longer, the wine I picked up from the grocery store dwindling, I wonder whether Irene and Joe notice how cold the house gets when it's only the three of us. In the unusual chill, I feel Kennedy's silent companionship.

I keep looking for glimpses of her, but right now, I'm not surprised to not find them. Understandably, Kennedy's parents' inability to see her depressed her during their first few dutiful drop-ins.

I think she's listening, though. I hope she is. The warmth of reminiscence is enough to make *me* feel human for a few hours. I hope Kennedy feels the same.

It's past midnight when I walk Irene and Joe down to their car under the goldenrod glow of my hillside's old streetlights. "Thank you for having us, Sawyer. We had a wonderful evening. And please tell Morgan it was a pleasure meeting her," Irene insists.

I smile. Honestly, I myself hadn't expected how much Morgan's presence would enliven the evening. Morgan is charming, obviously. But it's more than that. Having her here made it less like the unfinished version of nights Kennedy and I spent with her family. "She knows," I say. "Don't worry."

We've reached their car, the new Subaru they got last year. Kennedy's parents pause. Knowing what passes wordlessly in the look they exchange, I preempt them.

"We're really not together," I say, meaning me and Morgan. "I haven't . . ." I falter under the confession's weight. "I haven't moved on," I say quietly.

I haven't moved on.

When I was new to haunting, I tried, just once, at Kennedy's insistence, to re-create the dinner parties Kennedy and I would host, gathering our CalArts friends, commiserating over gallery rejections or unemployment frustrations, celebrating someone's pregnancy or a new commission, gossiping over new relationships or weird stuff our old professors said on social media. The house was much more unfinished, with whole sections of open drywall, exposed wiring everywhere, and sawdust carpeting the floor. I felt the same. Gutted. Unready. Hosting them the best I could.

Kennedy's specter hung out, half included, seeing but unseen. Over dan dan noodles, our friends did their best to balance their behavior toward me. Their condolences I knew were sincere—the last time I'd seen them was Kennedy's funeral, which no one missed. When they ushered the evening forth, I felt their heartbreakingly well-intentioned effort to remind me "life will go on," or some shit.

The whole night, I felt like my watch had stopped running. Like the rest of them could feel time's passage, but not me. For me, everything stood still.

I wonder if they knew. If they could see it in my face or hear it in my voice that it would be our final dinner party.

I haven't moved on.

Sympathy softens Irene's features. I've long found this quality of Kennedy's mother interesting, her open-faced, even overdramatic emotional readability. It's so unlike Kennedy's captivating, sometimes cryptic reserve.

"You know you can, though, right?" she says.

Now I can't meet Irene's eyes. I skirt my gaze to the front yard, to the empty space where they doubtless noticed the uprooted jacaranda. Kennedy's tree. Guilt sweeps over me despite Kennedy's parents wishing me the exact opposite.

Joe doesn't get into the car. We're just outside the reach of the streetlights. He watches me from their shadows. "Kennedy would want you to," he replies.

The streetlight flickers overhead.

The sign sets my heart racing. *Kennedy*. She's here. She has to be.

"She wouldn't want you holding on to her when she's gone," Joe musters, with pained strength I recognize. I've spoken to them in the same tortured tones. "You know that, right?"

I look down. I don't know what I know. I *knew* life ended with death until I met my fiancée's ghost. Now . . .

"And you're not getting rid of us even when you do move on." Irene takes my arm. "You may not have gotten the chance to marry Kennedy, but we see you as our son just the same."

She pulls me into a hug, which is when I realize how much I needed one. Even when Kennedy was with us, I felt such hope with her parents. The promise of the family I'd longed for. Irene and Joe Raymond could have filled in for the failings of my miserable, manipulative parents.

It was another reason I couldn't wait for our wedding. When Kennedy and I were married, I could finally call them my own.

I clench my eyes closed, fighting my tears. Over the years, I've let so many connections unravel, so many working pieces of myself fall into disrepair. Kennedy's parents haven't let me. They haven't let me lose them.

I feel so, so lucky for it. A gift, one of many, from my Kennedy.

Finally, I feel strong enough to release her. My . . . oh, fuck it. My mother-in-law. Not the way we ever expected. *Our* way. Believing it makes it true, like Irene's saying. I've believed more unlikely things.

Irene smiles, tearful. She unlocks the Subaru.

"Wait," I say, remembering. "The photo album. You left it inside—"

"We didn't come for the photos," Joe says softly. "We were worried about you."

"We have them all scanned," Irene reminds me. "Just return our calls next time."

I nod, unable to say more. Guilty and grateful, I wave them off while they start the engine under the streetlight's continued flickering. I wait until the car disappears down the curve of the hillside.

Finally, the streetlight stops flickering. Under its dull comforting glow in the black night, I walk back home.

20

MORGAN

Text me when you get home.

I reread the note I find on my cottage door twice, bemused. Under the simple instruction, I find Sawyer's phone number. There's no way the note came from someone other than him. It's just . . . well, we live pretty much next door. We haven't had much need for texting.

Over the past three weeks since Kennedy's family visited, we've settled into our own routines. I go to work. Sawyer continues refurbishing the house. When I return home, we prep the yard for the plants I chose, working with comfortably minimal chatter in heavy gloves to prepare the yard for planting.

Zach offers sometimes welcome, sometimes unsolicited creative counsel, popping up to recommend "the red one there" or pointing to the yard's rounded perimeter, noting, "It would be sweet if you hit that shit with some herbs."

We're like the world's most morbid sitcom. *Two and a Half Roommates.*

Sawyer and I have graduated from mac and cheese driven by necessity to the occasional shared dinner, though despite my mention of the nearby pizza place, Sawyer seems to prefer Korean or Mexican. I update him on my yard-work plans and regale him with the nonstop excitement of rescheduling cleanups and processing orders for DiCrescenzo Landscaping. Sometimes I even share stories of the more *unusual* people I've met in my interstate lifestyle. When I make Sawyer laugh, I feel like I've won points in a game he doesn't know we're playing.

No texting, though. With Sawyer constantly in the house whenever I've needed him, all I had to do was knock.

Smiling slightly, I pull down the Scotch-taped note. I wonder what's changed.

I head inside, inputting my roommate's number before I've even dropped my work bag to the floor.

> Hello, landlord. What can your favorite
> tenant do for you?

Sawyer replies quickly, which I guess shouldn't surprise me.

> Favorite living tenant, that is.

I laugh. Depositing my bag on my kitchenette countertop, I continue to my bed. I lie down, phone in hand.

I straighten up in surprise when my shoulder strikes something hard. Reaching under my pillow, I find the dragon mug Sawyer made. The one Zach found in here and started fiddling with on the day I moved in. Now he's nestled it into my pillows for some reason. Rolling my eyes, I move the mug to my nightstand, then message Sawyer back.

You're only saying that because if you don't
say Zach is your favorite, he'll burst a pipe or
something

You don't have to be a ghost to burst a pipe,
you know

I didn't know my favor was worth property
damage to you. I'm oddly touched by your
threats to my home.

Sawyer's texting style is very him. I notice the complete sentences with correct punctuation. He probably judges emojis with suspicion and scorn, the way medieval clerics viewed the printing press.

Just for fun, when I save Sawyer to my contacts, I put the ghost with its tongue out next to his name. Hilarious to me.

Just keep it in mind

Was there something you needed or did you
just want to chat from different rooms
twenty feet apart?

I watch the typing bubble pop up, then disappear. Stubbornly, I focus on the phone screen, waiting for his reply. Yes, I *could* dawdle over to social media. I could go Zillow-hunting for houses with yards I will never in one million gazillion years afford.

I don't. I wait.

So far, I am enjoying chatting from different
rooms twenty feet apart. But yes, I was

> wondering if there was a time I could use the
> studio for a couple hours.

Now I sit up in disbelief. Sawyer hasn't made pottery since Kennedy died. He's shared with me how her loss—understandably—plunged him into something like writer's block, ceramics edition. Despite knowing Sawyer for only the past couple months, I understand immediately how huge it is that he wants to return to his craft.

I want to know why. Obviously. But I don't want to make him skittish by interrogating him.

Instead, I measure my reply carefully. I want to come off welcoming but low pressure.

> It's your studio. You can use it whenever you
> want.

Punctuation is rubbing off on me, I guess.

> I wanted to respect your privacy. Just tell me
> a time when it would be convenient to you—
> maybe when you plan to be out for a bit.

I chew the inside of my cheek. The thing is . . . I don't *want* to be out of the house when Sawyer returns to his clay. I want to watch him work.

Inhaling in preparation, I send off my reply. Sometimes shooting your shot with the reclusive artist who lives sort of next door looks like this.

> Is now okay?

Seconds pass. No typing bubble. No reply from Sawyer comes.

It's only fair, right? I prepare to reason with him. *You've seen me landscape. Plus, shouldn't one of the perks of living in the pottery studio be watching the sculptor work? It's like running water or electricity.*

I'm putting fingers to keys, readying my persuasions, when I hear light knocking. Leaving my phone on my bed, I hop to my front door.

Outside, I find Sawyer. He's holding a potted plant. It's a gorgeous purple coleus with spade-shaped leaves the color of dark lipstick.

More importantly—it's the plant I kept eyeing when we went to the nursery. I didn't know Sawyer noticed.

"Happy housewarming," he says. "Sorry it's so late."

I smile, genuinely touched. "Guesthouse-warming," I reply.

"Hmm, still counts."

Gently I receive the plant from him. The rich maroon is stunning. "When?" I ask him simply.

"I went back while you were at work," he says.

I swallow, wanting to hide the sudden rush of emotion. It's just . . . I've ghosted from city to city forever—chasing possibility or running from emptiness. I've forgotten how long it's been since someone remembered to pick something out for me. Thought of me. I haven't given them much chance to. But Sawyer found an opportunity to anyway.

"You didn't have to," I manage.

"No," he concurs, holding my gaze. "I wanted to."

I hug the plant closer to my chest and gesture to the pottery wheel in the corner of my guesthouse. Sawyer walks over, pulls the mechanism out from the wall, then returns outside.

While I watch, Sawyer brings in clay he must have procured

today. He preps his station, dusting off the seat, then uses the kitchenette sink to fill a bucket with water, which he sprinkles over his clay.

I move my coleus to the windowsill, evaluating how the sunlight in the spot will change over the course of the day. "Do you know what you're going to make?" I ask Sawyer.

"Nothing in particular," he replies. "I just want to get back to it. To . . . see what takes shape. Your work out front is inspiring."

My eyebrows lift. "You going to sculpt some . . . drought-tolerant herbs and grasses?"

Sawyer has separated out the hefty chunk of clay he intends to use. He places it on the wheel with long, sturdy, experienced fingers and wets his hands.

"Not the plants," he replies. "You."

I still.

"Seeing your passion for your work," Sawyer continues. "I want to feel that again."

Quietly moved, I smile softly. I never imagined *I* would play some part in inspiring him. I figured I was just the loud haunted girl who demanded his stove for mac-and-cheese purposes. Learning I helped Sawyer rediscover this piece of himself . . .

Well, this purple coleus isn't the only gift Sawyer's just given me.

He starts pedaling. The wheel rotates in an even rhythm, the clay spinning smoothly under his hands.

I leave my plant on the windowsill to sit on my bed and watch him. The pottery wheel is nearly soundless, its revolutions filling the room with mechanical whispers.

Sawyer closes his eyes for a moment, just feeling the soft clay. Under his deft grasp, the clay rises and lowers, shapes coming to life and dissolving in his fingers. It's not long before light gray coats his hands.

"Is it time for us to have our *Ghost* moment?" a voice says behind me.

I whirl. "Zach! A little warning, please!" I exclaim. My ghost hover-perches on the countertop, looking pleased with himself.

Sawyer, to his credit, grins, letting the wheel slow. "Are you taking your shirt off or am I?" he replies.

Zach laughs and vanishes.

What does not vanish is the very shirtless image that has entered my head, which I fight while Sawyer sculpts. *Have some respect, Morgan. Have some freaking* dignity. *He's doing his pottery. He's . . .* He's guiding the clay with confident hands, shaping the supple material like a symphony I can see. His shoulders rippling, he holds one hand steady to keep the shape while the other reaches inside the forming vessel. When he seems satisfied, he pauses to wet his hands once more and starts finessing the lip.

I lean forward, chin propped in my hands, elbows on my knees.

His work is hypnotically beautiful—the circular motion of the wheel, the lines rising up and down the clay with his manipulation, the way his hair falls into his forehead, the way his hands look covered in clay . . . Yes, I understand very well how one could fall in love with Sawyer for those hands.

I'm mesmerized right until the clay explodes violently under his fingertips.

Gray gunk spatters everywhere. Pieces hit my cheeks and shirt with fast pinpricks of pressure.

"What the fuck?" Sawyer startles. Globs of clay have painted the room in Pollockian gray. He studies the pottery wheel, confused, then shakes off his stunned expression to check on me. "Are you okay? I have no idea what happened. It's not possible," he explains. "It's not how a pottery wheel works—"

I don't get the chance to reassure him. In quick succession, *every* piece of pottery lining the shelves above him shatters.

The detonated pots and vases spray porcelain shrapnel everywhere. I shriek, ducking down to the floor behind my bed. Sawyer, who is closer to the exploding pottery, flings his hands up to protect his face.

But just when the shattering seems to subside, the entire guesthouse starts to shake. The walls sway in menacing vibrations, and next to me, the kitchen window shatters. I scream. Rumbling leads to loud clanging under the sink. Suddenly, a pipe ruptures with a metallic slam, spraying water everywhere, dousing my hair.

"Shit," I hear Sawyer say. "Earthquake."

Peripatetic former Midwesterner that I am, I've never experienced an earthquake. I'm scared. I've experienced hurricanes, even tornadoes, but this feeling is horribly surreal—the ground moving underneath me, the walls of my shelter weaponized against me. I'm frozen, struggling to remember what to do in earthquakes. Get in doorways? Which one? Does it matter?

While the world ripples, panic constricting my chest, Sawyer rushes over. Disregarding the sink's spray, he grabs my elbow to pull me under the kitchen table. Joining me, he wedges his body close to mine so we both fit.

While my heartbeat hurtles, I realize I'm clutching his forearm.

I don't let go. I can't. My fingertips whiten the tan he's starting to get from our yard work in the sun.

Sawyer rubs his clay-coated thumb comfortingly over mine. "We'll be okay," he says soothingly. "We'll be fine."

His voice steadies me while everything else is unsteady. Outside the confines of our refuge, the shaking guesthouse does not, honestly, look fine. Plaster falls heavily from the ceiling, landing on the table above us and the floor around us. Water spews incessantly, soaking everything.

Then suddenly, the earthquake stops.

Everything is quiet. Only the whisper of the flow of water from the sink pipe fills the room.

While I'm petrified, still unmoving, Sawyer climbs out from under our cover. When he offers me his hand, his clay grip is enough to encourage me to crawl out.

I rise shakily to my feet, surveying the damage. The cottage is wrecked. The plaster has combined with the plumbing water into sludge flecked with vicious glass and ceramic shards. We're fortunate we're wearing shoes.

On second thought, *fortunate* might not be the word. Questions pound painfully in my head. *Are all my things ruined? The few items I've treasured enough to carry with me? Am I unsentimental enough to start over completely new? What about my singular plate? Where will I live?*

Sawyer is preoccupied himself. He's gone deathly pale. He rushes outside, thinking—I realize—of his finally near-complete erstwhile dream home. I follow him hurriedly, scared of what we're going to find.

Except outside, nothing is different. Every window is unbroken. Our yard work is exactly like we left it.

The hillside palm trees of Sawyer's neighborhood sway upright, the street free of fallen fronds, the bougainvillea blooms undisturbed. The trash cans remain standing. Even the shovel I leaned against the house didn't fall over.

"How . . . ?" I start to say, coming up next to Sawyer.

Sawyer's expression clouds. He pulls out his phone.

"What are you doing?" I ask.

"Checking social media," Sawyer replies. "If there's one thing people in LA love to do when an earthquake hits," he explains, "it's posting 'earthquake' on social media." He scrolls his feed. "Right now, there's nothing, which means . . ."

"It wasn't an earthquake," I say, starting to understand. Movement flickers in the corner of my vision, which makes me face the guesthouse.

Where I see Zach.

He looks like he did in Sawyer's spooky garage. Except worse. Gaunt. Unwell. His edges flicker, vibrating uneasily. He steps out of the ruined cottage, holding the dragon mug.

"What . . . happened?" he croaks out.

I exchange worried glances with Sawyer.

"Zach," I say, "do you remember causing the earthquake? Were you upset about something?"

Zach looks up, but his gaze seems to go right through us. Like *we're* the ghosts.

"I . . . no. I don't remember anything. You were doing pottery, and then . . . I don't—" He stares down, studying the dragon mug. He looks lost.

I look at Sawyer. "Something is seriously wrong," I murmur. I walk closer to Zach, Sawyer following behind me. Through Zach's flickering body, I peer into the cottage and find—

It's fixed. There's no broken pipe, no cracked plaster, no shattered window. My bedsheets are pristine. The only sign of the haunting is the splattered remains of Sawyer's clay.

Sawyer gapes at the scene. "But . . . the impacts were real. I felt the ceiling fall on the table."

I shiver in the calm daylight. Somehow the repaired damage is more unnerving than seeing my ruined residence.

"His haunting is getting worse," I say. "If we don't do something, I don't know what might happen the next time he loses control."

Sawyer doesn't need convincing. "You could have been hurt. Next time—" He swallows, clenching his jaw. "We have to find out what his unfinished business is *now*. Before it's too late."

The glass-sharp undercurrent in his voice catches me by surprise. He's scared. No . . . terrified. *For me.*

Of course he is. He's felt the fragility of life firsthand.

I reach out to reassure him, which is when I notice the thin line of red seeping through the side of his shirt.

21

Morgan pushes me inside. With no-nonsense urgency, she seats me at my dining table.

"First aid?" she demands.

I swallow, still dizzy with panic. My wound proves that what we experienced wasn't just a ghostly illusion. The danger was real. I knew Morgan was scared—if you're not used to earthquakes, they're really frightening—so I kept it together guiding her under the table in the guesthouse and ensuring we remained safely covered.

The whole time, I was freaking the fuck out myself. The fact is, Morgan Lane is the only person who's gotten close to me in years. The only person with whom I'm starting to feel the first semblance of healing and human connection. Yes, I've resisted it. Yes, I don't know what it represents in my landscape of grief.

Doesn't mean it doesn't make me fucking desperate to ensure nothing happens to her.

I'm relieved I'm the one injured. Not her. One more observation I do not voice out loud.

"I'm fine. It's nothing," I insist instead. "Are you bleeding anywhere?"

I should have expected the sternly raised eyebrow Morgan gives me in reply.

I sigh. "Under the sink in my bathroom."

"Don't move," Morgan orders. She runs—like a horror ingenue fleeing the killer runs—up the stairs.

While I wait, hearing her pounding footsteps above me, I inspect my wound. I didn't even feel the slice running horizontal on my side. I was consumed with fear, scared something might happen to someone else important to me, because Morgan, I'm forced to concede, *is* important to me.

Scared I was somehow . . . responsible. Not just haunted but cursed.

I can't lose her, too. I can't.

I press my hand to the wound, feeling the sting deepen. My palm comes away red.

Morgan returns, clutching the small metal kit of bandages and Neosporin I keep under my bathroom sink. "Take your shirt off," she demands.

"Zach told you to say that," I joke. If I downplay my own injury, I reason stubbornly, maybe I'll get straighter confirmation from Morgan that she's okay.

Morgan does not laugh. She does not smile. "I'm not kidding. You're injured," she says.

When her voice wavers, I realize she's worried, too. She hasn't had to lose someone like I have, which means, for her, the idea is unimaginable, and therefore endless.

She should never have to feel the pain I've felt. I want to protect her from it somehow. But I know I can't, so I settle for doing what Morgan says. I remove my shirt, unable to stop myself from hissing inwardly when the movement stretches my cut, wincing when the fabric rips away from the wound.

Morgan's eyes flash like she's personally offended by my pain.

She kneels by my side. Gently, she lifts my elbow so she can inspect the slash under my armpit. I honestly have no memory of when the injury occurred—when I was shielding my face from exploding pottery, I guess.

Morgan pops open my first aid kit. She removes the antiseptic, which she applies to the towel she carried down. When she presses the moist disinfectant to my cut, I manage to hold in my reaction to the searing stab. Morgan doesn't deserve to feel guilty for her medicinal efforts, and every time I wince, the lines deepen in her forehead. Part of me wants to reach up and smooth them out.

"We should probably go to the emergency room," she murmurs.

"And say what?" I reply, having more trouble than I should focusing on my injury. "There was an earthquake in my art studio? Oh, and it was caused by our ghost?"

Morgan purses her lips. She sees what I mean. "You could need stitches," she protests.

"I'm fine."

"You're bleeding through your towel," Morgan says. I glance down, finding she is, unfortunately, correct. Crimson is blossoming on the white terry cloth like the morbid imitation of the red flowers she chose for out front.

"Look," I say. "I haven't had health insurance since Kennedy died. We're not going to the hospital."

Morgan's expression scrunches with confusion and judgment. "You don't have health insurance?" she repeats. "What if something had happened to you?"

I don't reply.

In my silence, Morgan understands.

I didn't care. If something happened to me, if the universe wanted me closer to Kennedy, well . . .

On her knees, Morgan straightens. She looks fiercely right into my eyes.

"You're enrolling tonight," she says firmly.

Unexpectedly, this, not my side wound, makes my eyes water.

I hold her gaze without blinking. Her hand rests on my bare chest, right over my still-beating heart. I have the errant urge to lift my hand to cover hers. Holding her there. What was it Morgan said in Serving Spirits? *Proof of life.*

Instead, I nod. "Okay," I say. "I will. Assuming you stop the bleeding and I make it to then."

Her lips finally twitch. "Deal." Returning to my wound, she reluctantly removes the towel. Grimacing, she watches red droplets form on the edges of my skin. "I'm going to . . . bandage it, I guess," she says.

"Whatever you want, doctor," I reply.

Morgan lifts a playful eyebrow, pink rising in her cheeks. Was it the *doctor* or the *whatever you want* that flustered her? I refuse to ponder the answer.

She reaches into the kit, where she finds cotton gauze and spooled bandages. The bandage makes its sticky crunching sound when Morgan pulls up the end. Morgan packs my wound, then proceeds clumsily to hold the gauze in place while she wraps my torso in the bandage.

"I'm sorry if my hands are cold," she says.

My reply comes out a whisper. "They're not."

Morgan continues her work, maneuvering the bandage to constrict my cut. Her ministrations draw her head close to my chest, her hands brushing my side, her floral scent everywhere. I feel everything a thousand times more sharply than the pottery that slashed me.

I haven't been this close to someone in five years. And Morgan isn't just someone. I need a distraction, or I'll find myself dizzy for reasons having nothing to do with my injury.

Right on cue, Zach materializes over Morgan's shoulder.

While he hasn't fully recovered, when he observes what's happening in my kitchen, the sight seems to sober him into solidity. His dangerous shimmering edges relax. His opacity returns.

"Shit. I'm sorry, dude," he says with his usual earnestness. "We really need to find out what's going on with me. I don't want to hurt anyone."

I notice Morgan's shoulders relax nearly imperceptibly, as if she also welcomes our paranormal chaperone. "Have you remembered anything more about your life since we found out who you were?" she asks Zach.

The ghost stares outside, despondently watching the faint motion of the wind chimes. "Nothing useful. Just flashes from my childhood. Learning how to surf. When I bought my van."

Morgan cinches my bandage tight. I wince. "Sorry," she murmurs guiltily.

"You're fine," I say.

She glances up. Our eyes lock.

I *need extra bandages*, I consider requesting. *Wrapped more slowly.*

Morgan quickly pulls her gaze from mine. I fight to keep my chest from heaving with each breath. "We got the first clue about your life when we were in the garage and you saw the water heater," she reasons with determination. "We just need to find more stimuli that could reveal buried memories."

"Stimuli?" Zach repeats.

"Like cues," I say. In the same moment, Morgan's nails lightly scratch the sensitive skin of my side while she cuts and secures the bandage.

When Kennedy died, every good thing hurt. Every pretty sunset, every delicious piece of pizza, every interesting local museum exhibit I noticed on social media. Every joy pierced me with the reminder of who wasn't there to enjoy them with me. Every moment of happiness was a sugarcoated poison pill.

This is . . . the opposite. The pain of Morgan's contact with my skin is a *relief*. I'd forgotten what being touched felt like, and when she removes her hands, finished, I realize how much I missed it.

"Wait," I say suddenly.

Zach and Morgan look at me. *I'd forgotten what being touched felt like.* I follow the inspiration from my own forgotten memories.

"We can parade things in front of Zach for eternity, and still we might not find the right memory. But they're in him. We know they're in his subconscious somewhere," I say. "What if we don't try to bring the memories out of his subconscious but instead try to tap into his subconscious directly?"

Morgan sits back on her heels, intrigued, if skeptical. "You're not seriously suggesting we hypnotize a ghost, are you?"

I shrug. Honestly, I had not envisioned the methodology yet. "I know it sounds ridiculous, but—"

Morgan's eyes light up. "What about a Ouija board?"

"You don't need a Ouija board to communicate with me," Zach protests. "I'm right here."

Morgan shakes her head. "No. What if you put your hands on the console and see if there are any letters that . . . call out to your subconscious?"

Zach frowns, unconvinced. Then his eyes flit to my side, like he knows he can't dash our only hope. "I mean, I'll try anything," he concedes.

Morgan looks at me. "There was one in the ghost bar. We can go right now. Or wait—" She interrupts herself. She runs upstairs.

When she returns, she's holding my only black T-shirt, the shade chosen to mask stains if my bandages leak. Her eyes dip, lowering to my bare chest.

"We can go when you get dressed," she says.

I've kept in shape over the past years. Working out is solitary, occupies hours of my creativity-deprived days, and substitutes muscle pain for pain everywhere else. Morgan seems to notice. In a startled shock, I realize she's checking me out.

It's another feeling I'd forgotten I missed. It's . . . nice, which is confusing.

I suspect I would agree to anything she proposed in order to end the strange charge I've realized is very much between us.

I pull on the shirt. "Let's go."

"You're not going to get those goofy-ass ghost cakes, right?" Zach sniffs. "My culture is not your confection."

Morgan rolls her eyes on our way out the door. "You're a ghost, Zach. It's not your *culture*."

"We prefer *Apparition American*," Zach replies.

22

SAWYER

Unfortunately, the strange charge continues to haunt us when we reach Serving Spirits. I had no idea a ghost-themed liquor establishment could possibly feel so . . . romantic.

What happened to the cobwebs? I want to demand of the genial owner we met in the support group. *What happened to the cracked leather? The dusty windows? The scuffed countertop and furniture?*

Of course, none of it has changed, except the conspicuously cleaned cobwebs, which I don't mind. The rest of the room is very much in the state I remember from our previous visit. Yet somehow, the details feel richly inviting instead of irritatingly shabby. Enchantingly gothic instead of cheap horror.

Great.

Fortunately, Zach is with us. It can't be a date when you have a dead ex-hookup along.

My other consolation is Morgan, who seems similarly conscious of the vibe. When we enter, she quickly veers to order at the bar while I stake out one of the Ouija board tables. Zach lingers with me, passing smoothly through the table to sit next to me in the leather booth.

He clears his throat and runs his hand through his semitransparent sand-colored surfer hair.

"She totally has a crush on you," he informs me.

I determinedly say nothing, not daring to process those words.

Zach shakes his head insistently. "Uh-uh. No way. Don't just pretend I'm invisible again because I'm saying stuff you're afraid to hear."

"We're in a public place," I mutter calmly. "People will stare if I look like I'm talking to myself."

Zach considers. His expression changes, and I worry when Socratic zeal lights his eyes. "Good point," he says. "I can say whatever I want to you without you replying." While I fight to ignore him, Zach leans forward, resting his chin on his palm with his elbow on the Ouija board. "It's okay if you like her, too, you know," he says. "You're allowed to move on. Kennedy is gone."

I keep ignoring him.

Part of me doesn't want to. Part of me wonders whether Zach has some deeper understanding of ghostly comings and goings. *Is* Kennedy gone? I haven't seen her ghost since she urged me to go to the support group.

Why is she so absent?

Morgan returns, distracting me from the uneasy questions. Her drink is fuming with ghostly fog from dry ice. I have no doubt it's monikered with some paranormal pun. Man-haunt-tan or Ghost-hito.

Morgan is welcomely businesslike. *Good.* When she sits, I unfold the Ouija board. It's seen better days, its corners dented, some of the letters so worn they're nearly illegible. It smells like beer.

I don't care. "Let's do this," I say.

Morgan nods. I place one hand on one side of the viewfinder. Morgan does the same. We make sure to position our fingers on opposite edges of the carved wooden pointer, not entertaining the risk of more charged contact.

"Zach, try to tap into your ghostliness," Morgan instructs.

Zach squints doubtfully at the letters. "And do what?"

"I don't know," Morgan says, frustrated. "Follow your . . . unconscious desires."

Zach hesitates. "Here goes nothing," he grumbles. Then, while I hold the viewfinder with Morgan, he rises from his seat, hovering over the tabletop.

He screws his eyes closed. We wait. He emits a very disturbing moan of effort. Seriously, I'm very glad his paranormal presence is not public right now.

Nothing happens.

Finally, Zach's shoulders sag. He opens his eyes and removes his ephemeral hands from the table. "Dude. It's not working," he complains.

"Move your hands over the board," I recommend gently. *For real, whatever does not involve making that noise.* "Do any of the letters call to you?"

Zach scrutinizes the faded inscriptions. "The *P* is missing the top loop and looks like an *I*. That's all that stands out to me," he retorts.

"Please take this seriously," Morgan reprimands him. Her Man-haunt-tan has expended its ghostly dry ice. Even the fogless vermilion liquid manages to look disappointed in our efforts.

Zach throws his hands up. "I'm trying, but what do you want me to do? I can't move stuff!"

"Yes, you can," Morgan insists. "You move that dragon mug all the time."

"I can't *control* it, though," Zach says. "It just happens."

"That's exactly what we need," I say more gently. There's no use lecturing him. "Try to put your hands on ours and see if your subconscious takes over."

Zach's expression droops. Moan or no moan, I feel for him. I know he wants to do this for us. He's frustrated with his own limitations.

Ever the good sport, he grudgingly moves his ghostly hands to rest on top of ours. Of course, we feel no sensation of his weightless grip. He closes his eyes. No untoward noises escape him. In fact, he finally looks peaceful. Focused.

The room grows colder.

Instantly, I meet Morgan's eyes over the Ouija viewfinder. The startled urgency in her expression says I'm not the only one feeling the ghostly chill. Neither one of us speaks, not wanting to disturb Zach.

The jukebox in the corner skips. The lighted display flickers. When the music returns, it's "Call Me Maybe."

Now Morgan smiles. Zach continues to concentrate over the Ouija board. The temperature continues to lower, the cold fingers of supernatural concentration prickling palpably over my skin. Showtime. I look down, feeling my fingertips tingling—

The Ouija pointer starts to move.

My heart pounds. Zach's eyes remain closed, his mouth thin with focus. The pointer inches toward the letters . . .

"Maybe we should ask a question," I whisper to Morgan. "That's how this is usually done, right?"

Morgan nods. "Zach," she says softly, "was there anything you wanted to do before you died? Anything you left unfinished?"

Zach says nothing. The pointer continues to move . . .

Our combined direction settles on *A*. When we reach the stately letter in the left corner, the console stops beneath Morgan's and my hands.

We pause there. Then, sharply, the pointer sweeps down—Zach's power is increasing. *N.* Excitement mounts in me. I feel myself starting to smile. *Holy fucking shit. This is working. Ouija boards really work.*

Under Zach's focused direction, our hands continue to move . . . retracing their path. Coming to end where we started. *A.*

Zach is really communicating. I start to piece out his message. *A-N-A—*

The console starts to move to the right—

Morgan withdraws her hands sharply, grimacing in indignation. "Gross, Zach!" she exclaims. "No. Wouldn't have even happened when you were alive and definitely won't happen now."

Zach opens his eyes, seemingly pulled from somewhere deep within. "What?" he asks.

"A-N-A?" Morgan repeats witheringly. "No chance there was an *L* coming next?"

In earnest contemplation, Zach studies the Ouija lettering while Morgan glares. "Admittedly, I would have liked—"

"*No.* You did not skip out on eternal rest for *anal,*" Morgan says loudly.

In this moment, I recall that while Zach's portion of our discussions remains concealed in the hereafter, everyone can hear Morgan's and mine.

And there is only one other person she could be speaking to. I sink lower in our booth.

"Maybe I did! You don't know!" Zach protests while I smile weakly at the patrons now eyeing us. "What if that's it? Only one way to find out," Zach ventures.

"No. There's not," Morgan says with menacing finality.

Zach laughs. "No, I mean we put our hands back and find out what the rest of the word is," he clarifies. "Besides. Who says I'd want to have anal with you anyway?"

Morgan straightens. "What's *that* supposed to mean?"

I pretend I don't notice the smirk Zach shoots me. If he keeps up this Morgan-has-a-crush-on-me shit, I'm . . . well, I will have one *more* reason to want him to pass peacefully on, his unfinished business finished. Hurriedly, I put my fingers on the viewfinder. "Let's just see what it says," I offer.

Morgan drops the point, grudgingly returning her hands to the console. "Please take this seriously," she warns Zach.

"Hey, the heart wants what the heart wants," he replies, winking at me.

He closes his eyes. The chill creeps over us. Once more, the Ouija viewfinder starts to move.

Except . . . now Zach's supernatural efforts only lead the carved console to the starting place in the center underneath the letters.

Zach opens his eyes, looking confused yet certain. "I . . . think that's it," he says. "A-N-A."

"Ana," I say.

"Did I know an Ana?" Zach wonders out loud.

Morgan—looking grateful to pull her fingers from the viewfinder, where her hand was close to mine, and grateful Zach's haunted message did not involve sexual favors—holds her chin contemplatively. "Your dad didn't mention an Ana, and he was pretty detailed in his stories of your family and friends," she says. "If you had some secret girlfriend who was your unfinished business, surely you'd be haunting her, right?"

Zach nods. It's a good point.

Thinking, I pull out my phone. I open social media, where I type in Zach's username. Of course, when we learned Zach's last name, it was one of the first resources we investigated. Zach—to his credit, in my curmudgeonly opinion—only posted about a dozen times over the years. His content was vague, unhelpfully 2010-style posts. Sunsets, the ocean. Despite Zach's spare captioning, however, family and friends liked and responded faithfully.

When I scroll past his final beach photo, I notice an *Ariana_Scuba87* commented, "Reminds me of our trips when we were kids."

I click on the name, something Zach's father said registering in my memory.

Yes—*Ariana Harrison* is the full name on the profile. Like Harrison's Hardware. Like Zach Harrison. I remember Mr. Harrison's proud recollection of Zach's fondness and protectiveness for his older sister, Ari.

"A-N-A is a pretty unique spelling of Ana. It almost seems like a nickname." I show Zach the profile. "Your sister, right? Your dad called her Ari, but her full name is Ariana."

"Ari. Ana." Morgan pieces it out. "You and she were close. Maybe you had a special nickname for her."

Zach narrows his gaze. "It's not jogging any memories, but what else could it be?" he says. The futility of the question seems to frustrate him. The Ouija board rattles, then starts to levitate from the table.

Morgan and I press it downward frantically. We don't need to deal with patrons suspecting the presence of real ghosts in this ghost bar. "Ari is our best lead," I point out. "We should at least ask her if you called her Ana."

Morgan pulls out her phone. Across the table, I see her DM Ariana_Scuba87. "Hopefully she replies quickly," Morgan says.

"Should we order more drinks while we wait?" Zach's mood suddenly seems lifted. When he continues, I realize why. "Maybe we can see what both of your subconsciouses are pulled to in the Ouija board."

"No," Morgan and I say in unison.

Zach grins. I do not. No, no need to reveal what my subconscious is up to, through occult means or otherwise. Ghosts like Zach should understand perfectly well that some things should stay buried.

Still, when we stand to leave, Morgan having finished her thematic drink, I can't help myself. I put my hand on the small of her back to guide her from the booth.

23

MORGAN

Life returns to normal for the next week. Or as normal as possible when you're living with a ghost in the guesthouse-slash-pottery-studio of the guy you find completely and entirely confusing.

Sawyer and I each pretend nothing is different or weird or complicated. I pretend I didn't feel guilty, intense desire while I bandaged the sturdy chest of the wounded widower who wants nothing but his past to return to life. I pretend I didn't wonder, even for a split second, whether I felt the ghost of want in Sawyer's eyes when he noticed me checking him out—which, fine, I was—or in his gentle hand on my back.

I wait in vain for Ariana to reply. I go to work every morning, leaving Sawyer instructions on how to manage the soil, rock, and turf deliveries I'll need for the next stages of the yard renovation.

Every day, when I come home from my exhilarating workday of sorting out flagstone reschedules or itemizing fertilizer receipts, I find he's made more progress on the house. He cleans the over-grown plants from the side path and pressure-washes the wall. I'm silently grateful he leaves the climbing bougainvillea untouched. Inside, he patches and paints. He seems possessed by productivity.

Seems. I suspect it's not merely the renovative excitement driving him. No, I'm pretty sure Sawyer wants everything finished so I can get out of here.

He avoids me like *I'm* the one who caused the indoor earthquake in his pottery sanctuary. He doesn't text. He doesn't use the pottery wheel. I find no handwritten notes left on my door.

I pretend—to myself, because I don't exactly have time or money for socializing right now—it doesn't make me lonely. It shouldn't. I've known Sawyer for, like, two months.

And yet . . .

My purple coleus on the windowsill flourishes in the sunlight. I remember sometimes how little it needs to subsist—sun, water, soil—but if you remove even one of those precious resources, it withers into nothing.

I don't know why he's keeping his distance. Sure, *I* felt a spark with him after the Zach attack, but there's no way Sawyer felt the same. Even if he did, nothing would ever come of it. I don't get involved with emotionally unavailable men—at least, not intentionally—and a guy grieving his fiancée is pretty much the pinnacle of emotionally unavailable.

Whatever. It's fine. I probably *will* be gone soon, once we resolve Zach's unfinished business. I'll find my way to some new city, some new job. Sawyer and Zach will become ghosts only of memory. I decide to practice now and just leave Sawyer alone.

Or so I'm planning until Zach slams my laptop shut while I'm unwinding for the night with my favorite reality show.

"Okay, I'm sorry I was watching without you," I preempt him. "I didn't know if you were materializing tonight—"

"No," Zach says, then reconsiders. "I mean, yes, that was uncool of you. But you need to go into the main house," he demands.

The urgency is surprising on Zach. But I'm stubborn. Sawyer has made himself clear. What's more, my favorite couple was just getting back together in the episode I was watching. "No, I don't," I reply.

"Yes. You do," Zach urges me. "Sawyer is being weird."

"He's always weird," I say.

Zach paces, walking through the kitchen table in his distraction. "Not like this," he counters. "Stop avoiding him."

I reopen my laptop, patience dwindling. I had to deal with two double-bookings today. I *just* want to watch my show. "For your information," I say, "Sawyer is avoiding me."

The leaves on my coleus shake. A gust blows through the guesthouse, nearly knocking my computer off my lap onto the floor. I catch the MacBook just in time.

"I'm worried about him," Zach says.

Recovering from the nearly disastrous MacBook incident—for real, if I lose my connection to reality TV, I will lose my connection to *reality* in this isolated guesthouse—I find Zach's semitransparent eyes. He really is worried. Nervousness creases his uncreaseable forehead.

It's hard to worry a ghost. If Zach is concerned, something must really be wrong with Sawyer.

Resigned, I stand. "*Don't* watch without me," I warn Zach, who I notice floating nearer to my open laptop.

Stepping out into the night, I hear my show start to play over the rustling palms in the dark sky.

Glaring, I stomp from the studio toward Sawyer's house. Even with the improvements Sawyer has made, the dark house remains sort of spooky. Silver Lake is in the hills surrounding Los Angeles, where light pollution is minimal and sparse streetlights provide only pinpricks in the pitch.

In the night, the foliage casts ominous shadows on the ground. The insects humming in the hedges sound a little close for comfort.

I hasten across the patio, remembering ruefully how, mere minutes ago, I was watching my favorite couple. On their honeymoon episode! How could Sawyer, honestly? Why couldn't he act weird any *other* night?

I knock on the kitchen door, impatient. There's no answer. Only indistinct humming from inside.

When I press my ear to the door, I hear it clearer. Music playing in the house. Muffled, the melody is warped and—well, I shouldn't say haunting.

I knock again. Nothing.

Peering into the kitchen, I find the room dark. Nevertheless, the music pervades. Despite myself, chills having nothing to do with the California night shiver down my arms. Something *is* weird here. I'm just not sure it's Sawyer.

I knock once more, and still he doesn't emerge.

He's probably fine, I think, reassuring myself. In fact, I'm sure season five, episode twelve of *The Honeymoon Experiment* would concur that Sawyer is definitely, undoubtedly, one hundred percent fine.

Unfortunately, I can't quite convince myself. Zach's words—my ghost's very real concern—linger with me. I jog the handle, but the door is locked.

Okay, I decide, *nothing I can do*. My sweatpants don't have pockets, so I left my phone in the guesthouse. Not that I expect Sawyer would reply if I message him saying, *Hey, Zach thinks you're being weird, even though I told him that's just what you're like*. But I have to try.

I start my retreat—

The chill of the night deepens, shocking my neck. The feeling freezes me where I stand.

I hear metallic clicking behind me. Then Sawyer's kitchen door creaks open on its own.

Through my supernaturally repaired window, I can still see Zach making himself very comfortable on my bed. The mysterious unlocking wasn't his doing.

I turn to face the open door. The darkness seems to invite me inside, the music's murmured melody drawing me deeper.

Pulling my sweater close around my shoulders, I step into the house. Obviously, this is the part of every horror movie where the angry spirits kill their first victim—a pretty but foolish young woman. Believe me, I'm screaming at myself to turn around.

Instead, I continue into the kitchen, past the unlit stove where I cooked dinner last week. The music swells louder. I recognize the melody now—"A Sunday Kind of Love."

Kennedy's favorite.

Sawyer said at the support group it's the song her ghostly presence would leave in his head. The ethereal, romantic melody filling the dark house is unnerving. Holding on to determination combined with curiosity, I fight down the fear quickening my heartbeat.

Fortunately—I mean, I hope it's fortunately—light shines from the living room. I walk slowly forward, not knowing what to expect.

What I find is Sawyer.

He sits on the couch, head in his hands. His posture is hunched from the weight of some enormous invisible load. He looks defeated or defensive.

The music emanates from the old record player in the corner. On the TV, *Roman Holiday* plays. The sounds clash chaotically, filling the room with Etta James's voice over Audrey Hepburn's. On the coffee table in front of Sawyer, two wineglasses wait untouched.

I dare to speak. "Sawyer?"

He looks up, startled, his eyes bloodshot. He didn't notice me come in over the cacophony. He blinks, disoriented, like he doesn't recognize me. Or—

Or I'm not who he was expecting.

"Sorry," I say hurriedly. If Sawyer isn't visibly possessed or something, I'm eager to leave him to whatever is going on here. "Zach told me I had to check on you. But you seem . . . good! Great! Totally normal. So I'll just go."

His rough voice stops me. "What if she's already gone?"

The sheer pain in his words pierces my heart. He looks stripped. Ruined. In an instant, I know I can't leave him. Not now. Something *is* possessing him—just not something supernatural.

"What if I was . . . too distracted to notice?" Guilt warps his voice. He can't look at me. Instead, his gaze clings onto the wedding invitation framed in the entryway.

I move hesitantly closer to Sawyer. Sawyer, who remembered my purple coleus. Sawyer, who volunteered to help Zach's father process his grief for no reason except his own empathy. "I don't think she's gone," I say honestly, meaning Kennedy. "I think she just let me into the house, actually."

This transforms Sawyer. Rising quickly from the couch, he rushes into the kitchen. I wait, hoping for Sawyer's sake that Kennedy gives the wind chimes a go.

When Sawyer returns to the room, however, he's visibly dejected. "It was probably just a draft," he mutters. He returns to the couch, where he seats himself heavily.

Everything in me is crying out to leave him be. I don't, though.

I push past the voices in my head, the ones whispering, *Commitment-phobic*, and *He doesn't need you*, and *You'll just make it worse*. I sit down next to him.

I don't know if Sawyer needs me. Sawyer didn't know if Mr. Harrison needed him. It didn't matter. He *deserves* the best, clumsy, shitty consolation I can give him. The comforts I can piece together and meld with the gold of good intentions. Kintsugi kindness.

I turn off the TV, needing to reduce the sensory overload in here. Respectfully, I don't think Ms. Hepburn is helping Sawyer or Kennedy right now. "I'm guessing that was her favorite movie," I say.

Sawyer slouches, hands in front of him helplessly. Like he wishes he could mold the world with his two greatest creative tools but knows it doesn't work that way. "I was trying to do her favorite things, hoping to lure her out. But . . . nothing," he says shakily. "Maybe she hates me now. Maybe that's why she's refusing to appear to me. Maybe I waited too long to help her, or maybe I've betrayed—"

He stops himself, like emotion has clenched hard on his windpipe. He hangs his head to his chest, exhaling one shuddering sigh.

I sit down next to him. Earlier this week, I survived a 9.5 million magnitude earthquake on the ghost Richter scale. So why is emotional intimacy so frightening? "She doesn't hate you," I say, managing to keep my voice firm. "No one could hate you, Sawyer. You're kind and loyal, and you care very deeply for people."

Not letting myself lose my nerve, I reach forward and take his hand.

Slowly, Sawyer's fingers start to close on mine.

The music suddenly shudders. Etta James cuts in and out, her winsome vocals skittering. I stiffen, startled. Sawyer does the same. His eyes widen, but he does not release my hand, nor I his.

When I feel familiar cold creep over my neck, I say nothing.

Sawyer speaks instead, holding my hand tighter. "I . . . I don't know what to do anymore," he admits. "I don't know how to hold on to someone who isn't here."

He meets my gaze, his expression wracked. His eyes search mine desperately, like I'm the answer to his questions—or the cause of them.

"No one who loves you would want you to hold on to them forever," I whisper. Honesty makes my words come easier now. "You have to live your life again."

Sawyer breaks down crying so quickly it surprises me. His other hand, the one I'm not holding, moves clumsily to his face, like he's trying to hide his grief with an insufficient grasp. Like he's scared of the messiness of his own pain.

Impulsively, I lean forward. Sawyer moves to meet me. He presses his face into my neck, the now familiar chiseled lines of his features jutting into the softness surrounding my collarbone.

I hold him, letting him sob into my sweater as he clings to me, feeling at once helpless and like his last resort. I look up at the ceiling, fighting my own tears, just wanting to make him whole. Wanting to fix his shattered edges as he violently shakes against me. *He's* the earthquake, and I hold on tight.

When his breathing starts to even, he doesn't pull away. He still clings to me. I exhale, and Sawyer nuzzles deeper into my neck.

I let him. I do more than let him. I feel myself lean into him, lost in the fragile moment. His hands are warm and wanting.

My breath catches when he drags his face slowly up my neck, his nose softly grazing my skin. Etta James fills the room with haunting, intoxicating, devastating notes. Sawyer is . . . I can feel him on the edge of something powerful. Passionate. Reckless.

What he needs, maybe. What he wants, definitely. He shivers in my arms once more.

My heart hammers. I just want him to stop hurting. He's suffered alone for so long. I know, somehow, that he doesn't even realize how desperately he's gripping me. He may be my earthquake, but I'm his shelter.

His face stops close to mine, his eyes closed. His cheeks are flushed. His sigh is ragged, and then—

Then Sawyer kisses me.

Only the faintest brush of lips. The phantom of a kiss. But it's enough to send a shuddering sensation down Sawyer's whole body while my eyes flutter closed, the spirit of something powerful and rogue reaching out in me. His lips are feverish, the temperature shocking through my whole body.

I feel wide awake and like I'm dreaming at once. *Sawyer* is kissing me. I want him to keep kissing me. I want to take his pain away, to hold him, to let him hold me. I sigh.

The lights go out, cloaking us in darkness. Etta James cuts to silence.

Sawyer withdraws instantly. "Fuck," he says. "I'm so sorry. I . . . I don't know what I—I'm sorry," he stammers. He stands, his silhouette filling the dark room.

"It's okay, Sawyer," I rush to reassure him. His mouth only lightly touched mine, and still I feel my lips burning in this cold room. "It's okay."

"It's not," he insists. "It's not fair to you or to her. Clearly." He gestures to the shadows surrounding us. "Clearly she's pissed. She just cut the lights. I shouldn't have—"

I chew the inside of my cheek, restraining myself from pointing out it almost feels like Kennedy was giving us privacy. Like she didn't want this moment mixed up in Sawyer's painful memories.

I remember the way she made her first manifestation with the record player when I clasped Sawyer's hand. Warning me? Or encouraging us?

Another realization interrupts my speculation. "Wait, are you saying you haven't kissed *anyone* since Kennedy died?"

In the darkness, Sawyer's eyes fall to the floor. "How could I?" he whispers. "She's still here. I'm so lucky she's still—" He falters, unable to finish.

I hear what he's really saying. The retreat in his words. The regret.

And I realize it's better when I *don't* linger in the lives of people who don't need me. When I don't intrude on history I don't understand. I was right the first however many times. I should have left as soon as I found him here, surrounding himself with the paraphernalia of his pain. I shouldn't have sat next to him on the couch he chose with his lost love.

Because now, I'm not only leaving Sawyer worse than I found him. I'm stuck knowing just how much more of him I want. And how I'll never have him.

I stand on shaky legs. "You can't be engaged to a ghost, Sawyer." Then I leave him the way I found him—alone.

24

MORGAN

There is someone in my room when I wake in the middle of the night.

My terror is instinctual and instant. The feeling of being watched grips me, shooting chills up my spine. I search the darkness, hoping I'm half dreaming, or imagining things. Or hey, possibly Sawyer is here for some nocturnal pottery—

No.

I feel my heart seize in my chest when I find a shadowy figure standing at the end of my bed. Not Zach. It's a woman.

And I . . . recognize her.

Her dark hair, the shade matching the night outside my window. Her elegant cheekbones, her bow lips. She's young, and beautiful.

I've never met the shadow woman in my life. No, I know her from the photographs in Sawyer's house. CalArts graduation shots, road-trip pictures. Engagement photos on the Santa Monica Pier.

I'm face to ghostly face with Kennedy.

Unlike Zach, Kennedy is not semitransparent. Her only ghostly feature is her skin glowing in the moonlight, like she was sculpted of some spectral substance. Otherwise, Kennedy looks real. Full of life. I have to remind myself she's not.

Given Sawyer's concern over her not manifesting to him recently, I figured Kennedy was weakening, her grasp on the mortal plane insubstantial. I even wondered if the effort of clearing Sawyer's dead yard had exhausted her.

I guess not. She still has plenty of paranormal strength to scare the living shit out of me.

Kennedy no doubt notices I'm clutching my blanket, wide-eyed like the hunted sea lions in Zach's goriest *Shark Week* episodes. "I'm sorry for frightening you," she says sincerely. Similar to her physical manifestation, her voice is unusually normal, with no hint of supernatural distance or echo. She sounds like we're chatting. Girl time with my neighbor's ghost. "I didn't want to risk Sawyer seeing me through the bedroom window, so I had to wait for him to fall asleep. It took . . . a long time."

I pull my covers higher when I sit up in bed. It's freezing in here.

"You *have* been avoiding him, then," I say, choosing not to dwell on Sawyer's sleeplessness.

Kennedy winces. I didn't mean to guilt her . . . except, I guess I sort of did. *I* was the one holding Sawyer while he wept, only for him to reject my compassion and our moment of connection. Not her.

"Why?" I press Kennedy, whispering. "Why appear to *me*?"

Kennedy perches on the edge of my comforter. While I feel no weight, I'm surprised watching how she moves. The normalcy of her interactions with the material world is like Zach in my haunting's first week. Simpler times.

"I've been trying to for some time," she confesses. She sighs. "I thought your connection with Sawyer would let you see me the way Sawyer sees Zach. But it took some time for you to know *me*."

Your connection with Sawyer. This part of what Kennedy's saying clangs loudly in my head. I scour her ghostly tone for judgment or recrimination. *Your connection including kissing him. Your very flirty one-way exchange of* Coleus scutellarioides *connection.*

Kennedy, however, remains earnest and focused. Her expression doesn't change while her eyes search the ways I've made the pottery guesthouse home. Undoubtedly, she notices said coleus.

Then I concentrate on the rest of what she said.

Some time for you to know me.

I've never met Kennedy until just now. Yet tonight, Kennedy—not to mention the supernatural powers that be—have concluded I *know* Kennedy like I didn't before. Sawyer doesn't share much of his fiancée's personality or their life together. It's not like I've uncovered her hidden past the way we learned of Zach's, either. The only thing that happened tonight was . . .

"I sensed what you wanted tonight," I say, realizing. "When you cut the lights. I told Sawyer that you wouldn't want him to hold on to you forever."

Kennedy smiles. The moon seems to strike her just right, setting her glow to shining. "You know me, Morgan Lane," she says. "And I know you. You are his opposite in important ways. Ways that have helped you break through to Sawyer like I haven't been able to for five years."

I know she means it to be complimentary, but the reminder of the length of Sawyer's haunting—to say nothing of the length of the relationship, the engagement, that preceded Kennedy's ethereal limbo—settles on me wrongly, chilling under my covers. I can't meet Kennedy's eyes.

How do you talk to the dead fiancée of the man you might have a crush on?

"He loves you," I croak out.

Now Kennedy looks sad. Not winsome or disappointed. Deeply, wrenchingly sad. If even the smallest part of me wondered whether Sawyer was spending haunted years clinging onto his love for a woman who, when she was alive, didn't love him as much as he loved her, I know I was wrong.

I feel very small. Very out of place. Like—like maybe, despite the living heart pounding in my chest, I'm the unwelcome intruder haunting Sawyer's life. *Their* life.

I should leave, I decide. It's my natural gift, isn't it? The Morgan Lane special. Of all the times when I picked up and left everything behind, now makes the most sense.

Yet somehow, I know deep down I . . . can't. I can't leave Sawyer in his misery. It feels impossible. As impossible as walking through walls or vanishing like Zach or Kennedy.

"I will always love him," Kennedy explains, "and I know part of him will always love me, but what we had is over. Only the ghost of it remains." She smiles sadly, hearing the pun. "Sawyer knows. For years, I've told him what we had is only a memory."

I meet her eyes now. She looks sad but determined. Her glow has diminished, but not her opacity. She looks no less human.

"I want him to be happy. With love like ours . . . I want him to be happy," she repeats. "It's time for him to move on. Honestly, it was time long ago, though I confess I put it off longer than I should have. For a while, I thought we could live in this half existence, but as the years drew on and his life remained the same, I knew I was stealing his life the way the world stole mine." She frowns. "It wasn't fair to me. It's not fair to him, either."

I remember what I said to Sawyer tonight. *You have to live your life again.*

Yes—yes, I suppose I do know Kennedy.

"So, you just stopped appearing to him?" I reply. "Why not explain this to him?"

Emotion crosses Kennedy's face. Her glow sharpens. The leaves of my coleus waver. I'd just unconsciously let go of the last flickers of fear in my chest, but they return when I see the impatience that flashes on the ghost's face.

"Don't you think I've tried?" she snaps. "He won't listen to me. You know him. How is he supposed to respond to me telling him to let me go?"

Sympathy passes over me—I understand Kennedy's frustration, I do. Her connection to the mortal world is fragile, yet impossible to fight. It must be exhausting.

But . . . she's had five years to work this out maturely with Sawyer.

"When he met you, I thought . . ." She trails off.

"You want *me* to do it?" I say, incredulous. "*Just forget your dead fiancée, Sawyer,*" I pantomime. "*Trust me, it's what she wants.* Come on. I can't say that to him. Not when I want—" I swallow, stopping sharply.

I don't need to finish the sentence. Kennedy eyes me, understanding perfectly. She does know me. She knows my feelings for Sawyer, too. She *was* there tonight, manipulating the music, killing the lights. She knows everything.

"You don't need to tell him anything," Kennedy says, softer now. Peaceful, even. "Having you in his life is enough. Already, he is starting to live again. He returned to pottery. He's fixing up the house. He's . . . starting to move on. It's for the best." The ghost chokes out her final words. But the emotion in her voice is undeniable. She really means them.

He's starting to move on. It's for the best.

My indignation vanishes. Despite the lack of judgment or jealousy in Kennedy's words, shame suddenly roars in me. Who the hell am I to be impatient with someone who has literally nothing left to do on earth except watch the man she loves move on without her? "I'm sorry," I blurt.

Kennedy's smile is sharp and painful. The leaves of my coleus don't move, however. "It's not your fault," she replies evenly. "Do I love the thought of him . . . being with someone else? Of course not. But five years of watching him be with no one has shown me there are much worse things."

I say nothing. The fact is, if Kennedy hadn't died, I wouldn't be here. I would never have met Sawyer. Sawyer would never have met me. He would be happy with his wife, his life—the life they were building with every paint stroke and piece of drywall they put into this home.

Suddenly, I feel very sad that this woman is dead. Kennedy wasn't just a *piece* of Sawyer's now shattered life. She isn't just grief in ghost form. She was *herself*. She was every part of her own life.

Now she's . . . just this.

Kennedy sighs and smooths her expression. "It's why I've stopped appearing to him since he met you. I don't want to hold him back from what's in front of him. But when I'm not here, I'm . . . nowhere," she explains. I don't miss the new undercurrent in her voice. "I'm afraid eventually I'll forget myself completely," she confesses.

"Why don't you . . ." I start gently.

Then everything comes together. Kennedy's power over the garden, employed only five years after her death. Her conspicuous disappearance while Sawyer, reinvigorated, picked up his renovations where he left off. *I don't want to hold him back from what's in front of him.*

"You're not waiting for Sawyer to finish the house," I say.

Kennedy's stare bores into mine. She shakes her head.

Everything makes sense. Supernatural, grief-stricken sense. I sit up straighter, letting the blanket fall. "You need Sawyer to move on. That's the real reason you've been stuck in limbo for five years," I say. "*That's* your unfinished business."

The words threaten to close my throat with emotion, because Kennedy's final wish is proof of just how deep the couple's love is. Kennedy has clung onto the mortal plane for *five years* just to ensure the man she loves moves on and continues to live his life? It's the ultimate veil-crossing selflessness. It's heartbreakingly romantic.

"There have been two ghosts living in this house for too long," Kennedy replies. "Soon, I hope there will be none."

She smiles, and for the first time, her moonlit face looks hopeful.

I wipe my eyes, feeling overwhelmed.

But when I've blinked past my tears—Kennedy is gone. My room is dark. The moonlight through my window paints only serene shapes on the floor. My plant's purple leaves remain motionless in the empty night.

I stay sitting up. What Kennedy's told me is deeply moving, undeniably right . . . and impossible.

I can't just *tell* Sawyer his unfinished business is moving on from Kennedy. Moving on doesn't work that way. I remember when I frantically looked up haunting remedies early in my supernatural situation with Zach—finding online counsel recommending I simply *tell the ghost to go away.* This is no different. Grief, I'm learning, is nothing but the cleverest of ghosts.

Sawyer wouldn't listen, either, like Kennedy said. He doesn't hear reason or even compassion when it comes to letting go of Kennedy. He resists and guilts himself. He could barely talk about kissing anyone else tonight. If I shared with him my conversation with Kennedy, I'd probably ruin the progress he has made. He would cling harder to Kennedy, consciously or not.

And then there's the whole conflict-of-interest issue. It's even obvious *to the dead* that I have feelings for Sawyer. No doubt Sawyer knows. How selfish and manipulative would I sound trying to convince him the late love of his life wants him to move on *with me*?

No. I can't.

Not yet.

With the questions haunting me, I know I won't sleep. Instead, I settle for staring into the darkness.

25

SAWYER

I would have stayed in bed all day. Sleeping. Hiding.

Whether from the memory of sobbing into Morgan's shirt or kissing her—or the admittedly horribly pathetic combination of those two events—I don't know. It isn't worth sorting out. It's all daunting. What could she possibly think of me now? What do I *want* her to be thinking? How do you ever get out of bed after crying on, then kissing the girl you're trying not to admit you have feelings for?

The answer to that existential question turned out to be rather simple.

She texts you.

At first, I was afraid to check the message. I read my phone like someone watching a horror movie—eyes squinting, hand covering most of my view. I'm not proud. Add it to the list of choices I regret.

Thankfully, Morgan's message didn't mention last night. It was brief. Logistical.

Ariana replied to Morgan's DM last night. We're invited to a party Zach's sister is having at her house today in Santa Monica.

I choose not to examine whether it was the prospect of helping Zach or just the chance to see Morgan again that ultimately pulled me from bed.

As I shower, my relief that we weren't discussing last night turns to worry. Maybe she's avoiding the subject because she's horrified and doesn't know how to reject a crying almost widower. While brushing my teeth, I consider the cowardly route of seeking out Zach and asking him what Morgan thought.

But looking at my swollen eyes in the mirror, I resolve to stop making choices I'll regret. I decide to channel Morgan's bravery while facing down a haunted water heater.

While getting dressed, I examine the slash in my side, or what remains of it. Only a thin, straight scab stretched across my skin. It's incredible, seemingly supernatural, how quickly something so painful can start to fade away. Without Morgan, how much longer would the healing have taken?

With fresh coffee in each hand, I wait for her on the patio between our doors.

When she emerges, she's dressed in a flowery sundress with a circle cut into the back that makes her bare skin look like the sun itself. Her hair is up. She looks tired but beautiful.

Beautiful. I'm forced to finally admit the observation to myself. Morgan *is* beautiful. I'm captivated by her, despite the grief-stricken maelstrom in me. By her hair, by her eyes, the divots in her shoulders, the color in her cheeks. I have been since I first saw her, I think.

I don't know if I'm ready to move on. I don't even know *how* to move on. But I do know that kissing the girl I like while crying over another woman was not the way to begin anything.

I hold out one of the thermoses to Morgan.

She appears to not even see me. Only the coffee. "Oh, thank god," she says, reaching for it.

Well, she's not pissed, I console myself. Maybe kissing me was out of pity and she has no feelings about it whatsoever. It was a favor, like taking out the trash.

"Poor sleep?" I ask.

Suddenly, she doesn't meet my eyes. "Zach woke me up in the middle of the night," she says to the cracked flagstone between us.

She's lying. I know she is. It has to have been my fault. She was up all night worrying I would expect something more from her today than she wanted to give. Or maybe she was just tossing and turning, unable to escape the memory of what she considers the worst kiss of her life.

I find I'm frowning and force myself not to. As we start walking to the street, I suck in a deep breath. Time to face my fear full on. No hiding under the covers.

I stop sharply on the curb. "Morgan?" I begin, then clear my throat. "I just wanted to apologize for last night. I know I crossed some lines, and I feel awful."

Morgan blinks, her brow furrowed. She studies me like I'm an impossible-to-understand supernatural phenomenon. Then her gaze sharpens. "This is apology coffee, isn't it?" She holds up her drink in distaste.

"I—" I look at her travel mug, puzzled. "Yes?"

She shoves the coffee into my hand. "You don't need to apologize for anything," she says, sounding annoyed. "I know—" She stops herself, her posture sagging. Her eyes find mine. "No. I *don't* know because I *can't* know how hard of a position you're in. I'm just . . . well, I'm here for you." She fidgets like there's more she wants to say.

I wait.

"And . . ." Her mouth twists, and she digs her foot into the cement. "I'm not rushing you to figure out what you want."

Without waiting for me to reply or even react, she spins and walks quickly to her car.

I stand, stunned for a moment. *I'm not rushing you* sounds a lot like *I'll wait for you.* Does she . . . want something with me? Is it possible kissing me wasn't just out of misguided pity? That it was as unforgettable and profound for her as it was for me?

Awkwardly holding a coffee in each hand, I chase after her.

"Wait, does that mean you know what *you* want?" I ask to her back.

Resting an elbow on her open door, she peers at me over the top of her car. "Always," she replies simply.

The word electrifies me. "What—"

"Nope." She cuts me off. "No way. You cried on my shoulder and then kissed me. Pretty much the most mixed of messages a person can give. I wouldn't spell my feelings out for you even if you had a Ouija board."

I deserve the dig at my behavior last night, I really do. Still, somehow her accusation doesn't sting. Somehow, I'm not embarrassed anymore. It's some strange power Morgan has, to put me at ease, to accept me. To make me want to risk more than I should.

I shouldn't. I know how bad, how utterly destroying this road can be. I don't know if I can even walk it again. But god, I want to know what her feelings are.

I hold her travel mug up over her car. "Can I interest you in bribe coffee, then?"

While the sound of her laugh pierces me through with happiness, she gets into the driver's seat without replying.

I follow. "Fair enough," I say, watching her plug in Ariana's address to her phone and start the car. "What about a thank-you coffee?" I propose, hoping to get a laugh, a smile, even a glance from her.

She pauses with her hand on the gear shift to look at me. She lifts an eyebrow, waiting.

I'm not afraid now. "Thank you for last night, Morgan," I say, my eyes open, my vision clear, wanting to see every bit of her. "For all of it."

She holds my gaze, and I know she hears the indication meant in my words. The moment stretches, long but not fragile. I could sit here all day. I think maybe she could, too.

Finally, smirking, she holds her hand out for the coffee. I give it to her, feeling my heart thud painfully.

After a sip, she places the travel mug in the cupholder. We're both smiling as she pulls the car into the street.

"Cute, guys," I hear Zach say from the back seat. "But let's focus on me now."

26

We make decent time to Santa Monica. Or decent by Los Angeles standards. In twenty-five minutes, we're parking outside Ariana Harrison's house. Thank you, Saturday-morning traffic-free highways.

Morgan reaches for her purse in the back seat. She seems to startle, and while I watch her in uncomprehending interest, she looks back over her shoulder to inspect the contents she's rummaging through.

Withdrawing her hand, she holds the dragon mug. "Zach, why?"

Zach looks sheepish. "I don't know. I just do it without thinking," he says, rubbing his elbow. "Can we go in? What if my unfinished business is at this party?"

Morgan's gaze finds mine. We exchange a glance like we're the annoyed but adoring parents of a grown ghost child.

"Of course," Morgan replies. She returns the mug to her purse for safekeeping.

The home is lovely. It's the sort of Spanish Colonial meets suburban style I saw Kennedy work on often. Morgan admires the lively combination of hedges and cacti as we walk. On the front steps, the scent of home-cooked food wafts through the heavy wooden front door. I follow Morgan inside, where we notice streamers and HAPPY BIRTHDAY banners hanging over doorways.

"Zach," Morgan murmurs, "is today Ariana's birthday?"

Zach walks with us into the entryway. His footsteps hover just over the rust-colored tile. His stare sweeps the room intently, like he's searching the home for clues. "I . . . can't remember," he confesses. "Maybe?"

It feels promising. I wonder if Zach's Ouija board message has led us here so he can get some closure with his sister on her birthday. I'm not usually one for optimism, but everything this morning with Morgan has me feeling unexpectedly upbeat.

We continue through the house and into the backyard, following the sound of voices. In the home's expansive, welcoming backyard, kids play on a small swing set while the adults have gathered around an unlit firepit. The scene is picturesque. The Technicolor green grass, the cooler stacked with ice, the cans of seltzer and craft soda condensing on the concrete cylinder of the firepit.

Confused glances greet us. Since no one can see Zach, I know we look like random strangers wandering into this birthday party.

Until Bill Harrison notices us. Zach's father's worn features light up. "Sawyer! Morgan!" He gets up from his deck chair. "These are Zach's friends," he explains to surrounding family. "I'm so glad you came!"

Mr. Harrison hustles our way from the patio. He sweeps us both into a hug.

It's unexpectedly meaningful. My heart does this unusual wobbly thing I've noticed lately. I'm touched. Morgan has a similar lopsided smile, and I know she is, too.

"How are you?" Bill inquires like he really wants to know.

"We're good, Mr. Harrison," Morgan replies earnestly.

"Really good," I hear myself concur. "How are you?"

Bill gets teary, which I understand well. When Kennedy died, the simplest things could send my emotions into overdrive. The happiest reprieves were still sad. "I'm good, too," Bill replies. "Today is a happy day."

On cue, the hostess herself emerges from inside the house. I recognize Ariana_Scuba87 from her social media. Compared to Zach, Ariana Harrison is strikingly grown-up, effortlessly put together in understated California style.

What she shares with her sibling is her smile. When she spots her newest guests, her expression lights up, matching her father's enthusiasm despite her having never met us. She deposits the ice she's carrying in the drink cooler, then veers toward us.

Zach stands in her path. He stares, looking overwhelmed, like every memory of one of the most important people in his life has just returned to him.

"Ari—" he starts to say.

His sister walks right through him.

Zach's form shimmers. He's understandably stunned.

Morgan recovers seamlessly. "Hey, Ariana!" she greets Zach's sister. "Thank you so much for inviting us."

"Oh, of course. Please, feel free to get some food," she says. "Zach's friends are always welcome."

Past my eagerness for that smoky, spicy scent, I feel Ari's invitation deep in my chest. *Zach's friends.* The most idyllic part of this scene isn't the emerald grass or the laughter in the sunshine. It's the feeling of community. I haven't been part of one in years, and Zach's family doesn't even know me. Yet their kindness has me feeling impossibly welcome.

Feeling like I shouldn't have ignored my lost friends' outreach. Feeling like I should have left my haunted house long ago.

"So, um," Ari prompts us pleasantly, "you wanted to ask me some stuff about Zach?" Sudden mortification casts over her. "Please don't tell me he owes you money."

Morgan smiles. "I mean, he did break my shower curtain, but no. It was worth replacing just to hang out with him."

"Aw, Morgan." Zach has recomposed himself. He materializes, sitting on the edge of the firepit near us. "That's the nicest thing you've ever said about me."

Morgan ignores him.

Ari looks relieved. "Good," she says. "We had a GoFundMe for his funeral, but I'm not sure 'Pay Zach's ex the cost of his freeloading' would get the same community support."

Zach laughs.

"Hey," Bill interjects. "Don't talk about your brother like that."

"Why not?" Ari shrugs, and I see more of Zach in her. The irreverence. The love found in honesty. "I was always ragging on him. And he ragged on me. Just because he's dead doesn't mean I'm going to treat him any different. He wouldn't want it that way. It would be way too sad."

Zach has grown serious hearing Ari's explanation. "She's right," he says to me and Morgan. "It would legit suck if my sister stopped making fun of me. Then I'd feel *really* dead."

I feel compelled to speak up where the ghost can't. "Zach was a good sport," I say. "Teasing just meant he was the center of attention, which of course—"

"He loved," Ari finishes.

Her smile is wide and uncomplicated. Like a cloudless sky.

It seems impossible to me. I watch Zach's sister closely, feeling like she's holding the key to some equation or long-secret code. I've just . . . never experienced this form of grief. When Kennedy died,

I shut down. I isolated myself from people and experiences. I lived in loss for so long I never saw how it looks on the other side.

Now I do. Zach's family still misses him, but they're making more joyful memories. They're remembering Zach with jokes and smiles.

They've figured out how to reverse the chronology of what I recognized in Bill. Yes, no joy is without sadness. But here, Zach's family has learned how to wrap sadness in the warm embrace of joy. If Zach weren't invisible in our midst, I suspect he would still feel close right now.

Fortunately, while I'm contemplating grief, Morgan remembers our objective. "We were wondering if there was anything you needed help with? Anything Zach maybe left in the middle of doing that you could use some help resolving?" she says, plying Ari gently.

Zach's sister looks grateful and surprised. "That's really sweet." She pauses. "I guess . . ."

We hold our breath. Even Zach.

"You wouldn't happen to know where his car keys are, would you? I haven't been able to find them, and he left his van parked in my driveway," Ari explains with a hint of humor. She looks to the sky. "Nothing like free parking for all eternity, right, bud?"

"Whoops." Zach rubs his chin. "Totally forgot about that."

Morgan and I deflate. I hope Ariana doesn't notice. Inconvenient parking? This isn't unfinished business worth living in limbo for.

I fight hopelessness. It's what Zach would want. *Does want?* I'll inquire with the man himself on whether he prefers past tense these days. "We'll see if we can find them," I reassure Ari. "Anything else we could do for you, or for Zach? Anything that might help lay his memory to rest?"

Ari looks like she wants to help. Like she understands the importance of our interrogation. *Oh, if only.*

"You're really devoted friends," she says. "But of course you are. Zach was the kind of guy you let break your shower curtain and park in your driveway forever, wasn't he? No," she says reluctantly. "Nothing else. Zach was happy." She gestures to the table on the patio. "Please, have some cake before you leave. For Zach."

Morgan hides her disappointment effortlessly, but I know her well enough to know she's doing it. "We will," she promises.

Honestly, I could go for some cake. My whole breakfast was thank-you coffee this morning.

Glancing where Ari gestured, I find the cake table. The tablecloth is dragon-patterned.

I survey the yard, intrigued. Dragon streamers, dragon-shaped paper plates, dragon napkins. Even the cake depicts the remaining half of a green dragon's face. Unless she's really into fantasy novels, I realize, this party is not for Ariana.

"Wow," I venture. "I've never seen so many dragons in my life."

Ari grins proudly. "It's my son, Henry. He's turning seven today." She points out a dark-haired boy pushing a little girl on the swings. "We've read every book that features dragons in the library multiple times," Ari assures us.

Morgan watches Henry wide-eyed.

I do the same.

She finds her voice first. "If . . . if it's okay with you, Zach gave me something to give Henry."

"He—" Ari swallows. Past the tears that leap into her eyes, she looks puzzled. "He did?"

Zach seems overcome looking at his nephew. The sunlight shines through him for a moment, making him seem like he's glowing. I can't imagine how many memories are returning to him.

"Yes," Morgan replies, clearly thinking fast. "When we were . . . He mentioned Henry to me. He—we found this amazing artist," Morgan elaborates. "Zach had something made. He knew his nephew would love it."

Ari wipes her eyes. "Please." She clears her throat like she's fighting her tears. "Please, give it to him. Oh, Zach," she says to herself.

While I hang back, Morgan ventures to the nearby swing set, where she kneels down. "Hey, Henry. Your Uncle Zach gave me this to give to you," she says gently to Zach's nephew. "He wanted you to have the best birthday."

Henry steps closer. He looks shy but interested. The mention of Zach makes him drop his gaze to his shoes, until Morgan produces the dragon mug from her purse.

Excitement transforms Henry's downcast expression. His eyes go wide. "Cool!" he exclaims, and Morgan beams, handing the mug carefully over, while next to me, Ariana stifles her sobs. Her shoulders shake.

I join Morgan, leaving Ariana some privacy. I hear her racked whisper to her father. "He should be here . . ."

I should have known, I chasten myself. There is no *other side* to loss. Grief is never gone, even if family and community and companionship can help fill the world with more and more joy. Shadows remain, waiting for whenever the light of someone's life casts the wrong way.

I reach Morgan as Henry dashes off to show off his dragon mug to his friends. Instinctually, I know—from the shape of her back, the uncharacteristic hunched motionlessness of her posture—that she's going to cry.

I'm there when she does. I sweep her into a hug in the corner of the yard under a tree and stroke her back until her breathing settles.

Sometimes there is no fighting the shadows or finding the joy. Sometimes there's only this.

Eventually, her breathing evens. I hold on anyway.

"Guess we're even now," Morgan says, withdrawing and nodding to the wet spots near my shirt's collar.

"My shoulder is always available for more crying," I say honestly.

Morgan sniffles. She doesn't smile, but she seems sturdier. More okay. "Mine too," she says.

I open my mouth, then close it. Then—no, fuck it. No more choices I regret, right? "You make me too happy for me to cry on you again," I confess.

Morgan looks up. The sun catches those brown eyes, setting the gold in them to dancing. She opens her mouth to speak—

Zach materializes right next to us. "This has got to be it, right?" he enthuses.

I draw back from Morgan, startled. She does the same.

"My unfinished business," Zach continues, obliviously enthusiastic. "I had to give my nephew one final birthday gift. Ever since I saw the dragon mug, I've been unconsciously moving it toward Morgan. Then the Ouija board sent us here. Everything was just to give Henry the perfect gift. How incredibly sweet." He grins, seeming sincerely moved by his own ghostly thoughtfulness. "Now I can pass peacefully on to whatever is next, and I know my family knows I love them."

I smile. "It's beautiful, Zach," I say.

"Really perfectly done," Morgan adds.

Zach bows grandly. "Of course, I couldn't have done it without you two," he generously concedes, Oscar-speech-style. "Sawyer, thank you for making that mug and for not letting Morgan hire priests to exorcise me even when I caused an earthquake in your house. That was cool of you, man."

"No problem," I laugh.

"Most of all, shout out to your messy love life for the entertainment I needed in my afterlife," Zach commends me.

I roll my eyes playfully, forcing myself not to look at Morgan for her reaction to Zach's very unsubtle reference. I'd prefer another ghostly earthquake to seeing her respond negatively to that.

"Morgan," Zach continues, "thank you for giving me my last-ever hookup and for being sort of the best roommate I've ever had. I know it seemed like our date didn't go anywhere, but actually it brought me a really dope friend."

Morgan's eyes water. "Me too, Zach," she manages. "I'll miss you. I'll think of you every time my shower suddenly turns cold."

Zach places his hand over where his heart once beat, looking sincerely grateful. "I would fist-bump you right now if I could," he says.

"I know, Zach," Morgan replies. "I know."

Zach inhales and exhales in peaceful preparation. "I'm off!" he declares. "Take care of each other in your grief for me!"

He looks to the sky. The sun is shining perfectly down on us. We wait.

Nothing happens. Zach shifts on his feet. "Time to pass on!" he states loudly. He stomps his foot, like he can shoot himself sky-ward or something.

Still nothing.

Out of the corner of my eye, I notice dragon napkins scattering. A cold breeze is sweeping through the yard. The swings sway ominously. I lock eyes with Morgan. By now, we recognize the paranormal indications of Zach's frustration.

Still, the ghost goes nowhere. He stares up, exasperated. The swings creak, then start to move more deliberately, swinging on their own. The effect is, well, haunting.

"We have to go," Morgan says to me. "Now. Before Zach unintentionally traumatizes this kid on his birthday."

The branches of our tree creak. The tablecloth flaps. Morgan and I have no time for sentimental goodbyes. We walk quickly through the house, Zach drifting with us, preternaturally popping every balloon he passes. We get out front just in time for his outburst.

"I don't understand!" he exclaims. "We did it! My unfinished business. What else could it possibly have been?"

He sits down dramatically on the curb in front of Ariana's house. I hear the taut undercurrent in his impatience—the fear. He knows how long Kennedy has lingered in my life. He wants peace. He wants resolution. He's starting to reckon with the possibility that we won't know how to release him from his ghostly existence.

"I really thought we had it, too," I say, sitting down next to him. Morgan joins me.

"We don't have any other leads," Zach says hollowly.

"We'll try the Ouija board again," I promise him. "Maybe we can get more clarity or more instruction. Maybe . . ." I speculate. "Maybe this *was* important. There's just more we have to do still."

Morgan reaches out to pat him comfortingly on the shoulder—only for her hand to pass right through him. She loses her balance, wobbling where she's seated on the steps. Her elbow strikes the concrete.

"Shit, you okay?" I reach for her.

But Morgan says nothing. Her eyes have found the old Volkswagen van sitting in the driveway behind us. Zach's van, I realize, remembering Ari's joking irritation with her sibling's final parking choice. The van is cool, frankly, a sky-blue VW bus with just the right level of wear and tear.

"Zach, when you saw Ariana, you called her *Ari*," Morgan says, remembering. "I don't think she's the clue. Look," she gasps. "The license plate."

I follow Morgan's rapt stare to the plate on the front of the scuffed van.

Its middle three letters read ANA.

27

MORGAN

Zach's unfinished business can't be simply moving his car. If it were, wouldn't he haunt someone with a tow truck? Or maybe even a friendly car thief?

No. It has to be more than that. The car is a clue.

We peer into the dark and dusty windows of the van. Maybe the glove box contains a letter to a loved one he needs to deliver, or a key to a safety deposit box is stored in the armrest, or hidden under the seat, his laptop holds an unfinished novel no one ever read. Something, *anything*, worthy of Zach's purgatory.

It's impossible to make out much through the windows, though. There are some papers that look like receipts on the passenger seat and a sweatshirt balled up on the floor. In the expansive back, we can make out several large unusual shapes, but they're covered with a Mexican blanket.

Zach even drifts through the van's doors to get a better look, but being unable to lift or move anything, he doesn't discover more.

Ten useless minutes later, we postpone our efforts. If we don't want to risk having to explain to Ari why we're breaking into her deceased brother's car, we're going to need to find the keys.

We resolve to do just that. For the next week, we search *everywhere*.

Sawyer and I divide up Zach's frequent haunts—living, that is. Sawyer returns to the hardware store to scour the back room. I talk my way into Zach's lifeguard tower. I was prepared to fake a jellyfish sting in order to be taken inside for first aid, but it turned out all I had to do was imply I was Zach's girlfriend, and his coworkers were more than happy to show me around.

While we don't turn up the keys, we do manage to uncover more leads—the coffee shop the lifeguards all go to before their shifts, the gym across the street from Zach's former apartment, the surf shop he worked in when he wanted some extra hours.

I drive from Palms down the coast to Hermosa Beach, from Brentwood to Koreatown.

It's a scavenger hunt of Zach's life scattered across all of Los Angeles, a city that, I'm realizing, has a little bit of everything.

It's fun, if unsuccessful. I haven't explored much of LA's sprawl beyond my own neighborhood since moving here. Zach explained when we were stuck in traffic on "the 10"—this nomenclature for freeways, instead of "I-10," is mysteriously very important to locals—that he must have really liked my profile to drive out from his place in Playa Vista to West Hollywood for our date.

I laugh, even if I don't share his frustration with the traffic. I've always liked driving, and it's sort of amazing to see how these highways, these veins, course and splinter through the city.

Eventually, we find Zach's apartment listed on rental websites, courtesy of one of the lifeguards with whom Zach carpooled—in the vexing van, no less. The small studio has already been cleared out and is being shown to potential renters.

Sawyer and I decide to investigate together. If the property manager is on the premises, one of us will need to distract him while the other snoops.

I plan to meet Sawyer outside the Playa Vista complex one evening when I get off work. Zach won't be joining us. Whenever I pulled up the pictures online, he would get melancholy and spooky. He informed me he wouldn't manifest until I got home and put on the *Hunters of the Deep* documentary he found on streaming.

I understood. No matter how many times I've moved, looking back one last time on the empty view of where I no longer live is depressing—and that's without the dying part.

Unfortunately, Zach's absence means I have no help parallel parking on the street where he used to live. I somewhat successfully wedge myself in, managing not to scrape my fender, sorely missing my supernatural companion.

Sawyer waits outside the complex's front steps, framed in the sun setting over the concrete. The sky surrounds him in dazzling gold.

He's not scrolling his phone or lost in thought. He simply stares out into the sunset, until he notices my approach. "Hey," he greets me. "Hope traffic wasn't too bad."

"Not terrible. Only forty minutes," I reply.

"Spoken like a true Angeleno," he comments.

I smile lightly, not hating the unexpected compliment. I never stay in the cities where I live long enough to feel like a native, long enough to say "the 10" or discover date spots more original than repetitions of rock climbing. Instead, I've acted more like Zach or Kennedy, with one foot in my next life.

I wonder how long I'll stay here.

The question makes me a little sad. I hide the feeling, following Sawyer up the chipped slate inlaid steps to Zach Harrison's old apartment. Sawyer holds the door open for me, and we walk into the lobby. "We're here to see 409," he says to the woman behind the glass in the small property manager's office, who is perusing *Us Weekly*.

"It's open," she replies with the droning disinterest of someone who's repeated this exact conversation more often than she'd like. "Just let me know if you want to fill out an application when you leave."

She waves us toward the elevators.

"I guess I didn't need to drag you out here after work," Sawyer concedes when the elevator doors open for us.

I step in next to him. "I don't mind," I say honestly as the doors slide shut.

The compartment isn't spacious. I find myself standing close to him as the elevator rises. Its uninterrupted ascent half surprises me—we make it the whole way up to the fourth floor with no flickering lights, worrisome lurches, or unexplained stops. I laugh quietly, and Sawyer responds inquisitively with a raised eyebrow.

"I think this is the first time we've actually been alone together," I explain. "No ghosts."

In the echo of my words, his eyes catch mine. His gaze lingers.

Only the elevator door opening interrupts us. I step first into the silent hallway.

"Clearly, this is our chance to talk about Zach behind his back," Sawyer says, following me out.

His easy humor surprises me. I laugh, enjoying how the sound rings out in the empty hall. Sawyer is . . . different right now, in ways hard to put into words. Relaxed. Slyly charming. Outside his haunted home, with no specters hanging over him, he's just himself.

It's nice. I wonder if he knows.

"You're right," I say, playing along. "Hmm. Only problem is—and I can't believe I'm saying this—I sort of like Zach, honestly."

Sawyer grins. "Yeah," he says. "Me too."

We reach 409, where the unlocked door opens easily. I fight discouragement when we see what's inside. It's empty—in every sense. Clean, unfurnished. Exorcised of personality or life. The place feels like . . . nothing. No scrap of Zach remains.

Of course not, I know. It's not his home anymore. A haunted house in Silver Lake is.

Still, we owe him every effort to find his keys. "Looks like everything was professionally cleaned," Sawyer ventures when we walk in and close the front door. He's practiced in hiding dismay under his withdrawn emotionlessness. I get the feeling it's what he's doing now. "The odds of finding keys here are . . . low," he adds in the murmur I remember from our first support-group meeting.

I'm not convinced. "If the cleaning crew had found keys, surely they would've told someone," I say. "We should check the places that are hard to reach. Under the fridge, behind the stove."

Sawyer doesn't debate me. He continues down the short hallway, which opens up after a couple feet into the studio. It's small but recently updated, with modern lighting over the clean countertops. The view from the main window would let in welcome sunlight in the daytime, even glimpses of the ocean.

"He probably could have checked the swells from his bed in the morning," I can't help noting.

Sawyer smiles sadly. While I'm not sorry we're here, the reminder hurts—that Zach was his own whole person. I felt the same when Kennedy visited me the other night.

"If things had worked out with him, would you have moved in here?" Sawyer asks.

I snort. "God, no. I mean, this place is nice. No disrespect for the dead. No offense to Zach, either. I just haven't had the urge to cohabitate with a man since . . ." I swallow, realizing I've strayed onto a subject I didn't mean to dig up. "Well," I say with weak finality.

Sawyer kneels down next to the stove.

"Your fiancé," he says in his low, measured way.

I nod. Shining my phone flashlight, I peer under the fridge. While it's definitely dusty, my search yields no Volkswagen keys. I straighten, forcing myself to concentrate, but Sawyer's nonchalant reference has my mind stuck on Michael Hanover-Erickson.

"I really screwed him over when I left," I can't help commenting.

The sudden force of Sawyer's reply startles me. "You didn't screw him over, Morgan," he says firmly. "You know it wasn't my plan to live in a half-finished house alone. It's not Kennedy's fault, though."

I peer behind the fridge so Sawyer doesn't see my frown. It's just, well-meaning or not, his reply is the kind of naivete it's not easy to take to heart. "Kennedy died," I say. "I bailed. It's different." I move to the kitchen cupboards, opening them to rummage on the high shelves. "It's easier if I just keep my life unattached and uninvolved," I insist. "Then I can pick up and leave whenever I get cold feet, and no one gets hurt."

Sawyer has started pulling the oven out from the wall. He pauses with my explanation. "Except you," he replies.

I stop short.

Slowly, I close the cupboard. I've never . . . In years of deliberate noncommitment, of resenting my shitty decision-making, of feeling guilty for the people I disappointed, I've never considered myself the victim of my choices. No, the wretched honor goes to Michael, my parents, *his* parents. The people I let down.

But . . . I did get hurt, didn't I?

Except you.

Yeah, well, whatever. Fuck my hurt. "I deserve it," I remind Sawyer, repeating the words I've rehearsed on so many sleepless nights in different cities, holding on to my reasons for running from my destructive patterns.

Sawyer just shakes his head, impossibly calm while he reaches past the oven. "You can't think like that," he says.

"Like what?"

Finding nothing, Sawyer uses his shoulder to force the oven back into its proper position. "We don't deserve the sad things that happen to us. Zach and Kennedy didn't deserve to die. I didn't deserve to lose her. Believe me, I went through years where I was sure I did, where I was convinced her death was somehow cosmically *my* fault."

He faces me. His eyes lock onto mine.

"It wasn't, though," he says with sureness I sorely wish I felt. "And you didn't mean to hurt anyone." He paces to the window. "I know you feel guilty for your parents' finances or disappointing your fiancé or whatever it is you punish yourself for," he says quietly. "You shouldn't."

His reassurance makes me want to scoff. "I made such a mess," I say to him instead. "Of everything." I feel like I'm pleading with him. Like if I can get him to understand why I need to be this way, I'll know I was right to spend my nights lonely and my days restless.

But Sawyer won't let me.

"You needed help, Morgan," he says. "You needed people to care for you when you were struggling or when you made mistakes. That doesn't mean you forfeit your right to commitment or connection. Or I hope it doesn't." He gazes out, illuminated in sunset. "*You* deserve to be happy, Morgan. You deserve real, great love. You don't lose the right to happiness just because you need help."

I face away from him, not ready for him to see the tears in my eyes. "Thanks, Sawyer," I whisper.

"People aren't just the sum of their mistakes. If you woke up tomorrow and said you couldn't finish the yard, I want you to know I wouldn't be upset. You're your own person."

Now I dare to look up, letting him see my fragility. "I've thought about quitting a couple times," I admit. Not that I need to. With everything Sawyer knows, he's probably expected my hasty, shitty retreat for weeks now.

"I know," he says.

"I haven't, though."

"No," Sawyer says. "You haven't."

For once, I try holding on to my quiet pride. Not even my growing closeness to Sawyer, with all its complications, has driven me from his home or his city. I've even endured ghostly earthquakes and haunted water heaters. I haven't run out on Sawyer or Zach or even Kennedy.

"I don't want to let you down," I finally get out, feeling Sawyer's expectant eyes on me. I think sometimes recognizing your worth, your goodness, is harder than recognizing your flaws. Sawyer is pushing me to rise to the challenge. Not letting me undervalue myself.

He moves to the kitchen counter. The evening half-light seems to hum with his fragile closeness to me.

I don't move. He hesitates, then takes my hand.

"You'll never let me down, Morgan," he says.

His words stop my breath for a moment. His calloused, experienced palm is electrifyingly warm. No lights flicker overhead, though. No closets rattle. No cupboards slam. There are no ghosts between us.

"I owe you more than you could know," he continues. "You've already changed . . . my whole life."

How? I desperately want to know.

Sawyer denies me the satisfaction. He withdraws his hand, not waiting for my reply. "Shall we?" he says softly.

Startled, I flush. He's near enough to . . . *Shall we?* His words repeat in my head, laden with meaning. I'm fixated on his hand at his side, the one that was just touching mine. "Shall we what?" I manage.

Sawyer gestures casually into the studio's living room. "Zach's keys aren't here. Shall we go? I could pick up Thai on the way home," he offers.

The heat rushes from me, welcoming embarrassment in its place. *Of course he meant "Shall we leave?"* I chastise myself fiercely. "Oh. Yeah, yes." I recover. "Thai sounds great."

Sawyer smiles. He heads for the front door, making no indication whatsoever that he recognizes the new longing clutching unrepentant in my chest.

I follow him out, hitting the lights in Zach's former home on my way, forced to admit to myself just how much I wanted to kiss Sawyer in the dying daylight, when no one was crying. When it was just for the living.

28

On Saturday morning, Sawyer is on key duty, following the semi-promising lead of the park where Zach would play ultimate Frisbee with his friends and coworkers. Without work, and having no profound yearning to visit Zach's favorite Frisbee course, I can rest a little before I start gardening. I plan a luxurious extra thirty minutes of sleep. I may even snooze my alarm once or twice.

Except, I don't get to sleep in *or* snooze my alarm. My wake-up call ends up being an irritated ghost rattling all my cabinets loud enough to rouse me when the sunlight gently glowing through my blinds tells me I'm entitled to still be sleeping.

Groggily, I open my eyes to find Zach standing right by my bed.

I don't startle. I just close my eyes and will him to dematerialize for a bit.

"Your alarm should have gone off thirty minutes ago."

I feel the soft edges of sleep slipping from me. I roll over, mumbling into my pillowcase, "I turned it off so I could sleep in."

Suddenly, I'm very cold, and then Zach appears on the other side of the bed in front of me once more. He drifted *through me*.

"Not cool, man," I murmur irately. Of course I won't be able to sleep now. I need to shower for a hundred years to get the feeling of Zach off my skin.

Zach crosses his arms, unapologetic. "You'll thank me later because Sawyer is on his way over here," he announces. "I've been trying to work up the psychic energy to make a loud enough noise to wake you up when I realized your alarm didn't go off. You sleep like the dead, dude."

Now I sit up straight. "Sawyer is coming over here? Why?"

Is he home from Playa Vista already? When did he set out, five a.m.? Immediately, I feel torn in half. The thought of seeing Sawyer sets what feels suspiciously like butterflies fluttering in my stomach.

Until I remember Kennedy. It feels awful to realize my joy only exists because of her pain. It's like a strange survivor's guilt for a tragedy I didn't even live through.

But Sawyer did. Doesn't he deserve to be happy again, too?

The questions have run through my head since our visit to Zach's old apartment, making me grateful for the distraction of everything I've had to do. Even if I've hung onto the things Sawyer said to me like my own secret source of sunlight when I needed it. *You deserve to be happy. I owe you more than you could know.*

"I told him you're up by seven thirty. We have a lead to check out," Zach says, his voice high-pitched and urgent.

"Let him check it out on his own," I say, stifling a yawn.

Zach's eyes flit to the side. He shifts his nonexistent weight. "He can't."

I narrow my eyes into a glare. I'm not sure if all ghosts are terrible liars or if it's just Zach. "What are you hiding?" I ask. If we're *both* needed to check out a lead, it has to be either difficult or embarrassing or—I don't even know. The fact he's hiding the reason from me is enough for me to know I won't like whatever it is.

"Morgan, you're wearing a see-through tank top and Sawyer is going to be here any minute."

I look down, realizing—*shit*. He's right. This top is so ancient the threading is nearly translucent. It's one thing for my dead ex to see this; it's another for Sawyer. I groan and leap out of bed, hurrying to get dressed faster than I ever have before. I put on an old, fitted, and very opaque red T-shirt and the first pair of jean shorts I can find. I'm just pulling on my socks when I hear his knock on the front door.

Zach jumps like he'll answer it, then seems to remember. He slouches as I pass him, half hopping as I stomp my feet into my sneakers.

This time, when I open the door, Sawyer isn't just holding coffee. He has a bagel, too. The kind he must have gotten from a cool food truck. It smells incredible. Actually, it smells like my exact bagel order—everything-bagel sandwich with cream cheese, egg, and sausage.

"How?" I ask.

Sawyer keeps his cool, looking smug. "I have a man on the inside passing me intel."

I whirl to face Zach. He shrugs, and seems to blush, if that's even possible for a ghost. I didn't realize Zach noticed my order every time he complained about me stopping to get breakfast before work. I turn back to Sawyer and take the still-warm piece of heaven out of his hands, my stomach growling. Or maybe those are just more butterflies.

"Since you're bringing me breakfast, I'm guessing this new lead is going to be a long drive?" I ask, wondering if I sound hopeful.

Sawyer's not wearing a sweater today. For the first time, he's dressed for the summer in a linen shirt. My eyes are pulled to the hard lines of his chest beneath the soft fabric.

His grin is slanted. *Okay, yes, it's definitely butterflies.*

"Don't worry," Sawyer assures me. "Zach promised to be our car DJ."

Thirty minutes of Zach's chaotic music selections later, Sawyer pulls into a large outdoor parking lot. HUNTINGTON GARDENS, the sign reads. Of course I know of the gardens. I suspect even if I wasn't a plant girl, I'd know about them. They're a somewhat famous location in Los Angeles, a rare carve-out inland for nature, and unsurprisingly a frequent movie and TV filming location. I've wanted to go since I moved here, but I haven't made the time.

I glance at Sawyer when he parks in one of the few shady spots under a tree. "There's no way Zach's car keys are at the Huntington Gardens," I say, not comprehending this strange plan. "I didn't know him that well, but if he'd had any interest in going to a botanical garden *ever*, we might have had a better first date."

Sawyer's eyes light up like this delights him. His cheek dimples like he's biting the inside. When he puts on his sunglasses, he looks particularly handsome, or maybe that's just the amusement transforming his features.

I find myself quite annoyed. What right does he have to look this good when I'm not sure how to even act around him?

"Hmm," Sawyer muses like he's actually considering my point. "Should we go inside and look anyway?"

I don't take off my seat belt. "No," I reply, incredulous. "Why are we really here? Why did you pull me out of bed for a dead-end lead? I could be asleep right now." I try to sound convincing, I really do. But I know it's clear in my tone just how not upset I am to be here right now.

Suddenly, Zach leans forward between the seats from his floating perch in the back. "I told you she'd be stubborn," he says to Sawyer.

"I can't be stubborn when I don't know what I'm being stubborn about," I say, staring Sawyer down.

He sighs. "Fine, yes, Zach's keys aren't here."

"No shit," I reply.

Zach leans even farther onto the armrest between us. "This isn't for me at all, actually," he says happily.

Sawyer cranes his head around our ghost to see me. "We just wanted to thank you," he says, his tone gentling with sincerity. "You've been working so hard this week to help both of us. We really appreciate it, and we wanted to give something back to you for once."

I glance between them, my ghost ex and my haunted crush. "You're . . . taking me to the Huntington Gardens?"

Excitement starts to curl my lips. I'm not going to do yard work today. Instead, I'm going to spend the day in nature I can simply enjoy. With Sawyer and—

Zach interrupts my thoughts. "*He's* taking you," my ghost says. "Have fun!" He waves cheekily and then disappears from the back seat.

Leaving Sawyer and me alone.

What was it I just said? *If he'd had any interest in going to a botanical garden ever, we might have had a better first date.*

29

If Morgan in the nursery was something to behold, Morgan in the botanical garden is overwhelming.

While we walk every section of the Huntington Gardens, her face lights up in a million ways. I wish I could memorize every look of hers—her sunflower smile, her lily solemnity in front of the large ponds, her orchid eagerness. I could stay in each moment forever without ever seeing enough.

Naturally, Morgan looks like she feels the same for the plant life surrounding us. We continue slowly from section to section, Morgan considering every garden's composition while I follow, content to observe everything with my horticulturally inexperienced eye.

Even though it's early in the morning, it's getting hot in Pasadena's inland hills. The sun shines directly overhead, uninterrupted by oceanic fog. The garden isn't crowded yet, though. Peaceful silence greets us when we enter the desert garden, where our path entwines with stout cacti and large rocks.

While it's pleasant enough, the squat, unshowy plants have

nothing on the dramatic rose garden I saw on the website. Honestly, I'm kind of underwhelmed.

Not Morgan. Her eyes light up with cactus cheer.

I have to smile. "I suppose you work a lot with desert flora here," I venture.

"I try to," she replies immediately. "They're great for the environment, of course. And look at them!"

I do. I really do. I squint with my whole soul, searching for hidden spiny wonder.

Nope. Still . . . cacti.

"They're beautiful," Morgan gushes, her eyes roving over the desert display.

I follow her gaze, trying to see the unimposing cacti the way my companion does. It's her gift, no doubt. I make sculptures out of clay. Morgan makes spectacles out of succulents.

Morgan seems to notice my struggle to muster enthusiasm for the low-lying desert foliage. She raises an undaunted eyebrow. "Not impressed?"

"It's lovely, of course," I reply diligently.

Morgan rolls her eyes, but she's smiling when she elbows me as we continue down the path. "Lovely," she repeats, "but . . . ?"

"They're so prickly," I say, struggling to explain myself. "So isolated." They look oddly lonely. I remember the massive cactus at the nursery weeks ago, statuesque in solitude. A proud lone giant.

The cacti here look no different. Even surrounded by others like them, they seem somehow standoffish. The garden is so sparse, so empty of lushness or life, I feel suddenly sad in a way I can't explain.

Morgan grins. "Well, sure," she replies. "It's how they survive the impossible. It doesn't mean they're not still beautiful."

Now her eyes find mine, her gaze indicative, and I realize she doesn't just mean the cactus.

In fact, I'm very lucky Morgan Lane likes prickly, lonely living things. I'm lucky Morgan sees a garden in a desert, a home in a haunted house. A life in a wasteland of loss.

I decide I need to see things the way she does. If I did, maybe . . . maybe my life would look more like the Harrisons'. More like community, companionship, and even hope.

If I can believe in ghosts, I can believe in the power of Morgan's gold-dusted gaze to remake the world.

"Look," she says.

Morgan wanders to where she's pointing, where a flower springs from the dusty landscape. The pink-hemmed petals look innocently joyful, like they know nothing of the harsh climate surrounding them.

"Even the desert has roses," she comments. "We're here at a good time for them, too."

If I'm going to see the world the way Morgan does, I need to practice. I need to start sculpting my gaze the way I shaped hundreds, maybe thousands of misshapen pots in school workshops, honing my craft.

The desert surrounding me is strong, I decide. Not dangerous or isolated. It survived the unsurvivable, with pockets of unexpected color if you look closely for them.

I kneel down next to Morgan. Next to the desert rose. "You're very clever," I concede.

Morgan's lips remind me of the petals. Defiantly happy. She shrugs. "I don't know what you're talking about," she replies. But when she stands, leaving the flower flourishing in the desert, she winks.

We dust off our knees and continue our unhurried progress, eventually exiting the desert garden. The mouth of the path returns us to the main road, where the shaggy limbs of enormous trees reach for the sun. Only their gentle rustle fills the receding morning. "So, if I'm a cactus," I say, challenging Morgan, "what are you?"

When she laughs, delighted, my stomach swoops. I feel like I'm seeing colors I forgot light could make. "That's tough," she says, contemplating the question seriously. "I love the jacaranda trees that bloom here. Anything that has seasons, I guess. Maybe something that blooms twice a year, like a bougainvillea."

I startle. "There's bougainvillea on my back patio," I say. Of course, Morgan knows this. One cannot overlook the relentless high-winding plant, not to mention the endless sea of papery pink petals it deposits on my flagstones.

"You might have noticed I haven't torn it out," she replies.

"It's beautiful," I say earnestly. "Though it does make a mess."

The moment I hear the words exit my mouth, I know how they sound.

Morgan scoffs, pretending she's indignant. "I call you a beautiful cactus and I'm a messy bougainvillea. I see how it is."

I only grin. Morgan doesn't seem to mind being the messy bougainvillea of the two of us. Her pace picks up on our way to the next garden, unhidden excitement in her steps. I follow, and comfortable silence settles over us.

The gardens are wonderfully serene, uninterrupted by conversation or cars honking or city noise. The soundtrack is entirely natural, with soft undercurrents of stream water rippling under the hush of wind-rustled foliage. When Morgan points out favorite plants to me, her voice seems part of the collage.

"We had those outside when I lived in Florida," she says, pointing up. "I would go to work way early in the morning, waitressing in Miami. The sunlight would pass through them right in front of my car."

The tall, overhanging trees she's pointing to sway in the Pasadena sun like they're corroborating her story. Like they remember, too.

Morgan points out more pieces of her past while we walk. The yuccas, she says, remind her of where she most recently lived, in Phoenix. Every weekend she would go hiking, except when the weather was perilously hot, which was often. Instead, she would "hike" to the ice cream place she lived near. Spiny yuccas stood in the planters of the strip mall where she enjoyed mint chocolate chip waffle cones.

The rose garden reminds Morgan of the flower shop where she worked her first job in high school. The carnations of elementary school science, where she would color their petals by watering them with dye.

I start to understand the human kaleidoscope Morgan is. The garden of memory she cultivates effortlessly. She may have moved many times, but she's never left those pieces of herself behind.

In fact, with everything Morgan shows me, I start to understand *why* she moves so much. Morgan isn't just running, even if she thinks she is. No, her lifestyle isn't simply because she fears commitment. It's because she loves change.

She sees the beauty in change. In growth. Change is vital to gardening, her passion. The rose garden we passed hasn't bloomed yet, but if we were to return here later in the year, we could stand where we do now and see something completely different.

Contemplating the inherent reality of nature, I realize I just considered what would happen if *we* returned here. Not *I*.

How's that for change?

Morgan leads us into the heart of the Huntington Gardens, where huge trees literally reach their hanging foliage to the ground, ensconcing their trunks in rounded canopies of seclusion.

If one loves gardening like Morgan does, I reason, one must love change. It's a welcome way to live, I think. Learning to love change, when change is everywhere, uniting every living thing. Only death ever stays the same forever.

Morgan slows under the trees' concealing cover. Their draped leaves surround us on every side, enclosing us in peaceful shade. Right when Morgan looks up, meeting my eyes, the wind blows gently through, rustling the leaves, sending stray petals from outside dancing to our feet.

It feels . . . paranormal.

When some of the petals catch in Morgan's hair, she laughs that same dauntless, silver-sunshine laugh. She sweeps her hand through her chestnut locks, picking for petals with mediocre success.

Undeniably drawn to her, I step closer. I reach up tenderly.

Morgan's breathing stills. Her eyes hold my gaze while I pluck each rose petal. Her lips open in imitation of their shape, her cheeks matching their cream-pink hue.

My heart pounds painfully in my chest. Change is coming. I feel it throughout my whole body. My first kiss with Morgan was confused, impulsive, grief-racked.

It wasn't perfect, which means it wasn't enough.

I lean in, cradling Morgan's head in my hands, perfectly positioned from where my fingers roamed her hair. Now they caress her pinkening skin.

Morgan holds my stare. Her mouth slants up.

When my lips meet hers, she gasps. I think I do the same. Every moment feels like passion in bloom, like something once concealed underground now unfolding into gorgeous color. I'm swept up in the beauty of change—the surreal sweetness of kissing this woman who feels like life herself.

For just one moment, I let it leave me weightless.

30

SAWYER

I wake the next morning to the sound of birdsong outside my window. I've never noticed it before. It's beautiful, the perfect complement to the sunlight peeking through my curtains.

My room is bright and warm. I stretch in my sheets, savoring the moment. Something feels distinctly different today. It's like I've only half woken. My body may be in reality, but my mind is still in the lingering embrace of dreams.

Except, the longer I blink sleep from my eyes, the feeling doesn't disappear. It's not a dream, I realize. It's something else. Something as intangible and intoxicating. Something transformative.

Hope.

For the first time in years, I'm *hopeful*. The day awaiting me outside my windows is lovely. How many lovely days have I ignored? I won't ignore this one.

Springing from my bed, I pull the curtains aside, hungry for sunlight. It's been so long since my room felt warm. I feel the heat everywhere on my skin like it's radiating from within me. Like kissing Morgan under the dappled canopy of the Huntington Gardens has lit anew the kiln in my heart, the fire ready to shape hope and imagination into something real. Just for a second, I close my eyes.

When I open them, I smile. Morgan is visible through my window. She's in the yard shoveling earth.

Suddenly, I vividly remember another morning weeks ago just like this one, except not. It's like warped déjà vu. On Morgan's first morning here, I woke up and saw her in the yard through my window. She had her hair up in a clip bun just like it is now.

And yet, *everything* is different, even though only the yard has changed. Only the yard . . . and me. On that morning, I was angry. Scared, even. I glared, frightened deep down of the disturbance in my isolation.

Not today. Today I'm hopeful. Happy.

Morgan spots me over her shovel, and I wave. She's stunning, shining with sweat and sun. Dirt freckles her face, dusts her arms. When she beams at me, I feel it like a punch to the heart.

It hurts, but only because it forces me to remember how alive I am. How fragile yet precious the rhythm in my chest, the rushing in my veins. I want to feel it all.

Warmth spreads through me—warmth and light. Hope is addictive, and I can't get enough. I can't wait to join Morgan outside, to make her laugh, to see her tomorrow, to—

Suddenly, my world slants sideways. I stagger backward. My breath catches. This isn't merely happiness. It's overwhelming. Dangerous. I feel a shift in my room. The sunlight flickers. The air hums. I turn, gasping sharply.

Kennedy stands in my doorway.

It's been weeks since I've seen her, and yet it feels like it's been years. Five, to be exact. Her raven hair is loose, dangling down her shoulders. Her expression is serene despite the tear slipping down her cheek. She's glowing with ethereal light. A moon in my sunlit day.

I rush to her. Something is very wrong. Panic clutches my heart, constricting everything in me.

Kennedy doesn't react. She doesn't look afraid. "I'll always love you, Sawyer," she says. Her voice is hushed and yet so loud in my silent room. When did the birds stop singing? "Thank you for giving me a love so few people ever experience in their lives. I don't have a single regret."

I can't process what she's saying. Why is she here now, after staying absent for so long? It's all I can focus on. "What?" I ask, trying to clear my head. "Stop. Slow down. You sound like you're saying goodbye. We haven't even finished the yard yet."

Kennedy smiles softly. "I *am* saying goodbye. What a gift it is to have the chance. It's time. I'm ready." Her voice doesn't waver. "You are, too," she continues, sounding confident. "I'm so happy, Sawyer. For the first time in years, I'm happy. You deserve everything."

In a painful burst, my heart restarts. I realize what she's saying. Devastation sweeps through me.

"Kennedy," I plead. Her name comes out strangled. "No. No! What's happening? Stay. Explain what this is. I don't understand." My voice breaks. I desperately hope I'm not understanding, at least. She can't be leaving. *Moving on.* She can't be. Not now.

I was supposed to know when it would be. I was supposed to prepare. We have weeks left on the yard. If I'd known today, then—

I can't contemplate how I'd have spent my last day with her. It's too painful.

I remember our first kiss. She tasted like lemonade. The day I proposed. Sunset after the rain. Every happy day wasn't just leading to *this*. It wasn't. It wasn't supposed to end this soon. In this room, unceremonious, without warning. Dreams shattered by morning light.

My heart breaks all over again. Newly healed scar tissue shreds in seconds. I don't know how to make sense of the conflicts in me. I kissed Morgan yesterday. Today I'm desperate to hold on to Kennedy. I know I can't have both. Sun and moon at once.

I could figure it out, though, I insist to myself, desperate. I could process my new feelings for Morgan and the feelings I'll forever have for Kennedy. I could piece myself together. I just need time.

Kennedy grows brighter.

I don't have time. *We* don't have time. We've never had enough. Not from the first lemonade kiss.

I choke out a sob. If these are my last moments with my first love, I don't want to regret them. I won't spend them stuck in what should have been or reasoning with the unreasonable forces of the universe. I need to be here, with her. For all that we have left.

"I'll always love you, Kennedy," I say. I force my breathing to steady. I can crumble later. After . . . after . . . "You'll always be with me. *Always.* I'll never forget—" There's so much I want to say. Millions of moments that have made a lifetime in our too-short romance. Moments that I'm grateful for despite the pain I now know loomed behind them. I can't get them out, not fast enough.

Kennedy seems to know. She reaches for me, and for the first time in years, I can *feel* her touch. She squeezes my hand, her skin more than a memory.

"I know," she tells me. "I know."

She's really here with me. It's wonderful and horrible, because I know this truly is the end.

The light grows brighter. I stare into her eyes, forcing out the blinding pain for just as long as I can to look at her. I want to memorize everything about her. The faint lines at the corners of her eyes that never got to become wrinkles, the shadows of her eye-lashes, the shade of her lips. If I can just have one second more, another, one more—

I close my eyes as white envelops the room. Holding on to her, I squeeze her hand. I won't let go. I can't—

The light fades. I open my eyes.

Kennedy is gone.

31

MORGAN

When the front door slams open, I spin to find Sawyer.

His hair is mussed, like he's run his hand frantically through the brown waves. His shirt is askew, his eyes wide with panic. Racked exhaustion vibrates on his features.

I rush to him, knowing something is wrong. "What happened?"

Sawyer stops short of me. Like he wants me nowhere near him. The sunlight glares harshly on our non-reunion. "She's gone," he says.

His hollow intonation clenches my chest. I need no confirmation of who he's referring to or how he feels. What Sawyer's saying is hauntingly clear.

"Kennedy," he continues, exhaling shakily. "She . . . she said her goodbyes and she's gone. Really gone. Forever."

He mouths over the words like he's eating glass. *Forever.*

He doesn't cry. He looks like he's in too much shock. While Sawyer's world collapses, the garden paints the scene garishly— the clean white home gleaming, the palm fronds swaying gently overhead.

I want to comfort him the way I did the night of our first kiss. Feeling useless in my gardening gloves, I reach out for him. "Sawyer, I'm so, so sorry—"

He steps back. Something sharp pierces the shock in his eyes. "It doesn't make sense," he insists. "We never finished the yard. Her unfinished business is still unfinished."

Her unfinished business.

Realizations rip into me. Kennedy's unfinished business was not Sawyer's untangled garden. I know it wasn't.

But Sawyer doesn't.

I have to explain to him what Kennedy shared with me, but the very idea makes words lodge in my throat. I don't know how I'll possibly tell Sawyer that what Kennedy really wanted was for Sawyer to move on. To embrace the possibility of new life, of new love . . . with me.

The fact Kennedy has finally passed on is paranormal proof of Sawyer's feelings for me. It's a haunted love note written in vanishing ink. His unspoken confession sculpted in the supernatural.

I remember passing a car crash driving on the 405 freeway. Metal on metal, collided forms wrecked into unrecognizable shapes. To say my heart feels like the collision is an understatement.

I *want* to feel the happiness this means for me. Living city to city, I never expect to matter much to neighbors, coworkers, one-night stands or one-month flings. The rotating cast of my mutable life.

With Sawyer, it's different. With Sawyer, I not only fell in love. I fell into the reckless hope that I might matter to him the way he does to me.

Now I know I do. Every moment of closeness opened his heart the way he won mine. Every connection was reciprocated. Our kiss under the Huntington Gardens' weeping peppermint trees—the greatest of my life—captivated him the way it undid me. *He loves me.*

I want to feel this joy with him. But I can't. Not yet.

"Sawyer, the yard was never Kennedy's unfinished business," I say carefully. "She didn't stay for the house. She stayed for you."

He watches me, clearly sensing there's something I haven't revealed yet. "How do you know that?" he asks.

I'm proud of myself for holding his gaze. I want to skip this part. I want to escape this conversation into my secluded guesthouse, my gardening with plants who never, ever ask impossible questions.

Sawyer deserves the truth, I remind myself, mustering my nerves. He deserved the truth a long time ago.

"The night we . . ." I start.

I can't quite force the word *kissed*. Sawyer's stare won't let me. The only way out of this mess, I know, is to keep going. I can't stop in the middle and expect ghosts to clear away this debris.

"Kennedy came to me. She told me she needed you to move on," I say.

Sawyer's jaw clenches, his posture stiffening under the palms. When he replies, he's clearly restraining his voice. "You didn't— neither of you—told me." His eyes water. Like his indignation, his rage, has found the only outlet they could.

"I'm so sorry," I rush to say. "We should have. Kennedy believed you wouldn't listen to her. That if she told you, it would just close your heart to—"

To me.

"I didn't know how to tell you, either," I say, speaking quickly, skipping what I can't bear to have him reject. "I didn't want you to think I was encouraging you to forget her, to choose . . . someone else," I finally say. "I—I'm sorry."

Sawyer does not look forgiving.

Familiar grief cracks his features now. His face contorts until he controls himself. "I don't understand," he says. "Why now? Nothing changed. We kissed yesterday, but . . . it wasn't . . . It can't be because of that, or she would have left yesterday. It has to be something else."

I hate the jealous voice whispering in my heart. *It wasn't what?*

I never wanted to be part of a love triangle with a ghost. I never signed up to pull Sawyer from his tragic true love. When I proposed we figure out our hauntings together, I envisioned swapping notes on occult rituals or recommending witchy tomes to each other.

Not this.

Instantly, my jealousy leads me to embarrassment. Wasn't I just overjoyed that I—the wonderful, memorable Morgan Lane—had healed Sawyer with the overwhelming power of our love? *Who the fuck was I kidding?*

I honestly thought Sawyer wanted something deeper with me. I thought the softest, most tender kiss I've ever experienced meant he saw something special enough in me to help him past his grief. *Of course* he would rather hold on to his ghost fiancée instead. I'm not Sawyer's love. I'm his fucking consolation prize.

Which Kennedy knew. It's why she never told him. She said so herself. Sawyer could never want me if he knew he might lose her.

Shame blooms red in my face.

"What were you doing right before Kennedy said goodbye?" I manage.

Sawyer looks uncomprehending. "I . . . I waved to you."

I stifle my wounded indignation. "Well, like you said, I guess it's not about me or us or whatever. Waving at me isn't anything," I return.

I falter when Sawyer goes pale. He looks like Zach when he lost control in the ghost-quake.

"It was," he replies. "I thought you were gorgeous, and I couldn't wait to go outside and start the day with you."

My breath catches in my chest.

Sawyer reels like speaking the words has physically wounded him. I'm no ghostly love note, I realize. I'm the shards of something once beautiful, now shattered and embedded in his heart.

Sawyer stumbles backward. He sits down hard on his front steps. His eyes fill with tears. Looking lightheaded, he emptily surveys the yard. The horticultural canvas he offered me, unfinished now.

Stunned, I feel my own tears stinging my eyes. Sawyer didn't use the words, but the feeling he's described—*I couldn't wait to go outside and start the day with you*—that's love.

It panics me, because Sawyer looks . . . miserable. God, it's just like the night we first kissed, isn't it? Why don't we get some ghostly Etta James playing? Sawyer loves me and hates himself for how he feels. He hates loving me.

This isn't how we should share our feelings for each other. It's horrible. It's so desperately unfair.

Sawyer looks at me, his eyes red-rimmed. I can't meet his wretched stare. "It's my fault," he says, realization making his voice empty. "I'm falling in love with you. I love you, and it's cost me the final piece of Kennedy forever."

I love you.

I want to plead with him not to say those three words. Not when they do this to him. Love shouldn't do this.

I fall to my knees in front of him and remove my gardening gloves. Venturing to reach out, I put one comforting—I hope— hand on his forearm. "It's not your fault. You're human, Sawyer," I say. "You can't stop how you feel. You can't stop your own heart."

His stare goes vacant. "If I'd never met you, she'd still be here," he says. "It's like I've killed her." He drops his head into his hands.

My heart splits. I want to hold him, kiss him, help him. I know Sawyer wants none of those things, though. On my knees, I have nothing except my words. "You can't kill someone who isn't alive," I say. "She was already gone, Sawyer. She wanted to leave. She was ready."

Sawyer doesn't speak. He doesn't need to. His silence, his posture, screams everything. *He* wasn't ready.

I stay kneeling, feeling like I've found a wounded animal on the side of the road. Desperate to help yet having no idea how.

Finally, Sawyer's breathing slows. I'm relieved, until he looks up.

Something I've never seen shadows over his face. Sawyer hasn't healed his pain. He's smothered it in fury. "You should have told me," he says. Every word is deliberate, unflinching. "If you'd told me that night, I would have asked you to leave. I would have saved Kennedy. I would have kept her here."

My knees weaken under me. His words rip through me, shredding my heart until it looks just like his.

I knew he would choose her. I knew he would choose her, I remind myself ferociously. Maybe, I reason, I can make myself hurt less the way Sawyer did—by changing pain into anger. I rage at my naivete, my unimportance in the tragic schemes of the lives of others, my foolishness in imagining I could have meant more to him.

"You did save Kennedy," I say, voice wavering. "By letting her go."

Sawyer doesn't react. The silence in the sunshine is crushing.

He isn't hearing me. He can't.

When he speaks, his voice comes out clear and empty. Sculpted and hollow, like one of his ceramic creations. "With Kennedy gone, the yard doesn't ever need to be finished. Your work here is done," he says. "You should leave."

I let his rejection crash over me. I use the hurt to feed my anger. "You're right. I certainly have no other reason to stay," I reply.

Sawyer offers no objection.

I grab my gardening gloves off the ground, feeling infuriatingly helpless. I remember how optimistic Sawyer made me. Not just hopeful. *Optimistic.*

Un-fucking-believable.

I should never have stayed here. I should never have stayed in Sawyer's life. Staying isn't what I do.

I'm free to do whatever I want, I remind myself resentfully. If what Sawyer wants is to live in his house that no longer has a ghost but is certainly still haunted, then fine. I'm done.

Fighting down sobs, I return to the cottage, ready to pack my whole life up once again.

32

MORGAN

"You know he didn't mean what he said." Zach follows me from my car up the concrete path where I'm prohibited from gardening. While I wish his comfort reassured me, instead I can't help remembering how *often* my ghost has repeated similar sentiments. *Sawyer has feelings for you, he just won't say it. He's just scared. He'll come around.*

Will he, Zach?

The echoed consolations make them feel like Zach himself, floating up next to me on the walk to my old apartment—transparent.

Sunset is scorching over West Hollywood when I open the rusty metal gate. It's comically gorgeous, the sky on fire, showing off in shameless mockery of my miserable homecoming. We parked on the street, not far, funny enough, from where my first hookup with Zach occurred.

"It doesn't matter," I reply. "*I* meant what *I* said."

On the drive home, I dug deeper into my heartache. I reminded myself why I never get committed. To cities, to people, to romantic versions of myself. I remember the upside-down gift of my un-abashedly migratory lifestyle—it keeps me from *this*.

Zach, for his part, remains uncharacteristically serious. "No. You didn't. You should have some compassion for the guy," he re-plies. "Imagine what he's going through."

I've never heard Zach this accusatory. Not just frustrated with his own paranormal limbo. Not just irritated when I won't watch Netflix with him instead of performing my paid employment. Zach has been reprimanding me the entire way over while I ignore him.

"I've had compassion," I shoot back. "I've been nothing but compassionate. I didn't ask to be the thing that ruined his fucking life. I didn't ask for any of this."

Zach vanishes momentarily. He rematerializes suddenly on the stairwell in front of me, startling me.

"Sawyer said he loves you," Zach insists. "Does that mean any-thing to you?"

When my heart rate slows from Zach's disappearing stunt, I glare. "Yeah," I retort. "Then he kicked me out of his house and his life. *That* means plenty."

"It shouldn't," Zach insists.

I do *not* need this right now. What I need right now is mint chocolate chip ice cream and non-haunted time to scroll puppy videos on social media and cry. Not the ghost I can't get rid of re-minding me of every hurt I would like to ignore.

Instead of debating Zach, I walk right through him.

When the unpleasant cold ebbs from my skin, I round expec-tantly only for Zach to disintegrate while regarding me with disap-pointment.

Whatever.

I continue up the stairs with heavy footsteps. When I unlock the door with my old key, I find Savannah washing dishes inside. She looks up sympathetically. "Hey, you okay?"

I told her everything over the phone on the drive. Sawyer, Kennedy, *everything*. "I will be," I reply honestly.

Savannah smiles weakly. "Still haunted?"

Entering my old temporary home, I drop my keys in the entryway dish. The routine is painfully familiar. Like I never left. Thanks, universe, for the reminder of just how insignificant my weeks with Sawyer were.

"You have no idea," I say. The words come out so heavily even I wince a little.

When Savannah has no reply—she holds the soapy pan she was working on, watching me worriedly—I heft my suitcase in the door and resolve to lighten my disposition.

"I won't be here long, I promise," I reassure her, knowing commiseration was not the reason Savannah inquired into my supernatural state.

She looks conflictedly relieved. "Where will you go?"

The old furnishings of my bedroom greet me when I drag my suitcase inside. They're exactly how I remember, yet distant. Just because I know this place does not mean it feels like home. It's horrible how quickly somewhere else did—somewhere with a pottery wheel in the corner and a monstrous garden outside.

Noticing my old windowsill, I realize I forgot my purple coleus.

"Anywhere," I say. Then I shut the door.

Zach rematerializes when I unzip my suitcase. I'm grateful for the effort not to surprise me this time. He watches me, dismayed. I ignore him.

Leaving everything else packed, I pull my laptop from my luggage. Without hesitation, I open my computer on my old desk and set to work.

I search landscaping job listings in other states. I scroll, hunting for wherever is hiring soonest. I don't care where. New Hampshire, New Orleans, Newport. New Morgan, new life. It's the only way I know to escape the hopelessness settling over me.

Zach's distraught expression, shimmering semiopaque in the corner of my vision, makes me feel guilty for giving up on his unfinished business. But why should I derail my life for someone else again? Look where that got me today. I probably wouldn't even help Zach. I would just ruin someone else's life—or afterlife.

"Looks like you're stuck with me," I say. "Surely you could do worse, right?"

Zach floats forlornly through the wall in reply.

33

SAWYER

My guesthouse is haunted.

Not with the ghost of Zach, the spectral new friend I had the genuine pleasure of welcoming into my life. Not even with Kennedy. The onetime love of my life is now, finally, nothing except ashes.

No, it's not a ghost that haunts my pottery studio. Only a memory.

Stepping inside, I find myself wishing I could exorcise Morgan from this place. I wish there was some ritual I could perform to forget the day we sheltered under the table—earthquake water soaking her clothing and tangling her hair—or to expel the many times she greeted me at her door, hair up and eyes bright, or to erase the nights I would help carry in her gardening supplies, hoping my understated humor might make her laugh.

Without her, the silence in the studio is punishing. The lack of joy is oppressive. The sunlight, which once reminded me of Morgan herself, now seems only to emphasize the room's emptiness.

She left her purple coleus on the windowsill. I deserve that insult, I guess. That doesn't mean I know how to heal from it.

I ignore the innocent plant. What would even be the point of moving it? The whole front yard is a cemetery of Morgan memories. My house, my refuge from the world, is now what I seek to escape.

My unease has led me out here into the studio. The guesthouse I couldn't confront until now, so sparse without Morgan's MacBook on the counter, her charger on the nightstand, her laughter in the daylight.

I'm glad she washed her sheets on her way out. I couldn't bear the smell of her lingering where she isn't.

I haven't dared come out here in the five wretched days since I told her to leave, wrapped up in guilt, righteousness, and loneliness. Fuck, I don't even know why I'm here now. I'm hurt. Confused. Lost. Fleeing from myself, I guess. With nowhere to go except this mausoleum.

Perfect conditions for throwing pottery, my subconscious has decided. It makes no sense. I avoided pottery for so long, and now, after losing Kennedy and Morgan in one day, I hope desperately art will somehow help heal the impossible wounds of my heart.

Moving mechanically, I pull the wheel out from the corner. *Like when I showed Morgan*, I can't help remembering, then chastise myself. *Not everything is about Morgan.*

I sit. I put clay on the wheel, wet my hands, and breathe in deeply. I don't know what I'm going to make. The best I can do is . . . follow my instincts. Let my hands show me what I need. I don't even care what—I just need to create something, to shape something new. Instead of only wrecking everything.

Putting my foot to the pedal, I work the wheel steadily, rhythmically, watching nothing in front of me spin.

Then I place my hands on the gray form. The clay undulates under my grip, coating me quickly in residue the color of ash. Of earth. What everyone becomes in the end. What Kennedy is now.

I shape and sculpt, and it's like crying the tears I no longer have. I've run out, leaving my eyes swollen and my head throbbing.

I let the wheel pick up momentum, spinning the clay under my hands with unnatural life. It's hypnotizing, terrifying, thrilling. I could do anything. I could do nothing.

Like an exhale, I make my first choice, cutting into the clay with my thumb and my palm. Slowly, miraculously, nothing turns into something in front of me.

I close my eyes and let it ground me. Finding my way home to my craft, I start to imagine I'm not just lost. Not just stuck. Like I'm moving *toward* something. Some shining light, some nearing sun.

Like I felt with—

No. I focus on the clay, choosing to feel my way onward.

It helps. The pain lessens, just a little, as I'm forced to hold on to a shape I can't see. Finally, my instincts stay my work, like phantom hands on mine—figuratively speaking, for once—pulling my fingertips from the thing I've formed.

I open my eyes.

It's . . . not nothing at all. In fact, I recognize it instantly. Surprise rips through my sadness, because I know *exactly* what my subconscious has pulled from the earth.

34

MORGAN

I savor the satisfying rip of packing tape as I seal my first box shut. I wish I could pack away my heartbreak as cleanly as I can my gardening tools.

It's been two weeks since I left Sawyer's. Two weeks in which I've applied and interviewed for every landscaping and gardening job I could find. This morning, I got my first offer. It's in Massachusetts. The pay is shit and the company is uninspiring, but it's corporate landscaping and they want me to start as soon as I can relocate.

They have no idea how soon Morgan Lane can relocate.

I went out and bought moving boxes immediately. It's a Friday afternoon, so I figure I'll pack all weekend, then tell my current job I've received a new offer on Monday morning. I can be out of this cursed city by the end of the week. Just the thought of shipping my possessions across the country makes me breathe a little easier. I don't want to leave a single trace of myself behind here.

Of course, I'm an excellent packer. I can look at any room and know exactly how many boxes to buy and in what sizes. I know how much weight I can pack before I risk damaging the contents or being unable to lift the box by myself.

Usually, leaving a city is bittersweet. I don't like to stay, but I allow myself some sentimentality. It's how I've ended up with small souvenirs from every place I've lived despite my spartan existence. Art, local jewelry, decor—things that last.

I have nothing from Los Angeles. It would have been the purple coleus, but I left it at Sawyer's and there's no way I'm returning for it.

Besides, I couldn't stand to look at it. Sawyer likes to surround himself with misery. He can keep it. I'd rather forget Los Angeles anyway.

The Sharpie I'm reaching for rolls spontaneously off my bed.

Okay, it's not entirely true that I have no mementos from my time here. I have a ghost. Who needs a souvenir when you have your dead ex for the rest of eternity?

I reach for the Sharpie, glaring where I hope Zach can see me. He's going to be a hindrance to my packing, I can tell. He makes few things in my life easier, and after he's spent the past weeks guilting me, I have every reason to expect packing up my room will be my biggest challenge yet.

I do feel bad. I know I'm taking him away from his home, his unfinished business, his family. But I have to live my life. His existence isn't worth more than mine just because he's dead. Arguably, that's even more justification for not letting him derail my *actual* existence.

Still, I want him to be happy, even if I can't do everything he wants. I reminded him that the beaches in Massachusetts are where *Jaws* was filmed, and this cheered him a little. Then I told him it's only temporary. Everything in my life is temporary. Except for him.

He's welcome to choose the next city we live in, I promised. Maybe he can still get something out of this afterlife. We can travel to every beach he wanted to surf, go whale-watching, follow Carly Rae Jepsen on tour, maybe even try living on a houseboat or something. I can make anything work but Los Angeles.

He'll be okay. We both will.

I finish labeling my box and return my Sharpie to the bed. It promptly rolls off again, then continues to roll all the way under my closet shutters.

I sigh. I hope in my next place, Zach's haunted nook isn't where I keep my most expensive sweaters. Maybe he could haunt the cabinet under the bathroom sink or something.

I decide I might as well tackle my paranormal hot spot now. All the clothes I didn't bring to Sawyer's, like my winter gear, are in danger of Zach's "accidental" psychic shredding until I can fold them neatly in boxes. In Massachusetts, ruined sweaters won't do me any good when winter comes.

I prep a new box, using the exactly perfect amount of tape needed, while my hangers rattle ominously behind the wooden slats I always keep shut now. Yes, better to do this now, while the sun is still up.

Steeling my nerves—and pushing away all memories of facing down Zach in a dark garage while wearing Sawyer's shoes—I throw open the closet doors.

Quickly, I grab hangers without seeing them and toss them carelessly back onto my bed. My heart pounds. It's not that I'm afraid of Zach, exactly. When he's *Zach*, my ghost friend, I'm not startled at all to see him floating through my walls. But over the past couple days, there have been more instances of him doing serious ghost shit. He's stood in dark corners, staring through me and talking nonsense to himself. I woke up one morning to water dripping on my face. The frozen pizza I made the other day caught fire as I pulled it from the oven.

I think he's upset because we're leaving, and his subconscious is lashing out psychically. When we move, it'll be better, I hope. Or maybe I can condition myself to ghost scares by watching every horror movie ever since this is the rest of my life now.

With my sweaters rescued and no ghost goo or phantom plasma in sight, I decide to push my luck. I drop to all fours to pull out my shoes. It's suddenly ten degrees colder on the carpet. I shiver, remembering my hair dripping down my back while Sawyer guided me carefully through the dark—

I pull myself out of the past, focusing on my purple heels. Frantically, I fling shoes behind me. In the very back of the closet, behind my now empty shoe rack, I find my gym bag. Inside are the rock-climbing shoes I was looking for a month ago.

The bag is icy to the touch. I hiss in shock, dropping it sharply. The contents spill out across the carpet.

I suppose it makes sense. Zach has a lot of psychic energy attached to the gym bag. It's familiar to him. I brought it to our first and only date. It's actually the only part of my life that intersected with Zach's while he was alive.

I consider leaving it behind entirely, but I don't know how ghost powers are affected by cross-country moves. I can't risk Savannah's next roommate having a haunted gym bag in their room.

I back out of the closet, instantly feeling warmer, and grab a scarf I tossed onto the ground. Wrapping it around my hand, I clasp the frozen gym bag and shove it in the bottom of my box, then cover it with my snow boots and parka. Next, I turn to the contents that spilled onto the carpet. My rock-climbing shoes, of course, some Band-Aids, my water bottle, tampons, and—

I feel suddenly cold again. Frozen in shock, I stare at something that *definitely* isn't mine on my carpet.

A set of keys with a shark key chain.

"Hey, those are mine!" Zach exclaims chipperly, appearing inside the closet. For a moment, he flickers spookily, but as his eyes lock on the keys, his appearance sharpens. "Morgan," he says, his voice shaking. "Those are the keys to my van."

My heart races in my chest. "Why are they in my bag?" I get out, swallowing hard. All this time, they were *here*. It doesn't make sense. It can't. I reach for the keys, prepared for them to feel burning or icy. They don't. I pick them up, still moving slowly with disbelief. I've never seen these keys before in my life.

"I put them in your bag while we were climbing because I didn't want to forget them in the gym, and you were giving me a ride anyway, and then I—" His eyes widen as he realizes.

I straighten, gripping the keys hard enough for the jagged edges to dig into my skin. "You forgot," I say.

He gave me his keys, and he forgot, and I never knew, and I didn't go on another rock-climbing date until—until after he was dead and his paranormal activity kept me from my gym bag.

"To be fair," Zach says, "I forgot and then I also *died*."

My hands start to shake. "The closet was a clue all along," I murmur. "It was right here."

And we ignored it. Zach may have forgotten, but something in him remembered, causing his supernatural powers to flare whenever I was close to what he needed.

"If you hadn't driven my date away a month ago, I would have found your keys. None of this would have happened . . ." My voice breaks, crushed beneath my realization.

If I'd gone on that rock-climbing date, I would have found the keys. I would have returned them to Zach's family. I never would have needed to go to the haunting support group. I never would have met Sawyer. I never would have driven Kennedy away.

I wouldn't be heartbroken right now. Neither would he.

"That's not true," Zach replies sternly, his gaze finally leaving the keys to look at me. "If you'd found the keys then, you'd have had no idea what to do with them. Without Sawyer, we wouldn't have learned about the hardware store. We wouldn't have looked up my family. You wouldn't have talked to Ari or heard about my car. You wouldn't even know unfinished business is how to send a ghost on. You probably would have found the keys and thrown them out. I'd be stuck with you forever." His voice softens. "Not to mention, if you hadn't met Sawyer, he and Kennedy would still be stuck—"

I hold up my hand, not wanting him to finish that sentence. I hate that he has a point. About everything, except Sawyer and Kennedy, obviously.

"I guess we don't know what would have happened, and there's no point wondering about it," I say, eager to end this discussion.

Zach narrows his gaze. He knows I'm deflecting. I don't let him call me on it.

"Zach." I hold up his keys. "This is it. This is why you've been haunting me."

It wasn't random bad luck or because I was the last person he kissed. It wasn't that we had some special connection, like Sawyer suggested. I didn't steal his ghost from his family and loved ones, like I feared. I only stole his car keys.

I laugh suddenly, overcome. Fate isn't some invisible, incomprehensible force hurtling you into pain and frustration.

Fate is just a puzzle you don't have all the pieces to yet. With enough time, enough information, the picture starts to make sense. Maybe the picture of Sawyer and me will make sense one day, too.

I sink onto the edge of my bed. Maybe I *wasn't* just another senseless tragedy in Sawyer's life. Maybe I'm the lost car keys in his closet. Unfinished business. A missing piece.

God, I hope I'm a missing piece.

I don't know why Kennedy had to die. The truth is, she didn't. But she *did* have to move on. If I hadn't come into Sawyer's life, someone else would have. He's too good, too worth loving, to spend the rest of his life lost forever. I know that. It just sucks that the cost was my heart.

Still, with Zach hovering in front of me, I know there are worse prices to pay in this world.

He's silent beside me. He doesn't even seem like a ghost right now. For just a second, I let myself believe he's not. I let myself imagine he's alive. He's my friend. He's part of my future, not just my past.

That picture is a lie, though.

I look up at him, summoning a much stronger bravery than packing up haunted closets.

"Are you ready?" I ask, my voice a whisper.

Zach sits next to me on the bed. Between us are the keys—the literal keys to whatever is next for him. For a moment, we're silent.

Finally, he shakes his head.

"We don't have to unlock your car," I tell him. "We can go to Massachusetts, then in a year or so, we can go wherever you want next. Like we said. You don't *have* to finish this unfinished business." I hear it in my voice. Hope. Impossible hope. Maybe part of me does want to keep this one souvenir from a city I can't quite forget.

Zach meets my eyes. He smiles sadly, and my heart sinks. "I need to go," he says. "I can't explain it, but being here, it's like"—he looks around the room, the place his car keys brought him—"it's like I'm always wearing someone else's clothes. Nothing quite fits. This isn't my life, even if it is a life I might enjoy." He reaches for my hand, his touch slipping through me.

"I understand." I try to return his smile. I can't.

I didn't expect to like Zach by the time he moved on. I didn't expect to have to do this part alone, either. When he moves on, I'll be . . .

"You can take some time if you need. I can decline the new job. I haven't even put in my notice. We can stay as long as you want," I offer.

Zach stands. My ceiling fan spins lazily above him, disturbing none of his unruly hair. "I want to unlock my car," he says, his voice decisive. "I want to find out what I left behind. I just . . . I don't want to do this without . . ." He looks tentative. Like he has impossible hope, too.

"I know," I say, resigned. Now, I do smile, just a little. "You don't want to do this without him."

35

SAWYER

The summer heat is punishing.

I'd forgotten how it felt to toss and turn in too-hot sheets, to take lukewarm showers, to shove my sweaters into the farthest corner of my dresser. I've had to delve deep into the supply of old T-shirts I've barely worn in the past five years while Los Angeles swelters in ninety-degree sunshine.

It's not just the climate I find stifling. The house is . . . different. Everything is different. It's like with more emptiness, the space has become more suffocating. More like a tomb.

I would find the feeling ironic if I could have a sense of humor about my situation. Instead, I ignore the deeper problems like I ignore the purple coleus on the studio windowsill.

Sweating through my wardrobe of necessity, I hustle downstairs to meet my takeout delivery. My days consist even more now of solitary routines. Cooking, home maintenance, pottery. Repeat. Repeat. Repeat. Food deliveries offer pitiful interruptions from the monotony I have more or less embraced, like I'm some future post-apocalyptic refugee.

When I open the door, I'm almost hoping the DoorDash driver took long enough for my pad Thai to have gone cold, given the weather.

Hand still on the doorknob, I stop.

On my doorstep is not my dinner delivery.

Zach stands in front of me. He's semitransparent, as usual, but through his ghostly form, I see—

Morgan.

"Hey, man! I missed you!" Zach exclaims.

I can't stop staring through his translucent edges. "Zach, hi," I reply. "Is . . . something wrong?"

Of course something's wrong! my grief-won pessimism screams at me. I don't fight it. There's no other reason Morgan would ever deign to return here, right? There must've been some sort of ghost emergency. My heart skips a beat—*the earthquake.* Was there another Zach attack? Was Morgan hurt?

I resist peering closer around my spectral friend. I don't need to. Morgan steps aside grudgingly. She looks uninjured—in the physical sense.

There's no mistaking the reservation in her eyes, like fog finally settling over the golden light I found in them when I was close enough to have the chance. She does not look pleased to see me. She looks closed off.

Fine. Resentment kicks on in me. Yes, I didn't react perfectly to my fiancée essentially dying on me for the second time. Yes, I blamed Morgan instead of blaming myself. Forgive me.

In my minimalist boho tomb, I've had plenty of time to magnify my mistakes. I know I didn't handle Kennedy's final disappearance gracefully. But if Morgan really cared for me the way I very fucking obviously care about her, she would have had more grace for me.

I'm still pissed she didn't tell me what Kennedy's real unfinished business was. I know why she didn't; it's just . . . not only did Kennedy's departure hit me out of nowhere. Now I know the last week I ever had with Kennedy, she was hiding something from me.

With Morgan's help.

How can I not resent the woman standing in front of me?

Above it all, and hardest to confront, I hate how my feelings were exposed by tragedy ripping ragged edges in my life once again. I hate that the way Morgan found out I love—*loved*—her was Kennedy leaving. Why couldn't I just have one uncomplicated, normal thing in my life?

It doesn't matter now, I remind myself when Morgan crosses her arms in uncomfortable confrontation. It's dead and buried, like Kennedy. The look on Morgan's face says everything.

"I found Zach's car keys," she states.

Surprise makes me falter in my diligent defiance. The week I spent with Morgan hunting for Zach's lost keys was one of the most hopeful I can remember. The opposite of grief-won pessimism. Chasing possibilities with Morgan around Los Angeles felt like . . .

Like life.

Now Morgan holds those hopes in her hand. Literally, I notice. Metal glints from her fingertips.

"Zach wants you to come with us to go search the van," she continues.

Zach coughs pointedly. "*We* want you to come with us," he says. "It's not just me."

Morgan glares at him. Zach either doesn't notice or, more likely, doesn't care.

I look slowly to Morgan. Yes, I'm wondering whether Zach's positive spin holds even a hint of accuracy. "If you want me to come, then I'll come," I finally say icily.

Now it's me who earns Zach's exasperation. He rolls his eyes indulgently, his surfer's hair flopping to one side. "Guys, no one is going to die if you admit you miss each other," he chastens us.

Silence greets his choice of words.

"Bad joke. Sorry," Zach demurs.

Not even ghost puns can pull Morgan or me from our stern standoff. Neither of us looks at each other.

"I think I've admitted enough," I say, unable to keep from hearing my own anguished voice in my head. *I love you.* The way I spoke those words, they sounded like the sort of confession that leads to a guilty verdict and a gallows sentence, not . . . I don't know what. I don't know what I ever imagined with Morgan.

She scoffs. It irritates me.

"More than some, anyway," I add, sharpening my voice with accusation.

It works—momentarily. Morgan shrinks from my insinuation, then finds her fight. "You look flushed, Sawyer. Maybe it's time to install some AC. Or wait, no," she snaps. "Wouldn't want something in this house to actually change."

Zach steps into our fraught midst. "I think lots of great constructive feedback is going around. Nice work, you two," he says enthusiastically with very forced patience. "Let's think about those points on the road."

Morgan remains faintly visible past him. I drag my eyes from her.

"I'll come with," I declare. "For Zach."

36

Focus on Zach. Focus on Zach. Focus on Zach.

I repeat my stubborn mantra in my head the whole way to Santa Monica. Of course, Morgan and I drive separately out to Ariana's home on the sunset streets of the suburb. With no Morgan—no Zach himself, cheering my progress in my rearview mirror—my car feels painfully quiet.

But reminding myself of my postmortem friend motivates me. If we do finish Zach's unfinished business, he'll be leaving, just like Kennedy. So I should enjoy whatever final time we have left, like I couldn't with Kennedy. Even if it means dealing with Morgan.

I've survived worse. I can sort things out with her later. Or not. She isn't going anywhere.

I park behind Morgan underneath the two towering palm trees on the block. When I step outside, I'm pleasantly surprised—it's ten degrees cooler out here than on the Eastside. Santa Monica faces the ocean, ushering cool wind over the verdant streets. If nothing else comes of our visit to Zach's van, I'll count myself grateful for the reprieve from Silver Lake's unwelcoming climate.

The van in question waits in the driveway. I follow Morgan to Zach's sister's door. It really is lovely outside. If Morgan and I weren't fighting, I would suggest we walk to the pier. I haven't been since . . . I don't even know when. We could get ice cream or—anything but return to my sweltering, lonely house.

When Morgan knocks, no one comes to greet us. Not surprising, I guess. It's Friday night. Ari and her family probably have plans.

The memory of Zach stealing the dragon mug for his nephew leaps into my head. Knowing myself, I wait for it to sadden me. One more reminder of Zach's generosity of spirit, one more remembrance of what his disappearance will take with it from the world.

It doesn't. I only remember Henry's joy. I wonder if when people leave our lives, they eventually become nothing but the gifts they gave us.

Morgan knocks once more, then pulls a note from her purse, evidently prepared for this scenario. She slides the folded paper into Ari's mail slot.

"Should we come back another time?" I ask, hardly looking at her.

"No way," Morgan replies shortly. "We're getting this over with."

Well, nothing like some romantic scorn to dispel meditations on grief.

"Isn't it going to look a little odd if we're going through someone else's car?" I point out when Morgan, dauntless, walks into the driveway.

Zach glides down the steps, pretending he's sliding down the railing. I decide I give up on understanding ghost physics. "To be fair, it *is* my car," he says in Morgan's defense.

"You're dead," I reply. "I don't think *my friend's ghost told me to break into someone else's property* is going to hold up in court."

"Could be cool to try, though," Zach says without hesitation. "Courtroom drama meets *Ghost*."

I smile despite myself. Morgan does not. In fact, she looks like every second in my presence is ruining her day, while I was just welcoming the pleasant sunset. It's like we've switched places or something.

"We're not breaking into anything," she says primly. "We have the keys."

Without waiting for me to object, she unlocks the driver's side door. Zach shoots me a commiserative shrug.

Despite my misgivings, I find myself coming closer to the car. I'm not going to lie, I'm curious what unfinished business waits inside Zach Harrison's shiny, scuffed, sky-blue Volkswagen bus. Morgan opens the door—

"Oh," she says suddenly.

My heart rate speeds. "What?" I peer past her.

"It . . . still smells like him," Morgan says, half to herself. She sounds surprised and sad.

No scorn in the world can stop the wave of sympathy I feel for her now. Sense memory is powerful, often making the quotidian parts of loss the most painful. Doing the final load of Kennedy's laundry, erasing her scent from our home, was one of the worst experiences of my life.

Nevertheless, I stop myself from reaching out to comfort Morgan. It's not like she would want me to.

"Wish I could smell still. Bet it's great," Zach states proudly.

This manages to earn a smile from Morgan. "A mix of cologne and the beach," she says.

She climbs inside, then unlocks the doors. I pop open the side while Morgan searches the glove compartment.

Immediately, I'm hit with the scent Morgan just described. It saddens me for different reasons. I *don't* remember the smell. I never got the chance to know Zach when he was alive. While he feels like my friend, he's not, not exactly. He's dead, like I just reminded him. He won't be here much longer.

Determinedly I focus on what we're doing here. What I learned from losing Kennedy is that there will be *plenty* of time for grief later. Right now, I need to hold on to what I still have.

Surveying the van, I find Zach's car is surprisingly . . . clean, aside from some sand kicked into the carpet. I see no fast-food wrappers, no water bottles. "Nothing up here except a lot of sunscreen and sex wax and a couple receipts," Morgan reports.

"Sunscreen and sex wax and a couple receipts!" Zach repeats enthusiastically. "Sounds like a day well spent!"

I hide my smile. My pride won't let me let Morgan think I'm having fun.

She ignores his exuberance. "You really did like spicy food," she says, examining the receipts.

Zach climbs into the van and sits in the passenger seat. He looks, ironically, a little out of place. Which I guess he is. He's no longer the man who owned this car. Not really.

I diligently push past the thought, reaching for the blanket-covered shape I remember Zach noticed when he floated through the car on our first visit here.

Underneath the woven cloth, I find a surfboard secured to the wall of the van. Otherwise, a towel, a small bag with a change of clothes, swim trunks, and a toothbrush sit in the rear of the car. Pretty standard stuff for the van of a surfer. The surfboard snags Zach's interest—I notice him eyeing the fiberglass form wistfully.

"There has to be something here," Morgan insists, sounding frustrated. She snaps the glove compartment closed. "He wrote

A-N-A on the Ouija board. He haunted my closet until I found his keys."

"Maybe *he*"—Zach imitates Morgan's impersonal phrasing—"just wants to go surfing again."

"How are we going to get a ghost to go surfing?" I wonder out loud. Honestly, it sounds like the sort of movie Hollywood made in the sixties. *Surfin' Ghost Bonanza! Starring Zachary Harrison!*

Zach's forlorn expression compels me to keep this comment to myself. I reach for the surfboard, finding the shiny shape warm to the touch.

It's a promising, paranormal indication. I unhook the surfboard from the wall. When I lay the board down on its fin to view the top, the car shakes once, suddenly.

I meet Morgan's eyes. I have her full focus now.

While Zach and Morgan watch closely, I examine the surfboard. It's worn, covered in wax, but the art is unique. Over the red stripe down the center, dozens of hand-drawn squiggles and doodles cover the surface.

They look like . . . signatures.

"The Perfect Weekend!" Zach exclaims.

Morgan and I look at him.

"It's a tradition I used to have with my friends from high school," he explains eagerly. "For years, no matter where college and jobs and life took us, we made time to go back to the beach we spent our teen summers surfing at. But as everyone started to have kids or have more demanding jobs, it fell apart. We were bringing it back this year, though. Man, those trips were the best."

He reaches for the surfboard. Only when his hand nearly brushes the fiberglass does he remember he can't make contact. Like tradition—like everything—Zach possesses only the illusion of solidity.

"I really wish I could go one last time," he says.

He withdraws his hand, smiling fondly.

Then his expression transforms. In the same moment, the three of us realize what Zach's just said.

"Holy shit," he continues. "*I really wish I could go one last time.*"

"Your unfinished business," I say, locking eyes with Morgan. For the first time today, the sun in her gaze has parted the pissed-off clouds.

Of course, I realize, working backward. None of Zach's family knew of his surfing weekend because it was a lapsed tradition, years forgotten. Except not by Zach or his oldest friends. They brought it back to life. It makes perfect sense—and is so perfectly Zach—that returning to his cherished Perfect Weekend with his friends was something he wanted to do before he died.

"When is the trip?" I ask him.

"The last weekend in August," Zach declares, then looks stunned. Despite the inconsistent grip we've learned that ghosts have on memory and the passage of time, he remembered the trip schedule effortlessly.

"This weekend," Morgan exhales. "*This* is why your haunting started getting more intense when August began. We were approaching your trip and we didn't know."

She's right. Zach's erratic episodes, his losses of memory. He wasn't upset or fading. Something in him or surrounding him—I don't fucking know—was reaching out in the only way it knew how.

Even more incredibly . . . it *worked*. Everything led us here. Like Zach was crying out for help without knowing it, only for fate to deliver him exactly who he needed.

"But," I say, "we didn't miss it."

The relief is bittersweet. We've found Zach's unfinished business. It's within reach, which means Zach's departure is, too. I remind myself to stay present—future grief is not the same as grief—but damn it, does it feel that way.

I remember my vow. *Focus on Zach. Focus on Zach.* "Where is the trip?" I ask him.

"It's a beach in San Diego called San Onofre," Zach says quickly. "You can camp right next to the sand."

"San Diego isn't a far drive. I'll drive you out tomorrow," Morgan says.

Not *we*. Panic lances into me. I speak without overthinking and without my stupid fucking pride. "I'm coming with."

I look at Zach, doing what I never got the chance with Kennedy. Memorizing his friendly features, his sense of humor, the shape of his thumbs—sculpting them into memory with the hard chisel of knowing the last time is near. I focus on the fun we'll have on this trip. The memories I'll hold on to even when he's gone.

Zach grins, thrilled by my suggestion.

"That's not necessary," Morgan replies. "I'm sure you're . . . busy."

I hear the pointedness in her remark. *Busy doing nothing, in your empty house. Busy pointlessly mourning the past.*

"With Kennedy, she was gone as soon as her *business* was complete," I shoot back, making sure Morgan hears the reference to her own duplicity. "I'm not risking the likely possibility that Zach doesn't come back from this trip."

"Aw, man, I love you, too," the ghost himself interjects. He faces Morgan. "I want Sawyer to come."

Morgan is unwavering. "You guys can hang out all night tonight," she says to Zach with firm professionality. "Have a boys' night. I'll sleep in the pottery studio one last night. He"—she won't even say my name—"doesn't need to come with."

"Morgan."

I hear my own voice, stripped raw. I drop my rancor, my sarcasm, my defensiveness, my judgment.

When she reluctantly returns her gaze to me, I let everything I'm feeling onto my face. I show her every shattered piece.

"Please," I plead. "Don't. I've already had enough goodbyes sprung on me. Please just . . . let me do this one on my own terms."

Finally, sympathy flickers in Morgan's expression. Then regret. Over her shoulder, the Santa Monica sun slips past the horizon. "Fine," she concedes softly. "You can come."

My relief leaves me breathless. "Thank you."

Morgan doesn't smile, but she doesn't quite manage to frown, either. I'll take it.

For his part, Zach claps his semiopaque hands. "Fantastic. Oh, this is going to be the best. You guys are going to love the Perfect Weekend, and I can't wait for you to meet everyone. And the swells are fantastic. Oh, and the sunsets and the bonfires. Dude," he concludes. "It's the best."

Hearing his excitement, Morgan and I exchange a smile, only to quickly remember we're not on good terms. I drop my gaze to the van's carpet. Morgan stares determinedly down the street.

"Plus," Zach ventures. "You two on a road trip together. Spending the night on the sand—"

"We'll get a hotel," Morgan says stiffly.

"Definitely. Two rooms. Far apart," I corroborate.

Irritatingly, this only makes Zach grin. "Sure, sure," he reassures us, sounding like he knows something we don't. "I'm just glad I'll have both my friends with me for the end. Man, I couldn't think of a better way to go out," he says fondly, shaking his head. "It's going to be hilarious watching Morgan take a road trip with *two* of her exes."

37

MORGAN

The vibe is decidedly not chill in the van for our ghost road trip.

We set out early this morning. When I heard from Zach's sister last night granting us permission to drive his van to his favorite beach for a final tribute, we decided we wanted to maximize our time with Zach's friends. Sawyer took a cab to the van this morning, then drove over to my place under the cover of darkness to pick us up.

My phone read 5:07 a.m. when Sawyer's one-line message summoned me to my driveway.

Here

I should have deleted our texting history. It's too easy to scroll through our earlier conversations. *Favorite living tenant* lingers in iMessage, evidence of everything now ruined. It's the irony of our connection to Zach and Kennedy. Resolving their unfinished business will help them but not us. Love leaves ghosts everywhere.

Given the ungodly hour, I was prepared to sleep on the drive.

But when I opened the passenger door, scents from inside weakened my defenses. Everything-bagel spice and vanilla cappuccino. Sawyer had my coffee and breakfast order waiting for me.

I didn't say hello. Neither did he.

Still, I didn't sleep.

As we head onto the 405, the round headlights of Zach's van illuminate the darkness on the empty freeway leaving Los Angeles. I sip my coffee, feeling slightly less shitty. We're the only people out here, and I feel like we've stumbled into some ghostly plane of existence ourselves. The predawn night still covers the freeway in deep blue. The sound of our tires on the concrete feels small in the silent world outside.

Zach materializes in the rear of the van, his spectral cold making me shiver when he "leans" on my shoulder. If Zach fears his passage into the hereafter, he hasn't shown it. His presence has remained calm since our discoveries yesterday.

No complaints from me. It was nice to shower in normal-temperature water without fear of erratic heat fluctuations, and more importantly, I'll be free to go to Massachusetts without him.

With Zach's unfinished business still unfinished, deep down, I know I couldn't have left LA. The guilt would have pulled me back. He could travel and travel, from Massachusetts to Memphis to Montana, without ever leaving *here*. He would be stuck. I couldn't have stomached the cruelty of holding him here forever or until he vanished into nothing like Kennedy would have.

Now, when Zach is gone, I'll be completely free to move on. There will be nothing at all holding me here. Nothing to come back to.

I cling to that conviction as the clay and woodsy smell of Sawyer fills Zach's van.

"So, do you guys want to play the license plate game? I'd love to see Iowa before I die," he jokes wistfully, like he was reading my mind while I was ruminating on traveling from state to state. *Wait, can he read minds?* I reassure myself he could not have kept this ghost power secret if he possessed it.

"It's too early for road-trip games," I grumble, curling in my seat. It's not that I'm against the game itself. I just don't know how to spend two hours making conversation and joking around with Sawyer. Now I wish I'd ignored his coffee. I could have pretended to sleep. Foiled by my love for vanilla cappuccino, unfortunately.

Zach fakes offense. "I might be gone in a couple hours and you would deny me my road-trip games?"

"Yes."

"Cold," he complains.

"I'll play a road-trip game with you, Zach," Sawyer offers.

I would conclude Sawyer is fucking with me, except, irritatingly, he sounds like he's being sincerely friendly to our ghostly companion. "Don't bother," I interject impatiently. Is it healthy or normal not to want Sawyer to win points with Zach like divorced parents competing over our ghost child? No, it is not.

Do I feel that way? Yes. Yes, I do.

"He doesn't even want to play," I inform Sawyer. "He's just trying to get us to talk to each other. It won't work," I say to Zach, hoping he does not point out that it did, in fact, just sort of work.

Zach only winks in unashamed confirmation of his ulterior motives. He leans the other way to talk to Sawyer. "So, catch us up on your life since we moved out. How's the house?"

I notice Sawyer's knuckles tighten on the wheel. *Good.* "I've been spending more time in the studio than the house, actually," he says.

"Really?" Zach looks over. "Wow, isn't that interesting, Morgan?"

Okay, admittedly, it is interesting. The idea of our final fight, or

Kennedy's disappearance, releasing Sawyer's inhibitions in his pottery . . . I wish I didn't care about Sawyer enough for it to intrigue me.

So I pretend it doesn't. I won't walk into Zach's obvious manipulations. I'm here for *him*, to spend more time with my supernatural friend before he leaves, but my shit with Sawyer is mine to deal with or ignore as I see fit. Zach isn't caught between mortality and what lies beyond just to mess with my romantic life. That was Kennedy's thing.

I drink a deep sip of vanilla cappuccino instead of replying.

Zach presses Sawyer, dauntless. "You're making pottery again?"

Sawyer's eyes flash to Zach in the rearview mirror. "Every day," he says. "The studio is full of it. It's like I can't stop. Like everything I should have made for five years is flowing out of me. I've started reaching out to my old vendors, too. I have a couple commissions coming in."

I whip around to face him. "What have you been making?"

Wow, I chastise myself instantly. *Way to have zero impulse control or principled restraint.* Embarrassed, I face forward, pretending I did not just ask the question while a certain ghost gloats over my shoulder.

"Nothing," Sawyer replies.

Even if his lie stings, I can't help feeling a little relieved. Clearly he's no more interested in reconciling than I am. We don't have to pretend to make small talk.

He clears his throat like he's forcing friendliness. It reminds me of our first meeting. *Ghosts everywhere*. "I mean, it's not really anything that great," he explains. "Just whatever comes to me. You could come see—"

He stops himself. The silence hangs precariously in the car.

"You should totally go look at what he's made, Morgan." Zach very deliberately finishes what Sawyer clearly wanted left unsaid. "You need your Los Angeles memento anyway," he adds.

Well played, Zach, I nearly say when Sawyer's gaze flits to me.

"Memento?" he repeats, returning his eyes to the road. "Why would you need a memento?"

I grit my teeth, furious with Zach. You know what, forget my vanilla cappuccino. If I need to pretend to sleep to escape ghost-mandated therapy, I will. I close my eyes in quiet confrontation.

Naturally, Zach replies for me. "Morgan is moving," he informs Sawyer matter-of-factly.

I hear Sawyer scoff. "Of course she is."

My eyes fly open. Leave it to Sawyer to dispel my indignant pretend sleep. What right does he have to be dismissive of my choices? I fix my stare on him, the new object of my fury.

"I can't wait, actually. Massachusetts," I say proudly, hoping he hears the challenge in my voice. "I've never lived there, and I'm such a big fan of clam chowder and . . ." Okay, I'm struggling here. *Massachusetts. Massachusetts . . .* Inspiration strikes. "Dunkin' Donuts," I say.

"We have Dunkin' here," Sawyer says.

"It's not the same. I crave authenticity."

Sawyer shifts in his seat. His restless movement is the physical equivalent of grumbling. "So, you're moving because you have a sudden urge for *authentic* Dunkin' Donuts?"

I set my drink in the cupholder, ready to fight now. The fact is, Sawyer fucking *knows* why I'm leaving Los Angeles. He and his haunting have left me heartbroken. Just because it's not his fault doesn't mean it didn't happen, and he doesn't get to pretend my flight response to my fragile, messy life is some shameful character flaw.

If he's going to call out my Massachusetts bullshit, I'll give him what he doesn't want—the truth. "It's time for a change," I say. "I think I've gotten all I can out of LA."

Sawyer's grip clenches on the wheel. "Of course you have. Tell me, which plant will you reduce your time here to? Or since you're running away, does LA not get a plant?"

My cheeks heat. *Not cool.* While we walked the paths of the Huntington Gardens, I shared my life with him in the most honest, personal way I could. I dared to let him in on how I see my life like one vast garden, rooted in me but ever-changing, with room to nurture new blooms or tend to old reminiscences. Now he's thrown my happy memories—*our* happy memories, of kissing under peppermint shade, surrounded by so much life—in my face.

Clearly the moment is nothing but a point in an argument for him. Something to use to make me feel bad. Rocks to throw in my garden.

Well, two can play that road-trip game.

"Like you're any better than I am," I return. "I may be running away, but at least I'm running. You're not going anywhere."

Sawyer's jaw clenches, reminding me how horribly often I've seen him tense. It consumes him. I once thought Sawyer was chiseled of stone. He's not—he's encased in it. He's trapped in himself, miserable.

I don't give him the chance to reply. It feels good to get out my feelings. Perhaps this is the exorcism I've been looking for. "You have no dreams, no hopes, while you sit in your crumbling house wanting nothing but what's behind you," I say.

"If living in a crumbling house is the cost of feeling something real, it's worth it. You wouldn't know," Sawyer snaps. The stone cracks—the dam of his resentment bursts. He rages on, unable to stop. "You've never let yourself care about anything enough to be haunted by it. Who would you haunt if you were to die?" His voice is pinched with pain. His breathing is shallow with wounded fury.

I don't care. I don't even care how much his words sting. It feels good to hurt each other while we still can. One of the gifts of being alive, I guess.

"Hey," Zach chimes in. "Don't you just love the radio? Let's see what we got." He reaches forward, like he's hoping his paranormal proximity will summon some Kesha out of his old van stereo. He's obviously realized his efforts to conjure conversation from me and Sawyer have backfired spectacularly.

His ghostly powers work—smooth surf guitar emanates from the radio. Or maybe the van just likes him.

I don't react. Neither does Sawyer. We're not done yet. "Well," I say, "if *you* were to die, you'd have no unfinished business at all." I remember Kennedy's words. *Two ghosts living in this house for too long.* No. Sawyer, I've learned, is something more and something less than ghostly. Human but hollow.

"Good," he shoots back. "We wouldn't even be in this spot if Kennedy and Zach didn't have unfinished business. We wouldn't have even met."

The windshield wipers engage, their rubber thump momentarily startling on the dry glass while we rush forward into the dawn. *Zach.*

"If only we'd been so lucky!" I nearly shout. The words wrack my voice, because honestly, I don't mean them. I only wish I did. I fucking *wish* I hadn't felt every wonderful thing I did with Sawyer.

Now, I'll know what I'm longing for every day I don't have it. I'll remember what bloom in my garden he ripped up. It's gone now, but while it wasn't, it *lived*, flourishing in inimitable color.

He shakes his head, furious, looking like he wants to outdo me, to find something even more ruthless to say than regretting our ever meeting. He opens his mouth, his every muscle rigid. Suddenly—

Headlights explode from the near darkness. We round the freeway curve, moving fast, too fast, while they glare through the windshield, too close. Much too close. I should have known the freeway wouldn't be empty. This isn't purgatory. It's Los Angeles.

Sawyer pumps his foot furiously. "The brakes," he says. He stomps the floor of the old van. "They're not working!"

"What do you mean?" Panic flares hot in me. The headlights speed closer. Someone is driving on the wrong side of the empty freeway, speeding straight for us.

Sawyer releases his grip on the wheel with one hand.

While he flings his arm protectively across me, I scream into the oncoming light.

38

Morgan.

It's the only thought in my head. Everything else falls away. Memories don't flash in front of my eyes. I don't think about everything I regret, everything I still want to do. My life, at its end, isn't my focus.

Hers is.

I know I'm hurting her with how hard I pin her to her seat, but I need to keep her safe. It's the only thing I need. It feels comical, my arm against the weight of the world heading for her soft heart, as if I could possibly defy the laws of physics and nature.

But I've seen the laws of physics and nature defied before. I've seen Kennedy in my living room while her ashes rested in a box in my bedroom, my possessions moved without my ever having touched them. My car tire exploding, my garden cleared overnight, my house destroyed by an earthquake without a fault line.

There are forces stronger than the laws of nature. I'm determined to be one of them.

I have to be. I can't lose someone else. I can't lose *her*. Not the girl who makes me feel alive. The girl who brought me back from the dead.

I hold on tight, staring down our fate, then—

It passes through us.

I blink, focusing my sight on the road in front of us. There's . . . nothing. No car careening into us, no car behind us. The road is suddenly, completely empty, only our headlights breaking through the dawn.

In seconds that feel like hours, I become aware of my body. My heart thuds painfully; my lungs shudder. It's like I've been running full speed and told to stop in an instant. But nothing feels stopped.

Except, I realize we're slowing. The pedal has traction again, and I press it down, pulling to the shoulder.

My vision is still blotchy with panic as I flip on the hazard lights and unclench my aching knuckles from the wheel. I realize my right arm is still holding Morgan. It feels like breaking something in me to let her go, my body still convinced the danger will hit any moment. I don't know if I can.

Her face is too pale for me to look at, but I force myself to. I need to make sure she's okay. Her breath stirs the strands of her hair against her lips. The sight devastates and heals me. She's fine. Frightened but fine.

Shakily, I remove my arm and turn to Zach.

"What the *fuck*?" I demand. My voice is low with fury. "You could have killed us. What if I'd swerved into the divider or flipped the car trying to turn? That was completely irresponsible." Terrible what-ifs crash into my brain, leaving Morgan crushed in hundreds of horrible ways. My pulse thuds in my jaw. I feel like I can taste my own heartbeat.

The fear means I'm alive, I remind myself. I'm safe. Morgan is safe. But it feels like an illusion. Like those headlights. Every second of every day, tragedy lurks nearby. I can't believe I let myself forget it.

Zach doesn't look guilty, though I know he's the one to blame. "I had control of the wheel the whole time, just like the brakes. You were never in danger," he says, cavalier.

"It's not okay." My temper rises now, unfreezing me. "No backseat paranormal driving. What if we'd had heart attacks? You can't terrify us to get us to do what you want just because this might be your last day with us!" I shout. I'm picking up momentum. We didn't crash the car, but I'm still ready for collision. "We don't just exist to amuse you. We're your friends. Start acting like you fucking care about us."

I've never yelled at Zach before. I hate that I'm doing it now, on this day. But I owe it to our friendship to be real. I can't just hide my hurt so he goes peacefully. What would that leave for me? Only anger that will never fade.

"I *do* care," Zach fires back. "You think I did that for fun? You think me trying to get you to stop fighting for one day is out of *selfishness*? I won't even be here tomorrow. I have to make sure you two knuckleheads will be okay."

Emotion cracks his voice. He swallows, his eyes filling suddenly with unshed tears.

"You already have a reminder of how fucking short life is in the car with you right now." He hits his chest. His unbeating heart. "A literal ghost! And yet *still* you're wasting your precious, limited time arguing when you could be doing . . . anything. Making the most of the time you're lucky enough to have left!"

I've never seen Zach so upset. Sad, yes. Frustrated, sure. But he's scared. Maybe fear isn't a symptom of being alive after all. Maybe it's a sign of love.

I feel my anger fade as my pulse slows. I glance at Morgan.

Zach is right. I don't want to waste time with her. I already lost one love. Zach's stunt was reckless, but so is living. We're never truly safe. I should live every moment like headlights are bearing down on me.

Morgan draws a shaky breath, her first movement since the car stopped. She doesn't look at me. Instead, she twists in her seat belt to face Zach. "We're not wasting time," she says, her voice steady. "Sometimes arguing is important. It's part of living. Being here is . . . messy. It's imperfect. We're going to screw up, and we have to work through it when we do."

Her eyes flicker to me for just a heartbeat. "Fighting *is* making the most of our time here," she says defiantly.

I feel my breathing even. Her words weren't particularly kind. They weren't declarations of love. They weren't apologies. Still, I feel comforted by them. It's like what I was just thinking regarding Zach. How it wouldn't be right to the memory of our friendship to let him fade away without giving us a chance to work past my anger first.

Maybe living every moment like it's our last doesn't mean pretending nothing matters. It means pretending everything matters.

If we want to have any kind of future together, we have to fight. If we'd just wiped away the awful things we've said to each other for Zach, then when he's gone, we'd be left with something that might look like love, might sound like love. But it would be hollow, intangible. Only a shade.

Zach seems to consider Morgan's point with a level of thought I don't often see from him. He blinks his tears away. "That's fair," he says finally. "It's just . . . I need some indication that when I'm gone, you won't just cut each other out. I don't want to have been the only thing bringing you together. I don't want to go if that's the case, but I doubt I'll have a choice." He looks suddenly older. Like someone who's lived a whole life.

"You sure you don't just want us to ruin the Perfect Weekend for you?" I ask, summoning playfulness.

Zach smiles softly. "With your arguing, you have a decent chance. But then I'd just be here forever pestering you until you make up. I'm pretty sure Morgan would desecrate my grave or something."

Morgan laughs. The sound soothes everything in me. "How about this?" she says. "We promise not to ruin the Perfect Weekend with our arguments. We'll pick them up after you're gone. That way, you can go knowing that at the very worst, Sawyer and I will see each other again if only just to fight. That is, if Sawyer agrees." She turns her gaze.

Life fills my lungs. I smile. "It's a date, Morgan."

Our eyes lock. The moment stretches. Color returns to her cheeks once more. Rose red.

"You both said some seriously messed-up shit," Zach says happily, nodding as he thinks this over. "You definitely have a couple more rounds in you."

"Definitely," Morgan replies, still looking at me. She winks.

I pull my gaze from her, afraid of just how much I want to make the most of this moment. Not now, I tell myself. Later. I will defy any laws of nature that prevent a later.

When I restart the car, my hands are steady. I merge back onto the freeway, my heart pounding for a different reason now. I cherish every beat.

39

MORGAN

It's ironic, learning life lessons from a ghost. Yet Zach's words set in firmly with me and Sawyer, making us better behaved for the remainder of the hour-long drive.

We chat like old friends. Sawyer details more of his recent full-time return to pottery. I confess to forgetting my purple coleus in error, not to insult him. He promises I can come over to retrieve the plant before I leave.

We even play road-trip games with Zach. We spot license plates—Georgia, Washington, Nevada. Even my soon-to-be new home state. On the off-ramp to San Onofre, incredibly, we find Iowa. Zach cheers.

We watch the sun rise over the highway. My mood lightens with the morning sky. It's surprisingly easy with Sawyer to forget my resentment, my wounded indignation.

Not my regret, though. I wish I could take back what I said to him. Sawyer *does* have unfinished business. Every day must feel unfinished for him. Unlike our ghosts, what's missing from his world is something he can never regain, not with Kennedy gone for good. He's had to construct his new life on the shattered foundation of his old one.

I understand the fear it's left in him. I feel it in the bruise forming on my chest where he flung out his protective hand. An instinctual reaction betraying how unimaginable loss is never unimaginable for him.

But even more than that . . . I think it meant he might still care for me.

Yes, I know wanting to save someone from vehicular peril is not exactly equivalent to writing wedding vows. But in that moment, Sawyer's instinct was for me. It's not nothing.

I still care for him, I know I do. Despite everything, I do. I just don't know if it's enough, not with what he's been through. What *we've* been through. Zach or no Zach, Kennedy or no Kennedy, I'm pretty sure we're both haunted now by forces far more powerful than the paranormal.

It's why I'm leaving LA. Why I *have* to leave.

When Sawyer pulls the van into the sandy parking lot for San Onofre State Beach, I remember to focus on the now, not my impending departure. *Make the most of our time here*, like Zach said.

Our destination is intuitively obvious—the group of vans in one corner of the parking lot just like ours. I feel my heart quicken the way it did when I discovered Zach's keys. This time, this place . . . I've cherished my freedom in my decades of living everywhere, but I haven't often felt like I was where I was supposed to be.

It's nice.

Zach doesn't hesitate when Sawyer parks. The ghost glides through the wall of the van. "The swells are excellent already," he announces from outside.

Smiling, I reach for my seat belt.

Sawyer's hand on mine stops me. I look up, finding his gaze pained.

"Morgan, I—" he starts.

"It's okay," I preempt him. "Me too."

He nods, his relief visible. The inescapable tension in his posture relaxes a little.

"You make a pretty good seat belt, you know," I say.

Sawyer glances to where my shirt reveals red splotches on my skin from his forceful restraint. New mortification shadows over his features. "I'm sorry," he exhales. "I was so scared."

Reaching for the passenger door, I shrug. "I wasn't," I say. "Not with you."

Outside, San Onofre State Beach meets us in morning splendor. The shoreline is stunning. Not much has changed here for centuries, I would guess, except for the surfers enjoying the "excellent swells." Perfect light blue sky opens over the stretch of sand, the cliffs rising from the water with low grass covering their sculpted plateaus. The wind whispers over the coastline in the chilly morning.

While Sawyer is stepping out of the van, one of the surfers leaving the water pauses, seeing us. He picks up his pace, jogging in our direction while beckoning to friends on the shoreline. When he nears us, I hear what he's calling out.

"Ana!" he exclaims. "Guys, Ana is here!"

More surfers join him. Soon, everyone has assembled, surrounding us. Or rather, Zach's sky-hued van, Ana.

Zach watches the group, rapturous. They look like him, I notice. Not like relatives, but in the more important ways. They're his people. They share his sunlight-sharp, immediate exuberance.

"Everyone is here," Zach marvels, looking at each of his friends in turn. "Rick, Ben, Ashley, Layla, Otto. Wow, we all really grew up, I guess!"

The group's regard moves from the van to us. I understand the curiosity on everyone's faces.

I stretch out my hand toward the first person Zach mentioned. "Rick, right? I'm Morgan. This is Sawyer. We're friends of Zach's. He told us about the Perfect Weekend. We wanted to make sure to bring his van—um, Ana," I say, "and Zach's board out one last time."

Tears well in the widening eyes of the group. I prepare myself for their questions. *How did we know Zach? Why did he never mention us? Why didn't someone else, someone he told us about, drive his van out to the Perfect Weekend?*

The woman Zach called Layla steps forward. Without warning, she crushes me into a warm hug.

"Sorry if you're not a hugger," she says into my shoulder, sounding not sorry. I smile. "You just must have been really good friends of Zach's," she says. "Which means you're *our* friends now."

I hug Layla back, feeling tears of my own moistening my laughter. It's impossible how instantly I feel like I've known the Perfect Weekend crew for years.

I guess it's not the only impossibility of Zach's presence in my life, though.

"Yeah," I say wetly. "We were really good friends. Zach loved all of you guys so much. He told us how excited he was for this weekend with you all. How glad he was you'd brought the tradition back. He really wanted to go." While I can't tell them about his unfinished business, I can make sure they know just how important they were to him.

Zach smiles fondly. "Ask Ben how his kids are, and ask Ashley if she picked a wedding date yet," he requests. "Oh, and did Otto move to Boulder?"

I withdraw from Layla's embrace and look at the man next to Rick. "You're Ben," I say. He nods. "How are your kids?"

Ben sniffles. "They're good," he chokes out. "Really good. My daughter is into skateboarding. I think surfing will be next."

Zach laughs. "Hell yeah."

Sawyer steps up to my side. Like in Harrison's Hardware, his presence immediately steadies me. Solid, like the warming stone of the cliffs surrounding us. "And, Ashley," he says to the woman next to Rick. "You have a wedding coming up?"

Ashley beams. "Next summer. On the beach. Wish Zach could be there," she says, her voice wobbling.

Layla wraps her arm around her friend's shoulder. She really is a hugger. "He'll be there," she reassures Ashley, who nods like she's reminding herself.

I notice Sawyer watching their interaction with fresh pain clouding his features. I remember how he confessed to withdrawing when Kennedy died. The memories he regrets losing, the parts of Kennedy he never shared. The friendships he let vanish when he retreated into his haunted house.

I wonder if this is one of the ethereal gifts Zach might give Sawyer. When I'm gone from LA, maybe Sawyer will reach out to friends or family. Maybe he'll realize overcoming grief is easier when you manage it the way you might clear out a monstrous garden—with help.

"We'll bring a piece of him with us," Layla says to Ashley.

Zach straightens in inspiration. "My board!" he suggests.

I hear my cue. "You could take Zach's board if you want," I offer. "I know it's not the same, but it would be a piece of him."

Ashley looks up in wondrous disbelief. "Really?"

"Zach wouldn't have wanted it any other way," Sawyer says to her quietly.

Zach nods. I don't know if I'm just projecting or if Zach looks less insubstantial, more human. Like his ghostly form is responding to the fulfillment of his final wishes.

Recalling my last assignment from Zach, I look at the man who hasn't spoken, standing next to Layla.

"Otto," I venture. "Have you moved to Boulder yet?"

For some reason, everyone cracks up. Self-conscious, I look at Sawyer, whose confusion matches mine. Zach, for his part, is no help, grinning gleefully.

"Um, sorry if Zach was mistaken," I say.

"No," Rick replies. "No, Zach was right. See, dude?" he chides Otto. "Even beyond the grave, he knows you need to pull the trigger! It's been years! Do it for Zach!"

The chorus comes up from the crew—"Boulder! Boulder!" When they fall into rhythm, Zach joins in, first hesitant, then louder, though none of them can hear him.

Or maybe they can. Maybe he's a pop song stuck in their heads, a rattling in the cabinets of their hearts, a motionless earthquake in the sand under their feet.

Otto laughs, raising his hands in surrender. "Okay, okay!" he concedes.

Grinning, Layla looks at us. "Hey, Morgan, Sawyer. Do you guys surf?"

Sawyer shakes his head.

"I don't know how," I reply.

"I can teach you if you want," Layla says. "You could use Zach's board."

Zach's eyes round. He steps right in front of me, looking giddy. "Please," he implores. "Please take my board out, Morgan. Maybe"— he realizes—"maybe I can go with you. One last ride."

I hesitate. I hadn't planned on learning new water sports today, but . . . how could I deny Zach his Perfect Weekend dreams?

"Let's do it," I say. The group cheers. Zach fist-pumps. I guess I'm taking a ghost surfing.

I psych myself up—eighty percent of my recent living locales have been landlocked, and honestly, I'm sort of scared of the endless, powerful roll of the waves, the unflinching drag of the current.

Standing on the shore, though, I think of what really scares me. In the past months of my haunted life, my most frightened moments haven't been spooky supernatural occurrences or ghostly manifestations. They've been times of sharing the weight of grief or wondering whether I'd ruined someone's life or giving my heart to someone unexpected.

Sometimes fear is the ghost of love. The shadow drawn by the enormity of what it means to care for someone.

Zach needs this. So, for him, I'll get scared.

40

SAWYER

I sit on the beach, feeling the sea breeze ruffle my hair, the sand stick to my toes. Seagulls call above me, their cries and the crashing of the waves a symphony I could listen to all day.

It's hard to believe I was consumed by terror hours ago. I feel completely at peace now. Such a dramatic transformation seems like it should be impossible. And yet . . .

Change. The defining trait of living. Life might just defy the laws of nature, too.

No matter how bad it might get, how dark, how lost in grief, *this* is always possible. I want to sculpt something so I don't forget the serenity surrounding me. A vase with the texture of sand and the swirling colors of the ocean.

In front of me, Morgan is diligently listening to a five-person crash course on surfing. She nods, her brows knotted in concentration. She looks out at the vast ocean with apprehension, but she doesn't retreat. Gamely, she mimics what her instructors are telling her, pretending to paddle through the sand on her board, then hopping up in one fluid motion.

Everyone applauds and encourages her, like standing up on packed sand is anything at all like standing on the rolling waves of the ocean. Morgan swallows. She looks at Zach, who is smiling from ear to ear, and some of the fear leaves her face.

The surfers lead her out into the water. Zach crashes through the waves, looking like he's having the time of his life. Dipping her toes in, Morgan shivers, then seems to make a decision. I grin as she charges into the waves, dunking her head instantly. She comes up gasping for air and gorgeous.

As Zach's friends push Morgan into wave after wave, the tide surges. My feet get wet. This early in the morning, the water is cool. I don't mind it, though. The chill just makes me appreciate the sun on my face.

I lean forward, grabbing a handful of wet sand. Rocks eroded over millennia. *Earth*. Like clay. Like dust.

I mold it in my fingers into nothing but the shape of my palm, then release it into the tide, where it disintegrates and is swept out to sea, to Morgan. Nothing is ever really gone, I suppose. Only changed. Rock into sand. Us into dust. You can't erase a person completely, either. Kennedy's ghost is gone, but she's changed my world forever.

I hear a whoop from the sea and look up to see Morgan standing on the board for a triumphant five-second ride before she falls to the side. She comes up laughing.

I can't help smiling. Morgan is so fearless, so ready for new experiences, ready for everything. It's the opposite of how I've lived for five years. I was so afraid to let my world change, to lose Kennedy for good.

How foolish. I can *never* lose Kennedy. She changed my life every day I knew her, she made me *alive*, and then she changed it one last time. It was her final gift, I know now. To bring me to Morgan.

I want to be more like her. Morgan Lane is a force of nature, like the sun, the sea. An earthquake in my life, shaking my foundation until my walls crumble. Eroding my stone into sand and dust, leaving me exposed. I'm done pretending otherwise.

As I watch her cheering with Zach over her board, I feel like I did when I saw her in my garden. Heart-punched with longing, hope, affection. I know what the emotion is now.

Love.

I wait for the guilt to hit me. All I feel is the ocean at my feet, the breeze in my hair, the sun on my face.

The second love of my life learns to surf, turning a group of strangers into friends. She successfully rides waves, standing with one foot in front of the other, her mouth fixed in focus. I would happily watch her all day.

She's leaving, I have to remind myself.

But loss is only one part of love, I've learned. Losing someone doesn't make them any less worthy of holding on to while you can. I don't regret loving Kennedy for one second. And I won't regret loving Morgan, even if it's just for this weekend, just this day, just this minute. I can face the hurt later. I've survived it before. I'm not afraid.

When the sun is high in the sky, Morgan comes in from the ocean. Her hair is slick with salt water, her face golden in the sunlight, her smile wide. Zach jogs next to her, talking quickly and animatedly. I can't hear what he's saying, but I know he's happy.

I wave and stand to greet them.

"Dude," Zach says, "did you see her? She's a natural."

My eyes land on Morgan. "She was incredible," I reply softly.

She flushes. I think I might have actually flustered the fearless Morgan for a moment. She tightens her grip on her board, then turns to Zach, recovering. "Maybe our first date should have been surfing, not rock climbing."

Zach laughs, the sound another perfect strain of the day's melody. "Well, I'm really glad we got a do-over. As friends, obviously."

Morgan's eyes sparkle. "Me too. So what's next for the Perfect Weekend?"

"Anything and everything. Napping on the sand, listening to music, picking up sandwiches from the nearby deli, hanging out with friends. You can't do it wrong," Zach says.

"I think I can get into that," I say. "Here, let me take the board in for you so you can rinse off."

Morgan looks at me. She blinks. Can she tell how changed I am? How much she's inspired me? I hope so. "Thanks," she says, passing the surfboard to me.

It's wet still, but I don't mind how the salt water dampens my shirt.

I trail behind them with the board while Morgan and Zach run up the sand to the showers. When I reach the edge of the parking lot, I wedge the board upright in the sand the way the rest of our crew has. This close, I can make out all the doodles and signatures left by Zach's friends. I see where it looks like Ben's daughter wrote her name, the *E* in Emma written backward. Someone has drawn a snowboarder on a mountain—Otto, I think? *The Perfect Weekend 2014* is scrawled on the side.

"You should sign it, too," Layla says behind me. I turn to face her. "You were clearly special to him."

Emotion wells in my throat. I can't speak.

Layla seems to understand. "Here." She walks over to her van and leans into the open window. When she emerges, she's holding a thick Sharpie.

"Thank you," I manage to get out.

She smiles and walks over to the rest of the group setting up on towels in the sand, giving me my privacy.

I uncap the pen when I'm alone. It feels intimidating, leaving my mark on this part of Zach's life. But I want to. What we had is worth it.

So I summon Morgan's fearlessness. Just a little. Just enough to press pen to fiberglass.

Doodles spill out of me—pieces of Zach I've collected in our too-short time together. A blooming flower for Morgan, a dragon for his nephew, a screwdriver for his family. Ocean waves for his friends, a small house for me. It's not an urn, but it still feels like a part of Zach's spirit, a memorial of the love so many people have for him.

I was afraid to give this to Kennedy. I was so wrong. It's hard, but it's healing. Action instead of inaction. Taking control of something I have no control over. Changing.

I sign my name, and I start to say goodbye.

41

MORGAN

Throughout the day, Zach comes to life in new ways.

Not literally, I regret to say. Not even the San Onofre shore or introducing his hapless friend to surfing could reverse death.

He remains tethered to me, as usual, which means when I manage to catch waves, Zach is there to whoop into the ocean sun while my momentum carries us toward shore. In between the waves, though, Zach finds new life in the stories his friends tell. The memories they share of Perfect Weekends past. Even though they can't see him, everyone makes sure Zach's presence is felt.

When the sun sets, the surfers bring out pizza and beer and move to one of the beach's bonfires. Sawyer joins in easily, helping Ashley to build up the pyre. Fully lit, the fire leaps into the night while everyone sits around the crackling warmth.

I choose a seat across the flames from Sawyer. When I catch his eye, he smiles. We no longer feel like outsiders new to the group.

I know we need to leave to check into our hotel, but neither I nor Sawyer brings it up. We don't want to. We're enjoying ourselves

too much, weightless in the pleasure of the weekend. It's been—
well, perfect.

Besides . . . I don't know if leaving here will mean Zach leaves
us for good. I'm not ready. The thought seizes me with panic.

So, with the fire full of life in front of me, I try to keep the
thought from my head. I remember what Mr. Harrison said of his
son. How Zach lived in the moment, without hesitation or dissatisfaction. On what might be his final night, I chase Zach's spirit like
we're still riding those waves.

Sawyer seems to be doing the same. Watching him makes my
heart feel like the bonfire. He's looser, more calmly confident than
I've ever seen. He sips beer and laughs while Layla reminisces
about Zach in high school.

When Layla finishes, everyone looks to us. Zach's surprise
guests.

"How about you guys?" Rick asks. "Got any good Zach stories?"

Zach has perched himself on the beer cooler. He's played delighted invisible host to his own eulogies for the past memorable
hour. Now his eyes round, eager for Sawyer's and my unique trib-
utes. "Oh!" he exclaims. "Tell them about how you used a Ouija
board to communicate with me and thought I wanted anal."

Sawyer and I both have to hide our laughter. I clear my throat
behind my beer while Sawyer pretends to cough.

Wanting to share, I search my memories of my haunting—
hardware stores and crystal shops, unfinished business and *Shark
Week*. Honestly, where do I start? More importantly, how do I start
without sounding delusional?

"He told me about the last date he went on."

Sawyer speaking up surprises me. Everyone hushes, eager for
the story.

I watch Sawyer, captivated. The fire makes light and shadows dance on his face. His hair is ruffled by the breeze, his short-sleeve shirt unbuttoned at the collar.

He looks like himself, only different somehow. Like Zach isn't the only one who found new life on the shores of this weekend.

"This great girl he matched with online who he was willing to drive across the city to go rock climbing with," Sawyer elaborates. The way he says *great* makes me feel like I'm still surfing. Flying, on wonderful precarious momentum.

Zach grins, knowing where Sawyer's going with this.

"Zach rock climbs now?" Otto interjects. "Or I mean, he used to?" he corrects himself, his expression clouding.

Zach looks sympathetic, like he wishes he could comfort his old friend.

"Nope," Sawyer replies chipperly, ushering the moment past. "He just did it for her. That's the kind of guy Zach was. He was easy to share your interests in. We once stayed up for hours talking about pottery," he shares, smiling softly.

His gaze pauses on me. My breath catches—I had no idea. I've considered Zach *my* curse, then my mission, then my friend. But of course Zach had his own relationship with Sawyer. Sawyer was half right when he said it's the kind of guy Zach was. For us, it's the kind of guy Zach *is*.

"After hooking up in her car—" Sawyer goes on.

Ben whistles. "Attaboy." Everyone laughs.

Smiling, Sawyer gracefully finishes. "—they realized they were better off as friends. And they really did become friends, even roommates. He didn't stop there, though," Sawyer says, suddenly serious. "He introduced her to me."

His eyes find mine over the flames. Now, he doesn't just pause. He holds my gaze, his stare sculpted like a vessel to hold the memories of an impossible summer. I feel my heartbeat quicken.

"Every chance he got," Sawyer continues, "Zach pressed me to ask her out because he wanted to see us both happy. He knew we could be good—great—together. But I was . . . stupid." Sawyer shakes his head, real shame flickering on his expression. "He even played wingman on a couple of memorable occasions, one of which involved cutting the hot water in my place when they both had to stay with me for a bit. This girl showed up dripping wet in her towel to complain to me," Sawyer reminisces. "Later, Zach made sure I knew how much I owed him."

I laugh with the group, winking at Sawyer—only I know he means me.

"Everyone who knew Zach knew he was kind, generous, fun," Sawyer says, sobering. "He was also wise, though."

Even Zach looks somber now.

Sawyer's stare finds the invisible ghost. To Zach's friends, Sawyer must seem to be speaking only to the night. To the memory of Zach Harrison. I have this sharp, stabbing wish for them to understand how much Zach brought to the world not only in life but in death.

"I owe you, buddy," Sawyer says softly. He raises his beer in a toast. "I owe you everything."

I feel tears clutch my throat. *Everything.*

Zach, I notice, responds the exact same way. The ghost is overcome, and his eyes glitter in the firelight for only us to see.

"Dude," Layla interjects. "You better ask this girl out. Don't let Zach down."

Murmurs of encouragement come up from the crew. I wonder for a moment whether Sawyer's and my failed romance is going to get the reception Otto's Colorado dreams did. I can practically hear the chant echoing over the night-shaded sand—until Sawyer shakes his head, looking slyly self-deprecating.

"I'm not sure I have a chance with her anymore," he demurs.

I lean back, letting the flames warm my front. "I wouldn't count yourself out just yet."

Sawyer looks up, firelight in his eyes.

Everyone echoes my sentiment, even though they understand nothing of the context—our context. I hardly hear them. Heartbeats and roaring fire pass in Sawyer's and my conjoined gaze.

Innocently and inconspicuously, someone moves the conversation onto the next story about Zach, and the supernatural grip of Sawyer's and my shared past releases. I look away. The wind whispering over the ocean feels suddenly cold.

I find I'm . . . perfectly happy and so, so sad at once. I don't want to leave here. I don't want to say goodbye to Zach, my unlikeliest friend in more ways than just his unconventional relationship to mortality.

I don't want to let go.

I don't want to go home to LA. Just envisioning it makes me question the word. *Home?* What, my fifth apartment in six years? My roommate I never hang out with? My friendless city? It's not like I have family there—shit, I've spent more time with Zach's family lately than mine.

I hardly have more to hope for in Massachusetts, either, my vain cross-country effort to escape how much it fucking hurt to start to love someone. Every city, every new Morgan, is the same, even if I pretend they're not.

And Sawyer. What about Sawyer? Here he is, calling me *everything*, confessing to the flames how he wants *a chance*. Does he even mean it, or is he just giving Zach his final perfect day? If he does, will it be enough? When it's just us and life, without our ghosts, what will be left? What will hold us together?

It's not like some powerful connection or epic story united us in the first place. The wonders I've found in California would not have happened without pure chance. If I hadn't accidentally held on to Zach's car keys on our first date, I wouldn't even know Sawyer. How fragile, how happenstance the biggest parts of my life are is utterly terrifying.

And yet . . .

That chance led me to happiness I'll never forget. How many other connections have I let go and missed out on? How many memories have I never lived, how many loves forsaken, in my restless rush to escape my own insecurities?

It makes my heart hurt. I'm quietly a little drunk, and I feel my mood worsening. I don't want to upset Zach's Perfect Weekend.

Without explanation, while everyone is roaring with laughter over something involving Zach naked in a high school library, I inconspicuously excuse myself. When I retreat up the sand, I'm surprised how quickly the pinprick of friendly noise gets small, but I suppose I shouldn't be.

My footsteps in the sand eventually carry me to Zach's van, where I find his surfboard propped up on the beach. In the moonlight, I glance over the signatures, the dates, the scribbled illustrations, and—

New drawings.

Sawyer. This is his tribute. Rapt, like I'm Sawyer-starved, I examine everything he's left. Henry's dragon mug and the vines of Sawyer's garden. Screwdrivers and surfboards. Every memory I almost never experienced.

I'm sniffling, struggling to hold it together, when I hear footsteps behind me.

"I'm sorry if I made you uncomfortable back there," Sawyer starts, his voice hushed and low. "I was going for charming, but I'm rusty and—"

Then he notices how wounded I look. How ripped in half.

"Hey." Gently, without hesitating, he wraps me in a hug. His solid, powerful frame is suddenly everywhere. "Hey, I've got you."

Impressively, this only makes me feel worse. Morgan Lane, the ungrateful, wretched wonder. I step out of his embrace, unable to accept any more kindness. The chill of the night embraces me instead.

"You were right when you said I wouldn't have anyone to haunt. I'm like a living ghost," I say, the words suddenly pressing, demanding me to speak them aloud. I let everything flow out of me, dredging up every fear I've fought to ignore on this perfect day. "I don't want to leave," I say, "but I don't know how to stay. If I were to die today, the only person I could even think to haunt is *you*. And we only met because of a fluke."

"I wouldn't want you to haunt me," Sawyer says quietly.

I step back, stung like I've been slapped. Or like I've fallen off my surfboard to be swept endlessly out to sea.

"Okay," I say. "Fine. Whatever. I guess I could haunt the gas station clerk I bought jerky from today. She seemed nice."

So everything Sawyer said *was* just for Zach. Fuck, I mean, of course it is. We have too much unfinished business between us. None of it is the kind you can exorcise, and none of it is good. I pull myself straight, hugging my arms defensively.

Sawyer, infuriatingly, laughs. Like this is a joke. Like it's funny. Hurt and indignant, I glare.

When Sawyer meets my eyes, he's undaunted. "No, Morgan," he says evenly. "I wouldn't want you to haunt me because I wouldn't be content holding on to just your ghost. Not when I . . . I haven't—" He steadies himself. "Not when I want you now."

The wind whips harshly over the sand.

"The real you," he says. "And I know I can't really have you, not for long. You're leaving. I . . . don't want to waste any time. I'd be happy with as long as you want to give me, but if—if you're going, then I want to go with you."

His silhouette looks sharp in the distant firelight. My heart feels like it's stopped and like it's pounding double time at once. The life-in-death of my most fragile hope. Not optimism. Just hope. It flutters terrifyingly in my chest.

Stunned, I feel genuine weakness in my knees. "You—what?" I stammer. "But your house."

Pain rips through Sawyer's expression with my reminder. Instantly, I'm ready to give up my fragile, fluttering hope. While Sawyer's gesture is romantic, it's obviously impermanent, too. When it comes down to it, he's not going to leave his home, his dream home, for *me*, the girl who flits in and out of lives and cities.

Like kiln fire, new determination solidifies Sawyer's features. "The house . . . It won't be easy to say goodbye to it. But I built that house on old dreams," he says, looking me right in the eye. "My new ones are with you. I've fallen in love with you, Morgan," he admits. "We both know that. We've known it for a while now, and I'm sorry I let my grief get the better of me. I'm sorry I made you think loving you hurt me. It didn't hurt me. It healed me."

He steps forward. My back is nearly to the surfboard when Sawyer, with sureness and impossible tenderness, takes my hands.

"You brought me back to life," he says. "It's a gift I don't even know how to be grateful for."

New tears blur my vision now. Happy tears. Tears that feel like kissing under peppermint trees or riding waves for the first time. I've spent years running—running from myself, from the damage I was convinced my own wants or whims or careless, chaotic half commitments would cause. I expected I would never stop. I thought I was fine with that.

Instead, with a little supernatural intervention, I've found myself refusing to give up on Sawyer. I didn't run. I didn't panic. I found the strength to stay, and in Sawyer's own words, it didn't just hurt—it healed. Finally, in the form of someone I understand in every way, and who understands me, I have human proof that I'm not just the mess I considered myself. I'm so much more.

It's harder even than believing in ghosts. But I do. I finally do.

So I'm ready to stop running.

I dare to hold on tight to Sawyer's hands. He feels so warm, fresh from the fire.

"You were wrong," he whispers, and I hear emotion haunting every word. Years of loneliness, fear, and yearning finding release. "If we had died today," he says, "I *would* have had unfinished business. I needed to tell you how I feel. I needed to try."

Wiping my tears, I finally look at him—really look. Letting myself accept the embrace, in every way, of the man in front of me. Once broken, now whole. What I see is love, happiness, and peace in his expression.

"I needed to do this, too," he continues. "Just once more."

He leans forward, and I meet his lips, and gently he cups my head in his free hand and kisses me deeply. I taste the salt on my lips, the bonfire soot, the flavor of the perfect night, and it's like Sawyer said. *Everything.*

I sink into the warm rush of him, putting everything I feel into my touch. We caress with our mouths and confess with our tongues, everything we want, hope, even fear—*everything, everything, everything*—echoed in passion and compassion, until the wind gusts coolly over the sand, distracting us.

When we part, Zach is leaning against his memorial surfboard, ghostly and smug.

"This," he declares, "is the best Perfect Weekend *ever.*"

42

SAWYER

Kissing Morgan consumes me. I feel remade, renewed by the combination of expectation and culmination we shaped on each other's mouths.

I think of kintsugi pottery, of how the style doesn't just mean repairing something broken. The imperative ingredient is something *new*. Something clay could never have imagined on its own. It's not just restoration. It's transcendence.

We return to the fire, hand in hand, fingers loosely entwined. From there, the night surrounding us stretches long. Zach resumes his post on the beer cooler, looking, if possible, even more delighted than he did during his friends' reminiscences. The conversation moves on, returning sometimes to Zach but reaching out to other lives, other recollections, other plans and possibilities. Zach drinks them in, looking reassured by the evidence of life continuing on.

Eventually, the fire starts to die down. Layla turns to me and Morgan, inquiring whether we're camping overnight.

Of course, our hotel reservation waits for us. *Separate rooms*, we insisted when we decided to drive out here with Zach.

Right.

Morgan does not mention the hotel. Her eyes meet mine. The question in them is obvious.

"Yes," I reply to Layla, soft and clear. "We'll sleep here in the van."

Morgan smiles. Her cheeks pinken with eagerness in the fading firelight, and god, I want to go over there, wasting not even a moment, and kiss her right now.

Instead, we let anticipation smolder like the fire while we borrow some supplies from the group and find some pillows and a blanket in the back of Zach's van. Ana was outfitted for Perfect Weekend overnights, obviously.

I brush my teeth at the communal bathrooms, knowing exactly where this night is headed. I'm determined to enjoy every single second of it. Of Morgan, who, despite everything, has become the most vital part of my world. Life is precious—*she's* precious—and I won't waste even one moment. I won't waste a single gift I'm given, especially when said gift's laughter sounds like sunshine and her joy shines like gold.

When I return to the van, Morgan is under the blanket, partially reclined and half exposed. Her hair is loose, her tresses ocean-wild. Her tank top is desperately thin.

I'm lucky I need to crawl into the van on all fours. Otherwise, my knees might give out.

Morgan smiles shyly when I come closer. The moonlight makes her skin glow, urging my heartbeat faster. I wasn't lying when I confessed to some rustiness with flirtation, and Morgan has me overwhelmingly self-conscious. I wish I could sculpt her my feelings, somehow, instead of . . . What's the perfect way to tell her I need her, now, with every part of me? To tell her I want to give her everything.

"So, what do you guys want to do tonight? Swap ghost stories?"

Zach's voice startles me. Morgan looks similarly rattled. Our ghost watches us from the front seat, where he's just materialized, grinning his grandest Zach Harrison, Cheshire Cat grin.

Morgan and I lock eyes. Quite honestly, ghost stories were *not* part of our conjugal plans tonight, but—

"Oh, um." Morgan recovers first, finding her footing unevenly, like I imagine Zach did on their now infamous rock-climbing outing. "Of course. Whatever you want."

I force myself to look at my paranormal friend and not the beautiful girl half dressed right in front of me.

"Yeah, Zach, this is your weekend," I say in a passable imitation of Morgan's good cheer.

Zach looks from me to Morgan, Morgan to me, carefully considering how to keep the Perfect Weekend vibes going. Then he bursts out laughing. "You guys are the best. Honestly," he proclaims, "willing to give up this freaking perfect romantic night just to talk to me."

Relief crashes over me when I understand, which makes me embarrassed.

Morgan looks like she feels the same way. She straightens up from her reclining position on the pillows. "Seriously, Zach, we'd love to spend time with you," she insists. "Sawyer and I can . . ." She clears her throat, blushing intensely, not meeting my eyes.

Zach's brows rise in interest.

"We'll have other nights," she says, rerouting.

"No," Zach says firmly. He holds up one finger in pontificating urgency. "No. No *other nights* shit. A meteor could barrel down here at any moment. Live every day like it's your last," he demands. "I mean it. I lived that way, and I had the most beautiful life."

The peaceful weight of this statement seems to reach Zach only when he speaks it. The serenity in his expression isn't happy, exactly. Not many people get to reckon with the beauty of their life only once it's over. In fact, I've only met two. It can't be easy.

But Zach doesn't look mournful, either. He sees his spectral retrospective for what it is—a gift.

"So, you two definitely should bone tonight," he concludes.

I cough. Now my cheeks match Morgan's bashful color, I have no doubt. But I'm touched, too. We just heard for hours how self-less Zach Harrison is, how earnestly loyal. Encouraging his friends to "bone" during his last night on earth—yeah, he is.

"Zach, really," I plead weakly. "We don't need to."

Smiling, Zach starts to fade. "Ben stays up all night watching the waves. I'm going to sit with him," he informs us. "I want to be near the sea. Oh, and"—his visibility diminishing, he nods to the dashboard—"I left something in the glove compartment for you. Otto always has extras."

Then he's gone, leaving Morgan and me alone. The hushed sanctuary inside the van is comforting. The quiet shrouds us in a near-physical embrace. The beach is empty, everyone having set up tents or driven their vans to more secluded parking spaces.

Morgan is silent. She looks expectant, or—or maybe she's trep-idatious. Maybe Zach's intrusion, humorously intended though it was, has reminded her of impending loss or inexplicable guilt.

"You know we don't have to, um, bone, right?" I say.

I feel a rush of emotion when Morgan's expression clears. She smirks; there's no mistaking her meaning.

She rises to her knees, the blanket slipping off her, revealing more of the transparency of the worn material of her top.

Holy shit, my mind murmurs in jumbled ecstasy. I can't think straight. Morgan in her goddamn semitransparent top is deliver-ing sweet, shattering punishment to the coherence of my nervous system. *I'm* going to have to sit on the beach with Ben all night just to stay sane. Maybe I'll drift into the ocean for good measure.

Morgan is merciless. I want her so fucking bad. Her eyes half lidded, she crawls over to me. The closeness is . . . consuming. "Who are we," she murmurs, "to deny Zach's last wishes?"

I have to smile. When Morgan is inches from me, her scent overwhelming—florals, the sea, the complicated sweetness of her body—I put a hand on her shoulder, caressing her while holding her still. "Morgan," I insist.

"I want to," she promises me, her exhalation hardening and weakening me at once. "I understand if you're not ready, though," she says gently. "We can take this as slow as you want."

I look down, drawing her gaze to the prominent pressure in the front of my pants. "Oh, I'm ready," I reply.

Morgan laughs, and it's with her sunshine sound filling the van's cozy interior that I crash my mouth to hers. I want to capture that happiness, snare it in a kiss, swallow it in a drunken dream. I want Morgan's intoxicating joy to fill me up, and I want to give her the night of her life in return.

She meets me unhesitatingly, kissing me furiously, surging to her knees with her whole body coming to meet me. My other hand finds her, gripping her hips, pulling her into me while our tongues clash and devour. The obliterating power of one thought rips through my skull, hurtling down the empty freeway of my chest, past my heart, into where my desire swells for her. *I love this woman. I love her so much.*

Now it's Morgan shattering me, and it feels good.

I move fast, laying her down on the blankets to pin her beneath me. Morgan gasps from the sudden movement. I lose my shirt in supernatural haste, then reach for Morgan's. Her whisper-thin top falls to the floor, revealing her bare breasts, pure and soft and waiting.

I press my chest to hers, and she moans. Running my hand down the length of her, I want to touch her everywhere. She's so warm. Her heartbeat thrums in her chest, in her neck, pounding when I kiss the soft skin there. She's so alive, and with her, *I'm* so alive.

My heartbeat is fighting to catch up with hers, my mouth moving lower from her neck while my hand rises to cup her curvature when—

The glove compartment pops open.

We stop, startled, each of us simultaneously noticing the condom Zach left behind.

Otto always has extras. I laugh, grateful, reaching for the thin package.

"Having a ghost for a wingman really is useful," Morgan comments.

She takes it from my hands, while I undress her in the dark. Moonlight shapes the shadows inside the van, contouring our sanctuary in welcoming darkness with soft edges of pale white. Fighting the urge to rush, I draw Morgan's shorts down, her underwear coming with them.

When I move forward to kiss her once more, she puts her hands on me. Warm, impossibly gentle. Loving, like every caress I've given her. The wonderful rush of her familiar grasp on the length of me makes me lightheaded, nearly to collapsing. I haven't been touched in so long. Knowing it's Morgan's hands on me—finally— is overpowering.

Only by focusing on her do I stay within myself. I kiss her and kiss her and kiss her. I want to surrender to her completely, but in her tender grasp, I feel she's still hesitant to rush me.

I can't blame her. I've given her enough reasons to doubt that I'm ready for this. But god, I'm ready.

I urge her in every way I know how. With my mouth on her neck, tracing her pulse with my tongue, I reach down, putting my fingers to her, losing myself in her warmth. The whimpering encouragement she utters is enough to frenzy me, but I stay in control. I don't want to waste this night. No, I want to delve deep into every single one of these moments. I want to fight for them to last forever.

Morgan understands. She rolls the condom onto me, the waver in her fingers only impassioning me more. Unconsciously or not, she flexes forward when she opens her legs.

When I'm inside her, I press my head into her neck, entwining my hands with hers, wanting to touch her everywhere I can. *Morgan. My Morgan.*

I want everything, every part of her. Every day, every minute, every second.

My Morgan. My whole life.

43

MORGAN

Sawyer doesn't touch me like a man grieving. He touches me like a man possessed.

In his caress, his kisses—the deep strokes he makes inside me—I feel him starving for passion. I feed his need, fulfilling my own with the ecstasy I feel in his grip, his mouth, his body. He holds me like I'm clay in his hands he's caressing, shaping me to new heights. Like he's terrified of ever losing me.

It's hard not to feel insecure, being the first woman to sleep with him since his fiancée. But the truth is, Sawyer is who he is *because* of Kennedy, so I don't fight the thought of his ex. I love who Sawyer is, which means I'll remain grateful forever for her part in his life.

He moves with complete certainty, unmaking every concern I had for the pace of our relationship. We only have the one condom, so after, we spend the rest of the night telling each other how much we want this with our tongues, our fingertips, our heartbeats joining in a cleansing rhythm. We use every moment like it's something individually precious.

With the moonlight pouring over us in the quiet darkness, I'm his undoing. He is mine.

Waking in his embrace on the floor of the van, wrapped in blankets, I'm wonderfully happy for one perfect moment.

Then realization crashes over me, like the waves my ghostly best friend spent the night watching.

If Zach isn't gone yet, he won't have long.

Panic jumbles my sleep-softened senses. I'm hurting but whole. Ready but terrified. Of course I want Zach to resolve his unfinished business. It's why we're here, and when I watched him last night, experiencing the love his friends will carry forward for the rest of their lives, he looked so rapturously content. It's everything I ever wanted for him.

I even *want* to say goodbye, in my heart's purest resolve. It's what Zach needs, what he deserves.

I'm just not ready for the pain.

Holding on to the comfort of last night, I extricate myself from Sawyer's embrace. Outside, the sun is only just rising. The marine layer coats the shoreline in the early morning, making everything look hazy and soft.

What haunts me now is the list of lasts. Knowing what's coming, my mind organizes them with ruthless efficiency. This is the last sunrise Zach will ever see. His last sunset has passed. Soon, I will hear him laugh for the last time. I will look into my friend's eyes for the last shining moment before they disappear.

I will follow the current of time sweeping me into the world without him, knowing it will never be exactly the same.

"Don't leave me."

Sawyer's sleep-fogged voice pauses me. His eyes still closed, his hand finds mine.

I lift his knuckles to kiss them softly. "I'm not," I promise him. "I'll be right back."

He nods, then rolls onto my pillow, breathing in the scent of me.

I leave him to the serenity of the morning. Stepping out of the van, I continue down the sand to the seashore, listening to the gentle crash of the waves, looking for what I hope I'll find.

I do. He's there, sitting on the sand.

When I come closer, Zach doesn't look up. He keeps his gaze on the horizon, like he expected me. He looks . . . content. I don't know if I could manage this morning if he didn't, but this, I remind myself with every passing moment, is why we're here.

I sit down next to him, close enough to touch. To my surprise, ghostly cold doesn't emanate from him. Instead, he's warmer than the sand beneath us.

Without knowing how I know it's going to work, I lean on him. I find Zach solid. Soft, comforting, and impossibly real.

With my head on his shoulder, I hug his arm to me. He kisses the top of my hair, and I feel it. He's finally here. He's finally real.

Tears sear my vision, sadness streaked with joy, warping my vision of the water. "Zach . . ." I choke out.

It's horribly funny. I don't know what to say. I've had months, days, hours to prepare for the moment of Zach's departure, readiness many people never receive for the cold crash of loss. Still, I have no idea what to say.

Maybe nothing, I decide. Zach was one for living in the moment. Living every drop of life for its fullest experience, without examining or interrogating or memorializing. Maybe enjoying the silent sunlight with my friend is exactly the right way to conclude my list of lasts— to end my heartbreaking, healing haunting with Zach Harrison.

We watch the waves for a few minutes, until finally, I put my free hand into my sweatshirt pocket.

Zach eyes the packet of letters I pull out. My tribute.

"They're from . . . everyone," I say, my voice wavering. "Everyone who loved you." On top is Sawyer's familiar handwriting.

Zach receives them, holding them like they're fragile. "How?" he whispers.

The scariest, happiest parts of the past couple months return to me. "Everywhere we went," I explain, "I left notes behind, asking your friends and family, your neighbors, your coworkers, to write you a letter and mail it to me. I told them I would set them to sea in a tribute to you. But I think they'd all agree"—tears trickle down my cheeks—"handing them to you is even better."

Zach swallows hard. Even my happy-go-lucky ghost looks overcome. He crushes me to him in a hug.

"You'll take care of them, won't you?" he murmurs into my shoulder. "You'll check in on my family?"

I nod ferociously. It feels good to have something to hold on to. Not just hope. Not even just optimism. Something sure and certain, like the ghost made real in my embrace. Something pure and clear and real I can use to fend off the pain of losing this man I've grown to cherish.

"Good," Zach replies. "And Sawyer?"

"And Sawyer," I repeat readily. "I promise on your grave."

Zach laughs at this. *His last laugh.* I smile, and it's enough to stuff my sobs down a little longer. *Live in the moment,* I remind myself.

"You let him take care of you, too, okay?" Zach says. Withdrawing from his hug, I find real concern in his eyes. No, not just concern—love.

If it is the last look he ever gives me, I might just be okay.

"Yes," I whisper. "I think I can promise that."

Zach nods, each of us understanding there's nothing more to say. Neither of us wants to utter *Goodbye* or *I'll miss you.* Now is enough. The moment is enough.

I hug him one final time. Then, feeling like I'm tearing off a piece of myself, I stand. I honestly don't know how I'll get through this moment—only that I have to.

"Read your notes, Zach," I urge him. "See how much everyone loves you. How you'll never be forgotten."

"Morgan, I—" He falters, then composes himself. "Thank you. I can't thank you enough."

I smile. If it's the last look I give him, I think I'll be okay. "It was a privilege to be haunted by you, Zach Harrison."

Now Zach smiles back.

I force myself to turn, realizing that this is one last that I get to choose. I want my final memory of him to be that smile. Walking back up the beach, I hug myself in the morning cold. One step in front of the next, I continue on into the new world.

Finally, when I'm near the van, I look over my shoulder. Zach's form remains on the shoreline.

I watch him read his letters slowly, handling each folded message carefully while the sun rises, lighting the sky in front of him.

I wait. Finally, Zach stops flipping through the letters. He hugs them to his chest, and then he seems to glow brighter and brighter until, suddenly, he's gone.

The wind picks up the letters, carrying them in one gust out to the sea Zach loved. The beach is empty. I'm by myself.

But I'm not alone.

Sobs rip through me, overtaking me with every step up the rest of the sand. When I reach the parking lot, Sawyer climbs out of the van to meet me. With one look, he knows. I crumple into his arms.

Weak in Sawyer's embrace, I understand with perfect clarity that I'm confronting something I've never had to in my life of constant motion. This feeling—like my heart has been wrenched out of my chest, like the colors of the world have gone cold—only comes when you find something you're not ready to lose.

It scares the living shit out of me. Sawyer holds me fearlessly, and in his embrace, I remember he survived the unimaginable. Worse than the loss I'm experiencing, much worse. His healing was lengthy, unconventional, and haunted, yet still, he survived.

With him, I decide—with patience, with resilience, with love— I will survive this.

I sob until I have nothing left, letting myself lean on Sawyer. I empty myself out, cleansing the panic, the pain, the wretched *lasts* from my system.

Then, with the sun underlining the horizon in kintsugi gold, I draw the new day into my lungs.

"Let's go home, Sawyer," I say.

He kisses me on the forehead, intertwining his fingers with mine.

We bid our goodbyes to Zach's friends, knowing Zach's memory is kept forever in the hearts of those closest to him. We promise to come back next year. We load up the van, except for Zach's memorial surfboard, which we leave with the Perfect Weekend crew. It belongs with the people who helped make Zach who he was.

Not needing to speak, Sawyer and I return to the sky-blue van. I sit in the passenger seat, letting myself remember glove-compartment gifts and license plates spotted.

Sawyer quietly retakes the driver's seat, starting the car with the keys that began everything. He's looking over his shoulder to reverse out of the parking lot when the radio crackles to life.

"Call Me Maybe" is playing.

Sawyer and I lock eyes. Then we burst into teary laughter.

With the sunrise ahead of us, we sing Zach's favorite song—the whole thing—while Sawyer takes us to the open highway leading us home.

44

Two months have passed since Zach left. Two months of grieving. Two months of loving each other. Two months of something I never got the chance to do, or maybe never *took* the chance to do—confronting loss's long shadows with the light of someone else's spirit, courageous and compassionate.

When Morgan needs me, I'm there. When I need her, not only to deal with Zach's departure, but to struggle through the profound emptiness of Kennedy from this house she long inhabited, Morgan is there for me.

We plan a trip to visit her parents. She tells me she wants to see them more often. I start calling mine every Saturday. I ask old friends out to dinner. Even the ones I've neglected for too long are quick to invite me back into their lives.

I meant it when I said I would gladly move for Morgan, but she told me she'd found her home on the Silver Lake hillside. She was ready, in her words, to put down roots.

Morgan has many plates now. She stands in the kitchen, washing the dishes I made new for our home while I watch her from the doorway. We didn't leave Los Angeles—for Massachusetts or otherwise. Instead, Morgan moved into my once-haunted home on the hillside. The guesthouse is only for pottery these days.

I might have expected it to hurt, seeing Morgan where I'd once planned a lifetime with Kennedy. It doesn't. It heals me. I'm so grateful for them both, for the memories of Kennedy I have here and the ones of Morgan I'll make here.

Unlikely? Maybe, but I once drove a ghost to a seven-year-old's birthday party. Nothing surprises me these days.

The dreams I shared in this house with Kennedy haven't disappeared—dreams don't work like that. They're not just ideas from the past. They're living things. They change. They pick up new inspirations and joys and colors, like ceramic infused with gold. This isn't *my* dream home anymore. It's ours.

My gaze catches the framed photograph beside the window over the kitchen sink. It's from the Perfect Weekend. Layla captured it while Morgan and I weren't aware. Morgan looks gorgeous, laughing, effervescent with life. Beside her, lit in flames, I watch her with unconcealed infatuation. It's the perfect memory and the perfect prologue to us.

It's not why we love the photograph, though.

Over Morgan's shoulder in the photo shimmers a warped speck, an unusual lens flare. Distortion in the firelight.

Morgan gasped when she saw it. We both know it's the closest thing we have to a photograph with Zach, the three of us together.

Finishing washing the dishes, Morgan glances over. She shuts off the water, her eyes finding what I hold in my hands.

It's the first piece of pottery I made after she left here in the wake of Kennedy's vanishing. When we got home from San Onofre, I showed it to Morgan, just like Zach encouraged on the drive.

In their ungainly canister in my closet, my fiancée's ashes have waited for five years. Needing to make her urn myself kept me from pottery. It had to be me who crafted it. It *couldn't* be me. With what vessel could I possibly give voice to our life and love? To my loss? How could I endure the feeling of combining my greatest joy, my release, my soul's endeavor, with the deepest pain I'd ever felt? How could I go on making pottery after such a legacy?

The questions kept me from my craft for five years.

Until Morgan.

The day she moved out, furious, hurting, and freed, I went into my pottery studio and let my hands guide my heart. My grieving gave way to creation, to the piece I hold right now.

"You're sure?" Morgan asks.

I set it on the dining table, then pull Morgan close to kiss her swiftly. "I'm sure," I say.

She nods, touching my face softly. Her breath warms my cheek. She pulls back to head to the front of the house, and I delicately pick up my pottery.

It's not an urn, really. Or not a traditional one. It's a flowerpot, painted swirling midnight blue and black.

Joining Morgan on the porch, I carry Kennedy's final resting place. Together, we continue into the front yard, which is finished now, Morgan's vision complete in flourishing color. In the weeks since she moved in, she's worked to exhaustion pruning, tending, making routine trips to the nursery, until finally, this morning, she incorporated the final components—yuccas, carnations, sunflowers—the memories she shared with me when we went to the Huntington Gardens. Planting pieces of her own past in this sanctuary of our present and future. She's brought her homes here to mine. She's put down her roots in our garden.

It's perfect. The house Kennedy designed, I finished, and the yard, Morgan created. Pieces of all three of us, reified in one home.

Morgan leads me to the space we've chosen for the flowerpot, visible from our bedroom window. Once, Kennedy's jacaranda tree stood here, until Morgan helped me make space for new dreams instead of mourning old ones. Gently, I lower the hardened clay to the place Morgan sculpted of her preferred materials— soil, soft low grasses, and reinforcing rocks.

With her, I researched how flowers could be planted in ashes. We've chosen lilies. Where Morgan is my sun, Kennedy is the moon in my life. Her memory is the purest light in the deepest darkness I've ever known.

I don't cry while I empty the canister, Morgan helping me evenly mix the fine gray powder with the nourishing soil. Instead, as we plant something that will grow and change in her memory, I concentrate on every happy moment with Kennedy. On how much I loved her. So, so much.

On how loving Kennedy is the only reason I know how to love Morgan, the only reason we met. How loving Morgan is how I learned to let Kennedy go. Yet, in a way, in loving Morgan, I will always hold on to Kennedy. A living tribute, like these flowers.

We lower in the lilies. Morgan's expert hands cover the roots with utmost care, the most I could ever want. Under the pristine wide faces of the flowers, Kennedy looks like she's home, too.

She was half right. My kids will play in front of her flowers one day. I don't need her ghost here to know it's what she wanted.

With dirt on her fingertips, Morgan takes my hand. I hold on tight. In the perfect early evening, a soft wind picks up suddenly over the hills, gently blowing our hair and the petals of the lilies. I close my eyes, breathing deep.

"I think it's her," Morgan murmurs.

I peer down, meeting Morgan's eyes. "I think so, too."

Floating on the wind, music enters my head. The sweetest refrain, familiar and eternal. "A Sunday Kind of Love."

Holding on to Morgan's hand, I welcome the possibility of what this means. Maybe Kennedy is with us right now. Maybe Zach is, too.

Maybe no one ever really leaves. They just . . . change. From souls to soil, shattered pieces to loving completion, dreams to dust to memory. They live on, the ghosts of past lives made new forever.

Acknowledgments

Seeing Other People is a personal story—of memory and remembrance, of love and loss. It was also an ambitious undertaking in our writing journey, our first venture into putting speculative flourishes on contemporary romance. We're very grateful for everyone who helped it come alive.

Katie Shea Boutillier, our agent, first and foremost, thank you for trusting us and encouraging us to develop this unique story. Every year, with new inspirations, new challenges, new sparks of story, we remain grateful for the constancy of your championship, kindness, insight, rigor, and support. As ever, we look forward to many, many more with you!

Kristine Swartz, your care, keen eye, and editorial wisdom remind us every book why we love working with you. You chose Morgan and Sawyer (and Zach and Kennedy!) out of the ideas we submitted, and we feel incredibly fortunate you gave us the opportunity to make their story real. We're very grateful for your on-point notes guiding us to get to know these characters and their journey more deeply.

Vi-An Nguyen, you have outdone yourself. *Seeing Other People* is our favorite cover we have ever received on one of our Berkley romances, which we would not have thought possible given the wonderful work you have done over the years. Likewise, David de las Heras, we fell in love with your style at first sight. We could not be more thankful for the vibrant, captivating way you have captured our characters.

Five books in, we feel very honored to continue to call Berkley home. Our sincerest thanks go to the wonderful team who made these pages possible. Thank you to Will Tyler, Michael Brown, and Kendall Hinson for your careful, thoughtful read of every line. To Lindsey Tulloch and Christine Legon, thank you for your coordination and diligence in carrying this story from the manuscript on our computer to the book we hold in our hands. Mary Baker, thank you so much for your help, support, and feedback. Jessica Plummer and Hillary Tacuri, your wonderful work in reaching readers is unmatched, and we remain sincerely grateful to continue working with you. Yazmine Hassan, we're thrilled to have you on our team and thankful for your enthusiastic, incredible outreach.

Seeing Other People is the story of holding on to the people we love. We feel fortunate to surround ourselves with dear friends—Bridget Morrissey, Maura Milan, Gabrielle Gold, Gretchen Schreiber, Rebekah Faubion, Derek Milman, Brian Murray Williams, Yulin Kuang, Farrah Penn, Carlyn Greenwald, Kalie Holford, Sophie Sullivan, Kate Golden, thank you for everything. To the authors who have lent kind words to this book, we're thankful for and indebted to your invaluable support.

Finally, thank you to our family, without whom none of this would be possible.

SEEING OTHER PEOPLE

EMILY WIBBERLEY & AUSTIN SIEGEMUND-BROKA

READERS GUIDE

Discussion Questions

1. Have you ever visited a haunted house?

2. At the beginning of the story, Sawyer thinks he is lucky to be haunted—do you agree with him?

3. In what ways are both Morgan and Sawyer living like ghosts in their own lives?

4. Why do Morgan and Sawyer clash when they first meet? What do you think brings them together?

5. This is a romance novel with a constant third wheel in Zach. How do you think Morgan and Zach's friendship adds to the book?

6. How do you think the setting of sunny, hot Los Angeles contributes to this ghost story?

7. Sawyer feels betrayed when he finds out about Kennedy's real unfinished business. Do you think Kennedy and Morgan are

justified in believing that if he knew, he would have made sure he never moved on?

8. Love is the cause of grief. How does this book show that love is also the way to heal from grief?

9. Do you think Zach and Kennedy are truly gone at the end?

Keep reading for a preview of

THE ROUGHEST DRAFT

Available now!

KATRINA

The bookstore is nothing like I remember. They've remodeled, white paint covering the exposed bricks, light gray wooden shelves where there once were old metal ones. Cute candles and Jane Austen tote bags occupy the front table instead of used books.

I shouldn't be surprised it looks different. I've pretty much given up buying books in public in the past three years, including from Forewords, where I've only been once despite the bookstore being fifteen minutes from our house in Los Angeles's Hancock Park. I don't like being recognized. But I love books. Doing my book buying online has been torture.

Walking in, I eye the bookseller. She's in her early twenties, not much younger than me. Her brown hair's up in a messy bun, her green nose piercing catching the overhead lights. She doesn't look familiar. When she smiles from the checkout counter, I think I'm in the clear.

I smile back, walking past the bestseller shelf. *Only Once* sits imposingly right in the middle, its textured blue cover with clean white typography instantly identifiable. I ignore the book while I move deeper into the store.

This visit is something my therapist's been pushing me to do for months. Exposure therapy, conditioning myself to once more find comfortable the places I used to love. Pausing in the fiction section, I collect myself, remembering I'm doing fine. I'm calm. I'm just me, looking for something to read, with no expectations pressing on my shoulders or stresses jackhammering in my chest.

Covers run past me in rows, each waiting to be picked out. Everything is crisp with the scent of pages. I knew the Los Angeles independent bookstore scene well when Chris proposed we move here from New York for the job he was offered in the book department of one of Hollywood's biggest talent agencies. Each shop is varied and eccentric, indignant icons of literacy in a city people say never reads.

Which is why I've hated avoiding them. The past three years have been a catalogue of changes, facing realities of the life I no longer knew if I wanted and the one I decided I didn't. I've had to remember the quiet joys of my ordinary existence, and in doing so, I've had to forget. Forget how my dreams hit me with devastating impact, forget how horrible I felt coming close to what I'd once wanted. Forget Florida.

Everything's different now. But I pretend it's not.

The bookstore is part of the pretending. When I lived in New York on my own, before Chris, I would walk to Greenpoint's independent bookstores in the summer, sweating into the shoulder strap of my bag, and imagine the stories in the spines, wondering if they'd lend me inspiration, fuel for the creative fire I could never douse. Reading wasn't just enjoyment. It was studying.

I don't study now. But I never lost the enjoyment. I guess it's too integral a piece of me. Reading and loving books are the fingerprints of who I am—no matter how much I change, they'll stay the same, betraying me to myself for the rest of my life. And bringing me into this bookstore, wanting to find something new to read until Chris gets home in the evening.

"Can I help you find anything?"

I hear the bookseller's voice behind me. Instinctive nerves tighten my posture. I turn, hesitant. While she watches me welcomingly, I wait for the moment I've been dreading since I decided earlier today I needed something new to read *tonight*. Why should I wait for delivery?

The moment doesn't come. The bookseller's expression doesn't change.

"Oh," I say uncertainly, "I'm not sure. Just browsing."

The girl grins. "Do you like literary fiction?" she asks eagerly. "Or is there a subgenre you prefer?"

I relax. The relief hits me in a rush. This is great. No, wonderful. She has no idea who I am. It's not like people overreact in general to seeing celebrities in Los Angeles, where you might run into Chrissy Teigen outside Whole Foods or Seth Rogen in line for ice cream. Not that I'm a celebrity. It's really *just* bookstores where the possibilities of prying questions or overeager fans worry me. If this bookseller doesn't know who I am, I've just found my new favorite place. I start imagining my evening in eager detail—curling up with my new purchase on the couch, toes on our white fur rug, gently controlling James Joyce so his paws don't knock green tea everywhere and stroking him until he purrs.

"Yeah, literary fiction generally. Contemporary fiction more specifically," I say, excitement in my voice now. I'm going to enjoy telling Chris tonight that I went to Forewords and no one knew who I was. It'll probably piss him off, but I don't care. I'll be reading while he's working out his frustration on his Peloton bike.

"I have just the thing," the girl says. She's clearly delighted to have a customer who wants her recommendation.

When she rushes off, my nerves wind up once more. The horrible thought hits me—what if she returns, excited to pitch me the book she's chosen, and she's holding *Only Once*? I don't know what I'd say. The couple seconds I have right now aren't enough for me to come up with even the first draft of how I could extricate myself from the conversation.

Instead, it's worse.

"Try this." The clerk thrusts the hardcover she's chosen toward me. "It came out last week. I read it in, like, two days."

Under the one-word title, *Refraction*, imposed over moody black-and-white photography, I read the name. Nathan Van Huysen. I look to where she got the book from, and I don't know how I didn't notice when I walked in. The cardboard display near the front of the store holds rows of copies, waiting patiently for customers, which tells me two things: high publisher expenditure, and it's not selling.

His name hits me the way it does every time I see it. In *New York Times* reviews, in the profiles I try to keep out of my browser history—never with much success. The first is wishing those fifteen letters meant nothing to me, weren't intertwined with my life in ways I'll never untangle.

Underneath the wishing, I find harder, flintier feelings. Resentment, even hatred. No regret, except regretting ever going to the upstate New York writers' workshop where I met Nathan Van Huysen.

I was fresh out of college. When I graduated from the University of Virginia and into the job I'd found fetching coffee and making copies in a publishing house, I felt like my life hadn't really started. I'd enjoyed college, enjoyed the rush I got learning whatever I found genuinely interesting, no matter the subject—fungal plant structures, behavioral economics, the funeral practices of the Greco-Roman world. I just knew I wouldn't be who I wanted to be until I wrote and published. Then I went upstate and found Nathan, and he found me.

I remember walking out of the welcome dinner, hugging my coat to my collar in the cold, and finding him waiting for me. We'd met earlier in the day, and his eyes lit up when he caught me leaving the restaurant. We introduced ourselves in more depth. He mentioned he was engaged—I hadn't asked. I was single—I didn't volunteer the information. It wasn't like that between us. While we walked out to Susquehanna River Bridge in the night wind, we ended up exchanging favorite verses of poetry, reading them from online on our phones. We were friends.

For the whole lot of good it did us.

When I take the copy of *Refraction*, the clerk's voice drops conspiratorially. "It's not as good as *Only Once*. But I love Nathan Van Huysen's prose."

I don't reply, not wanting to say out loud his prose was the first thing I noticed about him. Even at twenty-two, he wrote with influences fused perfectly into his own style, like every English course he'd ever taken—and Nathan had taken quite a few—was flowing out of his fingertips. It made me feel the things writers love to feel. Inspired, and jealous.

In my silence, the clerk's expression changes. "Wait," she continues, "you have read *Only Once*, haven't you?"

"Um," I say, struggling with how to reply. *Why is conversation way easier on the page?*

"If you haven't"—she starts toward the bestseller shelf to fetch the paperback. I know what'll happen when she catches sight of the back cover. Under the embarrassingly long list of starred reviews, she'll see the author photos. Nathan's blue eyes beneath the immaculate black waves of his hair, the dimple he only trots out for promotional photos and press tours. Then, next to him, she'll find his coauthor, Katrina Freeling. Young woman, sharp shoulders, round features, full eyebrows she honestly loves. Professionally done makeup, dark brown hair pressed and polished, nothing like it looks when she steps out of the shower or she's reading on the patio on sweaty summer days.

The differences won't matter. The bookseller will recognize the woman right in front of her.

My capacity for speech finally returns. "No, I've read it," I manage.

"Of course," the girl gushes. "Everyone's read it. Well, *Refraction* is one of Nathan Van Huysen's solo books. Like I said, it's good, but I wish he and Katrina Freeling would go back to writing together. I've heard they haven't spoken in years, though. Freeling doesn't even write anymore."

I don't understand how this girl is interested enough in the writing duo to know the rumors without identifying one of them in her bookstore. It might be because I haven't done many signings or festivals in the past three years. Following the very minimal promotional schedule for Nathan's and my debut novel, *Connecting Flights*, and then the exhausting release tour for our second, *Only Once*—during which I made my only previous visit here, to Forewords—I more or less withdrew from writerly and promotional events. It was difficult because Chris's and my social life in New York centered on the writing community, and it's part of why I like living in LA, where our neighbors are screenwriters and studio executives. In LA, when people learn you're a novelist, they treat you like a tenured Ivy League professor or a potted plant. Either is preferable to the combination of jealousy and judgment I endured spending time with former friends and competitors in New York.

If you'd told me four years ago I would leave New York for the California coast, I would've frowned, or likelier, laughed. New York was the epicenter for dreams like mine, and Nathan's. But I didn't know then the publication of *Only Once* would fracture me and leave me reassembling the pieces of myself into someone new. Someone for whom living in Los Angeles made sense.

While grateful the Forewords bookseller hasn't identified me—I would've had one of those politely excited conversations, signed some copies of *Only Once*, then left without buying a book—I don't know how to navigate hearing my own professional life story secondhand. "Oh well," I fumble. "That's too bad." No more browsing for me. I decide I just want out of this conversation.

"I know." The girl's grin catches a little mischievousness. "I wonder what happened between them. I mean, why would such a successful partnership just split up right when they were really popular?"

The collar of my coat feels itchy, my pulse beginning to pound. This is my least favorite topic, like, ever. *Why did you split up?* I've heard the rumors. I've heard them from graceless interviewers, from comments I've happened to notice under online reviews. I've heard them from Chris.

If they're to be believed, we grew jealous of each other, or Nathan thought he was better than me, or I was difficult to work with. Or we had an affair. There'd been speculation before our split. Two young writers, working together on retreats to Florida, Italy, the Hamptons. Photos of us with our arms around each other from the *Connecting Flights* launch event—the only launch we ever did together. The fact *Only Once* centered on marital infidelity didn't help. Nor did the very non-fictional demise of Nathan's own very non-fictional marriage.

This is why I don't like being recognized. I like the excited introductions. I love interacting with readers. What I don't like is the endless repetition of this one question. Why did Katrina Freeling and Nathan Van Huysen quit writing together?

"Who knows?" I say hastily. "Thanks for your recommendation. I'll . . . take it." I reach for the copy of *Refraction*, which the girl hands over, glowing.

Five minutes later, I walk out of the bookstore holding the one book I didn't want.

Mike Yoon Photo

Emily Wibberley and **Austin Siegemund-Broka** met and fell in love in high school. Austin went on to graduate from Harvard, while Emily graduated from Princeton. Together, they are the authors of several novels about romance for teens and adults. Now married, they live in Los Angeles, California, where they continue to take daily inspiration from their own love story.

VISIT EMILY AND AUSTIN ONLINE

EmilyandAustinWrite.com

Ready to find
your next great read?

Let us help.

Visit prh.com/nextread

Penguin
Random
House